STRANGE ANGELS

✧ ✧ ✧ ✧ ✧ ✧ ✧ ✧ ✧ ✧ ✧

STRANGE
ANGELS

✧ ✧ ✧ Jonis Agee

Ticknor & Fields   NEW YORK   1993

For information about permission to reproduce selections
from this book, write to Permissions, Ticknor & Fields,
215 Park Avenue South, New York, New York 10003.

Library of Congress Cataloguing-in-Publication Data
Agee, Jonis.
Strange angels / Jonis Agee.
p.   cm.
ISBN 0-395-60835-X
1. Ranch life — Nebraska — Fiction. 2. Family — Nebraska
— Fiction.   I. Title.
PS3551.G4S77   1993
813'.54 — dc20   93-19441   CIP

Printed in the United States of America

MP 10 9 8 7 6 5 4 3 2 1

A number of quotations at the beginning of chapters are from
previously published works. Some of the quotations have been
changed slightly for the sake of conciseness.

Lakota Star Knowledge by Ronald Goodman, Sinte Gleska
College, Box 490, Rosebud Sioux Reservation, Rosebud, South
Dakota 57570, 1990.

Mitakuye Oyasin by Dr. A. C. Ross (Ehanamani), BEAR, Box
346, Kyle, South Dakota 57752, 1989.

Yuwipi by William K. Powers, University of Nebraska Press,
Lincoln, 1982.

The Medicine Men by Thomas H. Lewis, University of
Nebraska Press, Lincoln, 1990.

Mother Earth Spirituality by Ed Mcgaa, Eagle Man, Harper
San Francisco, 1989.

For my father, who read a book a day, never accepted his emotions or his life, and taught me to invent a home for my imagination.

For Marge Bobbitt, who gave me refuge and taught me that family and love could build that home.

And for Brenda Talbot, Lewis, Mike, Ross, Tara, and Blythe — the next generation.

"From this you see that — of necessity —
love is the seed in you of every virtue
and of all acts deserving punishment."

— DANTE
Purgatorio

STRANGE ANGELS

1 ✧ COWBOYING

Jackie Beavers and Group, a talent registry/casting service, are conducting a national talent search for riding, roping cowboys. They will hold an open audition Saturday, June 7, at the Omaha Marriott Hotel, 10220 Regency Circle, from 10:00 A.M. to 5:00 P.M.

Requirements are: ability to really ride and rope, 5'10" or taller, age 28 to 52, have a great build, have a rugged look, have been told by at least five women (not including mother) that you are handsome.

Applicants should take their cowboy hat but not their horse.

— *BABYLON CALLER*

When Cody swerved the truck to avoid the splash of sparrows ahead of them, the horses in the trailer shifted their weight and rocked the stock trailer back and forth. "Wish they'd stay off the damn road. They got the whole marsh to live in." He waved at the blue water and marshgrass on either side of the road where the red-winged blackbirds bobbed light as flies on the tips of reeds, their black bodies glistening in the sun.

"They were here first." Will looked at the younger man, whose face was showing the fatigue of spring cattle work — up at three-thirty every morning if he got to bed at all, what with the calving. "You out last night?" His voice was neutral, as if the sand and wind had worn the emotion out of him a long time ago.

Cody shrugged, but Will could tell from the tired slump of his wide bony shoulders that he was working against a hangover too. Cody had his tan cowboy hat pulled low, the way he'd learned to do when he first came to the ranch at fourteen and didn't want anyone reading his eyes. No one blamed him much. Heywood Bennett had kept his bastard son's ass out of jail for shooting somebody. There were all kinds of wild stories about that one, but Will mostly ignored them. He'd heard and seen enough to mind his own business most of the time. "Sufficient unto the day is the evil thereof," Will told the younger cowboys when they took to speculations. They never knew as much as they thought they did.

But Cody Kidwell wasn't like them. He hadn't even known Heywood Bennett was his father until the day his mother sent him to the ranch. Didn't know anything about ranching either. Never been out of his mama's sight. Crazy Caroline Kidwell. Dead now, but she was a real wild one. Kept Cody out of school, taught him herself. Heywood helped, teaching him how to shoot, how to ride a horse. Lucky he knew that much when he came to the ranch. Heywood wasn't around to help him then, to put any specialness on him. He was treated like everyone else, maybe worse because he was so young and green and the boss's son. Too bad nobody got a hold of Arthur, the other boy. He mighta turned out okay too.

Cody slowed the truck for the big wallow of milky water just ahead because the bottom might be deep sand and sink the truck. "Hold on," Will said, and Cody stopped the rig. They looked around at the green grasses on either side of the road. They'd passed the little lake and were even with a pasture already dotted black with cattle and new calves. The sandhills of western Nebraska marched away into the distance, disheveled and rough, as if the areas had been strip-mined, then abandoned.

"Think we should try the shoulder?" Cody asked, watching Will work the door handle open and climb stiffly out to stand on the running board. He was at the age where arthritis had set in, making the mornings particularly hard. His was a weathered face, nose jutting uneven and wide from the times it got broken, lips thin and chapped, small brown eyes alert in their yellowish sockets, skin matted with fine lines like the texture of an old bridle.

Just beyond Will, killdeer ran on their long thin legs, calling and trying to distract him from their eggs, which lay in clumps of bluestem and milkweed along the roadside. One went so far as to drag her wing and act hurt so he'd come after her instead of stepping on her nest.

Cody smiled. He could never figure out how any of them survived with cattle and horses and deer stomping around. They helped one another, though. The minute one called, others came running in their quick, jerky gait. He'd grown up watching the birds, the animals, the weather, and almost felt like they were part of his family. More than the Bennetts, now that his mother was dead. And his father.

Yes, Heywood was finally dead. Almost a month now. Cody scrubbed his face with his hands. Better to think about something else. Focus on the delicate little ribbon of white around the killdeers' tan necks; they reminded him of the old ladies in town, the ones in flowered dresses and gloves and chunky-heeled shoes, the ones who carried purses with gold clasps that clicked shut like their teeth when Cody or Kya, his sister, were around.

"Don't look good," Will's voice boomed out. "Bottom's outta the road. Shoulder's too soft. I think we should unload the horses and ride the resta the way to be on the safe side." He turned and spit tobacco juice into the ankle-high grass.

Cody looked at the mud hole ahead. It was still at least

five miles to Stannek's, and then another five back, and his body already felt like he'd been caught in a pen of wild steers all night. "Let's just try it. Get in." He shifted the truck into reverse, noting for the hundredth time how the transmission slipped when he pressed the gas pedal, then chugged backwards. He needed a new truck, but he knew cash was tight right now. They hadn't shipped calves last fall 'cause of low prices. He cursed and stepped harder on the gas, swinging the trailer too wide as a result, almost putting it in the ditch.

"Take it easy." Will looked at the younger man, who was beginning to sweat off the alcohol, so his faded blue work shirt was patchy with wet, his skin pale, and his eyes bloodshot. One of his knuckles was skinned, as if he'd hit something. Could be from cattle work, always banged up your hands. And Cody liked the physical abuse, as if he were glad for something to push his feelings against. "You want some advice?" Will stared straight ahead, but watched Cody shift the truck into low, pause, look at him startled, and shove the gas pedal to the floor, aiming for the center of the puddle. Will still told Cody, at twenty-nine, what to do, especially now that Heywood was dead. "Quit drinking so hard. You're not gonna see thirty, you keep this pace up." His words were flung to the roof of the cab as the truck seemed to shudder, land, and settle like a big boat suddenly becalmed.

"Shit." Cody jerked the shifter into reverse, rammed the gas pedal, and managed only to suck them a little deeper. The horses in back began rocking the trailer again as the water started creeping up through the floor slats. He put the truck in low again and stepped on the gas more carefully, but they didn't move. He grabbed the top of the steering wheel, his knuckles white as he gripped so hard the plastic seemed about to shatter, then he relaxed. "Got your life jacket?" He looked at Will and grinned.

"You ever hear of the *Titanic*? The *Andrea* effing *Doria*? Boy, where'd you learn to drive a rig?" Will opened the door, splashing milky brown water onto his boot. "Damn, Cody."

"You taught me everything I know. 'Sides, you haven't had a bath all winter, Will. Here's your chance." Cody shoved the other man's shoulder lightly and caught his thin arm at the same time. Will's battered black hat flew off and landed crown-up in the water.

"You silly so-and-so, that's my life work." Will reached down and picked it up, shaking it gently and brushing at the water so he wouldn't dislodge any of the feathers, toothpicks, and matchsticks stuck in the braided horsehair band. Behind them, the horses started a new round of stamping and shifting, their hooves ringing against the sides of the trailer.

"Must be learning to tap-dance back there. Have to get 'em new shoes, they keep this up." Will examined his hat critically, then set it on his head at just the angle he liked, square. As the oldest man, he also had the oldest hat, the rim uneven, crumpled, the crown torn. It was the best hat, nobody could dispute that; the other men looked at it with envy.

Cody stared at the muddy water ahead of them and the stretch of road beyond. "Now what?" Ed would be waiting for them, growing impatient. The CB in the truck was on the blink again. Kya had kicked it one night when he hauled her drunk ass home.

"Well," Will sighed, and reached for his dented steel thermos, "gonna have me a cup of coffee." He unscrewed the lid and poured the nearly white steaming liquid into it. "Then we unload and ride to Stannek's." He sipped and licked the foamy cream off his lips. "We'll send Ed back with a tractor. He's about as useful as a newborn calf anyway. He lost another one this week too."

Cody nodded absently, staring at the patch of yellow-headed blackbirds flying back and forth across the marsh on either side of them, chirping cheerfully.

"Better have something now," Will reminded him, shoving Cody's thermos of tea toward him.

Cody reached behind him to the half seat and flipped open the cooler, pulling a Pepsi out and popping the top. He took a long drag off the can, letting it burn and gurgle as it exploded with the alcohol still in his stomach. He'd tried to eat before they left, but could only get half a biscuit down before the crumbs filled his mouth like sawdust.

He took another pull on the pop, then put the can between his legs on the seat and reached for his thermos of tea. The combination would do it. He'd be awake at least, not as shaky as he was feeling now. Damn mud puddle.

Will watched the younger man alternate tea with pop and shook his head, wondering who the hell taught him to drink like that. Never ate a thing worth mentioning in the morning, then loaded up with that crap. He'd work hard, though, and never complain. It was in his nature. Even as a boy, when he didn't know the right side of a barn, he hadn't mouthed off about anything. In fact, a person could get downright lonely around Cody, stuck someplace tending cattle. He never carried much conversation in him; you had to ration it or you'd run out and be left with yourself. Heywood and Arthur were windy sons of guns, and the other men had their share of stories and things, once you got them started, but Cody kept it inside. Tight. Nothing extra. Not an ounce on him that wasn't muscle or bone. Except his face, too good looking with those wide lips. Gave him away. They always did. And those sad little boy pale blue eyes he knew enough to hide. Now they were looking out at something, staring off so far he was barely there.

A sage hen leading her chicks strutted into the road ahead of them and paused to peck at some seed or bug, spilling babies from their ranks in the momentary confusion. "Wish I had my rifle," Will said, and drained the last of his coffee.

It was a joke between the two of them, because Will hadn't

shot anything in years, since Cody had known him in fact. Nobody asked why. It wasn't courteous to question something personal like that.

Screwing the lid on his thermos, Will adjusted his hat and looked back at the rig they were pulling. "Well, time to get going. I sure hate working in wet boots." He swung his legs into the water and stood down. It hit him at the knees. "Damn, that's cold," he muttered, and slogged back toward the trailer, keeping a hand on the truck in case the footing gave way.

Cody threw the rest of his tea out the window and put the metal lid back on his thermos. Draining his Pepsi, he dropped the empty clanking into the pile on the floor behind him and opened his door. His work boots had cracked along the sides again and he'd forgotten to put duct tape on them. At first the water was just wet, then the chill of it filled his boots and crept all the way up his legs. The bottom kept shifting beneath him, and he understood how the truck got stuck. He should've listened to Will. It took both of them to force the rusty bolts loose on the back door of the stock trailer and open the gate. The horses were snorting suspiciously at the water, their eyes rolled white along the edges.

"For chrissakes," Will chided his buckskin, "you seen a hundred thousand mud puddles now." He climbed stiffly into the trailer, slipping a little on the wet boards and reaching to steady himself on the rump of his horse. He spoke in the casual, reassuring tone they all used with the horses, regardless of what they said to them. Working his hand forward on the buckskin's body, he reached up and scratched between its ears, the way it liked. The horse flung its head up, as if wanting to hold on to its worry, then relaxed. When the horse settled, Will untied the lead rope and backed it up. The animal reached the place where it had to step down the three-foot drop, stopped, shivering all over, and tried to bolt forward again. "No you don't." Will gave the halter a short jerk to get the horse's attention, then reached up and scratched its head again. "Come on, back up now, you big baby. Ain't nothing but a little ol' mud puddle."

Cody grabbed the horse's tail and patted its rump to help steer and reassure while Will pulled back on his lead and pushed his hand against the animal's chest. The horse stepped down with one reluctant hind leg, then another, and backed so it could lower its front end too. Both men patted it, and Will climbed down and led it to the side of the trailer and tied it while Cody went for the second horse. This was a young one he was almost finished training for Ed, and he hated to have a fight with it now, but the animal had to accept the idea that anything it was asked for, it would have to give. They couldn't afford to keep an animal around that couldn't be counted on to do its share of the work.

The little bay was already looking around anxiously for the other horse, shifting back and forth, testing the snub of the rope. It was only too happy to be untied, and the minute it felt freedom, it spun and lunged for the open door, leaping off into the water, pulling Cody behind it. Instinct told him not to let go of the rope, and the momentum dragged him sprawling head first. By the time he'd blown the water out of his nose and wiped his eyes, Will had the horse but was laughing so hard he was doubled over. Cody saw his hat floating beside him as the water lapped at his chest. "Shit. Shit. Shit."

"Still got that rope, boy?" Will gasped out.

Cody raised his hand clutching the rope securely. "Here." When Will took hold of the rope, Cody gave a sharp tug, pulling the older man off balance. He teetered as his feet sought purchase in the sand and grass, and his flailing arms startled the horse again, who jerked back — which was enough to topple Will into the water too. "You silly so-and-so," Will sputtered as he tried to wipe the water off his face with a muddy hand.

"You're just smearing it — try this." Cody put his face in the water and shook it.

"You're crazy." Will lunged for the younger man and pushed his head under before he had a chance to escape.

Cody had just wrestled free when he heard a voice: "Spring bath? Or did they just let you boys out for good behavior?"

Latta Jaboy was standing on the edge of the puddle, her small grey Ford tractor sputtering and growling behind her. She was dressed in lace-up boots with thick rubber soles and stained khaki coveralls over her other clothes.

"Miz Jaboy," Will said politely, and searched around for his hat as if he were caught naked in bed with someone else's wife.

"Water's not too cold once you get used to it," Cody said, and stood up, shaking his soaked hat as if it were only a matter of a few drops of water.

She frowned, but there was light in her brown eyes and a smile twitching at the corners of her mouth. He looked down and brushed at the mud streaks on his shirt that stuck to his bare skin like wet nylon.

"Need some help?" she asked, shoving her hands into the big pockets at the sides of her coveralls. She hadn't done up the top buttons, and Cody could see a faded red flannel shirt underneath that was also undone. She'd kept her figure over the years, and looked younger than forty. Today her short, dark brown hair swirled and twisted in curls around her face, and Cody decided he liked the intensity of her eyes. He thought he saw interest and humor in them too, along with the usual distance. Though her ranch bordered Bennett's, they never said much to each other.

Will waded out of the water and picked up the reins of the young horse that had forgotten about them completely when it discovered the new grass beside the road. "We could use a tug outta here." He took off his hat, looked at it, and squished it back on his head.

Latta nodded. "Looks like you could use a towel too."

"Cody likes an occasional mud bath for his complexion."

Will dug his Copenhagen out of his shirt pocket, rubbed the package off on his wet jeans, and opened it, pulling a few strands out and packing them in his cheek.

"If I can get around your rig, I can pull you out, I think. This little old tractor isn't very powerful, though."

All three of them looked at the narrow road ridged with holes and ruts, the shoulders, the marsh, and then the distant hills tumbling away from them. There was no evidence of human life aside from the fence posts and barbed wire. No houses, barns, signs. Just sandhills, raw and brown and green, and a watery milk-blue sky curving around them as if they were the last outpost of some distant moon. Just ahead, a crow started cawing from a stunted cottonwood, its body bobbing up and down with each burst of sound.

"You come down and drive this thing outta here, then," Will said to the bird. When the crow hushed, he said, "That's what I thought." He started for the buckskin, who was watching them with a sleepy look on its face that said the antics of men were just the price you had to pay in this world. "Cody, you ride with Miz Jaboy and hook up while I take the horses outta the way."

The sun was beginning to warm up, but the cold water had chilled Cody. He shivered and thought of his jacket in the back of the truck, but didn't want to waste the lady's time. Work to be done. He felt his stomach wanting to join the protest, but he quickly silenced it. It was going to be a long day, and when they got back, they'd have to get things ready for Arthur's branding party this weekend. He didn't know when he'd sleep again. Maybe it didn't even matter. He was always surprised by how far he could push himself. Drinking helped, he'd discovered, especially since Caroline died. Drink and work. Everyone left you alone, you left them alone. When things got dark and crazy, you just did more drinking or working or got in a fight, or found something to pound your fists on — like a wall. Old lady Clark had made him pay for two so far, and suspended him for a week last month from coming into her place.

He looked down at his skinned knuckles. He couldn't remember every single detail of last night, especially around the time he saw his sister, Kya. But if he'd done something really bad, he'd remember that, he reasoned, and climbed up behind Latta on the back of the tractor. The motion, as they started up and eased into the water, pushed him against her, and he had to grab one of her shoulders to keep from falling off as the vehicle jerked and bucked along. When he felt her stiffen beneath his hand, he quickly dropped it and leaned forward, saying "Sorry" in her ear. There was a certain scent that came off her neck like the taste of something very pleasant, not sweet exactly, he couldn't say what, vanilla maybe. He liked it.

He looked at her hands: short, strong fingers and wide palms gripping the old steering wheel, expertly turning it with the contours of the ground beneath them. They were almost past the truck when the tractor began to tilt, as one side of the shoulder, eroded by the washed-out road, started to cave in. Latta inched forward, watching the angle while Cody shifted his weight and leaned on the rear fender toward the higher side. But the angle kept increasing until she had to stop when the tractor began teetering dangerously. They both sat still for a minute, bracing to jump.

"Mrs. Jaboy? You need to slip off — carefully — dive — if you have to — or we'll end up under this thing." Cody spoke in a low, quiet voice. They all knew of people who'd been trapped, maimed, or killed under tractors.

She slid and dove into the water in one smooth motion, like an otter, and the tractor idled without tipping any farther. When she was out of range, she stood, dripping wet and muddy, and called, "What're you going to do?"

He was the problem. It was his weight that seemed to be counterbalancing the tractor, and he wasn't sure he could turn and jump off the high side fast enough, or dive off the low side either. It was interesting, he decided. Damn interesting. Will watched impassively, a horse in each hand, knowing better than to try and direct something like this. Cody began to inch his way along the big fender, keeping his weight centered. When he was closer to the steering wheel, he stopped, judging the distance to clear the tractor should it start to tumble. He wasn't sure he could make it. On the other hand, he wasn't sure he wouldn't, especially if he hit it just right as it started to go. Oh well. He slid into the seat, spinning the steering wheel as far to the right as he could and jamming the gas pedal to the floor. The tractor rocked and tilted even farther, hung there, then rocked back again and spurted into the water, righting itself as it stalled just ahead of the truck, when the water flooded the engine.

"That was a damn dumb cowboy thing to do," Latta said to his grin, and splashed past the tractor to the road beyond.

He climbed down. The thrust of the water against his legs actually felt warmer this time, since his wet clothes clung cold-ly against him. He walked to the dry road just ahead, sat down a few feet from her and pulled off his boots. His socks had holes in them as usual, and he could feel her disapproving gaze on the naked lavender of his big toe poking through the grey wet of the cotton. He sighed. "Sorry. Thought I could save the day. Guess we're all stuck, unless I can dry those spark plugs and —"

"We better mount up," Will said. "We can send Ed back with the big John Deere to pull us out. Miz Jaboy, you better ride with Cody — this old horse don't take kindly to two. It's just one of his rules, and I like him too much to argue. Lesson I shoulda learned long time ago, woulda kept my first wife." Will smiled, spit brown juice to the side of the road, and climbed on his horse, holding out the bay's reins.

Cody pulled on his boots, which grabbed against the socks so hard the holes in the toes widened and tore down to his instep when he stomped his heels home. He frowned at the feel of the wet leather against his bare feet. Taking the reins, he turned to Latta, who was stepping out of her coveralls. In worn Levi's, man's grey T-shirt, and flannel shirt, she was mostly dry underneath. "Wanna grab our jackets outta the truck?" Cody asked Will, and swung onto his horse.

While Cody put his denim jacket on, Latta rolled her coveralls and handed them to Will, who put them on the seat of the tractor. Cody dropped his left stirrup and held out a hand for Latta. She put her foot in and used his arm to swing up behind the saddle. The bay dropped his haunches beneath the extra weight and they sat very still until the horse blew out his nostrils and relaxed. Cody patted its shoulder and clucked. The horse took a few tentative steps before lengthening its stride and breaking into a trot so suddenly, Latta had to grab Cody's waist for balance. His stomach muscles tensed into ridges under her fingers and he could feel her breasts against his back. Cody reached behind for her leg and wrapped his hand around her thigh to keep her from bouncing off the back of the saddle but couldn't stop his wet, muddy hair from slapping her in the face as the horse grunted and pulled to run out its nerves.

A moment later it was over. The horse slowed to a walk as if nothing had happened, leaving Cody with the embarrassment of hanging on too long. She leaned back farther than necessary, to make it clear that she meant nothing, and he shifted in the saddle and spoke to the horse sternly. Both of them felt the rigid silence between their bodies, the result of touching someone you shouldn't, didn't know.

Cody cleared his throat. "He just has to work it out that way. Then he's fine. He's not a bad horse." He turned his head enough to look at her with his pale blue-grey eyes. From the front, his face appeared a bit broad and flat, but from the side, all the angles and bones emerged, showing a finely modeled chin and nose.

She nodded and he looked off across the sandhills, whose

ragged shapes were dotted with spiky green soapweed and bunchgrass. Where the erosion was bad, round green ears of cactus stood out against the pale sand. Last year's grasses waved tan and effervescent, as if it would take just one more wind to press them down permanently. The sky that just a bit ago was still pale and tentative was spreading thin spring blue, with only the white whisk of high clouds etching its distance.

Cody pointed to the place high above them where big white birds were riding a chimney draft up into the sky, spinning and whirling so their wings turned black and thin as table knives, then flattened white again. Sometimes the birds disappeared altogether into the sun, reappeared as single lines silvery and quick, then broadened and became wingspans and birds again. The pattern was repeated over and over, the birds trading places, front to back, side to side, precise and elegant until they disappeared, as if they had flown out of the world.

"They're beautiful, aren't they?" she murmured.

Will trotted up beside them. "Buckskin needs to get the kinks out." Cody nodded, a little relieved for some diversion. "Hang on," he said as they leapt into a lope after the buckskin. Latta just had time to wrap her arms around his hips. This time he tucked her arms under his, holding her tight against his sides and back, and put his free hand over hers, locking them onto his stomach, enjoying the feel of it. When the edge of his silver trophy buckle rubbed at her hand, she moved it higher on his chest. The horse was running flat out after the other one, ignoring the potholes and puddles and the double weight it carried. Instead of leaning forward to lessen the wind, Cody sat upright, almost leaning back into her, which made her tighten her arms around him.

When they slowed to a walk again to let the horse catch its breath, she dropped her hands and tried to put some space between their bodies. It was a gesture Cody was familiar with: he'd always been treated by older women as if they disapproved of him.

Up ahead of them, Will had stopped the buckskin and was half turned in his saddle. "We're saved," he called. Cody touched the horse into a trot, and Latta automatically grabbed his hips but tried not to press up against him. He stood a little in the stirrups to ease the roughness of the gait.

"Nice trot," she said as her teeth clattered together.

"That's why Ed's getting him." Cody turned his head and smiled at her, the left side of his mouth rising higher in a toothy way that made him look like a kid again.

She laughed. "Don't ever give me a horse, then." Her words came out jerkily between the bounces.

"Oh, I'd make sure you got a good one, Mrs. Jaboy." He smiled and pressed his lips together.

"I bet." She smiled. He laughed and touched the reins for a sudden halt, forcing Latta to grab him hard again.

Will shook his head and took out another strand of chew and packed his cheek. "Ed's coming up yonder. Musta figured we got stuck."

Cody was almost sorry to see the big green John Deere tractor chugging down the middle of the road toward them, scattering birds in its way. He wondered why the hell Ed decided to take this particular moment to show some initiative. He had half a mind to fire him, except they'd have a helluva time finding someone to take his place. Hardly anybody around wanted to cowboy anymore. Kids left the sandhills right after high school or college. The really good young hands got rodeo in their blood and took off half the year, working only to save money for entry fees and traveling. So he was stuck with Ed to run the Bennett operation at Stannek's old place. A person could tell just by looking at Ed's face that there wasn't much working behind it. His eyes were closely set and lopsided, as if they'd started to skid off the skull while he was being made. Everything else seemed just the poor side of finished — his small flat nose, his lobeless ears, his mouth with the flabby chin. Over his sparse tufts of pale hair he wore a seed cap with the emblem pulled off. You could still see its darker outline. Ed had a whole collection of what he called tractor hats, lined up on a shelf in the living room, each with the emblem removed because he "wasn't some free billboard."

"Ya fall in or go for a swim?" His unfinished face stretched with a smirk as he stopped the tractor in front of them and touched his cap for Mrs. Jaboy. Ed broke into an irritating high-pitched bray. Cody stared at the laughing jaws, lined with a jumble of stained teeth so crooked they looked like someone had stood back a few feet and pitched them at his mouth. He could feel Latta shifting uncomfortably behind him.

"If you knew the road was out, why the hell didn't you call?" Cody worked to keep his voice quiet and level, trying to forestall the headache that was starting to crack across his forehead.

Ed worked to pull his mouth straight and succeeded in a half-sly, half-embarrassed smile. "Guess I overslept a little."

Cody nudged the bay, who wanted to shy, up close to the tractor seat. Ed leaned away instinctively and grinned harder while trying to keep his lips together, as if he believed that the display of teeth would somehow cause his downfall.

"Cody —" Will said, riding up beside Ed on the other side.

"No, it's okay, isn't it, Ed? You get to sleep in, rest up, living out here by yourself rent-free. Keep your own schedule. Weather gets bad, you don't feel like working cattle, you lay around the house, eat, get fat — who gives a shit — Bennett cows are out there calving, no one's helping. It snows, no one's digging calves out or bringing hay. Hell, cattle are dumb animals — can't save 'em all, right? Who cares? You're doing fine, you're getting paid. Right?"

Ed looked uncertainly from Cody's cold face, rigid with anger, to Will's, but when he saw Latta's stare he dropped his eyes. "Cody, I'm sure sorry about —"

"Don't apologize to me. That doesn't bring the dead cows back to life. Why don't you get off your fat butt and do the work I hired you for. That's all I want — if you take the money, do the goddamned job. How hard is that to understand?"

Ed shivered at the ice pick of Cody's dislike in each word. He shook his head, then nodded, too confused to know what the answer was. Will had to duck his head to hide his smile.

Latta was so still, Cody could hear the catch of her breath behind him. Maybe he was upsetting her or something — the idea made him more angry at Ed. He shouldn't have to be doing this in front of her. "Now get down, take this horse I trained for your sorry ass, and go work cattle with Will while I go back on the tractor to clear the traffic jam." Latta slid off, bracing her hand on his thigh in a way he liked, and landed lightly beside the horse. Cody dismounted and held out the reins.

First Ed had a little tangle with his feet and the gears. Then it took him three tries to pull himself into the saddle, causing the bay to roll its eyes and to break a new sweat on its neck. Ed sat tentatively, his face creased with worry, his butt hanging over the cantle like a border of bagged custard.

"You haven't ridden a horse since you moved in here, I bet. He'll punch you to the moon, you bounce around on him." Cody looked at the man with disgust and climbed onto the tractor seat. With Latta resting on the big green fender, gripping the edges securely, he shifted gears, changing the engine idle from a low steady throb to a higher-pitched growl.

Out of the corner of his eye, Cody caught Latta's smile. "I'll catch up," he hollered over his shoulder. He pushed on the gas pedal, sending them chugging back down the road.

2 ✧ *BRANDING WEEKEND*

> The Bennett family ranch held their annual branding
> get-together last weekend, with visitors from Minnesota,
> Iowa, South Dakota, and Wyoming. They branded more
> than 400 calves. A record, according to Arthur Bennett.
>
> Truby Owen went to Hyannis Sunday and accompanied
> her daughter, Sallie, to Omaha for a doctor's appointment.
> They had sunshine the whole trip.
>
> — *BABYLON CALLER*

A t seven the next morning, the saddled and bridled horses
stood hipshot along the fence nearest Bennett's big east
pole barn, waiting for the riders. The slick new coats bore
the remains of winter hair in dull clumps along their bellies
and rumps, like the bunchgrass terrain climbing the sandhills
around them. The racket of crows in the big elms, cottonwoods,
and cedars around the main buildings seemed to break up the
dawn, the clatter of their calling back and forth some ritual
of reassurance as they collected, dispersed, collected, then finally headed out in four directions. At dusk they would collect
again, thick legs bouncing lightly on branches that would seem
barely able to bear the weight and size of these birds. With
chests the span of a man's hand, they strode the treetops as if
they were walking the decks of ships, while the dark, intelli-

gent eyes watched, heads cocked for the small edible something.

Cody stopped on the porch as he always did, taking the first deep breath of real air, noticing the dewy green of the new grass, the sweet and sour smell of the animals' manure, and the hint of perfume from the nearby golden pea and primrose. In the hydrangea bushes to his left, a small flock of grackles settled like fallen leaves on the new green, then ignited again and flipped up into the air, as if tossed like ashes by the burst of a fire. A great blue heron, its long neck crooked in flight, coasted just overhead, the shadow making Cody's eye lift momentarily to follow its soft glide to the pond in the wet meadows just south of the barns.

The morning chill that was causing the mist on the pond and distant marsh to curl up into the sun rested easily on his denim jacket and bare wrists. He knew it'd be warm enough in another hour that he'd shed the jacket, and maybe by noon he'd wish he could take off his shirt. He was dressed in his oldest chaps and clothes for working with the calves, and tried not to think about the end of the afternoon, when he'd be bruised, bloody, and coated with shit.

He checked his belt for the knife he'd be using, then stepped off the porch and walked across the small yard, out the fence gate, and toward the barn. Pausing, he looked down the driveway, which was really a twelve-mile-long unpaved road leading into the ranch from the county highway. Three pickups with stock trailers were pulling up, a sign that they'd be under way before long. Today they'd work the cattle closest to the ranch, then Sunday they'd go over to Stannek's and work on Ed's — if they could get through the washout. Otherwise, they'd go up and work the Clemmer place.

Cody looked for his saddle to determine which horse he was riding. On branding days, he left that decision to Will, who had to organize mounts for all of Arthur's guests too. When he found it was the rangy paint, he grimaced and mounted, letting the horse amble slowly toward the gate. Not particularly handy, the horse was useful because of its stamina. For some reason, the big, Roman-nosed gelding had never learned cattle work. It still had days when it even forgot what neck reining meant.

Will and Ed and Bless had set up the temporary pipe corrals and two squeeze chutes in the pasture beyond the main buildings where they'd do the work. A portable propane unit for branding rested beside each chute. Bless would have made sure the units and irons were in good shape. He wasn't good with the animals, but fifteen years ago Heywood Bennett had hired him to take care of the increasing amount of machinery on the main place, as well as on the other ranches they were acquiring. Having to haul a piece into town for repair could cost them days or weeks and much more money than keeping a man around to ensure things were in working order. Bless also repaired the windmills and checked on the wells. He was the only reason Cody's old Dodge pickup still ran, though Cody wasn't certain that was such a good deal.

Bless had projects of his own when he wasn't under a truck or tractor. This past spring he'd tried raising quail in the machine shed, but the barn cats had been raising a litter of kittens too. It'd taken him a month to figure out where his chicks were disappearing to. At least that problem took care of itself, not like when Bless had tried raising goats. The herd, left unchecked once they were put to pasture, multiplied rapidly. In their feral state, in the thousands of acres of sandhills, they soon started chasing anything they encountered. Heywood had just organized his first wild goat hunt with some neighbors when the herd inexplicably broke through the four strands of barbed-wire fencing and took themselves to the Burlington Northern tracks where the sum total were hit by a fully loaded coal train on its way out of Wyoming. Since it caused such a wreck, railroad officials were furious, and spent weeks trying to discover the origin of the goats, but no one said a word.

Everyone from Bennett's drove over that evening after chores to inspect the accident. The carnage was an odd mixture of black and red and white, with the crows tearing at meat already rotting in the sun. The smell was awful, yellow loops of guts and bowel torn open, spilling their green and brown contents, and the tarnished scent of blood and goat. The black fabric of flies were like flags placed discreetly over the fallen heads, the ripped throats, the ruptured bellies, the separated and stranded legs. Horrified and fascinated, Cody couldn't take his eyes away. When he threw up Will ignored him, silencing the other men with a look. That was before he was used to things, he now realized. He could see that same scene now and it wouldn't be more than a momentary curiosity. At least he thought so. You just put yourself someplace else, told yourself that this wasn't so bad, and walked through it.

"Looks like you got some sleep last night for a change." Will rode up beside him and leaned away to spit. "Got three youngsters coming up in a minute from Ross's, and Aubrey Foster and that Chris Young from Latta Jaboy's. We'll take this herd in three groups, I figure."

Cody nodded. "Bless pull the truck around for the culls?"

"Yup. And he set up the tables for us too. Vet'll be here by the time we get the first bunch penned, so let's be at it." Will set his spurs lightly to the buckskin's sides, loping away in an easy rocking motion.

Cody lifted the paint into a lope and followed Will up the hill and across the ridge to the other side, where the herd was resting and grazing in a dry meadow, chopping the last of the winter grass and pulling at the new green shoots. Only a few weeks ago, Cody and Will had been out in this same meadow trying to dig five new calves out of the snowdrifts dumped by a late April blizzard. It was the same storm during which Heywood had decided to die. When it all melted in a sudden wave of heat three days later, they found two calves they'd missed, and cursed themselves. Every time Cody had to tell

Arthur about a lost animal, his brother looked at him as if he had personally taken four hundred dollars and flushed it down the toilet on a whim.

Bluebells and purple spiderwort blinked color among the grasses as they came down the hill. The soft tan of last year's bluestem, grama, and switchgrass was gradually being overtaken with a tentative green. Soapweed's stiff, thick leaves and three-foot dried seed stalks poked aggressively into the sky. Right now, Cody thought, they were probably riding over a taproot five feet deep and an inch thick, with lateral roots spreading twenty-five feet wide and ten feet deep. The thing was so damn tough, you could never get rid of it.

He watched the land closely as they moved toward the cattle. It was important to discover erosion from water, wind, or animal disturbance as soon as possible, then begin the long battle to keep it from spreading by dumping tires, old hay, lumber, anything to hold the surface. It was an ongoing struggle, and the best way to preserve the land was to keep the surface covered with grasses that were needed for grazing cattle. The problem was the bureaucrats in Lincoln and Washington, and the environmentalists, who didn't understand the fragile relationships that had been established and maintained. When the government tried to open the land for farming a hundred years ago, the cattlemen fought back because the act of disturbing the land with plows quickly sent it to the wind. Fencing the land and controlling the grazing of animals had improved much of the region, and the ranchers themselves policed the number of cow-calf pairs their acreage could support, despite the distant politicians constantly trying to assert that they could graze many more. In truth, the legislators had no idea how anyone could live in the hills, let alone why. They would just as soon see the whole region turned into a national park, or abandoned altogether as some sort of vast desert, unnecessary and hostile to modern life. Cattle could just as easily be raised in much smaller areas, fed hormones and steroids to achieve growth, and be slaughtered more quickly. But the ranchers knew that the quality of the beef went down by hurrying the entire process.

By the time the sun had burned off the last of the mist and chill and the guests were stumbling down to breakfast in the house, the air was filled with the thick bawling of calves and the answering bellows of mamas. The men had to shout to talk over the noise, and most of their conversation was conducted in monosyllables and waves of an arm. Will, as the oldest cowboy, was on horseback in the middle of it, directing the younger men into different positions for separating the calves from the cows for branding. Aubrey Foster, a thickset blond with beefy shoulders and a full, sensual face, was roping calves that tried to escape. The other cowboys on foot drove the cows off with lengths of hose and board, whacking back ends and hollering at the stubborn ones. Dust rose and swirled around the men struggling to split the herd into two groups. Nervous cows splashed out puddles of hot green manure the men slid through before it soaked into the ground. The noise grew denser as more and more cow-calf pairs were separated, each animal calling and answering at a pitch just past what the human ear could tolerate without thinking of hell itself.

The area beyond the barns was filling up with cars and trucks pulling trailers. Just outside the fence, planks had been set up on sawhorses, and it wasn't long before the women covered the planks with coffee, tea, juice, biscuits, gravy, cornbread, rolls, coffee cakes, side meat, pork chops, small steaks, scrambled eggs, bacon, sausage, and fruit. The young men unloaded their horses and quickly sprang into the saddles, trotting to join the clamor and roar. Cody sent some of the new arrivals to a distant pasture for the next group of cattle, while he delegated the youngest men to the ground, where they would handle the calves. It was customary that visitors, young

men, and boys would take the worst job, which was corral-
ling new and yearling calves and driving them into the squeeze
chute.

Overhead, the sun had settled large and bright and hot, as
if it had caught itself on a nail. Cody was at the chute in the
first pen, Will at the second, each armed with a very sharp
knife, tags, and syringes. Old Colin Young from Jaboy's was
working the head for Cody. Chris, Colin's son, was on the
branding iron. The work flowed naturally from stage to stage.
One of the young cowboys on the ground selected a calf and
drove it into the chute, pulling its tail and banging on its
behind to keep it straight. When it reached the narrow part of
the chute, Colin at the front trapped the head in the squeeze
while the youngster at the rear held the tail high and crimped
to keep the calf's attention. Shoving his leg between the animal's hind legs to hold it, he was splattered with manure.

The calves had to be dehorned, vaccinated, branded, and
maybe castrated as quickly as possible. The boy at the back
hollered "Heifer!" when the work began. First Cody felt for the
nubbins of horn on the head and sliced them off with his knife.
The blood started oozing immediately, so he took the branding
iron Chris had waiting and cauterized the places. The brassy
stench of burning blood and horn made each man suck in his
breath, though by late morning they would be so used to it they
wouldn't bother. While Chris put that iron back in for reheating
and grabbed another to brand with, Cody injected the calf with
a broad-spectrum antibiotic and notched the ear. Chris pushed
the iron onto the hip of the calf, moving the iron up and down
slightly to make sure the brand burned clear and deep. The
cowboy on the tail pulled it higher and stuck his leg in farther,
receiving another squirt on his chaps for the trouble. He held
his face away, squeezing his eyes and breathing through his
mouth against the acrid smoke of burning hide and flesh. Since
the noise was so terrific, Cody used his hand to signal the man
at the tail that they were done, and Colin at the head to open

the squeeze lever. The calf stood dazed for a moment, then shook itself like a dog and trotted away, bawling for its mama as it rejoined the herd.

The next calf kicked the kid handling it in the balls, despite its tail being wrung. Though his face went pale, the boy didn't say a word, and Cody and Colin exchanged looks and grinned. That's why the older men let the younger macho cowboys and kids handle the calves. When the kid called "Bull," his voice was faint and squeaky, but he never let go of the calf or grabbed himself between the legs. Immediately after the vaccinating and branding, Colin flipped another lever and the calf was on its side on a waist-high table of rusty steel. When the door on the top dropped open, exposing the genitals, Cody pulled the sacs toward him and cut them off with one deft stroke. Without looking, he tossed them in the cardboard box behind him on the ground, where the flies quickly covered them. "That'll put your mind on grass, not ass," Cody muttered, and signaled Colin to flip the table and release the head. The calf walked off stiffly, with blood streaming down the insides of its legs, then picked up a trot as it distinguished the call of its mother from among all the others.

The work continued with mind-numbing regularity and speed. Aside from the cowboys yelling "Hee-haw," "Come on," and curses at the calves they half drove, half lifted into the chutes, there was no excess talking. When a bull calf chased a cowboy around the corral or mauled him briefly on the ground before he could jump up on the fence, there was laughter, but otherwise the work was too serious and costly to waste time.

After they had branded and handled more than a hundred calves and yearlings, Cody and Will signaled for the noon break. Carrying the boxes of testicles onto the porch, Cody caught John Long, who cooked and ran the Bennett household, on his way outside with a case of beer for the cowboys. "I'll dump these in the kitchen for later," he said, grinning at the other man's stricken face when he looked at the mass of bloody sacs dotted black with flies that clung drunkenly to the gelid surfaces. "Come on, you never had Rocky Mountain oysters? Ladies inside'll fry 'em up in a nice batter, you'll think you're eating mushrooms or chicken. Just a little less taste."

John shook his head and pushed his shoulder against the screen door. "I'll stick to the real thing."

Cody laughed and stepped into the kitchen, where women were cooking, unloading dishes of newly arrived food, and talking. When Vivicar Barnes noticed him, she gestured to a corner of bare countertop by the refrigerator, where she quickly slapped down a roaster pan to receive the contents of the boxes. Opal Treat, whose column in the Babylon Caller noted local society, was telling them about a murder-suicide over by Chadron, and after that, she promised to tell them about Andrew Redden's daughter, who had come home with AIDS.

Outside, the men who had spent the morning working were lying or sitting on the ground, eating plates of sandwiches, cold fried chicken and salads, and draining cans of beer and pop. The older men were too exhausted to talk, while the younger ones compared battle wounds and laughed. Arthur's guests sat on chairs and benches around makeshift picnic tables, suspect in their clean western clothes. Self-consciously they glanced at the filthy hands of the other men eating with quick pleasure, the food so much better than the usual "weenies and beanies" or sardines and crackers.

Balancing his plate of food and can of pop, Cody sat in the shade of the biggest elm, leaning against its thick corrugated trunk, rubbing back and forth to let the ridges work at the stiffness in his back. His fingers hurt from gripping the knife and syringes, but it was nothing to what the other men would be feeling by now, he knew. It had only been the last few years that he'd been allowed to move toward the front of the calf. He could still feel the kicks to the balls he'd taken while working the rear end.

He'd gotten kicked several times his first day of branding,

when he was fourteen, so by the time he lay down that night he could hardly walk, and his thighs and groin were black and blue. Joseph Starr had come to his bed when he was too sore and tired to eat and given him tips on how to avoid getting nailed so often. But the next day had been even worse. He'd accidentally pulled a heifer they'd missed from a group that had already been sprayed for flies, and when the branding iron was applied, her hide caught fire and within seconds she was a ball of howling flame, the men hollering and beating at her with their caps and hands. She was a smoldering heap of flesh before they could help her. Heywood had been furious, and made him drag her off, cut her up, and eat a piece of her every night for a month. The punishment had seemed mild compared to the nightmares the scene inflicted upon him afterward. Now he was too tired for death. Lucky, he thought.

"Need some help this afternoon?" Kya's boot toe nudged his side.

He opened his eyes and looked up. His sister had braided her long hair in two shiny black pigtails and wore an old denim work shirt open one button too far, jeans, and tan chaps he recognized as the pair he'd abandoned because they were too patched and holey. "Sure. Talk to Will."

She shoved her hands into her back pockets and looked across the yard to where Arthur was holding forth with two bankers from Omaha. "It's so boring here," she said. "I wish something would happen." She looked up into the trees, flattening the world with her gaze, as Cody watched. At six feet, she was almost as tall as he was, with straight thick hair and bottle-green eyes that seemed to pick up the light and dark around them. Her mother had been a Lakota from the Rosebud Reservation in South Dakota, fifty miles north of Bennett's.

"You know what Heywood always said, 'Boring people make things —' "

Kya toed his rib lightly and pouted her full lips. "I know. I can't help it. It's just — I don't know — since he died, it's like something's wrong. I can't explain it. Everything's gotten boring or weird. You know, we used to have fun, all of us, even Arthur and me. I miss him, Cody. He — I can't explain it — he liked me. I guess that's it. It felt good. And I don't usually care who likes me. I even miss seeing him out there in the corral, yelling at you about some cow thing. It'd be worth his piss-poor attitude to hear his big voice again. It just feels kind of empty without Heywood, doesn't it?"

Cody looked up at his sister, but couldn't hold her gaze and looked away, shrugging. "Guess I've been too busy to notice."

"You're always too busy or too tired these days. Don't you ever want to talk again, the way we used to as kids? Remember when you first moved here? And we'd get up in the middle of the night and meet out by the windmill and talk? God, I miss those times." Kya hugged herself and looked away, not noticing his quick glance at her face, his eyes finding the long slice that had scarred her jawline since childhood.

He nodded. "But —"

"Never mind. It's okay." She said it gently, as if she had to forgive him for something. He didn't understand why, but he felt sorry anyway. He was never right with his sister anymore. He seemed to let her down without understanding how or why.

A moment later, she was standing next to Arthur, flirting with the two bankers, stroking the end of a braid with her long fingers as if nothing in the world could feel as good as her own hair. Cody knew his sister missed their father. He just didn't have anything to offer her. Arthur should be saying something. He was better at that kind of thing — he always acted like he was, anyway. A surge of irritation at his half-brother passed through him, and made him climb quickly to his feet.

As if that were the signal everyone had been waiting for, the other cowboys also stood and filed tiredly out toward the corrals to begin the afternoon's work. The noise from the cattle had calmed since they'd finished with all the separated calves that morning, but as the process began again, new waves of ear-splitting bellering and almost human sobbing soaked the air.

They had just gotten back to work and Ty, Curt, and Haney Sykes, clumsy with their usual hangovers, were wrestling a particularly large yearling steer into the chute when it suddenly spurted forward, catching everyone by surprise. Colin pulled the lever to capture the head — a moment too late — and caught the shoulders and got his own hand tangled with the animal. By the time they'd released the steer to free Colin, the older man had a broken wrist. He looked at Cody apologetically and left for town to see if he could get someone to cast it at the little hospital. They were so short of doctors in the region, he might end up staying all day and all night before one showed up. Cody was about to put Aubrey on the head when Latta Jaboy filled in the space next to him. She looked at Cody with a cool challenge in her eyes, but he just shrugged and nodded at Ty, Curt, and Haney to shove the next one through.

"A load of mine will be coming through anyway." She leaned close to his ear to shout, and he looked up at her with surprise. She nodded. "Arthur's idea —" But the calf was being half pushed, half lifted into the chute and they had to pay attention.

She was quicker and more efficient than Colin, Cody noticed, her timing perfect. She even held the calf's ear still when he was notching, so there were fewer botched jobs. Her hands were steady and strong, and she worked without talking or complaining. He could feel growing approval for Latta. A couple of times when there was a slight lull, he glanced sideways at her face and clothes streaked with dirt. She wore a faded blue seed cap low on her forehead to protect herself from the sun, as many of the men did.

But then it started distracting him to have her there, which annoyed him because he needed to pay attention to the job he was doing. He almost felt like telling her to trade places with his sister, who had taken over the head position on the other chute, leaving Ed to direct the younger men on the ground with the cattle. After a while, he noticed some sort of vibration in the air between the two chutes. A couple of times when he looked up, Kya was glancing at Latta. And the animals started coming through almost faster than he could handle. He found himself slicing balls off so quickly he had to pull the last connection of skin away as the table was being uprighted again, almost smashing him in the jaw. "Watch it," he growled, and Latta yelled, "Get outta the way." It reminded him of Heywood, and he sank into his usual silence again, speeding up his hands to match the acceleration.

For two hours they worked at a pace that made their arms and shoulders bags of lead tied to their backs and kidneys, pushing in, pulling down, so that their bodies ached with spasms in every direction. Their heads pounded with the noise, their noses and eyes and mouths filled with dust and stink until everyone squinted against it, and spit continuously to get rid of the taste and grit. In long sleeves, gloves, and chaps for protection, their bodies felt as if they had been pushed into a furnace that was turned on just enough to slowly roast them to death.

The Sykes brothers, working in Cody's corral, were reaching a dangerous point where the alcohol in their blood was burning off too fast. Though Curt was doing okay, Ty and Haney both had the shakes, and it now took the two of them to load a calf into the chute. Cody was on the verge of telling them to call it a day before someone got hurt when Ty, at the tail of a big bull calf, started having real trouble. Cody was sawing at the last stubborn piece of horn and Chris Young was handing him the branding iron when the calf kicked Ty hard in the stomach. Dropping the tail, Ty staggered backwards, letting all hell break loose as the calf twisted to get away. The white-hot iron caught Latta on the arm, searing through her shirt while the knife sliced the inside of Cody's arm. The wound was deep enough that blood started seeping immediately after the skin separated, turned blue, then white and red.

Latta's arm bubbled where the iron had set the cloth on fire and melted it onto the skin. She stared at his blood, though, not her own arm. He was starting to feel a little lightheaded as he watched the skin layers separate and welt on her arm.

Judy, the vet, ran to her truck for bandages and antibiotics that she carried in case she got hurt on the job. Cody felt the noise recede a bit, as if the animals had decided to be considerate. He stepped back from the pen, holding his hand over the cut and squeezing to slow down the flow. Latta held her arm cradled against her chest like something small and fragile she had to nurse. Neither one of them expected help, and everyone knew better than to offer it. Ty and Haney Sykes followed the couple, their heads bowed in shame. Growing up, they'd always been good hands, but since the three brothers had taken up drinking as a full-time activity, they were more dangerous than an Omaha banker. Kya had stopped work and stood watching them, her face a mixture of concern and anger, as if Latta had been the cause of the whole thing. Will delegated another crew to help Kya, who took over the job of vaccinating, dehorning, and castrating while he took Cody's place.

Squatting under the cool of the eaves, Cody was washing his arm with the outside hose when a familiar voice said, "Better use hot water and soap, bub. Didn't I teach you anything?" He stood up too fast and wavered a bit. Joseph Starr reached out for his arm. "What's the matter, boy, little blood got you acting like a lady?"

The blood that had slowed with the cold water was oozing again in a long stream down his arm, dripping into the sparse grass and pale yellow soil at their feet. Cody smiled, feeling again the slight distance of the world at the moment.

"Trying to commit suicide just to get outta work. You young cowboys —" Joseph shook his head and picked up Cody's arm, wrapping his bandanna around it tightly and shoving it back at Cody's chest. "Now hold the damn thing up and get in there and clean it right, or next thing you'll be pulling on your boots with one hand."

Cody grinned some more. He couldn't stop, he was so happy to see his old friend. Joseph shook his head and put his arm around Cody's shoulders and walked him to the back steps, opened the door, and pushed him up and into the kitchen, following him. The women scattered as soon as they caught sight of Cody's blood and the Indian in the doorway behind him. "This boy needs someone to help him clean up. Doc says she'll stitch it if he gets the gunk out."

Opal Treat had been in the middle of discussing the latest on K. C. McNutt's long-standing affair with the wife of Jack Jolly, who owned Jack's Jolly Foods. K.C. owned the Absalom Food Center, and the affair had been started to undermine the competition, but had continued when the couple discovered more lust than commerce in each other's arms. Opal turned away and slipped out of the room. She'd get someone else to tell her the gruesome details for her weekly news column.

LaVeta Sheets, a small nervous woman who owned Simon's Hardware with her husband, Radney, surprised everyone by stepping calmly to the big stainless steel sink and turning on the hot water, mixing it with cold to get just the right temperature. "Here, I'll wash it." She held out a clean dish towel she'd pulled from the drawer as the men came through the door. "Radney's always banging and sawing on himself," she explained. "I see a lot of this kind of thing." Joseph stepped back, keeping his eyes down, as the women would expect of him.

When she slid the bandanna off his arm, the blood pulsed bright and hopeful, swirling in red strands with the water against the silver surface of the sink, then slipping down the dark hole of the drain. Cody concentrated on that, his face glowing with embarrassment at the situation that made him stand there with the tiny woman gently rubbing his filthy arm with a bar of white soap. Taking his hand, she scrubbed that too, using her small fingers in between his, the way his mother had washed his hands as a child. It's not my hand we have to worry about, he wanted to protest, but knew better. She probably figured you had to take a bath to get a couple of stitches. At least she was careful, he reminded himself, biting his lower lip as she returned to the cut, spreading the two sides to let the water irrigate it. You weren't supposed to feel it, and if you did, you weren't supposed to show it, but his eyes filled at the smart of pain, and he bit harder, sucking in his breath.

"I'm sorry," LaVeta said. "Want to make sure the wound's clean. Now wrap this around it, and Judy can just come in here where it's cleaner and sew that up." She turned to Joseph and said, "You tell her to come to the house, okay?" He nodded and left. She guided Cody to the kitchen table and sat him down. The women suddenly became busy again, clearing a space so the vet could work.

"Need a drink of water?" LaVeta looked at him, her small faded blue eyes the kind side of neutral. She hardly ever spoke to him in town, probably didn't even know who he was, but like most of the women out here, she could handle an emergency. He nodded and dropped his eyes.

Latta and Joseph followed Judy back into the kitchen. While the vet opened various packages, laying out coarse thread and needles and syringes, the other women left the room so only LaVeta and Latta remained.

"How's the burn?" Cody asked Latta in his soft voice. She stepped closer and lifted the ice-filled towel to reveal a three-inch V where the top of the triangle dot brand had caught her. It was so red and blistered, it almost looked bloody. "Hurt?" he asked, swallowing as Judy lifted his arm and laid it on the sterile pack she'd unrolled on the table.

Latta shrugged and nodded, then smiled. "You Bennetts have to put your damn brand on everything?"

He started to shake his head. "Hold still," Judy ordered, and swabbed the arm with alcohol. The cool felt good on his skin.

"I'm a Kidwell." He smiled. "Besides, Chris works for *you*."

Latta smiled, her large brown eyes locking his with the same interest and amusement they'd shown yesterday. The disinfectant hit the cut and he grimaced. "I'll have to speak to him about that," Latta said.

"Sure you don't want the town doctor to see if you caught any nerves or anything?" Judy straightened and rubbed the small of her back. She'd been working almost as long as he had, and although she'd cleaned her hands and arms thoroughly, the rest of her was as dirty and spattered as he was. She'd come to work at the veterinary clinic when the senior man had gone crazy and moved to a monastery in Wyoming. "Nothing'd be as lonely as these goddamned hills," he'd shouted as he packed.

Cody flexed his hand. "Feels fine. Just go ahead. I have to get back out there before they start trying to castrate the heifers."

Judy smiled. She was a good vet and not much of a talker, so people had quickly overlooked the fact that she was a woman.

"Novocain?" She held up the syringe, but he shook his head. He had to get back to work, and nothing would be more dangerous than a hand he couldn't quite feel.

He put his attention on the floor, on his boots, on the back of his skull, which felt wired with the needle each time it bit his skin and pulled. He didn't realize he was gripping his leg so hard until it went numb. Joseph and Latta ignored him, talking about horses and the recent winter, which he appreciated. At the end the vet gave him a tetanus shot and an antibiotic. She didn't tell him to take it easy, because she knew he couldn't. After she'd dressed the wound, she turned to Latta's burn and worked on it for a few minutes.

Filing out of the kitchen, Cody said, "Thank you, ma'am" to LaVeta.

Ignoring Ty and Haney Sykes, who were resting in the shade of the elms now, hastily draining cans of beer, Cody headed back to the corrals, where the work had slowed. With the vet taking care of the injuries, they could work only the new calves. He stopped for a moment to watch his sister. She was good, as good as any of them, working with a physical strength and energy that surprised people who had seen her just sitting around. She'd always been a good worker, until Heywood had caught too many men watching his daughter and ruled cattle work off limits for her. Now Kya slashed down with the knife, lifting it up with a swoop that flung drops of blood, wiping the blade off on her leg when it got too sticky. Her ear notches were precise and assured, not ragged like some of his. The flesh seemed to stand firm and ripe as fresh fruit for her stroke. Her fingers found the exact triangle of neck for the vaccination, the needle never faltering or breaking. There was a fluid pleasure in her motions as she dominated the chute, the animals, and the men around her.

While Latta was physically strong, she worked the way he did: to get it done, to get through it. Kya was something else. Even as a child, Kya had liked falling into the mud, sliding in it, covering herself with it. Sometimes, after their midnight swims in the stock tanks, she'd roll in the sand, then fall in the water again, as if she couldn't get the world close enough to her, as if her very skin were something that kept her from it. He never understood it exactly, just felt it.

Joseph stopped beside him. "Come on, Latta's gotta keep that burn iced. You work the chute, I'll be on the knife and needle." When Cody hesitated, Joseph grinned. "What's the matter, don't you trust me?"

"You can't be any worse than Ty Sykes," Cody said. The two men climbed the fence and stepped into the roar of noise again.

3 ✧ TIME TRAVELERS

Everyone had various amounts of rain and hail on Sunday late afternoon. Albert Smithson reported golf-sized hail and flooding in their basement.

Bill and Carla Lacy attended the memorial service for John Blake in Mullen. The Corey Lacy family were dinner guests at the Bill Lacy home Sunday. They planted potatoes after dinner. Nigel, Sue, Scoot, and Marge Kirk came on Tuesday to do repairwork on the Sid Kirk home.

— *BABYLON CALLER*

So, can you guess the number of Iowans want to be reincarnated as themselves?" Aubrey was on his fifth beer, telling jokes to Cody while they both watched the band set up beside the temporary dance platform in the side yard.

"Iowans?" Cody squinted thoughtfully at Aubrey Foster's red face.

"Yeah, sixty-four percent." He looked expectantly at Cody, who smiled, shook his head, and sipped at his beer.

"Where do you get this stuff?"

"Nashville Network's video shows. I tape 'em when I'm working and watch 'em at night. That and CMT, they do all videos. No talk. Sometimes I watch the Shopping Channel, but it doesn't do any good to tape that, I found out. Have to be right there to call in. Satellite, man. TV. I know I didn't miss it before, never thought about it. Now I can't believe I lived without it. The Weather Channel. Ever watch that? They have some pretty nice-looking girls on that one."

Cody stood up and stretched. His arm throbbed from the stitches, but the pain wasn't too bad with the beer he'd put between it and him. "I'm gonna grab a plate of something before the food's all gone."

Aubrey got up, setting the beer can down on the ground in front of his chair. "X marks the spot." He grinned and tugged at his mustache, then pushed Cody with his shoulder. "Four hundred fucking cows, man. A record, huh?" He nudged Cody with his shoulder again. He'd played football in high school and never got over the idea.

Standing in line, Cody saw Joseph and Latta just ahead of him, laughing and talking. He wondered when Joseph had gotten back. He'd been gone for almost a year. He'd left Jaboy's, saying he was going home, which everyone took to mean the Rosebud Reservation, since no matter how well they did off it, most Indians seemed to return eventually. In some ways Cody could understand that. If Caroline's house still stood, he'd go back there now. Maybe for good. Heywood had given her the house and land, or so she'd told him. Must have taken it back, then.

As Cody watched, Joseph helped spoon potato salad and cole slaw on the wobbly paper plate Latta held with her free hand. The other hand she kept tucked against her, protecting the burn. As soon as he was through the line, he'd find them and ask her how she was doing. Having Joseph there might help ease the conversation. She might be willing to talk to him again. He couldn't forget the something in her eyes after they'd gotten hurt together. The thought put him in such a good mood, he grew impatient waiting for the people in front of him to decide which of the five Jell-O salads they wanted, and he started to step around them. The fingers tightening over his cut almost made him drop his plate as he spun around. "What the hell . . ."

Arthur dropped his hand and turned, motioning for his brother to follow him. Cody paused, angry at his throbbing arm and Arthur's presumption. But he followed. Might as well get it over with.

The ranch office that Arthur had gradually taken over with the job of keeping the accounts during the past ten years was painted a deep forest green, with heavy, dark varnished mahogany bookcases and furniture, all a little too massive for the small room that struggled for the light sent in through the two curtained and shuttered windows. A brass library lamp with a green glass shade spilled a small pool of gloomy light on the desk, and made Arthur's shadow rise huge and distorted against the walls. Arthur was resting one big thigh on the corner of his desk, his arms folded across the expanse of snowy white shirt with bolo tie neatly drawn up to the buttoned collar. He was wearing a pair of Heywood's black lizard boots and black dress trousers. Arthur never wore jeans. His turned-up shirt cuffs, a concession to the casualness of the day, revealed tufts of reddish blond hair on his thick forearms and fingers. It made him resemble an albino bear, Kya had said once. His skin never tanned, just freckled in orange splotches. Arthur always claimed he was allergic to the sun, and Heywood had let him get away with it, leaving him inside to handle the business affairs while he and Cody did the physical work of the ranch. It had provided Arthur with a natural sense of superiority, since he didn't have to get dirty.

Cody watched his brother's mouth, the only feature shared by the three of them — the full, wide mouth the two brothers hated in each other and therefore in themselves. Cody sat in the barrel-shaped captain's chair in the dark corner opposite the desk. "Mind if I eat?"

Arthur ignored his question and continued to stare at him, as if his gaze would convey all he needed to, so words would be unnecessary. It was an old game, and though he felt uncomfortable under the scrutiny, Cody knew enough to feign indifference, which always irritated Arthur the most. Heywood had used the technique to much greater advantage, but then he was the one person they had all feared and respected.

After a few minutes, he was taking bites that were too big and having to swallow them half chewed, the silence was so overbearing. When a piece of meat threatened to lodge in his throat, he had to slow down.

"God, you eat like a pig," Arthur finally said, and turned to rummage on his desk.

"Fuck you, Arthur," Cody said without feeling. They'd been at this moment so often, neither of them had more than the form of it left.

"Aside from that, then, I just want to ask you something." Arthur paused and pressed his forehead with his hand as if the question needed to be squeezed out.

Cody watched him warily, swallowing the food and clearing his thoughts. He never had a clue what was on his brother's mind, but it was always something pissy.

"What the *hell* did you think you were doing letting those women work out there this afternoon? Why would you do something like that? Heywood *never* let Kya near the cattle, and Latta, you're lucky you didn't get her killed. She's forty years old. She had no business out there. We never let women work cattle on this ranch. On any Bennett ranch. Heywood laid down the law. You've been here long enough to know that. What do I have to do, repeat the rules every day or something?" Arthur's fists rested on his thick thighs, clenching and unclenching.

Cody set the plate down beside him on the dark red and green figured carpet. They'd already had one fistfight this year, the night they buried their father, and another was due, he figured. Maybe tonight was the night. "They *wanted* to work. I'm not their keeper. Mrs. Jaboy just stepped in. You think I'm gonna tell *her* what she can and can't do? And Kya — so what? It was stupid for Heywood to stop her from helping out in the first place. They're both grown women. So get off my ass unless you want to do something about it." He started to stand up, but Arthur waved him back down.

"Just relax. I wanted Kya to meet a man who's here from Minneapolis. I thought it would do her good to meet some men from somewhere else who don't make drinking and screwing around their life work. She's a beautiful young woman, she could take advantage of that. Get a life of some sort."

Cody leaned back and crossed his arms. "She *has* a life."

Arthur shook his head. "You don't see it because you're just like her, except you try to keep up with the work on top of it. Believe me, this is no life for her. She'll be dead from drinking and driving or something even worse before she's forty, at the rate she's going. I don't care what the hell you do, frankly, but I don't want to see that happen to Kya."

"You called me in here for this?"

Arthur sighed and eased off the edge of the desk. Walking around behind it, he rested a heavy hand on the back of the green leather chair, but didn't sit down. "Actually, I wanted to ask you to stay away from Latta Jaboy. Now before you go crazy, let me explain something." When he was talking like this, Arthur's voice carried the same edge of authority as Heywood's. "We're paying huge interest every month on the two other ranches and the cattle. We didn't sell calves last fall, so now we have to figure out how to make up for the cash loss."

Cody jiggled his foot nervously. "I know all this."

Arthur held up his hand. "Yes, but there's more — and remember, it was part of Heywood's plan, not just mine."

Cody stood and put his hands in the front pockets of his jeans and leaned against the bookcase. Whenever Arthur used their dead father as his backup, there was something fishy going on. He always heard it in his brother's voice, a little tinny ring, a rush and catch. Arthur thought himself such a good liar, but Cody had him figured out, and it had saved his ass a few times. He wondered what his brother was up to now.

"You know the farm we sent those three hundred yearlings to, down south of Broken Bow? Well, Heywood decided it was time to buy some farmland to winter-feed our own yearlings so we wouldn't be so dependent on calf prices in the fall. Eventually, he wanted us to become the biggest cattle operation in Nebraska. A one-stop shop, so to speak. We'd do the whole thing, cut out the middlemen, send the beef in line or on rail at the end. Whatever."

Cody shook his head. "We don't have the land. We're not set up that way. Can't do it here."

"Exactly. So we start acquiring farmland south of the sand-hills, and ship them down to our own places instead of paying for feedlotting or having to sell. There's just one problem." Arthur's eyes were moving restlessly over the prints that hung on the walls around him: people riding in carriages, dancing in great ballrooms, and walking along rainy city streets.

Cody knew something was off. He just hoped it wasn't more than the fact that this was probably more Arthur's idea than Heywood's. "Money."

Arthur nodded. "I'm borrowing the money for the down payment from Latta Jaboy. We're reading the will next week, but the banking sons of bitches won't do anything until the estate has cleared. That's what they came all the way out here to tell me. They eat my beef, they drink my liquor, they sleep in my beds, and they tell me they don't dare. The economy is too tight. The banking scandals are too close. Hell, they're waist deep in money. They're dropping the interest rates to nothing and begging people to borrow. If I wanted a goddamned new Chevrolet, I could get it in the blink of an eye, but I can't borrow to buy a farm that will make us all millionaires. It's a sick world, it really is. Any Indian off the res could have a new car or boat tomorrow, but I can't borrow money."

There was a certain amount of truth in what he was saying,

Cody recognized, but also a certain amount of play-acting. "So what does that have to do with me talking to Mrs. Jaboy?"

Arthur's head jerked up, and a wave of impatience passed over his face, making his blue eyes smaller. "That should be obvious. Don't piss her off so she drops the loan. We need the money. This is the first time the woman has been willing to consider being neighborly. You and Kya stay away from her, leave her alone."

Cody looked at his brother for a long moment, then walked to the door, yanked it open, and left. "Fuck you," he flung over his shoulder.

"Goddamned hillbilly," Arthur muttered.

When "white trash" and "hillbilly" had first been uttered by Arthur, Cody had resisted for a week or two before he began to think about it seriously. Then he looked at himself in the cracked bathroom mirror, trying to see the differences between himself and this half-brother which made one of them a hillbilly and the other a regular person. He'd thought it was the size of his crooked front teeth, or his eyes, washed blue and grey and yellow, or his pale brown hair, or the stringiness of his body, or the way he talked, ate, sat, thought, felt.

It was the first time in his life he had studied other people — not so he could belong, be like them, necessarily, but so he could discern the differences that permitted some people to be able to recognize instantly a type, a class, a whole way of being, without having to know anything about the person. He just didn't know how to do it. That was why he began to bring people like John Long back to the ranch, to introduce them to Arthur and Heywood, and to study how they reacted. It never started out as more than a whim, meeting someone drinking in a bar or hitchhiking, but it always ended with a momentary window into the workings of a society he could only guess at.

Arthur caught up with him in the dining room, just outside the kitchen door, grabbing his sore arm again. This time Cody swung around with his fist cocked. "Keep your hands off me."

Arthur stood his ground. The same height as Cody, he out-
weighed him by fifty pounds. Cody had to avoid the rush of
the beefy body that could pin him if he wasn't careful, but then
Cody was faster and more agile than his half-brother.

Arthur smiled at Cody's tension and said, "Chancy called
from Clemmer's. Spent the day with some sick cows and a
broken windmill. Says he needs Bless to come up or he'll have
to move half the herd. You better go check on the cows tonight.
He's worried."

Arthur brushed past him through the swinging kitchen
door, popping it hard enough that it came close to hitting his
brother. Cody was tempted to follow him and have it out, but
he knew he had to take care of Chancy's problems first. No
matter what, the ranch came first. Cattle and horses first. Heywood had pounded that into him, in more ways than one. No
matter how tired or sick he was, the animals were his responsibility.

Cody found John Long sitting in the kitchen, with his feet
stretched out on another chair and his arms locked behind
his head, staring at the grease-speckled rooster clock over the
stove. A glass of amber liquid and ice indicated the source of
his meditation. Without taking his eyes off the clock, John said,
"Shouldn't let him get to you, man." Cody looked at the glass
again, then spotted the bottle of Jack Daniel's on the counter.
He poured a shot and drained it, then poured one he could sip.
His arm was swelling, pulsating. He just hoped it didn't get
infected. When John didn't speak or move, Cody finally asked,
"What the hell are you doing?"

"Andy Warhol made a nine- or ten-hour film with the cam-
era facing the Empire State Building, just recording the way
time passed on it. I figure if you want to watch time pass, really
catch it at its stuff, you stare at a clock with a second hand.
The little brown specks of grease and fly shit help too. Time-
space continuum. We always do this circle thing. What if clocks
were long, like rulers, with inches we took off? We could have

one clock for the whole world, stretch it from here to there. We could break off the used-up part, make it edible, feed the masses or something." His hand picked up the glass of whiskey, brought it to his mouth, and he drank without taking his eyes off the clock. "I have to keep myself from blinking. That's a problem. We blink fifteen, twenty times a minute, and that uses up time."

"What are you on?" Cody smiled at the figure in the chair, his straight black hair tied in a ponytail that hung halfway down his back. His neat, well-muscled body never seemed to change from day to day, despite the lack of any hard work. John was a mixture of Irish and Chinese blood, his only physical flaw the deeply scarred texture of his face, from acne, which had attacked even his nose and earlobes and neck, but left the rest of his body smooth and clear. The ugliness produced was so violent it made him interesting looking.

"Well, I did score some peyote buttons finally. They were a little dry, but I think they're going to work. I feel a major lift-off coming. They said to drink, to keep the taste from making me throw up. You want some?" Without taking his eyes off the clock, John dug in his jeans and pulled out a mushroom button, which he spun across the table at Cody.

"No, I never —"

"You should try it. Good stuff. Or acid. Take that. Don't have any — ah, you see that? How long it took that second hand to move between those two specks on the five? God, I'm getting so hot, I gotta get out of some of these clothes." John began unbuttoning his shirt.

Cody laughed. It would be fun to let him run around naked, stoned out of his head, in front of everyone, but Arthur would fire his butt, and John probably didn't have anywhere to go yet.

"Hey, come on, we're going for a ride," Cody said. "I'm going up to Clemmer's, and you can go into the hills if you want, take your clothes off, hang out with the deer and the antelope. John? Okay, come on." Cody scooped the button off the table and pulled John to his feet, slipping the peyote back into his shirt pocket.

"Okay, just let me take that five down again — okay, there — yeah. Let's go." He backed out of the kitchen, letting Cody pull him so he didn't have to take his eyes off the clock face. When they got outside, the setting sun burst like a brilliant red and purple peony across the western sky. John collapsed on the steps, his jaw slack, his eyes fixed on the color.

"Wait here, man. I have to get Bless." Cody hurried toward the dance platform, where Bless always hung out, though he never danced.

Having sent the man on his way, Cody looked around briefly for Joseph Starr and Latta, but neither one was in sight. He hoped Joseph was going to be around for a few days. And Latta, he wanted to talk to her more than ever, now that he knew it irritated Arthur. Maybe they'd be around tomorrow.

John was missing from the stairs when Cody returned, but he found him sitting by the side of the house, staring at the sunset with Kya beside him. When she looked at Cody with unfocused, happy eyes, he groaned. "You didn't give her that shit, did you?"

John shook his head.

Kya giggled. "*I* gave *him* that shit. And he says you're taking us into the hills. I'm so excited." She put her arm through John's and the two of them struggled to their feet. "We're ready, aren't we?" They both giggled softly, already too far away for Cody to reason with. It was going to be one damn long night.

He sighed. "Okay, come on. The truck's parked —"

Kya held out a key ring, shaking it so the keys tinkled. "I got Arthur's Continental. We're riding in style."

Cody shook his head firmly.

"He gave me the keys — he *did*." Her voice was regressing, her face rearranging itself into the petulance of a ten-year-old. He knew there wasn't any point in arguing.

"Okay." He held out his hand and she dropped the keys into it, grabbing his good arm.

"I'll lead the way," she said. "I parked it for a fast getaway."

Kya got in front and John in back, and it wasn't until he'd started down the road that Cody realized there was another figure in the back seat too. He turned around quickly and caught the grinning face of a young girl from Babylon.

"What's this?"

"Relax." Kya patted his shoulder. "Bony — my, my, you better eat something. She got the peyote for us. She's doing it too, so I told her to wait in the car for John. Didn't know you were going to drive us. Better deal. Probably woulda wrecked this pig, and Arthur wouldna been happy. Not — at — all. Nope. Gotta keep old Arthur happy. That's truth. I know who *you* want to keep happy, little brother." She reached over and pushed his hat off his head, sending it careening into the back seat.

"Cut it out or I'm going back. I mean it." He slowed the car.

The hat came back and she put it on his head. "There, meanie. You care more about Latta Jaboy than me. I can tell. She's just some old hag. Not even pretty. She's mean too. Ask anyone. Nobody likes her. And —"

"Don't you want some music?" Cody flipped on the radio, but Kya pulled a tape from her shirt pocket and pushed it into the slot. The car filled with a somber chanting of eerie voices and instruments that made him shiver. "What is this?"

"Dead Can Dance," John announced dreamily from the back seat.

"Great," Cody muttered, and concentrated on keeping the car from sliding into the wheel-deep sand holes that threatened to belly them out.

"I see God, I see God, I see God —" Kya chanted.

"What?" Cody looked at her.

"Just kidding." She pushed his arm and laughed softly.

Half an hour later, he pulled up to the trailer that served as

Chancy's home on the Clemmer ranch. The house had been in such poor shape when they bought it, Heywood had bulldozed it and moved the trailer onto the property. "It's a double-wide," Heywood had announced proudly after his visit to the Repossessed Trailer Sales on the edge of town.

Kya, John, and the girl had been silent for ten minutes, and when Cody got out of the car, he simply left them there. He had no idea what was happening to their minds or bodies, but he had sick cows to tend to. Bless pulled in and parked his truck beside the Continental while Cody was banging at the trailer door. When no one answered, he went to the truck and got in on the passenger side. "Must be down at the barn."

Bless nodded and drove on the rutted road to where the lights shone from the dilapidated barn. The next thing that'd have to be replaced, Cody thought grimly, it never ends. They got out and found Chancy in the first stall, kneeling beside a cow whose distended belly and short gasping breath indicated pain. Cody dropped to his knees and put his ear to her stomach. The silence suggested colic. Some kind of blockage, maybe.

"You cleared her out behind?" he asked, and Chancy nodded. The three men stared at the cow laboring on the hay in front of them.

"Where's the other one?"

Chancy looked at him in surprise. "There's just the one cow sick. I told Arthur I thought I could handle it, but he said you'd be right up, so I waited. Think I shoulda gone ahead, though." The little man rose abruptly, as if some spring had gone off inside him, and left the stall.

"Dammit." Cody cursed quietly. He could be home in bed sleeping, getting ready for tomorrow when things got a little rougher from all the hangovers and partying the night before.

Chancy returned and held out a long thin knife. "Long as you're here —"

Cody took it reluctantly. "You tried everything else?"

Chancy nodded and kneeled down.

"Okay." Cody felt along the hard skin of distended belly for just the right place. When he found it, he took a deep breath and pushed the knife in slowly. The cow's cry of surprised pain ended in a sigh of relief as the gas whooshed out the puncture and the belly began to collapse as they watched.

The cow's breathing slowed and her eyelids, which had been stretched frantically before, began to droop. "You're gonna be okay now, little girl." Cody reached up and rubbed her neck affectionately, then looked at the amount of dead winter hair his hand collected. "She shedding slower than the others?"

"Thought she looked a little wormy the other day. But I knew we were going to be handling 'em sometime next week. Thought she'd keep."

Lucky the cow was with Chancy and not Ed, or she'd be out in the hills dying right now, Cody thought. "You stitch her up by yourself?" He rocked back on his heels.

"Yeah. Think I'll wait a couple hours, see how she's doing first."

Cody stood up. "Makes sense. Sorry you had to miss the party."

"Yeah, well, you know Connee don't like me going places without her." He grinned and ducked his head. The biggest surprise of Chancy's life had come at age thirty-five, when he'd met a young widow from Chadron. He was still thrilled with his luck, and half afraid it was pure fantasy. He'd been losing weight for two months, worrying about the wedding next week. Cody, Will, and Bless were all going to be in the ceremony.

"Wedding's still on, then?" Cody teased.

Chancy's head snapped up. "Lord, yes. That is, unless you heard something —"

Cody and Bless laughed. "No, I was just kidding. We'll be there. Providing you don't forget."

Chancy stood up too and grinned shyly, looking around as if he wanted to put his face away. "Not likely I'd forget that."

Cody slapped him lightly on the back. "Tell those cows out there they'd better behave themselves. Don't want this happening a week from now."

"I'll tell them that," Chancy said.

"Bless'll stay here and fix the windmill first thing tomorrow, okay?" Cody called as he and Bless left the barn.

Outside, the moon was just coming up, so thin and light a slice it looked like it was drifting off the gravitational curve of the earth. The sky hung like a blue-black cushion studded with silver pins, just far enough away so the two men below could stand and appreciate the good spring night, trickling with water from the Dismal River and ticking with insects, birds, and other small animals infinitely adjusting their positions and comforts. A breeze passed by, rattling the old manure-stained wood of the barn behind them, brushing down across the rushes along the river and up the far side, walking the land with the familiarity of a family member.

When he discovered his three passengers gone, the doors flung open, the dome light burning, Cody shut the car up and left the keys on the dashboard where they'd find them. After telling Bless to get a ride over with Chancy in the morning, Cody drove the man's pickup home, half asleep the whole way, and stumbled into bed in his clothes.

He woke with a feeling that something was in the room. Opening his eyes slowly, he blinked and tried to focus. It was a smell more than a thing he could see, though he had the distinct sense of something taking extra space at the foot of the bed. There was the same smoky, musky soap odor that had scented Heywood's clothes, his room, the air around him all his life. Even after Heywood had quit smoking, it seemed that the smell was permanently embedded in his skin, in the sacs of his lungs, not merely hardened and blocked, but crystallized. Then it became a growing thing that fled his mouth each time he spoke or breathed.

The smell flowed over Cody's bed as if driven on currents of air by a fan, paralyzing him. He stared at the foot of the bed, certain that it was darker there, as if matter itself were being sucked into a dimension of emptiness he couldn't imagine, let alone see. It never occurred to him to speak. His tongue was swollen cold, and his heart was pumping so out of control behind his eyes that it crowded away the words.

After a while he felt it leave, and he got up and went out to the hallway, leaning shakily against the door frame. In the morning, Cody tried to convince himself it was a bad dream.

*My mother got short and fat at the end, thick from bottom to top. I
couldn't understand for years except that there finally wasn't a man
around to make her stop. It must have surprised her too, the way
her body thickened up like tapioca. She had this little black dog, with
a short thick body, thin scrambling legs, skinny worried tail. Big
patches of hair kept falling out where he'd scratch himself. At night
when everything in the house was dark, I'd hear him in the next
room at the foot of Mama's bed, lapping at the spots, slopping them
raw with his rough pink tongue. And I'd hear her too, sucking her
teeth, even in her sleep, like there was something caught in them,
some last little bit of food.*

— Caroline
January 7, 1978

Juggling two drinks in to-go cups, Cody opened the weathered wooden door beside Richard's Pharmacy, Jewelry and
Fine Gifts, where everyone in Babylon registered for their weddings. Above him on the gloomy stairs to Selden Monk's sec-
ond-story law offices, Latta Jaboy paused and turned. She was
dressed in tight, worn jeans, dark blue cowboy boots, and a
checked western shirt. Her hair curled loosely around her face.
In the shadowy light, with her blouse open enough for him to
see the dark between her breasts, he noticed that she was more
attractive every time he saw her. His legs got a little stiff and
heavy as he started the climb up. "How're you?"

"Fine. How's the arm?" she asked as he reached her side. Looking down at her, he realized that she hadn't lost the soft- ened tone she'd used with him over the past weekend.

"Aches, but nothing to call the vet for. How's yours?"

She was just looking at him and smiling. "Okay."

"Want a margarita?" he asked, holding out the one he'd gotten for Kya. "John drove me in and we stopped at José's." She nodded and reached for the cup.

"Thanks. Guess we'll need these, huh?" she said, pulling on the straw.

As if he were obliged to do whatever she did, he took a sip too, almost forgetting to swallow, and the sour taste lined his mouth and made his lips pucker. God, he'd forgotten how much he hated José's margaritas.

"A little zippy. They ever hear of sugar?" She took another sip, closing her eyes, wrinkling her face, and lifting her square jaw as the sour went down.

He laughed and leaned back against the wall, propping one foot up. She wasn't bad, knew how to relax, he decided, watch- ing her work her way through the drink. "Might want to save some for the will reading."

"You ready?" she asked.

"Hell no." He liked her frank eyes, the rich shade of brown that surfaced when she laughed. He'd felt them when they were cold and appraising, and this version was a lot better.

She leaned against the opposite wall, propping her boot up too. Very cute, he decided. Very, very cute. Flirting. He felt it loosen him as the drink began to rise up his chest.

"I didn't think I should bother, then I had to come to town anyway, so I thought what the hell. I'm surprised he mentioned me at all." The thought seemed to change her, make her older, her face losing a little of its life.

"Doesn't surprise me." He smiled and raised his eyebrows, tilting back his head a little to look down at her through his hooded eyes.

Her eyes widened, softened, then she looked away quickly, and one hand went to brush at a wisp of her hair.

The door above them opened and Selden Monk appeared, squinting into the shadows of the stairs. "That you, Latta? Cody? Thought I heard voices. We're waiting on you."

Their arms touched as they started to walk up, and it felt like they weren't wearing clothes. He had to look at the walls, tinged yellow with age and dirt, and take another stinging gulp of the drink. Keep your eyes on the road, he ordered himself, and followed her up the stairs and through the door, hoping the swelling in his jeans wouldn't be apparent to the rest of them.

Selden Monk began reading after they'd all settled in their chairs. " 'I, Heywood L. Bennett, of the County of Cherry, State of Nebraska, being of full age and sound and disposing mind and memory, do hereby make, publish, and declare this to be my Last Will and Testament, hereby revoking all wills by me heretofore made and all codicils thereto.' " While Selden paused for a sip of water, Cody looked at Kya, whose face had grown sad at the mention of their father's name.

" 'Debts and Expenses,' " Selden continued. " 'It is my desire and I hereby order and direct that my Executor, my son Arthur Bennett, hereinafter named, pay all of my legally payable debts and expenses as soon after my decease as conveniently may be. I further direct that my remains be cremated.' "

"Uh-oh." Kya giggled and rolled her tear-filled eyes at Cody. They'd embalmed and buried their father instead.

Selden Monk was reading very slowly in a low voice with a slight stutter that seemed to catch the edge of a word, falter, stumble back, then pitch forward again. It made Cody restless. He finished his drink by the end of the first paragraph, shrugging at Kya when she raised her eyebrows and gestured for some. He couldn't very well tell her he'd given hers to Latta. They sat in a line — Kya, Cody, Latta, Arthur — staring at the lawyer. Selden Monk was a big, rawboned man, bigger than

Arthur but almost fleshless. His skin was rubbed red by his weekends and evenings at the small sheep ranch he ran just outside of town. A bachelor, he'd put himself through law school. The last of a line of ranchers and farmers living on the margin, he never lost the habit of being poor and wore his suits to shiny spots and white patches as the fabric gave. His white shirts were yellowed and frayed from years of hand washing in lye soap in the ranch house that still had no running hot water or indoor plumbing. Selden Monk was thoughtful about the law. Careful and honest. You just couldn't count on anything happening with any kind of speed. Like waiting a month before he read the will.

Cody looked over at Latta's big gold wristwatch. Oversized on her brown arm, he liked how it seemed right. He even found himself staring at the inch-and-a-half-long white scar on her wrist. And the burn she'd gotten a few days before. The strong fingers and the little tears around the ragged, blunt nails, where she'd chewed the skin off.

He looked to see if he could count how many pages were left. Ten? Fifteen? He'd be dead by then. He shifted in his chair, recrossing his legs and twisting so he sat half facing Latta Jaboy. This wasn't going to work. His head was aching now that he was bored. The pain seemed to have found the liner of his hat and skated its perfect ring around his head. He lifted his hat and set it lower over his eyes. What little alcohol was in the drink was already wearing off, leaving him feeling like he was going to have to reach across the desk and shake Selden Monk a couple of times to get him into fast forward.

Latta looked at him and smiled. Maybe she liked him. That was something. He wanted to touch the material of her shirt. He wanted to rub the cotton between his fingers, smell it. It might taste the way oats smelled, that nutty, musty, dusty odor when they were all piled up in the bin. Made him understand why horses liked them so much. He wanted to say her name in her ear. He shifted toward his sister.

Kya caught his eye and stuck her tongue in the side of her cheek and pushed it in Latta's direction. Their old signal. Cody pointed his finger at his head and his thumb at the door. Even Latta was shifting uncomfortably. The least the lawyer could do was spend some money on padded chairs for his clients, Cody thought.

It was Arthur who interrupted. "Selden, could you just summarize things for us, and give us our own copies to read later? Mrs. Jaboy here has things to do and I'm sure only a small part applies to her."

Everyone sat very still while Selden Monk concentrated on that thought, then finally nodded his head. "Mrs. Jaboy." He flipped several pages over, ran his finger down the page, and said, "Here it is. You are to have an item of your choosing as a gift for friendship over the years."

He looked at the other three, and flipped two more pages. "There are some miscellaneous small bequests. But the bulk, the main part of the estate, the Bennett ranch, livestock, stocks and bonds, et cetera, are left to the three offspring. You three. To be shared equally." He held up his hand as Arthur started to interrupt. "Arthur here is the executor, but the ranch cannot be sold or divided during your lifetimes. *Your* children, as heirs, may sell or divide after *they* reach the age of twenty-one. *Or* it reverts to the Nature Conservancy. He wanted to make certain that there would always be a Bennett ranch run by Bennetts. Or Kidwell-Bennetts, I guess. Or in Kya's case — she's asked to retain her Bennett name through the generations too. We can discuss that. Any questions?"

Cody was stunned. What the hell was this? Now he had to stay with Arthur for good or endanger Kya's future? The old man had had his say finally, the last word. He was even pushing them around from the grave. A helluva man. Never let go of anything or anyone he thought he owned. Cody wiped at his eyes and looked at Kya, who was watching Arthur.

Arthur stood up, staring at the lawyer as if he'd just issued a terminal diagnosis. "All three equally? This isn't the right will. You've got the wrong will, Selden. What's the date? Never mind, there's another will. He told me about it. I'll find it. You've got the wrong one —" His wide mouth closed against the angry accusations he was about to utter. Brushing against Cody, who had stood up too, he walked to the door, yanked it open, and pounded down the stairs.

Kya stood up, laughing. "It makes you miss him, doesn't it? He always made things exciting." She took Cody in her arms, giving him a long, tight squeeze. "Well, brother, see you later. I gotta see if I can catch Arthur before he takes off." She waved at the room, ignoring how Latta's jaw tightened.

When Latta and Cody got downstairs, he was surprised to see John Long and his jeep gone. Cody stuffed his hands in his jeans pockets, looking up and down the street in case he'd somehow missed the obvious. "John said he'd meet me here." Cody glanced at Latta's eyes. They were back to their cool, neutral place. "Honest. I guess I should go look for him or something."

"I can give you a ride," she said.

When they reached Latta's truck, Cody pulled the passenger door open and shoved at the mail cluttering the bench seat. Latta settled into the driver's seat, rested her arms on the steering wheel, and turned to him. "I guess I owe you a drink — how about Clark's?" He shrugged and she turned the key, the engine stumbled and caught. Stepping on the gas, she sent it backwards and spun the wheel.

It was just six o'clock, but Clark's parking lot was already a sprawl of cars and pickups. And when he looked behind them, there were a couple more trucks, the seats jammed with four cowboys apiece.

"All these cowboys must have spring fever, coming down here on a Tuesday night," Cody said. "Usually it's pretty quiet

midweek. You sure you want to go in there? I could just —"
He turned toward her.

"It's okay. I come here every once in a while just to remind
myself."

Aside from the strangeness of her remark, it was a little
embarrassing to come to a place like Clark's with Latta Jaboy. She didn't belong here; this was where cowboys came to
drink and screw around. A woman who wasn't looking for
it wouldn't go there. Especially a ranch owner. They went to
the Buckboard in town to dance and socialize, not out here
where things got down and dirty pretty fast. At the big battered oak door patched with plywood panels painted the dark
porch green that covered the rest of the building, Cody stepped
around and pulled it open so she had to duck under his arm.
When they got into the special red darkness of Clark's, they
stood there, letting their eyes adjust, searching the room. They
were drawing attention to themselves, and Cody always preferred to move unobtrusively into a scene.

"Let's get a booth." He pointed toward an empty spot opposite the front door, with a good view of the room. He wondered if Latta knew how many rooms there were here, and
what went on. Of course she did. Jaboy had known — everybody within a hundred miles knew. And there was that time
she'd followed her husband and Kya. Still, he wasn't comfortable bringing her here. Especially if Burch was around.

Passing the table where Colin Young sat with his two sons,
she nodded and smiled at her hired men. They touched their
hats, murmured hellos, and glued their eyes to their beers.
Then Chris Young looked up and gave Cody a hard stare. Cody
just nodded. He was a landowner now, so he shouldn't care
what the hands thought, he realized. But he knew he'd never
stop caring after so many years of working for a living just like
they did.

Cody and Latta slid into the duct tape–patched vinyl of the
booth bench, stretched their legs out, and leaned against the

wall so they could watch the room. When the barmaid came, she said "Hi" and giggled in a familiar way. Cody looked closer at her. Did he know her better than he thought? They both ordered JD straight up, with water backs.

The jukebox was still pretty low, since it was early yet. The serious fun always took a while. Weeknights in spring were free-for-all nights. Nobody came with anyone. Weekends were different. Friday night you coupled up, Saturday night you'd bring her again and probably have to fight for her, and Sunday you'd lie in bed half the day, fighting your belly and wondering if she'd kick you out or leave herself. Monday you started work again.

Now that spring had broken and the heat was starting to edge into the hills, there was a little extra something in the air besides the cigarette smoke and sweat. The women wore shorter skirts, tighter jeans, no matter how fat they were, and skimpy tops that bared their arms. The men rushed the afternoon work to get off early enough for a bath before the bar at night. They tried to brush the dust off their hats and caps on the way in the door. They drank beer and looked around the room slowly, hunting, letting their eyes bounce and land on a woman, like flies on steak. If she looked up and their eyes caught and held, they'd be sitting together within an hour, dancing locked to each other by midnight, swaying drunkenly out of sync with the band. Cody knew that feeling of burying your face in a neck full of sweet-smelling hair, and wrapping yourself around the soft flesh of a woman after a day of bone-bruising work. He wondered if the women guessed how the men felt. Maybe that's what made them act the way they did. Indifferent. Always looking for something better, it seemed.

When the drinks came, he took a crumpled five from his pocket and handed it to the girl. She blushed and giggled, flirting with him as if the money were a gesture of intimacy. "Burch Winants around?" he asked.

"No." Something changed in her face. She squeezed the bill

in her fist. "He heard Dwight Yoakam was playing in North Platte tonight — his girlfriend's crazy about Dwight. Old Mrs. C.'ll stretch both their hides on the back wall if she finds out. Anything else?" She looked wisely at Latta Jaboy for the first time, as if she knew the older woman didn't belong here.

When she left, Cody took a long sip of his JD, letting the flavor burn his mouth, then his throat, and finally his stomach. He followed with a drink of water, watching Latta do the same.

"Burch Winants married that middle Clark girl, born-again Evelyn, the one with the twin babies she keeps in Sunday clothes all the time?" Latta asked.

He nodded and took another sip of his Jack. Old Mrs. C. poured good-sized drinks here, not like at the Buckboard, where they always measured everything exactly.

"You surprised by Heywood's will?"

He shrugged, then nodded.

"Think Arthur's right — about another one?"

He twisted to look at her, but she was studying her glass. "I don't know. Does it matter?"

"Not my problem. Just hate to see people tearing each other apart over money or land."

She finished her drink quickly, and Cody held two fingers up as the barmaid ambled by, and ordered doubles. "Won't be me doing it — not my style," he said. "I guess I figured Arthur and Kya would get it all. I was just hanging around to make sure she was all right. Then —"

Latta looked at him sourly. "Oh, *she'll* always be *all right.* Your sister does just fine for herself. In a nuclear war, I'd bet on her walking out alive — and put good odds on it being her finger on the button to begin with."

"Yeah, I hear you." He didn't want an argument.

Colin's boys were keeping an eye on them, and he just hoped Latta kept calm. He really didn't want a fight tonight. After the second round appeared, Latta drank half the double immediately. Cody said, "Thirsty."

Latta raised her eyebrows and reached for her glass again. She stared at him until he grew embarrassed and let his eyes drop to the table, where the drinks were making wet rings on the burn-scarred Formica top.

"How did you get to be such a boy scout?"

He shrugged.

"Sorry," she murmured, and took a drink. "I got a mean streak in me."

He held the glass up in front of his face, sighting her in along the edge, watching the moods flicker in her eyes as she drained her drink and signaled for another round. She looked out across the room, her cheeks dark with feeling and the alcohol she was drinking too quickly, her mouth a tight line. He wanted to slug the liquor and get out of there before he got in trouble, but he'd started this business, now he had to wait for her.

He couldn't understand women, what they wanted. When a man was soft and gentle, they wanted him to be hard, and when he was hard, they yelled that he wasn't nice. It was so simple, it was complicated. He tried not to think about it. Not get too close. His mother was the person who taught him that.

For a long time, when it was just the two of them and Caroline was talking to herself, or arguing with people who weren't there, he thought that that was just the way things were. Then Heywood Bennett started coming around more, bringing books and stuff, a TV finally, though the screen showed snow and shadowy figures with voices.

Crazy Caroline mostly acted right when Heywood was around. She didn't hit her son or go into her long ranting diatribes, followed by hours of contrite crying. As a child, Cody loved and hated the man who could control his mother. When he'd grown up, women still made him feel helpless, doomed. But he couldn't stop himself from searching them out, wanting to lie with them, hold and be held. He couldn't cope with the rest — the talking, the complications. Horses were simple. Cattle simpler. The sandhills easiest of all.

Latta paid for the next round and immediately drank half. "Nobody owns me," she remarked to the booth as if she'd just discovered the fact.

Cody looked closely at her. Was she drunk? "Well, that's good."

She looked at him and smiled, flirting again. "You're awfully good looking, you know." She was sipping her JD slowly now, wetting the top of her tongue like a cat, curling it back into her mouth.

He ducked his head and looked across the room. He wasn't going to be in charge here, he could tell. But since everything he'd tried had turned out ridiculous so far, maybe it was better if she took over.

When her fingers touched his arm he wanted to say, Don't, just don't. Her fingers pressed in and he felt himself start to harden. There it was. What he'd felt earlier at Monk's. Christ, this woman was going to be trouble. If she could rock him with the tap of a finger, what would it be like when they took their clothes off? He tried not to look at her.

"Screw it." she said. Pulling back her hand, she finished her drink.

Was she arguing with herself or him? He looked at her. The drinks had loosened her expression, letting a younger, happier, more sensual woman out. Her eyes were large and dark, with the little lines in the corners he wanted to trace with his finger. And her strong nose with the bump in the middle. A break? The square jaw put interesting angles on her face. And he could imagine slowly pulling the thin wires of her gold hoop earrings through their tiny holes.

He swung his long legs off the bench seat, catching the watchful eyes of Latta's cowboys as he put both elbows on the table and rested his chin on his hands. "What now, Mrs. Jaboy?"

She smiled crookedly and looked toward the door. "Need a ride, cowboy?"

5 ✧ CODY AND LATTA

When they build a tipi, 3 poles come first. That 3-pole triangle is a star. Then 7 more poles — west, north, east, south, above, below and center. Fire at the center. Those 10 are the laws. Then 2 more poles outside, the "ears" for air, make 12 months. And once a year the people get together to pray at Sun Dance. Dancers make a tipi with their dancing, their sacrifice and their prayers around the holy tree. There's 12 stars: morning star, evening star, 7 stars in that Dipper, and those 3 stars (Orion's belt) and that makes 12, too — 12 stars, 12 months, 12 poles.

— *from LAKOTA STAR KNOWLEDGE*

*D*riving back through town on their way out County Road 11, Latta pulled into José's drive-through line. She said she wanted something to dilute the alcohol they'd had. Cody could tell that what she really wanted was to dilute the other thing that was alive and awkward in the front seat. He was watching her from some distance, as if the seat had stretched out another three yards and he could barely touch her even if he wanted to. He was half propped against the open window, his right arm framing it, his hat shadowing his eyes, his legs splayed. His left arm rested along the back of the seat, and he could feel the heat of her cheek on his waiting hand.

As they idled in line, she glanced at the pale hairs on his tanned wrist, his long beautiful wrist, exposed by the turned-up cuff. The kind of wrist that made her feel her heart would break. Men's bodies did that to her, she'd discovered, at seventeen when Jaboy's short powerful legs and hard round belly had broken her heart too. A piece of flesh or bone would call to her and she'd stare. But it'd been a while. She wondered why he didn't say something. She worried that she was mistaken about what he wanted.

"Can I take your order, please?"

Latta stared at the panel of pictures and words, faded to ghastly neon yellows, oranges, and greens that made the food impossible to imagine as edible.

"Four soft-shells, extra sauce, and two large margaritas with covers," his voice directed softly.

When she turned back, he smiled and let his body open and relax. He watched her body turn jerky with awareness. She had trouble shifting out of park to roll the truck toward the pickup window, until he reached over and started the engine for her. Her shoulder, her breath that close, made a soft heat rise in his stomach. She was digging in her purse for money when he handed her the bills. He wasn't talking, just letting the silence work. He knew she'd hate this part. How dumb she became, how if she didn't start chattering in a minute, she was going to have trouble steering the truck down the road. How she couldn't chew to eat, and nothing would be small enough to go down her throat. Fumbling with the change, the bag of food, and the carton of drinks at the window, she let him reach across her, his arm brushing her breasts, and take the food while she pressed herself thin against the seat back. He recognized that this kind of moment would be difficult for her — make her self-conscious to the point that she might not let anything happen. He wanted to calm her, to say something to help, but he couldn't. So he tried to slow his own body, put it under water, breathe as if he were falling asleep, ease the wild energy rising hysterically in the cab. If she would only let it happen, they would be drawn like two sleepers along a dream.

She smelled his sweet whiskey breath, and the other, the

soap and sweat and something else, horsey and male. "Here."
She handed him the wad of bills and coins, accidentally letting
them spill out onto the seat before he could grab them.

"You okay?" he asked as she put the truck in gear and
inched forward.

She nodded.

Was she going to take him home with her or not? He
couldn't ask. What words would he use? Hey, you want to go
to bed? I've been thinking about you for five days, since you
got your tractor stuck.

"You want me to drive, Mrs. Jaboy?" He kept his voice cool
and quiet.

She shook her head. She had to make this decision herself.
She wasn't going to let him do it for her. She pulled onto 20,
almost bumping the rear end of a downshifting cattle truck.

Cody took a deep breath and let it out slowly, then reached
for one of the drinks. Sticking a straw in the hole, he handed
it to her. He took one and tried a sip. More ice this time, and
the tequila was all on the bottom. Still sour.

"Music?" he asked between sips on his drink. They both
tried to ignore the leaking grease-stained white bag between
them that was filling the cab with the smell of lukewarm refried
beans, cheap meat, and taco sauce.

She shoved a tape into the player. Emmylou Harris's sad,
haunting voice wound itself around their heads and chests.
Latta couldn't quite catch the rhythm enough to hum with it.

Cody studied her, trying to see and memorize everything —
the way he always had to, because he'd learned a long time
ago that everything vanished except in your own mind. He saw
the angry burned arm, the way her shirt was a little faded and
damp under her arms, the way her nose wasn't straight — if
you looked at the nostrils from below, one hole would be
bigger than the other — the beginnings of those lines from the
nose to the mouth, and the ones around the mouth. Again he
noticed she had those small creases around the eyes that you

got in the hills by the time you were twenty, from squinting against the blowing sand, sun, snow, and sky. In the fading light he could just see how her skin was starting to get that matted look, with hundreds of fine lines like a piece of cowhide. Caroline had laughed at the way women got old like their handbags, their shoes. Did Latta see herself that way too? An old handbag of a woman no one could love? The young have no tolerance, Caroline used to say. They don't overlook anything physical, that's the problem, she'd told him.

But he didn't mind the way Latta's thighs were a little heavy, making the material of her jeans rub and wear white between her legs, though she rode horses every day of her life. As if she could feel his scrutiny, she took a quick breath and stepped harder on the gas, pushing the truck into the curve, catching some gravel with its rear end and wobbling as it slid out. She straightened the wheels and let her foot off. He was glad when she slowed: the winding road was full of deer this time of night.

He knew that things wouldn't be so bad if he'd just say something. How hard would that be? She probably hated men who did this — the strong, silent routine. But she wasn't talking either. Probably thought he was too young or poor or dumb. Hillbilly.

She wished he'd just reach over and grab her. She wished she was tough enough to pull his tight little cowboy ass across the bench seat, crushing the tacos, and the mail. Just put a hand on my knee, she urged silently. Maybe if she stretched her neck, rolled it in a circle like it ached, he'd take the hint and massage it.

The turnoff for the Bennett ranch was coming up over the next rise. He'd almost lost track of where they were. If she didn't take that road, they'd be going to her place. Should he ask? What if she laughed or said no — she'd had a long day. Hell, *he'd* had a long day.

By the side of the road two sets of gold eyes caught and

gleamed in the headlights. Deer. She slowed down, watching them carefully. They seemed content to graze where they were, walking along the ditch. But that was a trick they had, then they'd suddenly decide to spring across the road to the other side. So she oozed past, adding speed to the truck gradually, then gunning it. Over the hill and down the other side, the Bennett road at the bottom. Neither of them saying a word, she let the truck roll past the turnoff.

His fingers touched her neck. Just the tips at first, sending currents up his arm, down her back, making it hard for her to breathe. He inched closer. Not much, just enough to rub her neck. She slowed the truck to the rhythm of his fingers loosening the muscles, separating the strands of her hair, rubbing himself into her.

Now their silence worked another way, letting them feel the night air blowing into the cab from the hills, sweet with new grass and spring flowers, and smell the dampness from the day's rain that climbed the hills and spread across the valleys in long scarves of mist the truck sank into and burst out of as the road rose and fell, while the green glow of the panel lights seemed to blink and lead them like fireflies.

She stumbled on the first step of the porch, and he caught her arm and pulled her back against him. He felt like a shadow, a shape of her behind herself, dark and sensual, so full of her. She couldn't stand without falling, and he was there to catch her lightness. She led him up to the one room she had never slept in, with Jaboy or anyone. A strange room, all angles and curves from the patching on of a second story and an addition. A guest room, though she had never had any guests. Antique double bed, too narrow to really sleep in with another person.

"Wait," she said, and went for candles. And remembered bourbon and glasses and water, and wondered if she should change clothes, make sandwiches, brush her teeth, her hair, wait, she'd told him, and she filled her arms with things they would need for a long journey, wait, and she was afraid to go back without something to offer him. Something more. What was she missing — what would be the one thing? A sweet something for the tip of his tongue.

He was waiting. When he saw her arms full, her frantic eyes, he stood up and gently took the things, placing them on the floor. She was standing with empty arms when he laced her fingers with his and spread their arms against the wall, bending to kiss her, so long he was holding her up, and then he wasn't and they slid to the floor, mouths working slowly, as if time were a jar of honey dripping in the pantry sun, each bright drop distilling on the metal tongue of the saucepan below. Each new place he touched, he did it slowly, to ask permission, to let her give it to him, her breasts, the scars lining the inside of her wrist, the zipper on her jeans.

She felt so small and valuable against him, he was careful when he lifted her hips and brought her to him, rocked back on his heels and held her against him, rocking, rocking. He felt himself slip away, away, and she with him, to some smooth place where the voices stopped, and the quiet breathed small, then not at all.

The moonlight was blowing into the room through the trees, scattering dark leaves across the bed, his back, their legs. When she opened her eyes, Cody's head hung off the side of the bed, where they'd ended up sprawled after their lovemaking. Trying not to wake him, she pulled and lifted the shoulder nearest her to center him more. He muttered something and lifted his other arm as if to stave off someone, then rolled toward her, reaching and finding her, tucking her into the cup of his body, wrapping her into him. She had trouble breathing, with her face pressed against his chest, the hairs tickling her nose. She waited until his breathing evened out again, then gently extricated herself.

In the shadows of the dark room, his face looked so young

she wanted to cry. She watched his chest sinking and rising. There was the trail of a thick scar along his collarbone. She'd been there the day he'd broken it. She and Jaboy had just flown in from Europe and decided to come over to the spring round-up. She had been sickened when he broke the bone, the grating sound as Joseph adjusted his arm and strapped it to his side. She'd watched Cody, a sixteen-year-old boy white with pain, ride the next horse, biting his lip. She'd tried to get Heywood to stop it, but he'd just shaken his head, his hands tightening on the trophy belt the boy would soon win. She'd wondered what Caroline would think if she saw her boy passing out when the horse had stopped and he'd been lifted off. What would she do if she could see how they treated her darling boy? Put in the back of an old pickup and driven to town, bouncing with the tools and hay. Or later, when the bone had to be broken and reset again because there was no adult to stop him from working it too soon.

That was the worst part of what she'd done here: sleeping with a boy she'd watched grow up, who could almost be her own son. Was she crazy? Yet even looking at him asleep, she felt the animal pull that had led her to take him home.

His was almost a soundless world, she knew. He rarely spoke when she was around — or anytime, from what she could tell. But there was something else, the way he could look at a person, had looked at her. And the way he worked the horses. She'd noticed that years ago. He lacked the brutal efficiency that marked most of the men out here. There wasn't that love-hate thing she observed so often among the cowboys and ranchers. If anything, his ambivalence was with people, not animals. That was the difference. He'd fight almost anyone, didn't mind getting battered around, but she'd never known him to fight an animal.

People could make their own lives so small, she decided. So small that when someone like Jaboy came along, that seemed sufficient. Small like the sparrows who flew back and forth from the barns and trees to the manure piles, arguing in the boughs of the pines and evergreens on the north side of the house, plumping and coaxing and mating, day after day. If there was a special complication in the the weave of their motion, it was whether they perched on the dark green of the clothes post or the black utility wires running from the house to the barn.

Since meeting and marrying Jaboy, in that one swift act, she had moved her life from the world of her parents, from the hard, essential simplicity of their Christianity, from their disapproval. Until meeting her husband, she'd never known how much a person could enjoy, could give in to, impulse. Her parents had taught her that life was a struggle, a contention against layers of disapproval, from God on down. There was never any lasting achievement in the eyes of such judgment. One only failed by degrees.

With Jaboy, she discovered approval. He might reward her for a mistake, an impulse, as easily as for doing the right thing. It had confused her at first, but she had listened and imitated. Later she realized that these were the very gestures that gave him pleasure — the aping gratitude of a seventeen-year-old girl as he introduced her to the world. Watching her responses, their freshness, he was reborn, he told her. He trained her to suspend herself, her values, and follow appetites. Their whole marriage had been about appetite. He just turned out to be a much bigger eater than she was, in the end. It was an experience he had needed to repeat again and again, until Kya. She was another reason Latta shouldn't be here with Cody Kidwell.

This was truly a move Jaboy would've enjoyed. What bothered her was that she hadn't felt the switch, the thing that came over her when she had to find a stranger, a pair of eyes, a pair of hands. Something had happened with Cody on the stairs that afternoon. She hadn't been paying attention. Maybe she wanted to sleep with every single man in three counties, then there'd really be nothing left. Maybe she was trying to make her world so damn empty that she couldn't look anyone in the eyes. Then she'd say screw it and live — who needed eyes, anyway.

"Latta," he whispered in her ear, so quietly she thought she'd made a mistake hearing it. "Latta." He stroked her shoulder, her hip, her belly. "Latta," he said, letting the syllables ride the rhythm of his breathing as he made love to her. On top of him, she outlined his full lips with the tips of her fingers and kissed the inside of his wrists, the stitches on his arm like the black lashes of a closed eye.

"Cody," she whispered in his ear.

They didn't look away or close their eyes to shut each other out. It was like tunneling into some cave where the ice backlit the walls, a pale blueness of stars, an explosion in arctic waters when he probed her deeply, opening her, making her feel places she'd forgotten, until she began to feel the protest rising blunt inside her like a club, the thing that wasn't going to let this be. Too much here. Not safe. No. Not. But he, yes, and yes she let his voice take her in its persuasive arms.

6 ❖ AT THE LOST AND FOUND

Tuesday, Albert Kemp took Lewis and Talbot Flood fishing at Buryanek Bay on the Missouri. Mrs. Billy Flood helped dress chickens, Thursday, at the Kemps', and called on the Gene Kemps to see the new baby boy. The boys returned home with her.

Mr. and Mrs. Welch have moved their trailerhouse to the Robert Ferguson property.

Elmer and Lea Kornblum drove to Lincoln, Friday, to assist their daughter, Brenda, in moving to a different apartment. They returned home Monday.

— *BABYLON CALLER*

To take his mind off his anger, Arthur forced himself to go slowly through downtown Babylon. Looking at three blocks of stores and businesses, including those he had bought during the eighties when capital was scarce in the sandhills, helped to ease the anger he'd felt since yesterday when Selden Monk had read the will. Only Heywood had known the extent of his enterprise, his hard work and vigilance.

Arthur owned the buildings where the Buckboard squared off across from the Mustang Western Wear and Saddle Shop and the Sandhills Office Supply, all in storefronts with tin roofs and tin ceilings inside. And he owned the next building over, where Conver's Insurance and Sally's Pets and Used Books were clad in aluminum fronts and plastic green awnings originally intended to shelter shoppers.

Today his workers had started to strip off the aluminum, pulling the entrepreneurial hopes of earlier years from the storefronts. He saw them standing now, blinking with surprise and puzzlement as the building emerged like a locust after its unshelling.

As Arthur considered his properties, he was struck by the number of bars and liquor stores whose neon glare mocked his investments. The Buckboard could stay, but they should move the Midnite Rodeo and Frenchie's topless bar off Main Street, like they'd done in Gordon up the road. A person had to work a little harder to raise hell there, and they weren't doing it in plain sight of every tourist or family either. It cut down on the ruckus the Indians could raise too. Babylon had twice as many police calls as Gordon, he knew that for a fact.

Another fact that struck him was that he would not be able to buy the Nebraska Theater when it came up for auction next month. Showing a movie every Thursday through Sunday, it was always on the verge of bankruptcy. Owning it would help offset capital gains. And he would fix the marquee with its missing lights and baseball-sized hole in the white glass which was advertising *City Slic ers.* He would get enough letters to spell things out properly. But not now. He had to fix this will situation first.

Look at what Heywood had done, dammit. Now Arthur was stuck with Kya, a wild Indian woman who'd been out of control since he caught her swimming naked with Cody when she was sixteen. The way Heywood had allowed Kya to create her own character, there was little anyone could do to control her as an adult. He had given her a kind of freedom she couldn't come back from. She did as she wanted.

He didn't have a word for Cody. A hillbilly psychobrat, that was all he could think of. His father had whelped Cody in the wild, brought him home like an orphan calf, and told the rest of them to accept it. Only Cody wasn't as useful as a calf; he couldn't be turned into beef. And he always had that starved, dirt-crusted aura about him, like he did that first day when he climbed out of the truck and brought that sad-ass, tear-stained face into their lives. The brother he didn't want. He already had a sister he hadn't asked for, Arthur had tried to tell Heywood, who had just laughed, said they all needed family. There was nothing like family; it was the only thing a person could trust in the world.

His mother had taught him that the only thing saving them from being like hillbillies and Indians was acting respectable. It meant clean clothes, clean fingernails, going to church, and behaving in public. Even in death, she had managed not to make more of a scene than necessary.

Arthur hated remembering this, but the memory arrived full and breathing with a life of its own that demanded its little moment before it would go away. Marion Bennett had had trouble sleeping for years, until the night she took to her bed with a fifth of gin and a bottle of prescription sleeping pills her old family doctor back in Omaha kept her supplied with. As she wrote in her note Heywood gave him to read years later:

It's hard to have a car accident with a tree or bridge abutment because there aren't any, or a lake through thin ice or water at all since the rivers are shallow, the pond and lake shorelines are so marshy and soft a car mires before it can get you to deep water. Most opportunities are too violent or too slow — fire, freezing, liquor or guns. The automobile is almost no help, unless you don't mind taking someone else with you. Generally that's considered a low-class thing to do here — something drunk cowboys, hillbillies and Indians do — nothing a rancher's family, a Bennett, would consider, I suppose. Everything about the sandhills continues to force me to act alone. No one saves you and no one kills you here, so I'm doing this the best way I can, with the least amount of trouble for anyone. My mother told me ladies must always behave that way. Goodbye and good luck.

Mrs. Marion Howe Bennett

No mention of her son. That final thought stung him as it always did. Three short blocks beyond downtown, he pulled into the rutted driveway of the big white frame house, the old mortuary, that Heywood Bennett had bought for the family years ago. Arthur had tried for years to get people to start calling it the Bennett house instead of the old funeral parlor. He loved its stern New England uprightness. The tallest and widest house on the street, with its pillared front porch and three solid stories, it wielded authority over the surrounding houses.

He knew his mother had expected him to follow the other young people out of the hills. No one stayed if they could help it. They moved away to college and then to the larger cities, avoiding the hills as if they had been a penal colony. He'd missed that opportunity, though. His mother had become another grave in the hills, gone silent too soon, leaving him stranded where she had been, between his father's life and his own.

His father was a puzzle, a man whose disappearance from Arthur's life, when as a child his mother moved him to Babylon for school, had remained an eternal mystery, as obscure and silent as the hills they had fled for those long months. After his mother's death, Arthur had tried to find his father, but Heywood had been too far away. There'd always been someone, something else. Pulling open the back storm door and pushing the inside door open, he realized that his mother had lost her husband too — then killed herself because her son, Arthur, was simply not enough. He slammed the big door hard enough to rattle the glass.

There had been an incredible arrogance about Heywood Bennett, a confidence that seemed unshakable, emanating from someplace invisible and solid, as if he'd never made a mistake he hadn't planned on making. It always made Arthur feel stupid to be around his father. Cody just acted the same as always — dimwitted or tongue-tied. But for Arthur a real change had occurred, his mind went a little dry and blank. The relief of having Heywood dead was that he could feel comfortable with the knowledge that he was now the smartest person in the family.

He'd start by looking in the coffin showroom on the third floor — an attic, really — that Heywood had taken for storage when they had bought the mortuary and turned it back into the house it had originally been. Arthur had already done a cursory examination of the boxes of papers and goods a few years ago, and determined they contained everything Caroline Kidwell had left in the world, his own mother's papers and keepsakes, and Heywood's. There was a large box devoted to each of the children too, but Kya's was the only one containing much. Arthur had kept most of his own school papers and prizes, letters he'd received or sent and had retrieved. Cody's box was nearly empty. There was nothing from school, since he hadn't ever attended one formally. No letters that Arthur could discover. In Cody's box were simply the newspaper articles pertaining to the death of John Axel, the man he had shot, and to a series of small accidents he had had, and some rodeo columns listing his winnings.

Cody and Kya never bothered with the third floor — they never seemed interested in the past. So Arthur was the only one who knew about the way their father had arranged the cardboard boxes of the two women along opposing walls, with his own personal boxes centered between them like a presiding Old Testament king. It would be just like Heywood to hide the will in all that junk, for the fun of it.

It took Arthur four hours to sort through his father's papers and to discover no other will. He couldn't believe he'd been lied to. He sat back on his heels, rubbed the small of his back, and watched the sweat, which rolled down his face from the attic heat, drip on the old contracts for the original land the first Bennett had bought.

It had to be here. His father had prided himself on telling the truth. "I never lie about the ranch, about business," he'd bragged to his son. This *was* business, this was the whole business, Arthur protested as he looked around him. If he could get one of the small windows open for a breath of air in this late afternoon heat, he could stand to go through his mother's things. The other will must be in there. When he stood up, he staggered from the stiffness in both knees. Limbering his legs, he walked in a large uneven circle on the grey commercial carpet. When he got the money, he would rip this out, drive away the mice whose turds dotted the floor, and build storage closets for these damn boxes. He knew the other will was here, the thing that said it was his. His father had always meant it to be his.

The windows wouldn't open, and Arthur added it to the growing list of things to do — call a carpenter. Windows should always open. He wheezed and coughed as he stooped in front of his mother's things. But he'd been all through those boxes last fall, when Heywood was starting to get bad enough to stay in bed most days. Arthur had just wanted to see what his mother's life was about, in case he had questions before his father died. But he hadn't been able to understand anything — how much or how little she loved Heywood Bennett, or even her son. She was too ladylike, too respectable to put it on paper. No diary, no letters of revelation. It had been the one time her respectability had disappointed him.

He'd taken off his suit coat an hour ago, and now he unbuttoned his white shirt and took that off too, setting it down on the carpet with his coat, lining it up neatly across the oblong indentation outlining the weight of a coffin that had rested there for so long its presence was permanent. In his undershirt he felt the hot air, like a cool breeze, hit his wet skin and dry some of the sweat. He loosened his belt too, so bending at the waist would be easier. Then he looked at the opposite wall with its boxes he'd never bothered with before. He counted them: forty-eight boxes, one for every year of Caroline Kidwell's life. What kind of a person, he wanted to ask his father, would do something that deliberate?

At first he looked in random boxes, then decided that he had to go back to the beginning. The early years were nothing but girlish stuff — feathers, pressed flowers, letters, and keepsakes. It was the letters that began when she was fifteen that made him pay attention. Letters from Heywood Bennett, boarding at a military school not far from her tiny Missouri town.

April 25, 1945

My dearest Carrie,

Today I walked to that place by the natural bridge, and waited. I kept thinking you'd feel me calling you and come. I don't know, I just believed it. But you didn't come. I suppose your mother kept you busy, maybe she was the one who could feel it — like the other times when she's kept you in the house doing something she hadn't even done in years.

I waited. Almost to dark, but didn't want to have to find my way out of those woods that time of night. Didn't see any snakes. Not like that last time when that big old copperhead laid right down in the path and wouldn't budge. He knew who was boss, didn't he? I'm glad you told me not to kill him. When I told my buddy Damien he said they have their mates nearby and we would've had a whole other problem if we'd hurt the first one. Kind of like us, isn't it?

All afternoon I thought about that last time. I don't want you to worry, no matter what happens, I'll be there for you. You know that. Say the word and we can run away. I'm ready when you are. If things don't work out after what we did, well, you know you can count on me. If you'd say so, we could spend the rest of our lives together. We will anyway, you know that. We've known each other all our lives now — how could that change? No matter what happens in the war. Damien says it's almost over now, so I can stop worrying about leaving you when I get drafted.

You're in my heart,
Heywood

May 13, 1945

Dear dear Carrie,

Don't do this. What about these past two years? Remember that time I saved you when the Schuberts' pony came chasing down on you and I pulled you under the fence before it could hurt you? You were so sweet crying and stamping your foot because I took you away. I knew then, my heart was lost. I might just as well have pulled it right out of my chest then and there. Because I've known my whole life how I loved you, so don't do this, please. It will kill me. I can't stand it. Belford is about as useful as a one-armed fiddle player. You know I'm right. I can't believe you're doing this. I don't care what you've done. What your parents want. You know your heart is in mine. Please, please meet me at the rock bridge tomorrow afternoon. I'll be there after lunch and wait for dark. Please come.

Heywood

The intensity of their feelings was obvious and frightening; Arthur found his hands trembling so hard he had to put them down. His father, then, had always known Caroline Kidwell.

May 16, 1945

Caroline, my dearest,

I tried to come and meet you, but I think your parents have been talking to the school. Suddenly I was on the morning train for North Platte. I can only hope that you understand. I tried to slip off and come back but a teacher was with me apparently instructed to keep a sharp eye, because when I got up from the seat, he came, even to the washroom. My only hope is that I can slip by him. There's word the war is over, but I don't believe it. I'll always come back for you anyway, so don't, I mean, *don't* go with

Belford, no matter what your parents want. I remain your devoted, most true, most sad, love — I am nothing without you.

Heywood

P.S. The distance between us is only physical. I can feel you
breathing every minute of every day. I wouldn't want it any other
way, couldn't stand it. I still have the pistol in case it matters to
you.

He had removed the boxes from their stacks and lined them
across the wide room, pulling one letter after another from
them, only to discover that the long and tortuous affair his
father had had with Cody's mother spanned their lives. Over
and over, Heywood Bennett assured Caroline Kidwell that she
was the only person or thing he'd ever loved.

October 27, 1961

Dear Carrie,

Remember when we loved for free? I always told you, you'd
never get away. Not really. It's still true. Even now. Being with you
a few hours ago was the sweetest, saddest thing in my life since
that train ride home, all those years ago. I hope you understand
why I couldn't stop myself, why even with Belford in the next
room dying, I couldn't. Because we belong together. Can't you see
that now? I'll leave my wife if you want. I know we'll always find
each other, the way it happened this time. I just want you close
so I can help you. Touching you is the only thing I care about —
in my whole life — the only thing.

Love,
Heywood

June 6, 1964

Caroline,

It's happening like before and I don't think I can stand it again.
My wife is sick — the doctors say she's depressed. I can't leave
her now . . . not here in the sandhills where help is so far away.
She's been a good solid wife. Mother to Arthur, our son. She's
not you — but that's not a surprise. But I owe her, Carrie, do

you understand? After all those years, and she didn't complain, even knowing as she must have, that somehow things weren't right between us. Maybe she even knew that I loved someone else.

Five years is long enough. Please. I know I can get the Lundgren place. They're leaving. Now that Belford's dead, there's nothing to hold you there. Cody needs a father. Please. Marion hasn't spoken in months now, it's so lonely I can hardly stand it now. Sometimes I wonder what God has meant all these years keeping us apart like this. Won't you please come? The sandhills are beautiful this time of year. You'll fall in love with them — maybe that's why you don't come. Please. I dream of the day when we can forget the past, live together as we were meant to.

My love to you and Cody,
Heywood

Arthur thought he was having a heart attack. His chest seized up and he was panting so hard he had to lie down and close his eyes. He turned on his side and squeezed his arms hard against his chest to silence the pounding there, pinching his eyes against the too bright light of the late afternoon sun. Nothing about the world he had been raised in or believed in existed as a fact. His mother was an act of desperation and loneliness, his birth a mechanical application of generational logic. His childhood meant virtually nothing to his father. Heywood Bennett, his whole life, was obsessed by his love for Caroline Kidwell and nothing else. The birth of his son Cody was the fruition of that love, marked by the deepest wonder and joy Arthur had ever heard his father express. While Arthur and his mother spent winters in Babylon so the boy could go to a proper school, Heywood was with Caroline, and later Cody, riding and driving through terrible storms to bring them food, or simply his love. He remembered bitterly his father's unwillingness to come to Babylon during those winters to spend time with his wife and son. Too busy on the ranch, he always said.

August 30, 1965

Carrie,

Get packed. I'm coming. You are not going to endure any more from those neighbors or townspeople. I don't care. I will be there soon.

Heywood

P.S. I'm going to be a real father to Cody now.

Cody. Always Cody.

There had to be another will, then — maybe one naming Cody as the only heir, Arthur thought, and got up off the floor. He should burn all this, he decided. Get rid of the evidence. That way, when Arthur found the real will, Cody wouldn't be able to contest it with proof of his father's feelings.

But he didn't touch anything. Instead, Arthur shook out his fingers, and then his arms and shoulders, like a swimmer before a race, loosening the muscles, rolling his stiff neck and flexing his jaw. There had to be something for him, a voice inside insisted. There had to be a piece of his father's life for him. He would read every single scrap of paper in that attic. For all he knew, maybe Caroline Kidwell had another will hidden in her notebooks. That's probably where it was, he decided, and selected a box from around the time she'd moved to the hills with her infant son. Picking up a small spiral notebook, he shook its pages for any loose paper. Words scrawled in red caught his eye and he opened to the yellowing pages of cheap lined paper and read.

> How far can you go before you're abstract, how many miles do you drive before you're a concept: too like a Wyoming mountain range to be more than large beyond what we can see, with our eyes narrow — or small, vanishing, the idea of Omaha behind me —

Arthur flipped to another page:

> Grief is a string of pearls, black and white, they pull out of your throat. You feel each bump, each round whole of yourself. Once I

was young. Once I was unafraid. Once I loved and was loved by many, by many more than I can say. Now I sit in my slip in the evaporating walls of a house, crying too late for the love gone, too late for the wedding. I am the bride dressed all day because she was afraid.

This was the woman I brought to him. I can't get dressed because grief has taken my clothes, and the bride is afraid, boards the bus for school in her wedding dress, dragging the hem in the dirt.

A confusion of splendors is the peal of bells pearls make when they clank coming out of your throat, crossing your tongue in small round obsequies.

Arthur closed the notebook, squinting around him at the boxes. "God, what a crazy woman." He'd take a few of these journals downstairs and read them while he made something to eat. If it took a month, a year, he'd read every word in those boxes — Caroline's, Heywood's, and his mother's. He'd finally have the truth. Maybe there'd be proof that Cody wasn't even Heywood's, maybe another will would surface — anything seemed possible.

Arthur recalled a line in one of the letters from Heywood: "Is it true about Cody? My son?" He felt hope soothing his flesh again. There it was. All he had to do was figure out who Caroline Kidwell was, who she'd slept with, to find out just what kind of a bastard Cody was. He wasn't a Bennett — Heywood had doubted it, even — that was the mote of proof he was after. He smiled grimly as he picked up his suit coat and shirt and walked tiredly to the stairs. With luck, he'd be rid of Cody by Christmas. Things could go back to normal, the way they'd been when it was just Kya and Heywood and he fifteen years ago. A long time to wait, he realized as he clicked off the light switch at the bottom of the stairs. A long time, but worth it, now that he was so close.

7 ✦ OPPOSING DREAMS

*I*t was a clear day with a bright, cellophane blue sky that promised no more rain. The light was almost iridescent on the peonies and roses in the yard, momentarily turning their fragile lacquered shapes permanent. The driver had left the diesel running and was letting down the ramp in the middle of the van by the time Latta walked over. "I thought I told you not to rush when you called," she said.

He shrugged and lifted the right panel to form the chute and fastened it to the truck with a chain. Then he fastened the left side. He was moving too quickly, Latta thought. His hands were shaking, he had dark circles around his eyes, and his face had the drawn look truckers got from popping pills and driving too long. Running up the ramp, he startled the horses facing the aisle, who threw their heads and jerked on the chains fastened to each side of their halters. He pulled a heavy rolled mat of thick brown fiber to the top of the ramp and let it loose.

It fell precisely over the rubber-covered metal to make it less slippery.

At least he does that right, Latta thought. She felt Cody come up beside her, and out of the corner of her eye she saw him with a big square of cornbread in one hand and a Coke can in the other. Inez always told her: if you feed them, they stay around. "He's delivering my new stallion," she said in a low voice without turning to face Cody.

"Son of a bitch they gave me to ride shotgun got drunk in Kansas City, got in a fight, and ended up in the can. Dumb bastard. I sure wasn't going to bail him out. Now I gotta do it all."

It wasn't clear whether the man was talking to them or to himself as he snapped a rope on the halter of the big bay gelding standing closest to the door, slipped the metal bar at chest height out of its slots, dropping it loudly, and stepped up aggressively to unsnap the halter chains. When the horse tried to back away, the man growled "Hold still" and yanked on the rope. The horse obeyed, but his eyes were rimmed in white. When he felt his head free, the bay surged forward, pushing the man aside, and leaped from the top of the ramp to the ground, trailing the rope. He stood there a moment, head flung up, snorting the early morning air, searching the land for something familiar.

Latta was just going to step forward for the rope dangling from the halter when Cody walked slowly up to the horse, holding out his hand, rubbing his fingers as if he had something good to eat, talking low and gentle to the animal. At first the horse sidestepped nervously, but Cody stood and, without looking him directly in the eye, reached out and patted the big bay's shoulder, letting one hand rub his chest and up his neck while he quietly picked up the rope with the other. The horse lowered his nose to sniff at the hand being offered again, then blew out hard and shook himself all over like a big dog. Cody led the horse toward a patch of grass and said to Latta, "Hang on to this one." He climbed the ramp, picked up the man sitting where the horse had knocked him, and asked where the stallion was.

"Have to get all these dumb bastards outta here. Stud's in a box back there. Couldn't stop 'cause I didn't have no help. It's not my fault. That bay's a bastard too. Pulls that again, I'm gonna whale on him." He said it loud enough for the horse to hear, but the bay just flicked his ears and pulled hungrily at the grass. "Got a full load and no help," the man complained as he motioned toward the next horse in the row that had to be moved, a plain brown. The horse's head was drooping and he offered no resistance to the jerking motions of the driver. "This is the way they should all be," the man commented as he led the small horse down the ramp. At the bottom, the horse stumbled and almost went to its knees.

Cody walked purposefully to the horse's head and, lifting the upper lip, pushed on the pale gums. Then he pinched a piece of hide on the horse's neck, noting that it stood up rather than returning immediately. "Horse's dehydrated. Water's over there, in the corral. Better put it in there while we get the other ones out. Bet they could all use a drink, couldn't they?"

Though both men were tall and thin, Cody's body was all muscle and he was a good fifteen years younger. The driver was obviously considering what to do, then shrugged. "Water 'em yourself if you feel like it. I got a schedule to keep. Don't have time to baby a bunch of horses." He offered the rope to Cody, who just shook his head and folded his arms, rocking back.

"I'll get the others out. You water the horses." Cody said it quietly, though there was something in the tone that suggested problems if the driver disagreed. Latta could see the fists Cody was making, and the tightness bunching the muscles in his back. She hoped the driver wasn't too jacked up to pay attention to the signals. Some men were more dangerous when they became quiet.

The driver shrugged and gave a pull on the lead rope. "Suit yourself," he said over his shoulder. "Don't blame me if that stud gets loose. I told 'em, I got to have someone to help me with the damn horses." He muttered all the way to the corral, leading the tired horse, which lifted and set down each foot as if it weighed a thousand pounds.

"I'll get the chestnut next — think you can hold two? Or maybe put that bay in a pen. He'd like a roll and a drink too." Cody walked slowly up the ramp again as she led the bay toward the pens on either side of her main horse barn.

"I'll be right back," she called, and patted the big bay's neck. He stood well over sixteen hands and looked heavy-bodied enough to be a quarter horse–thoroughbred cross. She liked that look, but at that size some of them tended to be a little clumsy and slow for cow work. She wanted to breed a horse with guts and endurance and agility. She'd come across the idea of the Irish horses because they had to work cross-country, much the same as horses did in the sandhills, and they were bred as athletes, to run and jump huge ditches and obstacles. She figured to sell the horses for show, work, and pleasure. She wanted to create a whole new breed; it was her most private and only dream, the only thing left after Jaboy. Really, it was the first hope she'd had in years for making her life matter. She turned the horse into a pen and laughed because he made only one circle before dropping down in the good deep mud for a roll.

Cody met her halfway and handed over the chestnut's lead line. "Careful, he's a little sour." The horse's head shot out and teeth snapped empty air beside his shoulder. Cody's hand flicked out and caught the horse on the muzzle with a loud slap. The horse looked shocked and puzzled. "Cut it out," Cody said in his low voice. The horse turned to watch him go, then looked at Latta, who laughed again.

"Big bully, huh? Met your match this time." She led the horse to another pen without incident.

"Aw lady, you know I can't put 'em back on the truck fulla mud." The driver's whining was muffled by the tobacco he'd just stuffed in his cheek.

"I'll get someone to help you hose them off," she told him as she walked back to the van. "Why don't you turn the engine off. You can get some breakfast while I get one of the men to water the horses." When she heard the kicking and crashing of metal and wood, she broke into a run.

"Cody?" she called as she ran up the ramp, then stopped herself so suddenly that the driver, hobbling just behind, bumped into her.

The stallion was blowing into Cody's face, while he blew up the horse's nostrils. Rubbing the horse's neck, Cody worked to slide the chain end of the stallion's lead over his nose, through the ring, and back under the chin to snap it. That done, he said, "Just let me walk him down." Sliding the door over, he waited a moment, wanting the horse to surge forward and hit the chain that was a reminder of manners. Although the stallion was obviously eager to get out, he dropped his head to relieve the pressure on his nose and waited for Cody to step forward.

At the top of the ramp, the horse swelled up and let out a tremendous bellowing call, which caused the other horses on the van and in the nearby pens to jerk their heads up and stiffen. "That's enough," Cody said, and the animal dropped his head and walked calmly down the ramp as if he were a cow pony.

Latta let her eyes travel over the stallion's body, looking for the qualities she'd seen in the videotapes — thick strong bones, deep chest, powerful hindquarters, pasterns at an angle to give a comfortable ride. When she noticed the gash on his hind leg, she stepped forward. "Oh, no."

Cody patted the horse and looked back at the leg. "Must of done that when he fell. Knew he was home, tried to push his way out. Probably hasn't been outta that stall since he got on, from the looks of it." The driver chewed quickly on his tobacco, and spit toward the van's tires. It was clear that the stallion made him nervous. As if sensing that, the animal looked at him and pinned his ears. The man looked away.

"Doesn't look bad," Cody said. "Wash it later, put some blue powder on it. Where you want him?" Cody didn't offer to hand over the rope, and Latta was just as happy to let him lead the stallion until she got to know him. He'd been guaranteed a gentleman a lady could handle. But he was clearly full of himself prancing beside Cody, trying to be obedient and wanting to be wild, as he caught glimpses of the pastures and the hills rising around him. His grey coat, splotched with dark sweat, glittered in the sunshine like new silver.

"Stallion's pen is that corner one there, with the run in." She pointed to the six-foot pipe fencing.

Inside the pen, the horse waited patiently, legs spread stiffly while Cody slid the chain off. The minute the gate clanked shut in its slot, the stallion exploded, rearing and bucking and spinning, switching leads every few strides, jumping imaginary obstacles as he flew around and looped back through the mud. Latta and Cody laughed.

"Think he's glad to be here?" Cody said, his eyes shining as he watched the horse play. "He's a big sucker — sixteen-three or seventeen?"

Latta put her hands on the same pole Cody's were resting on, accidentally touching his. She didn't expect the warmth to come flooding through her quite so naturally. "Seventeen hands. Bigger than I wanted, but he had the other things going for him, and hasn't been throwing oversized babies, according to the breeder, so I think he'll be okay. I mean, ideally I wanted something a little smaller." It was suddenly important that he approve of her horse, her plans.

Cody nodded and let his little finger open and close on her hand. It brought back the nakedness of their bodies an hour before, the hard ridges of his stomach, the corded muscles of his arms as he'd braced himself above her. If he grabs me and kisses me, I'm going to have to let him stay, she promised herself, but he stepped away, and nodded toward the house instead. "I best be going. Think you can handle the rest of this?" He glanced at her with a serious look on his face, but the yellow flecks in his blue-grey eyes lightened his expression.

"Get out of here." She punched him in the shoulder. He laughed and grabbed her around the waist, pulling her against him. She was a little breathless when he leaned down and caught her face in his hands and kissed her, letting it grow so long and deep it brought tears to her eyes. When he released her she almost said, Don't go, but she pushed at his chest and frowned. She wasn't going to get this involved.

She could tell by the confusion on his face that he didn't know what to make of her. "I've got work to do," she said. "Take my truck." She started for the house, stopped, and turned. "Thanks for helping out here."

When she heard the truck tires spin and grind in the gravel, then roar off down her road, she caught her lower lip in her teeth, and avoided Inez's stare in the kitchen. Inez had been with Latta for years. She was more her grandmother than her housekeeper, more her friend than anyone else. And more her conscience than she wanted to admit. Inez wouldn't be able to help her with this one, though.

From what Latta had seen, Cody knew only one thing — make that two, she corrected herself — cowboying and making love. And he did both of those damn well. She just wasn't sure she could afford him, especially after he'd shown how good he could make her feel. What if she fell in love with him — then she'd be in real trouble. Better stick to one-nighters, men too boring to interest her, she ordered herself. But as if to point out her lie, the sweet sweaty scent of their lovemaking drifted up from her body.

She was sitting down to breakfast when Colin came in for the day's work orders. "Saw those deer again last night. Musta had a hard winter, hanging around like this." That was his way of asking if she was ready for him to shoot them so they didn't tear up the hay meadows. Latta ignored the remark. She tended to believe that they could coexist — and this was an ongoing debate she had with Colin.

"Stopped to look at that new stud of yours." He paused, a tiny smile pulling at the corners of his mouth. Latta was startled — was he talking about Cody? "What's his name?" Colin stood by the door, hat in hand, hair flat on top from the rim. Five wooden matches and two toothpicks were carefully tucked into the leather band. His face burned red under his deep tan as if he were uncomfortable. Of course he'd seen Cody and didn't like it, Latta realized. Cody slept with too many women, fought and drank too much, though a lot of men did that. But he was just plain different — strange even, and he'd killed a man by the time he was fourteen. People didn't trust or know him. Maybe that was part of the attraction. The hills people didn't like her either; they excluded her socially now that her rich husband was dead, and for her part, she wasn't above trying to scandalize them once in a while. Maybe that was all this was, really.

"What's his name?" Colin asked again.

"Oh. Stoney. Stone's Throw. What'd you think of him?" She smiled.

It was important for the men to like the horse. They'd have to help with the breeding until they found out how he behaved. If he was good, they'd turn him loose and let him pasture-breed the mares; otherwise, he'd have to be walked through each session. The Irish breeder and the American agent had assured Latta that he was kind and considerate with mares, but she didn't trust anyone about horses until she saw them with her own eyes. She'd been burned a lot when she first started out. Now caution supplemented her growing knowledge, especially with overseas breeders and agents. Hell, they didn't know her — nothing lost there, especially at the price she'd paid. But after her nomadic life with Jaboy, she avoided leaving the hills for any reason and had taken a huge chance with the horse rather than going to Ireland to check it out. The decision had kept her worried for months now.

"Looks all right. A little big, maybe." Colin looked hungrily at Inez's stack of cornbread.

"Sit down, Colin, I'm sorry. Thought you'd eaten." Latta knew the food the men cooked themselves was basic and poorly prepared. She paid a decent wage, gave them good housing, a side of beef each year. She even paid their medical insurance. That was more than some places did, but she'd long ago discovered that the last thing cowboys thought about was health. Jaboy had just fired anyone laid up. They'd fought about it until his death.

Colin murmured "Thanks" and sat at the table far enough from his boss to show respect. Behind them, Inez was dishing up plates of eggs and bacon.

"We'll give him a few days to settle down, then we'll see how many mares we can catch," Latta said. "Gonna be late foals this year, but it's better than too early, I guess. Besides, Red's worn out." She helped herself to bacon and cornbread.

"I don't notice him complaining any." Colin grinned, and yellow cornmeal crumbs peeked through his missing teeth.

Latta laughed. Red was her old quarter horse stallion she'd been breeding from for the past ten years. King ranch stock, he had stamped his babies with the old-fashioned sturdy body and mind he possessed. Now she wanted something with a little more size and style. "We'll use him to tease the mares."

"Hope he doesn't get too depressed." Colin spread the bottom half of a piece of cornbread with butter, loaded on two pieces of bacon, layered on a fried egg, and added the top half of the cornbread.

Inez sat down at the other end of the table to eat the bowl of grits she had every morning. A pasty white puddle with an island of butter floating on top, it reminded Latta of the Cream of Wheat and Malt-O-Meal her mother had forced her to eat on winter mornings. She looked up and out the big kitchen windows she'd put in after Jaboy died, when she'd started spending most of her indoors time in the kitchen or upstairs in her bedroom. The rest of the house was too much of a museum to be very interesting — it reminded her too much of him, anyway. Sometimes she wished she could just bulldoze the whole thing and start over, build herself something simple with clean modern angles and lines, lots of glass so she could watch the hills from all directions, and lots of insulation so the wind couldn't blow through so easily in the winter. Even so, with her remodeling, the windows in the kitchen took up half of one wall and almost all of another. It was easy for the two women to keep track of their world that way.

She was watching the barnyard when two pickups rolled in. The first truck was hers — with Will driving, from Bennett's — the other was Cody's Dodge.

Will stepped to the screen door and peered in. "Cody didn't want to trouble you none, Miz Jaboy. Said to thank you." He stepped down to climb into the battered Dodge.

When she looked, Cody gave her a two-finger salute and pulled his hat lower as he drove past the house. Can't have it both ways, Jaboy'd always told her that. Why not, she used to ask, but he'd only smiled at her, the malicious curve of his lips letting her know she wouldn't like it both ways anyhow. He'd spent his life having everything. He'd wanted to live at some edge of the world, he had told her, a place no one else could even find, let alone inhabit. He'd taken her close to it. She'd looked into the special darkness off the edge of a night-filled canyon, but she couldn't take the steps into thin air he took. She couldn't walk on blackness without falling. She wore proof of that — her fingers rubbed the lattice of scars on her left wrist. She felt like she'd seen every poor, corrupted place in the world, after traveling to Mexico with him. Anything could happen there, he'd told her. She shivered and stopped herself.

Before Jaboy died, she'd felt she remembered every single moment of her life. Every thing. Since then, she'd worked to forget most of it. She didn't care what horrors visited her sleep as long as she couldn't remember them. She didn't care that she'd lived a whole life she was gradually turning into greyness. When she stayed in the present, she was all right. She could keep things simple. Usually a cowboy was simple. Cody only appeared simple. That was the difference. That was why she'd have to work hard to stay away from him. He was some key that threatened to turn the lock behind which she'd placed most of her life. She just wanted a man who gave her sex. Cody would care. He was like that. Things would matter. She'd worked too hard to make sure they didn't.

She pushed her breakfast plate away, smelling their love-making again as she lifted her arms, then stood up and announced, "I'll be down later." She'd just go upstairs and take a long bath, soak his body off hers. As she left the room, Inez and Colin raised their eyebrows at each other.

8 ✦ OUTGOING CALLS

The wind's been blowing for a week and a half and no rain. The wind gusts and tears so you can't hear anything but yourself — hair flapping at your ear, faint bawl of cattle once in a while, birds blotted out until you realize what's been taken away. The wind blows everything away — the birds, insects that should speckle the windshield yellow and brown, the sand, the flowers, water —

— Caroline
May 3, 1965

When Rosalie Crater, the psychic and past-lives expert, came to town in early June, the Christians didn't offer more than token resistance and snuck out to their appointments just like everyone else. The psychic charged twenty-five dollars a visit, and had set herself up three doors down from the VFW on Bigger Street, in the old bakery that Emil Vullet had finally closed after thirty years because the drought in the eighties busted out plenty of folks.

LaVeta Sheets and Opal Treat, there late one afternoon for their private consultations, could still smell the sweet floury goods Vullet had been famous for as they waited on folding chairs in the newly swept front of the store. The wooden display cases barricading the doorway to the kitchen, where the actual baking had been done and where Rosalie now gave her readings, still held round greasy splotches where glistening rows of doughnuts and sweet rolls and cupcakes had rested.

The memory of those baked goods was greatly improved by the contrast to the cardboard- and plastic-encased objects shipped in nowadays to the two grocery stores. It no longer mattered that Emil's stiff grey beard hairs had sometimes been found nesting in the middle of his breads and cakes, or that when he was fighting with his wife or maiden daughter, he had rudely shouted at the customers. There remained on the town's palate the memory of an extraordinary taste of fresh baked goods fingering the tongue, reminding it that once things did have flavors that were distinct and alive.

Emil's wedding cakes were to dream about, the waiting women murmured. Every bride who could afford it had one, even if it meant sacrificing things like monogrammed matchbooks and napkins, because each cake was a drama of flavor, color, and detail. Emil often disregarded the order, after meeting with the bride, giving her something much grander, and stranger in some cases. Because he could see what her eyes told him, he bragged and created the creamy richness of butter-laced amaretto frosting or the almond- and raspberry- and grape-flavored flowers that wound their way along the layers as if they were garden paths.

LaVeta and Opal shook their heads. If he'd only been able to weather the hard times, until the return of the new traditionalism, as those bridal magazines were calling it. Girls wanted the big white weddings again. Emil would've thrived now, they agreed, sorting the dusty remnants of the shop from the luxury of the baked goods in their minds, and ignoring Greta Vullet, the baker's daughter, who slept quietly in the corner, her head leaning at an uncomfortable angle against the wall as she waited her turn.

Opal and LaVeta were waiting for Kayla Odell, who was well over her allotted fifty minutes. They'd already had their turns and were dying to take the cassette tapes out to Opal's car and play them on her tape player. Opal and LaVeta had known each other since girlhood, and shared everything, even their past and future lives, which had just been revealed to them. Opal had been told she was a ship's captain in a previous time, and now she understood why she loved the water so. And giving orders. LaVeta was once a nun, Rosalie had told her, which embarrassed LaVeta a bit, since she'd made fun of Catholics all her life. She didn't know whether it was okay to change her mind now, and she could hardly wait to share this knowledge with Opal and get her opinion.

LaVeta wanted to leave now, but she knew Opal wouldn't want to offend Kayla, who got hurt so easily. Especially since Kayla's husband, Jack, hadn't been around for the past week when she'd called the ranch, and hadn't been to town to visit Kayla and the kids for two weeks. He'd told her he'd be busy, so she shouldn't come out. Opal and LaVeta both thought he was having an affair with the hired man's wife, or that Burke woman down the road, whose husband was up in Rapid City drying out. These young wives didn't understand anything. The older women shook their heads: they'd lived there in Babylon for fifty-five years, and they'd seen it all, come and go, come and go. You just had to hold some hands; it was the only thing you could do.

When Kya Bennett burst in the sticky front door, she let it slam with a glass-clattering bang behind her. Naturally towering over the other women, she smiled and took a drag off her cigarette, ignoring Opal Treat's frown. She was dressed in tight Levi's and fancy red and black snakeskin boots that came halfway up her long calves, with the pants tucked in the tops. Around her left ankle was a bracelet of thick silver conchos and rings that jingled with every motion of her foot. As she looked around the room, her green eyes shone with that extra brightness that made people want to get out of her way, as if there were something unnatural about her.

In fact, her presence cut into the long goodbye Kayla Odell was having with Rosalie Crater, and sent the three women scurrying out the door. "I don't have much time," Kya explained, taking another long drag on the cigarette and letting the smoke out slowly over the heads of the two remaining women. When she did it she looked sexy, like women in commercials or forties movies.

Rosalie shrugged. "This lady's next." She cocked her head toward Greta Vullet, who had opened her eyes when the door slammed the second time, behind Opal, LaVeta, and Kayla.

"Can't wait," Kya said, and dropped the cigarette on the floor and flattened it with the toe of her boot. "Mind if I go first?"

When Kya turned the full light of her green eyes on them, people usually let her have her way. Greta shook her head.

Kya stared into her eyes, plundering her like a dog dismantling a basket of food. No one had ever told Kya not to stare, to keep her eyes out of other people's lives. "Thanks."

Kya crowded the heels of Rosalie Crater going back to the kitchen, and sat on the old brown metal folding chair as if she'd have to leap up in a minute. Crossing her long legs, she bumped the little table, sending Rosalie's deck of cards sprawling across the floor. Her body always seemed just that extra bit too big, and the idea irritated her as she bent down to pick up the cards. Rosalie, she noticed, sat down with a tired sigh and folded her hands on the table. Kya quickly jammed the cards into order and put the ragged stack on the table as she sat down again. She pulled a cigarette out of the pack in her shirt pocket and was just putting it to her lips when she hesitated, looking at the short woman across from her.

Rosalie shook her head. "Clouds my channels. So if you don't mind —"

Kya put the cigarette back in her pocket. She didn't really need it, she told herself. Not really. She wasn't like Heywood, who'd smoked like a chimney until his lungs gave out. Then he'd turned on smokers like some born-again. Except for Kya. He'd just smiled and said it probably wouldn't hurt her for a few more years. She wondered if he knew she'd been at it since she was twelve, trying to stunt her growth. Another lie they told you — she was a goddamned tree.

Shuffling and cutting the cards as Rosalie instructed, Kya tried to focus on her questions. She'd been having a burger and beer at the Liquor 'n' Lunch a few blocks away when she overheard a discussion about the psychic. The idea came with such clarity and force she'd simply put money on the counter and finished her food as she walked to Bigger Street. She'd left the beer bottle on the sidewalk outside the old bakery. LaVeta and Opal must have stepped around it. Kya smiled. Women always treated her like she had rabies, so she went out of her way to irritate them. She had no idea what made other women tick. Men were easy to handle — like animals, they always wanted approval, or something a swift kick in the butt could fix.

She put her elbows on the table and watched Rosalie lay out the cards, pausing over a couple and closing her eyes with her blunt fingers resting lightly on their faded surfaces. She was wearing blood-red fingernail polish, in odd contrast to the soft pastels of her little-fat-lady makeup. The flesh on her arms hung on the bones like unbaked dough, and Kya had a vision of pushing her into one of the big black ovens that lined the back wall.

Rosalie cleared her throat and drummed on the jack of spades in the left corner of the pattern she'd laid out. "A man, you've got trouble with a man. Let's see, this king, another one, and this jack here — another. That's a lot of men. Oh, and this here king and jack. It's unusual to see so many men in these positions. Like you're — I don't know — in some constellation with all of them." She rubbed the bodies of the cards gently as if they were live figures of tiny men.

"Yeah — okay — so what?" Kya peered into the half-turned face of the one-eyed jack. It didn't mean a damn thing to her. The old lady better come up with something more if she expected to get paid.

Rosalie opened and shut her mouth with a little huff, then spread her hands on the cards and closed her eyes. She wasn't much to look at, Kya decided, not unless you liked to look at people made out of squished balls of fat — from her round cheeks to the balloons of breasts and belly, with the pink polyester T-shirt nagging at the weight like overstretched rubber.

"You've spent your life surrounded by men. You were raised by a man, your father. You came here today to ask about your mother. You want to find her — you need to find her." The psychic looked at her expectantly, blinking her round blue eyes.

"Yeah." Lucky guess, Kya decided. "So where is she?"

The psychic looked at the cards, then at the ceiling, shaking her head slightly. "I'm not getting a clear picture. I'm not sure she's — she's not dead. No, I don't see her as dead. But I don't think she wants to be found. You'll look for her, but I don't know whether she'll be found. I see a place, lonely, open, few trees. You'll go there and find something —"

"Like the sandhills here?"

"No, another place. South Dakota. I see your mother with men, a lot of different men. She's laughing and drinking. She's not far. Another person is going to help you — a man, no, yes, a woman too. Both of them are necessary."

"This is stupid." Kya stood up and slapped at the huge copper mixing bowl hanging overhead. Its muffled sound echoed dully among the other bowls, spoons, and pans. She wanted to ring them all with her fist. Rosalie watched, a light flush rising from her throat and spreading across her cheeks.

"Tell me something real — tell me a detail, something nobody could know. Not this mumbo-jumbo." Kya leaned back against the butcher-block counter, cocking her knee and folding her arms.

Rosalie smiled and turned away to the small dirty window that let in just enough dusty light to give the kitchen a patina of decay. This girl needed a lesson. Sometimes they just wouldn't listen. She'd seen much more than she'd told and was trying to be tactful, careful.

"There's two brothers, different mothers — all of you have different mothers. They argue about everything, especially since your father died recently." She met the girl's hard green eyes.

"You could've heard that anywhere in town. That's no secret."

Rosalie shrugged. She didn't know why she bothered with people like this. "There's going to be a death — and you'll be the cause if you don't do something to change things."

"Who? Who's going to die?" Kya came toward the other woman, her fists clenched at her sides as if she'd batter the information out of her if she had to.

"It's not clear," the psychic lied. "But it's in your hands. You have it in you to change things, to channel your energies toward the positive." Rosalie let that sink in, then ordered, "Sit down."

Kya complied, surprised at the strength in the other woman's voice.

"One of your brothers is in danger. You'll need to protect him — not hurt him. The choice will be yours. You've spent your life doing pretty much what you wanted — things have to change. You need to think about other people. You need to get away from all these males. You don't have a single woman to talk to. Well, you better change that today. The first woman you meet, you make her your friend. You have a chance to beat this, but you can't do it the way you are now." She held up her hand to stop Kya's interruption. "See this card? That's your house, and it's coming down — and your brothers with it — and you. You need to look for a guide. Stop indulging yourself, start taking care of other people."

Kya felt the uncomfortable weight of judgment surround and threaten to sink her like the sand of a blowout in the hills. She didn't want to hear this. She didn't want any more death

— Heywood's was enough. She'd vowed after he died that she'd never stand still for death. She'd never wait around for it again — she'd run, make it catch her, take her down like an antelope with a .30 slug in its chest. Everyone was on her own. She reached for the cards.

Rosalie grabbed her wrist, pressing in with her nails. "Two years after he moved to your father's ranch, your brother Cody almost beat a man to death for torturing a crow he'd maimed behind the barn."

Kya felt the sting of truth against her eyes like they'd been whipped. She remembered watching from her tree house next to the farm as the bird dragged its crushed wing in circles, then tried to run away from the dirt clods that kept pelting it. Blood spattered the dust in dark drops like rain. The bird was panting so hard it couldn't cry out. When Cody came around the corner of the barn and saw it, he went crazy. It took three men to drag him off. The beaten man spent a month in the hospital. Her brother was crying when he took the brick and smashed the crow's head. He stopped only when Heywood slapped him hard enough to knock him down. She went to his bed that night, held him while he cried, but he wouldn't say why. She should have asked, but she never wanted to know. She was curious about the bird. She wondered how long it would have taken for it to give up and lay down and let the clods kill it.

Kya pulled a twenty and a five from her jeans and slapped them on top of the cards, sweeping them loose from their positions as she pulled her hand away. She hated Rosalie Crater, hated the whole world suddenly, hated the fear she felt hollowing her out so it rang her chest and head like a flawed bell.

She stood and pushed the metal chair so the legs squeaked on the concrete floor. Rosalie was gathering her cards together. The money had already disappeared.

"The whole world is a web of circumstance, Kya. One thing leads to another. You know that. There's deep wisdom buried inside you. Stop trying to hide from it. Find people to help you." The psychic spoke so softly, Kya had to hold her breath to hear every word.

"Bullshit." She turned and hurried out, ignoring the young woman sitting in the other room as she fumbled with the door handle. Kya was just considering putting her fist through the glass to get out when a much smaller hand reached under hers and jiggled the handle until the door popped.

"Always used to stick until Emil remembered to put lard on it," Greta Vullet explained.

Kya glanced at her as surprised as she would have been if one of the chairs had taken on life. Kya nodded and muttered thanks, fought to get through the screen door. Outside, she stopped at the beer bottle waiting on the sidewalk, paused, then booted it hard enough to send it spinning and bouncing across the street, where it shattered against the opposite curb. She hated spending money just to get depressed or angry. She didn't care about money for its own sake — like Arthur — or because it equaled work — like Cody — she liked it because it cheered her up, kept her in a good mood, let her have fun. She just hated this feeling she had now: the money had let her down, or she'd let it down, whichever way it was. It made her feel like a kid again. Now she'd have that woman's voice in her head for days, like Heywood's, telling her what to do.

As she walked back to her Blazer, she couldn't resist thinking about the bird. If the psychic knew about that, maybe the rest of it wasn't so idiotic. The idea kept nagging at her until she got in the truck and drove back to the bakery. At first it was Rosalie Crater she was waiting for, but when the psychic came out with Greta Vullet, finished what she was saying, and walked away, Kya found herself getting out and talking to Greta instead.

Greta wasn't paying attention as she stood blinking in the late afternoon sun, and Kya startled her when she stepped in front of her and said, "Wanna come to dinner?"

Greta frowned at the tall figure with the sun behind her in

such a way that her head seemed to explode with fiery sparks. While she wasn't sure she liked Kya, there was something irresistible about her that made the question more of an order.

"I have to get my, uh, father — what time is it?"

Kya shrugged and tossed her head impatiently. She didn't want to think about anything except taking care of the damn psychic's predictions. Get a woman friend. Here she was. A little mousy maybe, with her navy blue skirt and plain white blouse and nylons, but she was female all right.

Greta looked down the street toward the corner with the bank sign, which she could just make out. "Oh, five-thirty. I have to get him by six, when they close the Senior Citizens Center." She was nervous — what did Kya Bennett want with her?

Kya glanced at her, then back down the street, and nodded at her big black Blazer, which stood mud-caked, with its front bumper drooping, and the driver's side mirror dangling by its wires. "We can swing by and get him. You can both come out to the ranch for dinner."

When Greta stepped on the mud-clotted running board to swing into the seat, the dried dirt gave under her foot, and she would have slid down if Kya hadn't reached out for her flailing arm and pulled. It was a smooth gesture, with a male's casual strength that made Greta blush. Settling in, she stared at the inside of the truck, which was almost as dirty as the outside, with a crush of old wrappers and drink containers from José's and the Dairy Bar littering the floor and seats, as well as pop cans, money, clothes, boots, sneakers, halter and bridle, a brush, and paperback books.

"Just shove that shit out of the way and get comfy." Kya swept the seat between them with her forearm, pulling the debris toward her and onto the floor. "Cody usually cleans this out. He's been too busy lately."

Emil Vullet, Greta's father, spent his days at the Senior Citizens Center, giving free advice to the Meals on Wheels people about their baking. His wife had died right as the shop was closing down, and Greta still kept the little house on a dead-end side street just past the business district. Because his legs were bad from years of standing, Greta came to get him each afternoon on her old-fashioned bicycle with the thick tires and frame strong enough to hold them both as she struggled home, trying to keep the bike erect with his wobbling mass behind her. He'd talk all the way, recounting stories of his cakes, trials and tribulations of delivery, near disasters of weddings, mindless of how his daughter never responded to anything he said, not even a nod. As she pumped her thin legs slowly around, gasping for breath on the last block when she stood, steering and balancing her small body against his big one and the old bike, they resembled a high-wire circus act, with only the dull spokes and rust-splotched frame between their bodies and death. The Flying Vullets, people nicknamed them, and after a while it stuck and became a permanent moment in town time, which everyone took for granted and would only notice again when it disappeared.

In the winter, Greta came for Emil pulling a sled if the roads and sidewalks were icy or snowy, and she'd be seen tugging his bulk seated on the old wooden slab, as if he were a giant toddler out for an airing with his sister.

Greta spent her days cleaning house and working part time at the Sweete Shoppe, where she served day-old baked goods Wanita Cone bought at a discount from the Buckboard dining room each morning. With two small round tables, four chairs, and the owner's two babies crawling the chipped linoleum floor, the Sweete Shoppe, tucked on the edge of downtown, led a doomed existence that was largely ignored by its owner, who was convinced that success was simply a matter of the right gimmick. This year Wanita was trying a salad bar that consisted of three plastic gallon ice cream containers of aging potato salad, cole slaw, and macaroni salad, all turning shiny and dark on top as they waited patiently for customers in their little nests of ice beside the serving counter that also functioned for ordering, paying, and changing diapers. Wanita stayed in business because ladies could hold meetings there, with the extra folding chairs stored in the back room, and if you were really poor, too poor for the VFW even, and not religious, you could have a tiny wedding reception there.

At thirty-five, Greta still possessed the unlined face of the sleeper, unawakened by care and concern, or by emotion itself. Her blond hair streaked with silvery grey was worn in a simple straight cut that boxed her thin oval face, accentuated her strong, slightly hooked nose. No one noticed Greta really, most of the time, certainly not that she might be attractive at all. Her grey eyes never looked directly at anything or anyone as long as she was being watched, but when she wasn't, they stared with an intensity and sharpness that would have startled the town. Her small mouth with the curveless lips seemed prim and proper, but again, the lips reshaped themselves when she spoke, when she ate or drank, transforming her face with a natural beauty no one had yet guessed at.

Greta hadn't known what she wanted in life, and she'd always been the kind of practical person who needed to have a purpose, a goal, before she did something. She didn't want to waste herself or her parents' money on college, so she stayed home, waiting. Today, however, she'd decided that as silly and ridiculous and fake as it might turn out to be, she was going to do whatever the psychic told her to do. It was a chance thing anyway, she'd decided lately, leading one's life.

In Babylon, as in the hills around them, people were used to time taking forever, having to wait for everything, and then watching it pass in a moment, only to stretch out and make you wait again. Nothing happened by pushing at it. Nothing happened by chasing it — sand taught you that, and weather, and cattle. Everything did change; it just took so long sometimes, you forgot what it was you wanted by the time it happened.

9 ❖ *MISERY LOVES COMPANY*

Greta watched Kya stuff a tortilla filled with moo shu pork and fried rice in her mouth. Next to her, Cody was drinking beer steadily without eating, his face drawn under the tan. Arthur, one of the most powerful men in the region, seated at the head of the table, ignored everything but his food.

Greta looked around the table, which was silent except for the eating sounds. This was the way ranch people often ate

in town too. Silent meals, joyless and efficient, the men wearing a special solitude they carried with them like a frost on
their clothing. To Greta, the three Bennetts resembled cousins
rather than siblings. Each of their faces was unique, except that
they all shared full, sensual mouths, and eyes with the same
degree of odd coloration and an intensity a person would
avoid.

Looking around, she noticed that the dining room had not
undergone the more recent refurbishing of the rest of the
house. The walls were paneled in old, yellowing knotty pine
that ran halfway up to meet the aged paper depicting clusters
of fruit, once bright, now tarnished and faded as if the fruit
itself had begun to rot and mold. Such decay occurred over the
years, as if the walls existed in a slower, more methodical
world, one where change didn't jar and hurt a person. The dish
rail bisecting the walls held a hundred years of Bennett wives'
plates, everything from world's fair and state commemoratives
to a blue willow and a Limoges. In the china cabinet against
the south wall rested the accumulation of Bennett figurines and
objets d'art: a Jim Beam Elvis bottle, a coy shepherdess, and
rooster and hen salt-and-pepper shakers. Nothing was discrim-
inated against, nothing judged by its cost. There was a strict
egalitarianism practiced in this world of china, as if the article's
history gave it such value.

Kya followed Greta's gaze around the room. Should she
give her friend something? None of that stuff would ever belong to her, though. When she'd asked Heywood, he'd told her
that they were the house's. Like the land around them, they
couldn't be moved. As a child, she had believed that one day
something of hers would be added, and had looked anxiously
in Simon's Hardware for just the right thing.

By the time she was sixteen, she understood that she wasn't
really a Bennett, that she had nothing to leave in the company
of the other women. But she didn't care. She'd already figured
out that none of that glass had any life — it was too far away

from whoever had bought and cherished it. But her mother lived and mattered. Who was she? A native woman from Rosebud, Pine Ridge? Did she, Kya, look like her mother?

She tried to reconstruct a person she could call mother, but no one arrived. She wouldn't believe what that psychic had said about never finding her mother. She'd always been able to find Heywood, Cody, and Arthur when they disappeared. She just had to focus, that was all.

"Let's tell Cody what we did today," Kya said, putting her arm around her brother's shoulders and smiling at Greta.

Greta shook her head slightly and rolled her eyes at Emil, but Kya continued. "We went to a psychic who told us our past and future lives. Cost twenty-five dollars. Seemed like a bargain after what she told me about you two."

Emil stopped eating, gently set his fork down, and shifted in his chair to face his daughter. "What's this?"

Greta concentrated on his mouth. She couldn't look him in the eye and lie. "It was my money I saved." Her voice came out weak, and it made her angry.

"If you —" Emil said in a deep, measured voice that signaled a lecture.

"John, bring Cody some Pepsi, will you?" Kya called out. "Greta, you want one? Emil?" The can of pop appeared a minute later, along with a plate of biscuits and honey from breakfast. Kya and John exchanged knowing looks over Cody's head as he reached for the food.

"Mrs. Jaboy called this afternoon, Cody, I forgot to tell you," John said. "She wants you to come over and help her with her new stallion. She's having trouble breeding him, she said." He wiped his hands on the towel around his waist and pushed his long ponytail back over his shoulder.

"When'd she call?" Cody asked, his eyes on the biscuit in his hand.

"Well, after lunch and before dinner. I was too busy to write it down. Then I forgot." John picked up a bowl in each hand and smiled.

"What stallion's that?" Kya tipped her chair back.

"Something special, from what I hear," John said.

"Cody?"

"Too big to work cattle."

"Cost as much as ten good bulls," Arthur announced, as though she'd spent *his* money on the horse.

"Put together pretty good," Cody countered as if the two brothers had a personal stake in it. "Seventeen-hand grey. From Ireland."

"Seventeen hands? How's Latta Jaboy going to handle a stud that size?" Kya was making up her mind to go see him, whether Latta liked it or not. "You know, Arthur, I gotta get a new truck. I had to drive all the way out here in D3, and reverse is starting to drop out too." Kya leaned her elbows on the table and propped her chin up with her hands while she looked at her brother.

Arthur put down his fork, sighed, wiped his lips with his napkin, and pushed his plate away. Meals regularly ended this way, to his regret. He looked around at the others. Cody was the only one still eating. He was pulling each biscuit apart, slathering it with streams of honey from the plastic bear bottle and washing it down with Pepsi.

"That's disgusting," Arthur muttered.

"What'd the psychic say?" Cody asked between bites, ignoring his brother.

"Oh, yeah. Stuff about you two. Me. I went to ask her about finding my mother. She wasn't much help." She glanced at Greta, who shook her head more openly now. "What'd she tell you, Greta?"

"Your mother would —" Emil began, pushing the plate away too.

"Can't it be repaired, Kya?" Arthur asked.

"It's falling apart, Arthur. I can't even drive these people home tonight." Kya made her voice plaintive.

Arthur rubbed his face with his hands. "This isn't a good time. We can't free up much cash right now."

"In the old country —" Emil was saying.

"I know, Daddy, but I don't think it matters," Greta said to hush her father. She was trying to listen to these strange Bennetts, with their conversations in layers like her father's torte cakes.

"Look at your brother." Arthur gestured toward Cody, who was slouching on the table, his head propped in his hand as he slowly ate. "He hasn't had a new truck in ten years. We need to stick to our depreciation schedule on machinery."

"It never was new — you got it used to begin with," Cody said with his mouth full, so it came out in a mumble.

"Just like Germany, this superstitious nonsense, then it starts —" Emil pushed a big meaty hand through his bushy white hair and shook his head as if he could dislodge the wrongs burrowing in there.

"I know, Daddy." Greta was afraid that her father would get launched backwards in a spiraling litany that would make him sad for days.

"Even then, people don't listen, it doesn't matter." Emil's pale blue eyes were bright with memory. "Twenty-five dollars. Do you know how long it took me to save that when I first came to this country? There were winters when —"

"Dessert." John put down a plate of brownies, shrunken and black around the edges, and a plastic pail of cheap vanilla ice cream. From the kitchen floated the eerie melody of a Native American flute.

"The Blazer's a wreck, Arthur. Might as well face it." Kya grabbed a brownie. She looked at the Vullets. "Dig in, help yourself. Don't be shy."

"Please, just help yourself," Arthur said to Emil, who was seated next to him.

"Ice cream's icy," Kya warned, mouth full.

"We need a new freezer before we need to be buying new cars." Arthur dragged the plate of brownies toward him and picked one up, testing it on the rim of his plate for hardness.

"John isn't much of a baker," Kya said.

Cody laughed. "Probably another thing we need to replace."

"John is Cody's contribution to the household," Arthur said, as if the fact were condemnation enough.

"Still," Kya said as she crunched her brownie, "I need a new truck. You don't want me driving yours." She smiled, her teeth outlined with brown crumbs. "And you don't want me stranded here, do you?"

"No way," her brothers said in unison.

"Twenty-five dollars," Emil said loudly into the silence that followed.

"Oh, for chrissakes, she earns her own money at the Sweete Shoppe," Kya said, scraping the plate with her forefinger and licking it off.

"What?" Emil said the word slowly, as if each letter were its own syllable. Greta looked away from him, into the dark corners of the dining room where the polished wood of the spare chairs glinted, and the plates along the walls reflected back smudged versions of the scene.

"Daddy, please," Greta said.

"She's an adult who earns her own money — what's the big deal?" Kya said.

"Kya." Greta turned and stared hard at her. "Just don't say anything else, okay?"

"You should try working sometime, little sister. You wouldn't feel so free about wrecking things," Arthur said.

"What do *you* do? Cody's the only one who works for a living as far as I can see." Then Kya giggled. "Course, he doesn't make any money for it, so he's not such a good example, I guess."

Arthur laughed. Cody shook his head, pushed his chair back, and started to get up, as if this were the point in the evening when he always left.

Kya grabbed his arm and pulled him half off his chair to make him sit down. "Here." She stretched her legs out and dug into her jeans pocket. Pulling out a wad of bills, she shoved them across the table at Emil. "There's more than twenty-five dollars there."

The old man's face went white, then pink, as he tightened his lips and laid his fork down.

"Daddy," Greta said.

"Kya," Arthur and Cody said.

"I just hate talking about money all the time." Kya pouted and folded her arms across her chest.

Arthur shook his head. "I apologize, Mr. Vullet."

The old man fingered the silver fork handle for a moment. "I remember when you came into my store, a little girl with big eyes for my cookies, and I gave you one."

Kya nodded, and for the first time felt ashamed. "I'm sorry," she said. Emil waved it off, picking up the fork again. Everyone at the table sighed.

"We'll drive the Blazer to Abboud's tomorrow. Maybe he'll hold off on getting paid until the cattle checks come in. I assume that's all right with Cody?" Arthur looked at his brother, who was watching the floor again and only nodded.

Emil caught Arthur's eye and said, "Brownie too hard, break the teeth," gesturing toward his gold-capped teeth. As he drank, the old man's accent thickened.

"John isn't much of a cook, I'm afraid," Arthur said. He wondered if Emil was too old to go back to baking. An intriguing idea.

"I'm excellent cook." Emil nodded and drained the last of his beer.

"Daddy —" Greta put her hand on his arm, but he held up the stein anyway, and as if he could see through the walls and door, John reappeared with a fresh beer. The ease of it panicked Greta a little — apparently, anything could happen here.

"Daddy, that's enough now." Greta looked at his watery blue eyes, and turned to Kya. "I think we'd better go home. My father needs to go to bed."

"You're spending the night, aren't you? Arthur doesn't trust me with his car at night, and Cody's truck is too uncomfortable for your father. Stay, we have plenty of room." Kya couldn't explain the feeling she had at that moment, like she hadn't done the thing she was supposed to yet. She'd think of something to do in the morning, maybe take her shopping.

Arthur looked curiously at his sister. She was being more civilized than he'd seen her since before Heywood died. If having these people around made that much difference, he didn't mind at all. Besides, he could take Emil by the old bakery and have a talk. He had an option on the building he could exercise if the cash flow was there and the old man had some capital. "Of course, you should stay. I can drive you first thing in the morning. This house has more rooms than Buckingham Palace. Every Bennett for a hundred years has added on to it. I don't know what they were thinking — we'd field a football team or something — but we kind of rattle around in this thing most nights, so we're glad for some company to fill up a little of the emptiness. If you don't mind."

Surprised at his generosity, Kya smiled at him.

Greta looked from sister to brother and then to her father, whose eyes were in fact beginning to droop from the unaccustomed beer. "Thank you. We'd appreciate it. My father has to go to bed now." She pushed her chair back. "Come on, Daddy."

When Kya and Arthur got up to help, Greta glanced gratefully at them, thinking that maybe the Bennetts weren't so weird after all.

Cody's chest tightened as he watched. The scene was reminiscent of the last year with Heywood, when he'd be so weak sometimes that his sons would half carry him back to his bed, so he could take a breathing treatment or drag deeply on the oxygen or just lie there, moaning in pain from the bones that were growing brittle with the steroids they gave him for his lungs.

Cody got up and went to the liquor cabinet, poured himself a double shot of Irish whiskey, and went through the kitchen door so he could take the back way out while they were all busy.

The old carpet runner still retained enough of its texture and pile so that Kya could rub her feet along it as she went. Emil Vullet's snoring roared into the hallway like an old bear in a cave, snarkling bubbling snorts. She laughed quietly as she felt the heat of the burgundies and reds, the cool of the yellows and greens as they swirled and danced, meeting and dissolving. There were places where black ruled in thick dark twists she'd stub her toes on and skip over.

Dressed in a man's white T-shirt and a pair of Arthur's boxer shorts, Kya walked quickly to the first door and turned the knob. After the squeak, it gave and she slid through the opening. The heavy drapes were drawn against any potential light or noise, turning the room into a dark aquarium, confined and swimming with objects. Kya felt the chair before she stumbled over it, but when her feet found the rough terrain of Arthur's shoes, she fell forward into the side of his bed, landing with her arms outstretched on the mound of his body.

"My God," he cried out, and rolled away as if he were being attacked by demons.

Kya climbed into the warm hollow where he'd been sleeping and clutched her knees to her chest. "It's just me," she said to the panicked breathing next to her.

"Kya?" he whispered.

"No, your dead mother."

"It's not funny. You scared the bejesus out of me. What're you doing crawling around this time of night?" Arthur pulled the covers up to his chin and pushed himself halfway up the heavy oak headboard.

"I don't know." She shrugged. "I couldn't sleep, I got lonely. Kept thinking I was hearing things. Cody's truck isn't back yet. Jeez, it's dark in here, you know? How can you see anything?"

He sighed tiredly. "Usually I'm trying not to. That's the point. Light keeps me awake. You know, I just got to sleep. Now I'll be awake all night I bet."

Kya looked in the direction of the voice to see if she could make him out. There really was so little light, all she could pick up was a faint phosphorescent outline, and she couldn't be certain that it wasn't something she was making up in her mind against the blackness.

"What'd you think of Greta and Emil? Good, huh?"

"Sure. Wonderful. What's going on? Why'd you bring them out here? That Greta's not bad looking." He paused. "You're not trying to fix one of us up with her, are you?"

Kya reached over to touch Arthur. The idea of the voice coming at her from the darkness was bothering her. "Ow, stop it. What do you want?" Arthur pried her hand off his face and hung on to it.

"It's not such a bad idea. The psychic lady said we were all in danger. We needed to make peace. And it was up to me." Kya felt proud of her new role. "It's my calling, but I'm a little worried, I guess."

"God save us," Arthur said dryly.

"I could surprise you, Arthur. I know a lot more than you think I do."

"I'm sure you do, Kya. It's just that thing about too many cooks, you know?"

Kya snorted. "Well, I haven't noticed you and Cody doing such a great job so far."

Arthur shifted and pushed himself farther up the headboard. When she first came to the ranch as a small child, she'd visited him at night when she was bothered by bad dreams.

She'd needed the comfort she never got during the day, when she was too wild to tolerate much holding as long as she could be outside. Since Heywood was often gone at night, the two of them got into the habit of relying on each other, and not the grown-ups.

"We haven't talked like this in years, have we?" She sat alongside him, letting his arm encircle her and leaning her head back into his thick pajama-covered shoulder. "There. Feels good. God, I forgot how you used to do this and fall asleep sitting up just so I wouldn't be scared or alone. You were nice back then."

"You are the damnedest woman, Kya," Arthur said. "You're just —"

"I know, I'm a shit." She reached over and dug her fingers into his fleshy side, laughing as he squirmed to get away from her. "Still ticklish?"

"Cut it out." He took a couple of short gasps. "You know, if I started doing that to you —"

"I know. Keep your hands to yourself, Arthur."

"You're the only one gets to play?" he said.

"Yeah, well, I'm a grown woman. You should know better."

"Bull." Arthur tried to pull his arm from behind her, but she pressed back, trapping it there. He tried to push her away with his free hand, but she rocked back, grabbing at it. "You come in here and wake me up in the middle of the night to play games? Jesus, Kya." She could always match him, control him physically, as if her presence automatically weakened him. She'd hurt him on more than one occasion with her violent and sudden temper. He was actually a little afraid of her.

"Stop being such a baby, Arthur. Remember how much fun we used to have as kids? Like that time we stole Will's pickup so we could go to Mullen for some pop, and ended up in the pond. You changed after that."

"Not exactly. More like the minute Cody showed up, you didn't have the time of day for me."

"Well, you got so pissy, you weren't fun anymore. Didn't even stick around. Kept asking Heywood to send you places."

"Nobody wanted me around, if you'll remember. Suddenly we have a little murderer as the star Bennett attraction. I got the message." Arthur took a deep breath to battle the surge of boyhood wrong that was filling up his chest.

Kya fingered his hair lightly. It fascinated her that the three of them had such different textures to their hair and skin. "*I* never wanted you out of the way. You were imagining that. I wanted *both* of you to be my brothers."

"Well, we know *one* of us is —"

"Don't start in, Arthur. Cody's our brother. Just let it be, okay? Leave him alone. He's not bothering you. Focus on something else — like having fun and buying me a truck." She rubbed his skull with her knuckles hard enough to make him twist away.

"That's easy for you to say. I stuff money in your pockets every time I see you. Pay your bar and gas bills. That's all I do around here, pay bills. Who has time for anything else? Jesus, Kya, where do you think money comes from? Cody sure doesn't know. Now, instead of taking care of our work, he'll be off screwing around at Latta Jaboy's. That's all I need, him getting her all twisted around about something."

"Sorry. Didn't mean to start a big deal. Calm down."

"Maybe it's not that simple or easy for other people, Kya," Arthur said. "The world's not the way you and Cody imagine it."

She shrugged. "Whatever. I'm not Cody's keeper, and besides, I've told you before, Latta's an old bitch. That's all."

"And you're a young one, so there we have it."

"Yup, there we have it. Once a bitch, always a bitch." She crawled over him to slide out of bed.

"Watch it," Arthur said as she pushed too hard against his middle.

"Oops." She laughed. "See you in the movies, Arthur." She

slipped out of the room and down the hall to get dressed. She knew where Cody was now.

Cody sat in his truck watching the lights flick out one by one in the smaller house set just on the other side of the long, low machinery shed and garage next to the main house. He hadn't thought about what he would do. He was half a mile from her house when he'd turned off his headlights and killed the engine, hoping to keep his presence a secret. She'd called him — that had started it. He couldn't quite get it straight why he thought she'd want him there. She'd been so distant after the last time, he'd stayed away.

Tonight it just seemed natural to drive over, until he got there. When Colin and the boys were in bed finally, and there was just one upstairs light on in Latta's house, he decided to go only as far as the walk. Then the kitchen screen door was unlocked, of course, so it was just a matter of closing it softly. Nobody locked their doors out here. Weaving his way through the dark to the stairs, he put his foot on the first step, slowly sinking in his weight. When it squeaked, he put his other foot on the outside edge of the next stair. Looking up, he saw a Lakota ghost shirt encased in glass, gleaming palely on the wall of the landing. He hadn't noticed that the last time. The powdery blue around the neck glowed strangely, reminding him of the peculiar thing in his room the night before. Heywood again, always with the same smoky smell. This last time Cody had opened his eyes to a face or head with yawning mouth — whether in anger or fear, he couldn't tell.

The varnished banister was sticky under his hand. On the landing he paused and stared at the colored forms of butterflies, deer, moons, feathers, and stars on the shirt — things seen only in visions now, but which would return to the world when the white men were gone.

Cody looked up the short series of stairs. The line of light bisecting the edge of the hallway was coming from the left, two doors up from the room they'd used before. He was counting on it being her room and not Inez's. The older woman would probably club him to death if he made a mistake.

He reached the door and put his hand on the knob, held his breath, and listened for a sign of Latta. He sensed something of her emanating from the room and found himself having to let his breath out too soon. When he turned the knob and pushed the door open, her voice said, "Inez? Cody! What are you doing?"

She was sitting propped up in bed wearing a dingy cotton nightgown held up with small straps that had fallen off her shoulders, revealing the tops of her heavy breasts. The ragged gown was hiked up to her thighs. He couldn't think of a thing to say. She dropped the book she was reading, grabbed a sheet, and pulled it up around her waist as if her bare legs were indecent.

"*What* are you doing here?" she asked again, pulling the sheet higher.

He took a step forward, then looked around desperately. This wasn't going very well, he kept thinking. How was this supposed to happen? He came closer. "I called and asked you to come over tomorrow —"

Her eyes were watching his legs, then his hands, as he moved around the bed. He wasn't listening to anything as he sat down facing her on the edge of the bed.

"Cody —" Her voice dropped and stuck like there was a splinter it caught and hung on. "Don't —"

It wasn't words he needed; he'd known that when he'd seen her in bed. He ran his fingers up her arm, inspecting the fine down, the healing burn, the mole at the point of her shoulder, the little wrinkles of skin under her ear, and the fine wires of her curly hair. When his fingertips found her lips, she looked in his eyes and opened her mouth to his. Her breath stumbled in a half sob as he began.

·   ·   ·

"What does Latta Jaboy want with Cody, anyway?" Kya muttered to herself as she jumped off her horse and tied it to the door handle of Cody's pickup. She liked the way the thin clouds muted the moon tonight. She wasn't afraid of snakes or burrows. They weren't things she had to worry about. The animals and the land knew her, and she'd always felt comfortable with them.

She remembered being five years old and coming upon a big bull snake sunning itself one morning after a bad night of spring storms. He was lying in loose coils on the stump of a huge old cottonwood the wind had taken down. His skin was the shade of wet elm bark and shone sweaty like hot licorice. As she approached he watched her, sending a shiver that rippled down his long body like a little wave ringing back from a rock thrown in the water. He'd claimed that raw stump as his, she knew, and she just wanted to touch him. That's what she said, in a soft singsong voice she'd heard adults use.

When Heywood found her, the snake was in her lap, his weight like the big dictionary in the library. When the other men came, the snake simply eased itself off her lap and disappeared under the long grey trunk of the fallen tree. She waved goodbye to the last flicking inch of tail and looked up in time to catch a look of disgust and amusement on her father's face.

Opening the gate of the stallion's paddock, she slipped through and was turning to close it when she felt him behind her, snorting as he blew high to catch her scent. She turned slowly and blew at his face, laughing when he curled his lips and clicked his teeth.

As she led him out, he was the brightest object in the pasture. His coat shone like pounded tin, full of shadows and sharp planes of light. She slipped a bridle on over the halter and made him stand as she grabbed a handful of mane and swung on his back. He broke into a lope immediately, lengthening his body into a dead run at the urging of her boot heels in his sides.

When they reached the fence and cattle guard separating them from a pasture of brood mares with their new foals, Kya leaned forward, grabbing more mane, and kicked the stallion. He jumped the guard so effortlessly, she realized he could just as easily have cleared the four strands of barbed wire instead. The herd of mares greeted him with low questioning calls. Although he'd been taught not to behave like a stallion when he was being ridden, Kya could feel the swelling in his chest and the lift of his body as he tensed.

He was sweaty but hardly panting after his run. Lots of stamina and heart, she thought as she slid off, patted his neck, and brought his head down so she could pull off the bridle.

"Have a good time," she whispered, and eased the bit clanking past his teeth. The stallion stood for a moment and looked at her as if to question the rightness of this. When she slapped his neck and said "Go on," he trotted toward the waiting mares.

"You're a real piece of work, baby boy," she called. The horse stopped, looked back, blew at her, and trotted on. Kya didn't mind the walk back. It felt good to be in the hills, even if they were Latta's. And now she'd done something to even things up.

This was an old war between the two of them, dating back to the time Latta and Heywood caught her with Jaboy at Clark's. It had changed her forever in her father's eyes, and she could never forgive Latta for that. Now the other woman was trying to take her brothers too — doing one kind of business with Arthur and another with Cody. Latta was going to learn to stay away from Kya's world.

10 ✧ *SOMETHING TO MEET THE EYE*

A house is one room filled with mirrors and windows. Your face fades a little, grows trees, bushes, birds. You open your mouth and spit sun, clouds, cars riding the plate glass teeth, and finally your eyes. A man walks in, his curious mouth an elaborate curve of fullness, so beautiful you think just once to close his eyes so he can't see your trumpet announcing room.

— Caroline
July 12, 1976

Arthur was almost to Babylon, on his way back from Ainsworth where he'd checked on some land and a laundromat–bowling alley he was considering buying. He'd been thinking about the will again. He'd been searching for over a month, with no luck. Now interest rates were falling, and he should be buying stocks, property, anything to hedge against the low bank rates. Instead, the estate was tied up. The thought of Heywood's betrayal made the allergic tickle in his nose rise up and settle deep in his sinuses, sending waves of unbearable sneezes. He was having trouble keeping the car straight, and pulled over on the outskirts of town to blow his nose until it satisfied the tickle. Wiping his streaming eyes, he didn't see the figure outside the car until a knock on the window startled him. Wallace Moon, the sheriff, was squatting beside the car when Arthur pressed the button to lower the window. The sheriff's broad face waited patiently for Arthur to whank on his nose one more time.

"Having trouble this afternoon? Noticed you weaving a mile back, but you didn't see me." Sheriff Moon always spoke in a flat neutral voice, the sentence rising at the end with a lilt that further irritated Arthur.

"Allergies." Arthur gestured with the handkerchief and threw it on the seat beside him, sighing. He did not need a ticket.

"Uh-huh." Moon looked up toward the Repossessed Trailer Sales, sprawled in shabby neglect as if the misfortune of the lost households had brought their legacy with them. On the other side of the road, Harris Implement had placed planting and harvesting equipment out front like giant metal insects, colorful in their red, yellow, and green finishes.

"Why don't you step out here, Mr. Bennett, so we can talk." Moon stood up in one fluid motion. He was of average height, which made him less frightening to the voters, and bore little of the deference to whites that often marked the reservation Indians trying to do business in Babylon. He looked everyone in the eye and shook hands with the same authority he had practiced all his life. Moon had a reputation for being tough and fair, which had followed him through high school, to Vietnam, back to college, and to his days of coaching and teaching English when he was Babylon's first Indian teacher, and now the first Indian sheriff.

As he stepped out, Arthur noticed that Moon stood very close to him for a moment, then leaned back and relaxed against the car.

"I haven't been drinking."

Moon folded his arms and crossed his legs, permitting himself a small smile that thinned his lips even more. "Have to do my job, Mr. Bennett."

"I don't drink and drive. You should know that."

Moon just nodded and looked at the polished toe of his cowboy boot, as if he'd heard it all before. "Your sister? Kya?" he said quietly.

"What about her?" Arthur could feel the pain in his stomach start, and he couldn't even dig around on the front seat for his Mylanta tablets.

"She's —"

Radney Sheets, the locksmith, drove slowly by in his van, peering out at them. Sheriff Moon nodded to him and Arthur raised two fingers to his hat. Behind him was K. C. McNutt, followed by a semi full of cattle which rattled by before the sheriff spoke again. Arthur could just imagine how fast the news of this scene would travel on a boring summer morning.

"She's what?" Now that the traffic jam had cleared, he was impatient.

"She's up at the Oasis."

"She stays there sometimes." Arthur turned to open the door again.

"Yeah, but Burch Winants is there too. I got a call from someone this morning saying Mrs. Clark was going to wait one more day before she sets the dogs loose on her son-in-law. Just thought you'd like to know. Hate to see any trouble at the Oasis. Oliver has enough to worry about with his legs." Moon straightened, tucked his tan shirt in behind, then touched the brim of his hat and walked back to his car.

Arthur cursed and yanked the door open, almost bumping his head as he climbed in. He shifted out of park and pressed on the gas, spinning sand on the sheriff's car as he powered down the asphalt. Then he had to slam on the brakes past the Repossessed Trailer Sales because Moon had posted a twenty-five-mile-an-hour sign last week. Beyond the implement dealer, Boettcher's Monument Company was having a spring sale, fifty percent off on selected models. Just his luck Heywood had to die a week before the sale started. Housed in an old car dealership, the granite slabs stood facing the road through the long plate-glass showroom window. A few of them bore the names of people whose families had been in the sandhills for as long as the Bennetts. Others he didn't recognize. Maybe these were the rejects. He imagined Heywood Bennett's tombstone out there like that and had a momentary suspicion about Boettcher. Maybe he took so long getting the gravestones to the cemetery because they each stood their little round of duty in the showroom.

His soaked shirt stuck to his back, and sweat slid down his sides, gathering in the waistband of his pants. The air conditioner was hardly doing a thing against the July heat laying on top of him like a playground bully. He'd have to go to the house and call Cody at the ranch to come get Kya. He'd be damned if he'd make a fool of himself in broad daylight at the Oasis.

Before turning down Main, he drove by the Oasis, the most rundown motel in town, wearing faded pink paint and plastic shake shingles chipping at the eaves. The Oasis sign, with its palm tree and camel and pool of water, was so bleached only a ghost of the figures and letters remained. The screen doors on the rooms hung skewed, as if they'd gotten tired of the constant slamming and kicking.

Sure enough, Kya's new black Blazer stood like a horse baking in the July sun, which was stepping up the sky, growing hotter with each passing hour. Why couldn't she leave the married men alone? Go out with that Vullet girl she'd brought home in June, pick up single cowboys at least.

Arthur automatically glanced at the kitchen clock, surprised that it was so late in the day. He poured a glass of iced tea and phoned the ranch and left a message for Cody to call. Then he remembered that he had to call Minneapolis about the condo–golf club project, Holiday Ranches. The receptionist seemed to forget who he was every time and made him repeat his name before she tried to get him to just leave a number.

He'd learned from experience not to do that. He couldn't figure it out, though: didn't they want to do business up there? He drained the tea and glanced at the clock again. Five-thirty. Might already be too late.

"Sid Greenway." The voice was smooth and confident. It made Arthur envy the dark polished wood of the man's office, the windows that covered almost an entire wall, thirty stories above the city.

"Arthur Bennett."

"Art, glad you called. We were discussing your proposal at lunch today and it looks fine but —" Sid never rushed his words. Nor did he sniffle at the end of sentences from allergies. How could you have allergies in an office with pure cool air, a car whose air conditioning worked, and an elaborate condo overlooking the river across from downtown? "We just need to solve this one problem." The man paused.

Arthur let him dangle a moment before he said, "Yes —"

"We need to secure the mortgages on at least two of the ranches for our investors."

Arthur let the silence build again. He felt like hanging up. "What do you mean?" He struggled to keep his voice neutral so it wouldn't rise and crack.

"Well, Art, we did a little checking with your lawyer, and he feels, well, we feel, that is, our attorneys *feel* that with the will putting the estate in joint ownership, we have to have more depth, financially speaking, you understand."

Arthur held the phone away from him and rubbed his eyes, which stung from anger. When he stopped, he saw a blurry line weaving along the back of the counter between the sugar bowl and the windowsill over the sink. Was he seeing things?

"Art?" Sid's voice seemed to squeak tinnily from the receiver held at that distance.

"You don't think there'll be a problem giving you mortgages on jointly owned property." Arthur let his voice carry some weight of sarcasm as he leaned closer to the wavy line. Ants.

Hundreds — no, thousands — of tiny red sugar ants. He followed their path to his mother's old china sugar bowl, painted with thick creamy yellow flowers.

"No, since you're executor of the estate, *and* business manager, you can invest . . ."

He didn't want to pick up the lid, but he had to. There was a rim of dusty red motion along the lip it rested on.

". . . best if they sign on too, you understand, to avoid . . ."

He lifted the lid. His stomach fluttered.

". . . if you think there's any chance. Because we do want to move ahead on this project. We've had interest in Omaha from some corporations, Kansas City, Denver, and of course . . ."

Inside the sugar bowl was a mass of rusty specks, jittery with motion. He felt a little nauseous. He tried to remember if he'd sugared his tea. No, he'd put sugar in the pitcher a few days ago. Had he missed them then because he was too distracted?

"So if you take care of the paperwork at your end, fax us copies, and Fed Ex the actual documents, we'll be set, say, in the next ten to fourteen days. You can move faster than us — you know each other out there personally. That's a real advantage. Art, you can't imagine what *we* have to go through."

Arthur picked up the sugar bowl and dumped the contents into the drain. Even then, the ants clung stubbornly to the grains of sugar, like sailors going down with the ship. He turned on the water, watching the specks of struggling bodies swirl as they rounded the sink several times before disappearing down the dark hole.

"Art?"

He cradled the phone between his shoulder and chin. "Yeah, well, a Denver bank holds one mortgage, a bank in Rapid City another. We only have one here in town now. The main ranch is free and clear, as you know —"

"I'm sure you can make the arrangements. You're still interested, aren't you? I need to know now if —"

"Yes, *Sid*." Where'd this *Art* business come from? "You'll be hearing from me."

"Well, you know business deals are courtships, Art. We're past the holding-hands stage. We've had our first kiss. You know what's next, so don't wait too long or the suitor might get impatient."

Arthur wanted to laugh at the ridiculous analogy. He reached out and began pinching off sections of the ant line, which continued its march despite the missing sugar bowl. A few ants broke ranks, but most persevered, trying to get to or from the food that was now only imaginary. Sid Greenway was going to try to fuck him over, he could feel it. Whether Arthur could stop him was the question. "Okay, Sid, I'll get back to you." He hung up the phone, taking out his frustration by methodically obliterating the remaining ants.

The phone rang, startling him. It was Cody calling from the ranch. "What's so important?"

Arthur heard the clank of glass against the phone receiver, which meant that Cody was draining a beer as they talked. He was probably dropping grids of dried manure and sand all over the floor too. "What do you want?"

Cody sighed. "You told John I should call you when I got in." Another clink, and then the muffled request to John for another cold one. "We got over fifty cows with the scours, we lost five calves already, I spent a whole day wading in shit, and I got to go back and meet the vet in an hour. She's picking up some new stuff flying in from Laramie. I'm trying to keep the rest of the herd from coming down with it too. So just tell me what you want." There was a long gurgle of beer.

Taking a deep breath to organize his thoughts, Arthur said, "Kya's holed up at the Oasis with Burch Winants, and old lady Clark is sending her sons tomorrow. You need to go get her out of there tonight."

"Shit. I don't have time for this, Arthur. You're in town, you go get her."

Arthur felt another kind of heat rising in him. Why couldn't his brother just help out? Why did he always have to make such a big deal about everything? He liked to play the Lone Ranger — why couldn't he just break the goddamned door down and bring his sister home?

"Just do it," Arthur said, and slammed down the phone. He hated his brother. Saying it seemed so simple now — and relieving — as if he'd washed all the dirt and sweat of the day from his skin, and as if in so doing, something else had been rinsed away, something inside of him. His brother was worth hating.

He made his way to the third floor, stripped down to his undershirt, and turned on the fan he'd placed in one corner. There was something here, he kept reassuring himself. He knew he should search the brittle papers that filled each box, but he was drawn to the diaries that Caroline had kept. He felt that the key might be there too. Maybe she would confess that Cody was someone else's son, and his problem would be solved. He decided to go back to 1962, the year Cody was born:

I'm pregnant, but I haven't told anyone. I don't want to. He's mine. I know it's a boy — I dreamt the other night what he would look like, how he would talk to me. Sometimes I wonder if he'll hate me, if he'll know *how* to love me — I mean, I don't know how you *learn* those kinds of things. Did someone teach me? Was it my mother's wooden hairbrush against my back, or the scrape of my father's whiskers on my chin? They taught me that pleasure of hurting. Is that what he'll learn from me? Do I love Heywood or is it some darker form of desire? He tells me he loves me, the words just clatter like spoons in a drawer. I can't even say the words sometimes. They stop like pieces of cardboard in my mouth, choking me off, so I smile. Men are always satisfied with so little. Like Heywood. He'd rather believe anything than nothing. I give him the choice. I think that's why he keeps coming back, even though his wife will kill him when she finds out. Or maybe Belford. But he's too busy to notice, he's a man satisfied by a smile.

Arthur rocked back on his heels, tapping the page several times with his thick, blunt fingers. There it was. He just had to find out about Belford, her husband. Opal Treat. He hated to bring her big gossipy mouth into his life, but she was the genealogy expert and historian.

Poor stupid Heywood. Thought he knew it all. Thought he had it all under control, while Caroline Kidwell made a laughingstock out of him, screwing God knows who — maybe every man in Cherry County. It made him hate Cody even more, and he was surprised by how infinite a feeling hate could be.

Heywood had set up Caroline Kidwell to satisfy himself sexually. That had to be it. From the letters and diaries, it seemed they'd had a lot of sex. That was all it was.

"My sister here?" Cody asked Oliver, who was sitting in the easy chair behind the motel office desk, his swollen, weeping leg propped up on a wooden kitchen chair with a cushion while he watched a ball game.

"They're starting football soon. Gets earlier every year." The old man shook his head as if all of civilization were falling to confetti before his eyes. Cody waited. It wasn't going to happen any faster from this point on. Like swinging your leg over a horse you know is going to try its level best to buck you off, you did it slow, inevitably, and even then it felt too fast. Just a blur.

"Twenty. She's not alone." He answered without taking his eyes off the screen. "Will you look at that son of a bitch fly around them bases?"

Cody leaned heavily across the counter, searching the board for the key. When he found it, he flipped it off with his forefinger and turned to go.

"I don't wanna be calling the sheriff on you, Cody," the other man warned. "Take it easy in there."

There were only ten units in the motel, but Oliver started numbering at ten to make the place sound bigger. He skipped numbers he didn't like too. He said it was his motel, he could do any damn thing he wanted with it, and no one argued with him.

Room 20 was at the end of the first row, before the curve around the little horseshoe drive. It was probably a bad idea to walk in without warning, but he didn't want to give Burch a chance. So he turned the key and shoved his shoulder against the chain at the same time, wondering if he should've brought the pistol he kept in the glove compartment for stock emergencies, when he fell into the room.

"Jesus Christ, Cody, don't you ever knock?"

Kya was lying naked across the bed on her stomach, looking lazily at him over her shoulder. Her dark hair was spread in a tangle across the rumpled sheets. She should cover up. Something. His head was so thick with the image of his sister's body, he forgot to look for the man, who rose from the floor on the far side of the bed, buttoning his jeans.

"Time to come home, Kya," Cody announced in a muffled voice, as if he had a blanket over his head. He wished he did — that he wasn't seeing Burch lean over and slap her bare ass, or seeing her body as it turned toward the man, flashing a bare breast with its brown nipple, as she grabbed for his leg.

"She's staying here, Cody." Burch was grinning, his teeth perfect and even. His handsome face was brutal in its vacuousness and cunning. The intelligence in the eyes was the sort that planned only for its own pleasure; it had given up on everything else. "Sit down and have a drink before you go." Burch offered the orange chair with blond wood arms in the corner beside the table. On it were a half-empty bottle of Cuervo Gold, a six-pack of Corona, a quarter of lime, a cheap paring knife with the orange price sticker on its handle, and a brown plastic bucket of ice, which stood warming in little puddles of water on the peeling fake wood-grain tabletop.

For some reason, the sight of the liquor made him more angry. Cody knew it was wrong, what he was feeling, but he was enjoying the wrongness of it rising up inside him, the way anger could replace everything else. He remembered how much he liked anger, how long it had been since he'd let it loose — the dogs at the fence, simple to open the gate and stand aside.

A hand gripping his shoulder stopped him. "Get dressed, Kya. Burch, you sit down." The hand jerked him out of the doorway. "Get back in your truck."

Cody turned to face the sheriff, his fists cocked.

"Just take her home, Cody. She's too drunk to drive. Get in the truck and get out of here."

Turning, Cody saw the squad car, lights off, idling a few yards away. "Get in the truck now," the sheriff ordered, and Cody found himself opening Kya's door, then going to the driver's side and climbing in. Maybe he should go back and finish Burch, he thought unreasonably, and reached across to the glove compartment. Kya's hand shot out and covered the button. "No," she said, climbing into the truck.

Out of the corner of his eye, he saw Moon's hand reach in and turn the key in the ignition. "Put it in gear and get out of town. Now."

Cody sat up, hands on the wheel, staring at the dead insects dotting the dusty hood. Sheriff Moon was already at the door to room 20 when the Dodge rolled quietly past. Cody had gone three blocks before he realized he hadn't turned on his head-lights.

"You shouldn't run Arthur's errands for him," Kya said, stretching her legs out and propping her feet on the dashboard while she braced herself in the corner. She was still only wearing her T-shirt and underpants. The white cotton glowed bluish in the dark against her long tanned legs.

He put his eyes on the road. The anger was spreading and running off like spilled oil, leaving him aware of his body, of her body. He didn't want this. He wanted her to put her clothes on. To wear a bra like a decent woman, not let her breasts swing in the thin cotton of his worn-out T-shirt she'd cut the bottom off. Why do you keep taking my clothes, he wanted to ask her. He could smell her, all the smells of the room and Burch, and he pushed her feet off the dash.

"Grow up." She flung her shorts at him.

"Put your pants on."

"Mind your own business. You and Arthur both." She reached for the radio and twisted the knob, but only staticy music came on. "Jesus, this is a cheap piece of shit." She punched it with the heel of her hand, and the silver knob popped off and rolled under his boots.

"Quit breaking stuff. Settle down, for chrissakes. I don't need this crap tonight." He tried to sound worse than he felt. Actually, he was feeling pretty good, when he thought about it. He knew Burch would have to settle it next time they saw each other. He liked that idea a lot. It was just the post-adrenaline rush, but it felt good. He was ready to kick ass. Hadn't done it enough recently. He looked at his scarred knuckles on the steering wheel.

"Stop the truck."

"Forget it."

"No really. I have to pee. Stop."

He looked for a place where the weeds weren't too high by the side of the road, and stopped without bothering to pull over. Nobody else would be out here at this time of night. In the pastures around them, the crickets and frogs whirred and chirruped. Most nights it was comforting, and in winter their absence made the silence almost unbearable, especially when the wind blew steadily for days. Sometimes it made a person think he was going to be rushed away, head blown apart into a brown hiss of nothing. White and brown, the winter hills, and the dark humps of cattle nearby.

The warm green air wove through the cab of the truck. He closed his eyes and breathed deeply, smelling the new-cut hay from the flats a set of hills away, the marsh-brown suck of water in the pasture to the left, the hot furry hides of cattle somewhere close, and the pale perfume of flowers.

He opened his eyes. "Get in the truck, will you? I have to get some sleep tonight."

"Come and get me," she called from behind him.

He pounded the seat next to him, waited another minute, then climbed out of the truck. When she got like this, he didn't have a choice.

"Feels good, doesn't it? I was lying in that motel room, just thinking about floating in a stock tank like this." Kya was on her back, her arms and legs spread lazily across the middle of the water. Her green eyes glowed like an animal's from the moonlight overhead. Her hair stirred around her like seaweed, edging the thick mushy strands of moss that flowed from the sides and rose up from the bottom.

Cody had his arms hooked around the cool metal lip of the tank and his legs spread out in front of him. Every once in a while, his toe touched her thigh. He hadn't taken his jeans off, and their wetness bound his skin. His shirt and his boots lay on the ground. Kya had run barefoot across the pasture to the tank with the windmill pumping water into it, cool and fresh from the deep rock below. She'd simply jumped in before he could catch her. He leaned his head back, letting his neck rest on the rim. The hard coolness felt good, and for the first time in many days he felt clean, despite the slimy sides and the debris settled at the bottom. The water was always being pumped in fresh, the overflow soaking the sand around the tank so the cows could moisten their hooves while they drank, preventing cracks and lameness. You just had to be careful not to stir up the bottom.

"Remember how we used to do this? God, this feels good," Kya said. Turning over, she spread her arms and legs and hung her face in the water for so long Cody started to worry. She was capable of anything.

"Kya? Hey." He nudged her with his foot.

She pulled her face out, laughing, and paddled over, catching the side and turning to lean back beside him. Their long legs matched almost perfectly and they began to scissor them in a single motion, making bigger and bigger waves that pushed up their chests and finally splashed their faces, before they stopped.

"Remember that night Heywood caught us swimming naked?" Kya said. "Arthur ratted. He still doesn't get it. I thought the old man was gonna stroke out. What a stupid scene. I almost ran away, you know. Especially when he took you to Clark's. That was shitty."

Cody didn't want to remember that particular humiliation — being driven by his grim-faced father in the middle of the day to Clark's, put in a room with an older woman whose tired, practiced body gave him an erection she quickly dispensed with, leaving him with a kind of dispassionate hunger he'd been feeding ever since. A few days later, while everyone else had gone to the Fourth of July celebration, he'd found Kya sitting on the porch of the main house. She was smoking one of Heywood's Camels between little hiccups of dry sobs. No tears.

He'd taken a cigarette from the pack and smoked with her, until her silence made him want to smash something. He didn't know what Heywood had told her about him. Maybe everything. Maybe that he was evil, not to be trusted, that he was trying to make her have sex. After Clark's he was different. What he'd done had changed him, he could feel it. He could never swim naked with her again, never be close again. Heywood didn't have to say a word. Cody would stop it now. Send her away. She knew it too.

He hadn't been quite aware of doing it, but after a while he found himself touching his arm with the lit end of the cigarette. At first he hadn't felt anything, so he held it there longer, watching as if it were someone else's arm, as the hairs caught and crackled away, then the spot brightened, layers of skin separated and bubbled pink and white. The cigarette's miniature torch searching for something. When he stopped the pain came, a quick searing sting that stayed, pushing down into the muscle and bone until he started again. By then Kya was watching his arm and his face, fascinated enough to stop crying. This is for you, he'd wanted to say, I'm sorry.

When she grabbed the cigarette and ground it out, he put his arms around her as if he'd earned the right. A month later she started seeing Jaboy, and his mother died.

Now she touched the puckered round scar on his arm. "I thought you didn't like me anymore, that you wanted to be with real women after that. I was just a kid. I always thought we'd do everything together. Heywood had different ideas. Guess I surprised him with Jaboy. Surprised everyone." She laid his arm back on the tank rim and put hers over it, pressing his skin lightly into the icy metal.

"Surprised is one way to say it," Cody said, closing his eyes. Jaboy reminded him of Latta. He hadn't gone there two nights in a row yet, but maybe he'd risk it after he took Kya home. The water was soaking the tiredness out, and maybe she'd find his wet jeans exciting. For some reason women got turned on by things like sweat, dirt, and scars. Latta hadn't said a word in a month, just moaned with pleasure. That was good though. He couldn't complain. She was like a strange woman in a dream. Without talking or lights, they had found a way to satisfy themselves. He tried not to think of the day one of them changed it.

Joseph Starr had told him he had to draw a circle for himself that he couldn't cross, couldn't let other people cross no matter what. That was how you knew you were a grown man, an adult. He was still trying to figure that part out. Mostly he'd discovered if he just kept his world small, simple, he didn't have to make many decisions. There weren't so many mistakes, either. He hoped Latta saw how important that was.

"I don't understand why everyone has to make such a big deal out of sex. Especially mine. I wish everyone would stay out of it for once." She raised a leg and dropped it against the surface with a hard smack that splashed them again.

He thought of Latta. "Seems reasonable." Except when it comes to Burch, he added silently.

"How's Latta's stallion doing?"

He looked at his sister's face, resisting a laugh. "You're the one who turned him loose with those mares."

She smiled. "Maybe. Maybe not. He breeding okay now?"

"Oh yeah. Much happier these days."

"He's not the only one then, is he?" Kya said quietly and leaned back, closing her eyes.

Cody closed his eyes too, wishing they could talk directly again, the way they did when there weren't these secrets and lies.

"What happened to us, Cody? We used to be so close, like skin."

He nodded.

"Latta Jaboy. If that old bitch had kept her nose out of things —"

"You were sleeping with her husband," Cody said as neutrally as possible.

"He didn't want her anyway. Besides, why'd she have to tell Heywood? That was the worst part, the way they came marching into Clark's after us."

Cody took a deep breath. "You were sixteen, Kya. He was a dirty old man. Maybe she was trying to save you."

Kya laughed. "That's why she waited a week after she found out? No, you're blind, Cody. Your dick is leading you around again. She wanted to make the biggest stink possible. She was jealous of me. I'll just never forget how miserable I was afterwards. Worse than when Heywood found us swimming. At least you still cared about me. After Jaboy, even Arthur clammed up. It wasn't like I *killed* somebody or something." She slid down so the water rimmed her face, then pulled up and looked at her brother. "I'm sorry, Cody, I didn't mean it that way. I wasn't talking about you."

Cody just stared at the hills rising beyond them, silvery with sage and soapweed. He didn't answer her about the man he'd shot. He never talked about it with anyone. Even Heywood, that first day at the ranch when he'd whipped him for it. What was there to say? He'd done a thing and it changed him forever. Sometimes he wished he could understand Caroline's reaction better. That was all.

Overhead, a bat screeched and fluttered past them. Then there was a rush of large wings and an owl sailed by. After that, the insects and frogs picked up a steady throbbing, like a giant heartbeat, catching everything in its muscle and pushing it in and out, in and out, in its thick liquid pulse.

After a long time, they climbed out without a word. Toweling his feet with his shirt, Cody shook his boots out to dislodge any snakes, then pulled them on and picked his sister up and carried her back to the waiting truck.

In traditional Lakota culture each person had a purpose or plan
in life. A destiny. It was his duty to go on a vision quest to find
out what that purpose was. Parents allowed children to discover
answers for themselves. A child was never told how to do a task.
He was shown the task and then allowed to attempt it himself.

— *from* MITAKUYE OYASIN

After that night the heat settled on the hills like a panting
dog, scooching its haunches and its hot furry belly down
into the dirt, lying there for days. The mornings rose damp and
hot, and even sleeping naked did nothing to cool the skin. It
took hours for freshly washed hair to dry stiff from the salty
sweat rising up each strand. The cattle ate at dawn and long
into the night, but during the day they lay in clumps or stood
chest deep in the ponds and marshes, fighting flies, crowded
against each other, the heat pouring from their thick hides.
Horses stood nose to tail in any shade they could find, even
the thin sliver of a telephone pole striping their backs. Sweat
splotching their coats, they shook their heads dotted with black
sticky flies, and stamped their tired legs in slow motion.

Afternoons were silent except for the heavy buzzing insects
and the *hooot hooo hooo hooo* of a dove or the single exhausted
twert of a sparrow, as if the weight of the damp heat were
driving the birds to ground. At dusk, when the clouds re-

turned, the birds rose and began frantically grabbing at specks of grain and insects blown by the rising wind.

At night it rained heavy thick rains that drove petals off flowers, leaves out of trees, grasses to the ground in big heaving waves, as if bodies had fallen and lay there. Shingles on roofs that had blistered and buckled in the heat were lifted away. Windows and doors rattled in their frames as if the houses were imploding some exhausted temper baking within. Ratcheting against barn walls, scaling windmills, the wind banged and tossed and tore across the night's sleep. Dreams came dark and tangled.

The rains had come and paused, giving the air a brief cooling one night in early August when three figures drove a truck and stock trailer rattling up Jaboy's road, maneuvered a turnaround, and parked amid a row of machinery a quarter mile from the main house and horse barns. They walked purposefully but kept straining their eyes at the dark. Inside the barn, they moved quickly to the stallion box.

They were snapping the leads on the stallion's halter when they heard the truck tires on the gravel outside as it rolled to a stop with the lights and engine off. One of the men went to the window and peered out at the tall, lean cowboy who slid from his truck, closing the door gently with a click rather than a thud, and walked quietly through the gate, up the stairs, and pulled on the screen door. When it refused to open, he froze, put his head down as if listening for something, then tried again. He knocked lightly, his palm resting on the wood frame, and stood for a moment before turning away. On the front walk he paused, looking up at the dark windows on the second floor. Tugging his hat lower, he walked back to the truck with slumping shoulders. Once inside, he started the engine but didn't turn on the lights before driving away.

The grey stallion pulled back when his front feet touched the shaky floorboards of the old stock trailer, but one thief held on while another hushed the horse, coaxing him with a hand on his haunches. The rain started lightly and built momentum, traveling across the hills beyond in sheets that obscured everything. Suddenly the man slapped the horse's butt hard and yelled loudly, and the animal sprang into the trailer. The rain arrived in long sweeps, pushing through the open spaces between the slats on the sides, wetting the horse's face and neck in front and big haunches behind. He stepped back and forth to position himself away from it, but to no avail.

By the time they reached the cab they were soaked, and the engine sputtered and died a few times before it caught, the rain was coming down so heavy now. The windshield wipers merely brushed water against water, as if they were trying to part a lake. The wind rocked and lifted the truck and trailer, making the horse shift uneasily, throwing his weight from side to side and the truck with it.

By full light they were driving on another unpaved road, winding deep into pine-covered bluffs and hills where the light filtered dark and shadowed into the valleys. Finally they stopped, so far from anything that there were no signs of modern life. No utility wires ran from the small cabin backed against a pine-notched slope. Inside, it smelled as damp and sweet piney as the air outside. The corral showed signs of recent reinforcement, with freshly hacked saplings woven between the old rotting timbers. There was a three-sided shelter facing south, with a pine bough–covered roof. A person would have to be looking specifically for the place to discern it among the trees.

Unloading the horse and the bales of hay, and making certain the water tank was full, they threw hay to the stallion and drove back out to the highway.

If it hadn't been for the rain last night, she wouldn't have to drive to the sheriff's. Everything was so soaked, a pole must have fallen, knocking out the phones. She closed her eyes, gripped the steering wheel hard, and tried to collect herself. She had to organize, concentrate on the problem piercing her stomach like a big darning needle. She hardly noticed Opal Treat's insulting failure to wave as her car passed Latta's from the other direction.

They'd all had cattle stolen before, trucks driving up to a fence, cutting it, loading and hauling out in the middle of the night. The Bennetts were lucky because the blacktop ended long before their place, and the back way out was too boggy with sand for a heavy truck. But Jaboy had paid plenty for the blacktop to come as close as it did, so he could get out in the winter and spring, past the low areas, and keep the sand from blowing out on the ridges.

She felt like taking a bulldozer and skinning off all the asphalt like old wallpaper. She imagined the heavy gears shifting and the roar and tremble of the engine as she ripped up the road. A little late.

She opened her eyes and looked at the storefront with the little apartment on the second floor that served as the sheriff's office and home. He'd married the young gym teacher from Wichita last year. The slim, dark-haired woman could be seen jogging early mornings out on 20. Everyone knew who she was, since she was the only adult runner in town, but they refrained from honking — her actions seemed a kind of eccentric, maybe even dangerous, behavior they should ignore.

Getting out of the truck, Latta hoped the young wife was upstairs or out doing whatever it was gym teachers did in the summer. She felt vaguely embarrassed by the situation, as if the theft were a more intimate violation than a stolen horse. Just the idea of strangers on her property, in her barn touching things she had touched — it was like having unwanted hands on her body. Cody. He'd come just before the rain, but she'd locked him out. A week and no word, no visit. What did he think she was? Maybe he saw something.

The shiver that spiked her skin made her mad and she

yanked the door open and slammed it after herself. The office smelled of spicy grease. The sheriff's plate of eggs swimming in salsa was resting on a paper towel on his desk. He was leaning over, forking food in and chewing thoughtfully, staring at a small TV tuned to the CNN morning news. None of it good. It never was, it seemed to Latta, unless you liked sports, where someone was always winning and someone was always losing.

"You check with your neighbors?" he asked, patting his wide lips with a second paper towel, after she'd told him about the missing horse.

She glanced at the plate of yellow and red. It made her stomach lurch. "No, I don't think they'd steal."

The sheriff put the paper towel down and rolled the chair away from the desk. Leaning back, he cupped his hands behind his head. "I don't mean that. Did you ask them if they'd seen or heard anything?"

Latta shook her head and looked at his neatly combed hair, parted on the side, cut short enough that when he put his hat on, only the sideburns were visible.

"Did you talk to the people on your road?" He was watching the baseball scores roll quickly up the screen. "Damn. Twins lost."

"Isn't that *your* job?" She wanted to walk across the office and flip off the TV, but getting angry with him wouldn't work. It never did.

"I suppose you could say that, but you've been here long enough to know that folks like to take care of things themselves when they can. I got to cover too much territory to be chasing after every single cow and horse gets loose" — he raised his hands — "or stolen."

Latta stared at his full round face, perfectly seamless though they were approximately the same age. It wasn't fair.

"You having any trouble with anyone? Anyone who might want to — I don't know — play a trick or even things up or something?" The intelligence in his eyes contrasted with the innocent inquiry.

"What? You think a Bennett took my horse? You going to accuse them or should I?"

He crossed his legs and leaned back, smiling. "I wouldn't accuse anyone."

"Isn't fifty thousand grand larceny? I'll call the state cops and FBI if I have to. Unless you want to do your job."

The sheriff stared at the TV for a few moments, then nodded his head and stood up. "All right. You track down Arthur Bennett — he's in town — see if anyone heard or saw anything at his place. I'll call around. Fancy horse like that'd be hard to hide or sell."

On the sidewalk, she stood and blinked, surprised by the brightness, as if she'd forgotten it was morning, forgotten the world outside her anger. Why was her business always getting mixed up with the Bennetts'? Now she had to consult Arthur, who hadn't approved of her purchasing the horse to begin with. But the horse was everything — the promise of her future — without it, her life didn't make any sense.

Looking up and down Main, she spotted Cody's truck parked in front of Em's Café. He was in a booth at the back of the long narrow room, bent over a plate of food, his hat pulled so low it almost touched the table as he ate. He was wearing an old plaid cowboy shirt unbuttoned, revealing his smooth tanned chest.

He looked up, surprised, then embarrassed, and put his knife and fork down slowly. She wasn't going to do the friendly thing and pull up a chair. He probably knew about the horse too. Hell, the whole town probably knew about the horse.

"Someone stole Stoney, my stallion, last night. Do you know anything about it?" she demanded as she stood over him.

He sighed and pushed his plate toward the center of the table as if it had poisoned him. Since she was blocking the booth, he couldn't stand up and face her, so he swung around and leaned against the wall, looking at her. "What makes you think I'd know anything?"

She wanted to slap his face. She couldn't say why, except maybe he was too young, too pretty sitting there. And he'd started taking her for granted.

Cody rubbed his face with his hands, pushing his hat off his forehead. "I didn't see anything. I came —" He glanced quickly at her, his eyes dull with lack of sleep and a sadness that surprised her.

Latta sighed. Who knew the stud's value? where he was kept? "Think it was the driver maybe? That creepy man who delivered him?" She sat down across from Cody.

He nodded. "Could be. Tell Moon about him."

"You really didn't see or hear anything?" She said it quietly, looking around to make sure no one was listening.

He sat still, watching her. She noticed how hard his eyes had turned, as if they were iced glass, the kind the taxidermist put in the heads of animals he stuffed for the hunters who invaded the hills every fall.

Finally he spoke: "We're haying. I've been up to my ass in sick cows and hurt horses. No, I didn't see anything. I didn't steal your horse, Mrs. Jaboy."

Cody shifted his gaze to the front of the café. He looked tired, as if he'd been up all night too. Maybe stealing horses. Why? Because I locked him out, Latta thought bitterly. Because he needed money. Arthur was so stingy. The horse was easy money. He'd killed a man — how bad was stealing next to that? He hadn't even fought her when she'd sent him away last night, or knocked harder or broken the door down. He was relieved, she bet. She couldn't tell anyone now. The thought made her feel crazy, and she had to stop herself again. Don't get paranoid now, she cautioned. Keep it simple. Concentrate on getting the horse back.

"I have to get back to work," he spoke flatly, refusing to look her in the eyes again.

She felt disappointed, as if it really did matter what this half-assed cowboy thought of her. "I'll call Arthur."

He nodded and swung his legs around to slide out of the booth. "He's at Selden Monk's." He started for the door, shoulders high and stiff, slim hips swaying in the elegant rhythm of a man in cowboy boots. It was a confident walk, one that understood its own gestures, its own capabilities. Latta felt a familiar mixture of contempt and longing as she followed.

Walking down Main to Selden Monk's law office, she thought about how being angry had worked for so long, she didn't know whether she could stop. Maybe that was how things happened with people. Anything could become convenient, then pretty soon you weren't thinking about it anymore, and it became the most important thing you did, and you couldn't not do it. Like eating or sleeping, anger was her habit. The only time she wasn't pissed off at something was when she was alone. Or those nights with Cody.

Being with other men — that was different, that was a way of exercising anger, going to battle with it, letting it win, letting it take its pound of flesh so she could be free for a while. Go ahead, she had urged, hurt me, make me feel it, do it, do it. So everything they had done was just that tiny bit too much, and she had felt the way anger laced her skin, bit her hide and left its mark. Anger was a stranger panting, as they had stumbled and slid to an edge where feelings rose that frightened them both. They had looked out over some dark plain, and there was only more darkness there, shining, enameled with blue-black, as they had led each other across, taking each other, she urging him, he pushing her. Where they went, there was no morality, no feelings complicated by emotion. She was laid bare like an electric circuitry board, and a stranger had run her. And she had felt safe that way.

"There's another will, Selden, and I'll find it. So don't do *anything* yet. I'm the executor, and I want you to wait until we have the real will, got it?" Arthur's voice tumbled down the stairs to her. She could hear Selden's voice trying to placate him. Arthur was probably Selden's biggest client, with all his investing. Arthur seemed to have a finger in every deal that came up. Now he was getting her involved too, but that was going to stop as soon as she got her money back on his farm loan.

"Arthur?" She called loudly enough for him to stop talking. She didn't want to hear any more Bennett business as long as she lived. She was sorry for every dime she'd loaned him that had brought her back into contact with these people.

"Mrs. Jaboy." Selden Monk came around his desk and shook her hand. Arthur stood, smiling fiercely.

"My stallion's been stolen," she announced, looking directly at Arthur.

"Have you called the sheriff?" Selden asked.

She nodded. "And I just talked to Cody at Em's. I was wondering if anyone at your place heard or saw anything last night." Latta walked to the window facing north, half expecting to see her horse trotting down Main.

"My sister's been in Mission for the past week," Arthur said. "I just talked to her last night. She was going on to St. Francis to check the church baptismal records. The men have been haying till all hours." He ducked his head, folding his hands behind his back. "Cody's in town? He's supposed to be at Clemmer's. Left word yesterday he'd be there for the next few days. I wonder what he's doing in town?" Arthur joined her at the window, and they both watched Cody's old truck, pulling an empty stock trailer, drive past them heading south, stop at the T meeting Route 20, and turn west. "Where's he going now?" Arthur tapped his upper lip. "He was alone, wasn't he?"

Latta nodded, too shaken to say anything. What if he *was* the one? What if she'd helped Cody steal her own horse by giving him the opportunity *and* the alibi she'd be too embarrassed to want public?

"Mrs. Jaboy, did you send in the insurance forms I sent you, and the check?" Selden Monk had a file open on his desk when she turned.

She opened her mouth and shook her head. She'd been letting a lot of things slide recently. Cash had been tight. She'd intended to look around for cheaper rates. Selden always dealt with the same two or three companies. She looked at the frayed yellowing cuffs sticking out below his threadbare coat. He was cheap enough when it came to *his* insurance, she bet.

"Well, then, you'd best get Sheriff Moon to put the state police on alert," Selden said. "For all you know, that horse is in Canada or California by now. No doubt he's crossed state lines, so the FBI can step in too." He paused, closing and opening the file folder. "I *am* surprised at you, Mrs. Jaboy, not taking care of the insurance. This isn't like you. Is everything *else* all right? If there's anything I can do, or if you need to talk to someone —"

Latta shook her head, not trusting herself to speak for fear the anger that was rising from her chest would make her say something ugly. Selden, in his old bachelor way, was always overprotective and fussy.

"We'd better go see the sheriff, Selden. I'll be in touch later. Just do as I asked, please." Arthur placed his fingers lightly on the middle of her back and steered her out the door and down the stairs.

The only way I can break my son and make him cry is to beat him.
He's learned so much about silence, I can't do it any other way. He
has to see that, so I spread newspapers on the bed and make him lie
across them while I whip him with his father's old belt. He doesn't
know whose belt it is. I use it to remind myself to be harsh. I don't
stop until his flailing has shredded the papers, his tears have wet
them, and he comes into my comforting arms again.

— Caroline
October 25, 1971

Cody drove toward downtown Cheyenne and the Wagon
Wheel Motel complex, where his sister always stayed because the owners knew the Bennetts and she could charge it to
Arthur. Now that he was in town, he couldn't understand why
he'd thought the *horse* would be in Cheyenne. The horse would
be someplace else — that made sense. Unless they'd already
sold it.

After Latta had left, he'd called Clark's and found out that
Burch had taken off, telling his wife he was going to Wyoming for a while. The Antelope Motel in Mission said Kya had
checked out. Cody had figured it had to be them, and Kya
always liked Cheyenne.

Passing the bars and cheap motels that lined Lincolnway,
he remembered how much trouble he always had here, from
servicemen, oil refinery workers, or local rednecks. The thought

of what might be ahead made him pull up to the drive-in window of the liquor store attached to the Wagon Wheel. In Wyoming he could have an open bottle on the front seat as long as he wasn't drunk. Hell, he'd be parked before he was drunk. He drove around to the back and took two long slugs off the quart of JD before he got out and went to the front desk, walking through the complicated geography of the motel. The motel's air conditioning was so powerful, it wiped away any trace of heat he'd felt getting out of the cool of the truck.

When the clerk told him they'd mentioned going to Laramie for a few days, Cody gassed up, grabbed two burgers and fries at McDonald's, and started up 80.

Beyond Cheyenne, a refinery sat in a wasteland, with nothing around it, as if it were eating the landscape. The mountains behind it were like a promise to the eye that there was more beyond, and in no time the land began to curve and rise, in pale skim-milk blue, soft green-yellow, and tan. It looked like the ice age had just rolled off and the grass was coming back. When the mountains took on toothy edges, the soil turned pink and the land dropped in alluvial draws and valleys, with a thin coating of grass over billion-year-old granite. Pine trees rose dark and thick as the road neared Medicine Bow National Forest, and then it dropped down a steep grade, where trucks sometimes lost their brakes on the hill toward the valley where Laramie lay peaceful and green between mountain ranges.

The whiskey was working well with the burger, and by the time he reached the center of Laramie, Cody was feeling confident about finding his sister and convincing her to come back and give him the horse. Burch Winants would be a small problem, but Cody wasn't worried. Burch wasn't so tough. The important thing was to get it done before anyone discovered it was Kya. She'd gone too far this time.

Laramie was everything Cheyenne was missing. It had the authentic feel of a western town. The flatbed full of stacked deer and antelope hides outside the Cowboy Gas seemed good to Cody. The bumper sticker on the patched Suburban pulling it said GOD BLESS AMERICA, and he felt the rightness of that, though he wasn't sure if there was a God, or exactly what He'd have to do with America to begin with. Huge elk horns were mounted on the hood. Something to be proud of, he guessed, though he didn't do much hunting. Deer were a problem for the ranch when they came down to the stack yard in winter and tore the hay apart, dropping stinky piss and shit that made the cattle shy away. He'd have to shoot some to keep the herd down, though he'd just as soon send Will's dog to scare them away.

He was sightseeing and forgot to check the motels as he drove through town, so he had to circle back around looking for Burch's black Ford pickup.

He tried not to think about Latta. Disciplining his mind was something he'd learned a long time ago. You could put things away. They came back at night in your sleep, like Heywood had been doing all summer, but you sure as hell didn't have to torment yourself while you were awake. If nothing else worked, he would create a map, letting his mind's eye roll out every marker, every hill and gulley on the ranch, every scrub tree, bush, patch of soapweed, and blow out over thirty thousand acres, trying to put every variation in its place. He'd ride it on his horse, or walk it, in his mind.

But in Laramie, the neon, the traffic, and the busyness kept distracting him, and flashes of Latta came with every phrase of music on the radio. He found himself wanting to call her from his motel room later. He'd have a few more drinks and do it. Tell her: Mission accomplished, he'd found the horse. But he hadn't yet. But by then he would have, wouldn't he? She'd be grateful. His sister would be safe. No one would know. He'd have to have a talk with Latta.

He had another sip of whiskey, letting it turn cool and metallic in his throat. When he got back, he was going to straighten things out with her. They wanted each other. He couldn't get over their lovemaking, how perfectly they fit each other, how simple it had all become for a little while. How no words were needed, before or after. Not like with women usually, when only alcohol could replace talking, so he drank until he was hardness and need and what they wanted. Still, he shouldn't have kept coming at night, never talking.

But his mother had taught him how words fail, how language was a lie. He'd grown up in a house of words, of sounds, of Caroline's dialogues with the people who weren't there, her moaning and laughing with Bennett, her ranting lectures that led to her spiraling anger and beatings. He was plenty happy for silence when he ran from their house, sometimes flattening his hands over his ears to stop even the crowding of frogs, crickets, grasshoppers, wind, and birds that threatened him. Silence. Some nights he wanted to unplug the steady hum of the refrigerator, the broken flicker of the fluorescent light in the kitchen, the choke of water in the pipes, the *thwap thwap* of the lilac against the window. Just to hear nothing.

He punched off the radio and circled the end of the block again. He didn't want to see his sister, Burch, the horse. He really didn't want to do anything but sleep. It seemed like such a long, long time since he'd been alone, away from everything that needed him, really been alone, someplace where no one knew who he was. He felt the exhaustion begin to slide on top of him with the weight of the mountain he'd just come down.

Maybe Heywood would stay away too. Maybe he wouldn't know how to find him away from the ranch. Last night he'd slept in his truck, too tired and disappointed to go back to the ranch. He didn't know whether he was asleep or awake when the smoke came burning into his lungs. This time he'd seen an arm wearing his father's favorite red plaid shirt, resting on the window as if he were standing just outside the truck. He'd been too scared to speak, though he vowed he'd ask him what he wanted the next time. Cody wondered if Heywood came to Arthur or Kya. She would've said something, he was certain.

He'd get a room someplace, it didn't matter where, and he'd go to sleep for a few hours — it was five o'clock now — and then he'd get up and find them. They'd be staying close to the center of town, where the bars were. He pulled into the first place with a Vacancy sign.

It was dark when he opened his eyes again. The only sound was the noisy rattle of the window air conditioner, which put out just enough stale-smelling coolness to keep his body vaguely aware it was on the verge of sweating. With a groan, he swung his legs over the side of the bed and sat up. The sandy taste in his mouth was from the booze, and he got up to get a glass of water from the bathroom, feeling his way to the wall switch.

As soon as the water hit his stomach, he realized he was hungry. He'd have to eat before he started searching; no telling how long that would take. Looking at himself in the big streaky mirror over the low pine dresser, he smoothed his old long-sleeved shirt and brushed at his dirty jeans. He'd been dressed for work, not traveling, when Latta'd found him. He picked up his stained and dusty work hat lying on top of the dresser, and left.

He was watching the green sauce wet the paper placemat in a dark circle when the waitress set down the special combination plate, dripping with orange-colored oil. She stood over him, arms on her wide hips, and asked if there'd be anything else. He shook his head and watched her walk flat-footed and tired back to the kitchen, listing from side to side as if each leg carried an extra invisible cargo that had to be lugged along.

There were a number of tourist families having late suppers around him, the fathers with dark circles and lines on their faces from driving too long and too fast, the kids cranky and twisting in their chairs from not being let out of the cars enough, the mothers trying to put cheerful faces on everything, and reaching across to handle the crises. Watching them fascinated him. Families were another world.

The smallest child had just upset her milk at the table next to his, causing the family to scramble out of their chairs as it raced toward them, when Cody caught the motion of a familiar figure out of the corner of his eye. He turned to see the side of Burch Winants's face as he picked up a white bag of take-out food from the cashier's counter and pushed open the glass door to leave.

There wasn't time to grab the truck, and Burch seemed to be on foot himself, so Cody dumped money on the table and followed, trying to keep enough distance so the other man wouldn't notice him. They were apparently staying across the street from where he was, and when Burch closed his door, Cody stood outside trying to figure out what to do. Finally he went to the door and tried to listen. The TV was on, but he didn't hear any other voices. This wasn't Babylon; he'd have to knock and get them to open the door. He didn't want a fight now. He just wanted to get Kya to straighten it out.

He knocked and turned the knob at the same time, and was surprised when the door swung open as if it hadn't been locked. When he took a step into the room, he felt a hand on his arm and a stunning blow on the back of his head that sent him to his knees. Reaching out for something to support himself, he touched a leg just as the knee came up and caught his chin with a jarring snap that sent him to his side. When the kicks started, he tried to remember to curl, but that seemed too difficult, and he lay there, wondering abstractly if the toe of the boot had a steel shank, if it would find the third and fourth ribs after the first two gave. He was throwing up Mexican food in short gagging waves while someone on the TV cursed him in a steady stream. Down on his stomach, the boots found his back and legs and head until he slipped into the metal glint he thought he saw at the very tip, and let the black come over him.

When he woke, his eyes were so swollen he could only see through slits. The lights were on in the room and the same voices were talking on the TV. He hadn't been out for long. Maybe Burch and Kya were still around. He was afraid to move. His chest stabbed him every time he took even a shallow breath. Burch had stomped every square inch. He'd be a mass of bruises for weeks, even if he hadn't ruptured anything.

He knew how to do what he had to do next. Like getting up after a bull has stomped you, you put yourself outside and lifted your body up, no matter how much it hurt. You put your pain in the hole, stuffed it in, shook it down and off, away. Feet on the floor, eyes open as wide as possible, he staggered for the door. Ignoring the pain of broken ribs, the pain in his face, his legs threatening to collapse under him, he wobbled out the door, where the wall of heat strong enough to topple a healthy man pushed him back.

Somehow he found Burch's black truck in the parking lot. Somehow he climbed up the hitch, over the tailgate, fell into the truck bed, and burrowed into the empty feedbags and equipment before he passed out again. He woke once when the rain started as they headed up the mountain pass out of Laramie, and he was soaked, shivering himself to sleep again, thinking that the rain could wash the blood and pain away so he'd be good as new in the morning. That's the way it should work, he decided. He woke again in the morning when the truck turned onto a dim road through meadow and woods, bouncing around everything in the bed, jarring his bruised head and body until he was gasping with pain and trying not to take a deep breath for fear of his ribs hurting more. When the truck lunged and bucked in a particularly rocky, deep place, he yelled out, but they didn't even slow down. He almost cried with relief as the torture subsided when at last they stopped.

He was fully awake now, and he knew that Burch had hurt him, hurt him good. But he'd be okay — everything about the pain was familiar. Even the heat, the sweating, and the chills that had started a while before. That was normal. It'd take a week or two. In the meantime, he had to get the horse back. He knew he couldn't drive: he didn't think he could see well enough to steer, and his ribs were killing him. But maybe he could ride, let the stallion find its way while he hung on. Otherwise, he'd have to leave the horse and risk their moving it again before he got back. Inside a nearby cabin, he could hear two voices rising and falling in anger. And a third one. Must be somebody taking care of the horse. A Winants, probably. They were hillbillies like him, from around Valentine.

He should get out of the truck, he knew. He peeked over the side at the cabin in the clearing and the small corral and barn. If they'd settle down and get some sleep, he could do that. He made himself count backwards from a thousand while he listened, and by the time he'd done it three times, the sounds from the cabin had quieted. He did it once more, hoping that the crows in the pines and cedars around them would keep up their noise. He didn't think he could stay quiet enough to slip off the truck and hobble to the barn, as hurt as he was. If they thought they were being watched or followed, they'd be listening. But they didn't, did they? He argued with himself until finally he inched his way forward and dared to peer over the lip of the truck bed.

The stallion was watching him from the corral, several yards away. It looked drawn, as if it hadn't been fed or watered. Still, the eye was bright and intelligent and calm as it watched him struggle and half crawl to the stack of hay bales butting the wall of the three-sided shed at the back of the pen. Ignoring the possibility of snakes, Cody managed to burrow in between the wall and the hay, lying there with the spiny points poking his skin like hot needles. He'd wait until dark to take the horse. In the meantime, he would sleep, he decided — as if he could help it. The blackness was getting easier to find. Heywood was there sometimes too, beckoning and shaking his head.

The sound of the truck driving away woke him. It was dark, but he had to work to open his eyes into slits to make sure. For some reason the pain in his ribs and chest seemed to press harder on him, and he wondered if a bale of hay had fallen, but when he felt himself, there wasn't anything there. He noticed how clumsy his hands were and wondered if he'd be able to fasten the buckles on the bridle and saddle.

Although the cabin was quiet, he had no idea who'd left in the truck, so he waited a while longer. Listening to the horse's restless pacing, as if it too were waiting, Cody was comforted by the soft plop of each hoof, the sureness of the step. They'd need that tonight. Finally he inched forward out of his hiding place and pushed himself up the wall of the lean-to. His legs protested that they couldn't hold him, his back heaved in spasms, and his chest stabbed him, but he stood and braced himself while he looked overhead at the stars and moon to see if he could guess what time it was. Not late; ten or eleven. Starting to cloud up. He wouldn't be able to take the road out — a man on foot could follow too easily, and he might meet the truck coming back in. No, he decided, looking at the woods on the hill above the cabin, he'd go *that* way.

Bridling the horse was relatively easy, since the animal lowered its head until its chin rested on his knee, and took the bit eagerly, as if it knew this meant leaving confinement, escaping. The saddle was harder, and Cody debated riding bareback until he decided to climb the fence and drop it off the top rung onto the horse's back that way, hoping the animal wouldn't spook and dump it. The stallion shivered when the saddle thumped down, but stood bravely, even when Cody took ten minutes to fasten the girth, which he couldn't pull quite tight enough. It'd be a balance ride tonight, he thought, but maybe he could tighten it again once he was on, with more leverage from above. Getting on was a problem he solved by climbing the fence until he could step on even with the stirrup.

It was the clatter of the gate boards that he hadn't counted on. The way they fell out of the slots and rattled on the rocks piled around the gateposts made such a loud noise, Cody froze, then pushed the gate again with his foot and urged the horse through the little opening. When a hind ankle caught, the stallion kicked out, sending boards clattering. If anyone was in the cabin, he would be on his way out now, Cody realized, and pressed his legs weakly into the horse and clucked. Unwilling to hurry in the dark, the horse simply quickened its walk.

Just as the cabin door swung open and boots clumped on the steps behind them, the animal balked at the dark edge of the woods. "Fuck," Burch swore. Cody tried to slam his heels into the stallion's sides, but it was a woman's voice calling "Don't shoot" followed by the click and explosion of the rifle that sent them forward, just as he felt a blow like an ax blade slamming hard and deep into his back and shoulder. "Fuck you, Cody," Burch yelled. The horse was scrambling up the rocky shale when the next shot caught Cody's thigh, making him cry out and almost drop the reins as he leaned over the horse's neck, ignoring the pain in his chest as he pressed against the saddle horn. "You'll hit him, you moron," he heard the woman holler.

It had been raining softly on the cabin's cedar shake roof thick with pine needles, soft ticking noises that entered Joseph Starr's sleep as a familiar song, one his grandfather had taught him with the old ways, which came when the dream came. He was there because he needed to be. In his dream it was years since he'd left the cabin beside the little pool that stayed full from the spring in the hill. It was part of his life now that he go down on his hands and knees to cup the water fresh and lap it with the animals. Someone else owned the cabin and wanted pay for it. He tried to explain about finding it abandoned and repairing it, but the words kept having to be repeated. They didn't work. They weren't getting through. No reconciliation, the man insisted, and began to chop the corners of the cabin with an ax. The sound made a round shape Joseph thought he recognized. And deer came out of the woods, crowding up against the walls that were threatening to collapse, blowing through their nostrils in a high whinny like a horse. The noise startled him awake.

Something was out there. He waited past the tapping rain. Deer often came bodying up against the cabin, and coyotes sniffed the walls. This was different. He listened again. In the carpet of needles covering the ground outside, metal clanked on stone. Then another sound, moaning. Joseph sat up stiffly and swung his legs around, feeling for his moccasins with his bare toes.

He grabbed the rifle and knife from the floor beside the bed and stood for a moment by the door, listening. There was nothing but the tentative chirp of a bird and the wind hissing in the pines. He could distinguish the tap and click of the softly falling rain in the trees from other sounds now; he'd been there long enough. Opening the door cautiously, he was surprised by the size of the grey head and chest looking at him. Then he heard the moan again and realized it was coming from the other side, a figure hanging off the saddle, which had tipped and slid under the horse. The man was lying on the ground except for his hand, tied by the rein to the horn.

Joseph set his rifle down and patted the horse's neck and cooed so it wouldn't startle. The animal stood quietly as Joseph pried the fingers off the horn, unwrapped the leather strap, and let the injured figure down to the ground. Then he quickly went to the other side of the horse, unlaced the girth, and pulled the saddle off. At first he thought the dark streaks on the animal were its blood, then he realized it was the man's.

He'd have to do something with the horse before he brought the man inside. Taking the reins that hung to the ground, he turned the horse and led him to the side of the cabin where the ruins of an old corral stood tangled with saplings and weeds. Enough fence remained that if he hobbled the animal it'd probably stay. The stallion looked at him curiously, but seemed to recognize the hobbles when it tried to follow him out of the corral and had to stop. "Stay there, I'll be back to take care of you," he said quietly, and ran to the man on the ground.

The rain was cool on his bare skin as he half lifted, half dragged the injured man through the door of the cabin and laid him on the floor beside the fireplace. He looked around for a moment. His truck was parked ten miles out. He'd have to walk, then drive half an hour if he wanted to get help. Judging from the amount of blood on him, the wounded man could bleed to death soon if he didn't do something. Hot water. He'd start a fire in the fireplace. He lit the kindling and filled the cast-iron Dutch oven with water from the bucket he kept by the door, and hung it over the fire. He needed to see better. He was so used to the dark, to following the rhythm of waking and sleeping with the sun, he usually forgot about lighting the kerosene lamps.

With three lamps around him on the floor, he knelt and began to examine the body. A small bubbling hole in the chest. He rolled the body over and found the entrance wound in the back that had broken the shoulder blade. He bent and listened to the suck and gurgle. The lung had collapsed and was taking air in the diaphragm. He pushed wads of cloth in the front and back holes to stop the air flow. There was another bullet in the thigh that'd missed the bone, he thought, but nicked the artery or a vein. He'd pull the belt tourniquet off as soon as he could figure out an alternative.

Gutsy, having the presence of mind to do that, Joseph decided. Something about the ragged breathing seemed off too, and he pressed along the ribs, noting where the figure seemed to jerk. Broken ribs. He put his ear to the chest. He hoped a lung hadn't been punctured by a rib. There was something else about the man, something familiar. He'd seen this before, in the war, where men were blown to pieces by guns. But he'd seen this body too. He looked closely at the battered and swollen face. He knew who it was.

He rocked back on his heels for a moment, tucking his arms around himself. He wasn't equipped to save this life. In the field they'd have had the medevac near enough to fly out the wounded. They'd have had antibiotics, vacuum pumps, sutures, painkillers. He didn't even have a phone. He'd decided against that world, brought only what he'd needed to get started out here. He closed his eyes and took a deep breath. Then another. Cody would die if he sat here doing nothing.

It was well into dawn by the time Joseph finished. He'd found his medic bag with some tubing and stuck lengths of it in the holes, sucking the air out with the hand pump until the chest was clear, then clamping them off. He'd torn strips of a sheet for bandages to immobilize the shoulders, being careful of the tubing.

He squatted beside Cody, watching his face again. How the hell had he managed to get into this much trouble? Joseph had made tea and was just taking his first sip when the face below him changed and the eye slits opened enough that Joseph could tell he was awake. He did what Joseph would do, tried to lift the hand with the broken shoulder and moaned, then lifted the other weakly, and bent his knees as if to get up. Before he could make the attempt, Joseph touched his chest. "Stay still."

Cody closed his eyes and Joseph thought he'd passed out again, but in a moment he spoke. "Joseph?"

Joseph set the tea mug down and kneeled over Cody's face, peering into it so when the eyes opened again, he recognized the peculiar slate-blue with yellow streaks.

"Have a little problem," Cody whispered as he tried to grin.

"I can see that." Joseph rocked back and waited.

"Latta Jaboy's stud." He started to cough and grabbed his ribs with his good hand to stop himself. "Think Kya stole —"

"Busted ribs," Joseph said. "Don't talk, just makes you cough."

Cody shook his head slightly. "Burch Winants shot — don't sheriff. They'll put her jail. Nobody knows." Another round of coughing and pain made his face grey and he closed his eyes, then seemed to drift off, his body shaking with cold.

Joseph stood up quickly and went to grab the blankets off his cot. Tucking them around Cody, he said, "Don't worry. Rest." From the slackness of the lips, he knew Cody was unconscious again. He'd have to get him to a doctor or he'd die. They had to finish clearing the chest, make sure the lung was inflated. But Cody was right — if he took him to the hospital in Chadron or Babylon, the sheriff would be all over them because of the gunshot wounds. His sister would go to jail. Cody would rather die than hurt his sister. And Kya had always seemed to feel the same way, so he was surprised she'd let Burch shoot him. He'd probably beaten him too.

The Winantses were another reason Joseph had moved up to the cabin. Not the family in particular, but the type. The wasting, thrashing people he'd found all around him, stumbling and crashing through life. He'd tried cowboying, but he kept running into them there too. Nothing made sense after a while. Not even throwing the empty tube of toothpaste away and buying another. Not even the plastic teeth of the black pocket comb staring back at him as they chipped out and waited like seeds in the palm of his hand. Nothing to grow. He'd thought he was losing his mind. He'd left the Bennetts, hung around Jaboy's until the old man died, tried the reservation again, then left to study the old ways. But there'd been no reconciliation yet, his grandfather told him in the dream. He had sold his responsibility — his grandfather's ghost shirt. First he must buy it back. That was the way of it. The dream had said the same thing every night since he'd moved to the woods. And now it was bleeding over into his days.

Outside, he could hear a flock of crows move into the clearing. Cawing and flapping loud enough to snap the air with their wings, they landed on the trees and roof. Pacing with the weight and authority of men, making the rafters creak, they seemed to be giving him notice. Landlords, pushing him out. Rent due. Eviction. He'd have to get Cody to the truck. If it was willing, the stallion was strong enough to carry the two of them out. Then what would he do with the horse? He'd have to hobble him again and send someone back for him. Latta Jaboy would pay for someone to take care of an animal as valuable as that one. The first thing was to get Cody out and hope the move didn't kill him.

All that was left of the rain was a pale grey mist that hung in the air and clung to their skin and clothes as the horse carried them down out of the woods. At fifty, Joseph wasn't quite as strong as he'd been at twenty, but he was more determined, so he simply ignored muscles protesting the press of the body propped in front of him. The stallion had balked at the weight behind the saddle at first, but Joseph had spoken firmly enough that it had taken tiny steps forward until it could accept the weight and really move out.

By the time they reached the road where the truck was parked in a little turnout, Cody was starting to mutter deliriously, and the stud flicked its ears back and forth and bunched its hindquarters, ready to shy. When Joseph slid off, the horse abruptly stepped sideways, almost dumping Cody. It stood snorting, eyes wide, chest puffed. Joseph pulled Cody off and saw that the leg was bleeding again. The horse had smelled the blood.

Leaving the saddle on so people would see it belonged to someone, he led the stallion several yards off the road before hobbling it. Leaving it this way was dangerous, but he didn't have a choice. Almost no one used the road anyway, so with luck the horse wouldn't wander enough to get hit. He'd drive as fast as he could to the nearest phone. He was two, maybe three hours from Jaboy's by back roads, and with a little more luck he could reach Latta to have a doctor ready. She could make the decision about putting Cody in the hospital. It was her horse he'd tried to recover; she could take care of him. It never occurred to him to call Arthur.

Looking in the rearview mirror as he drove away, Joseph saw the crows that had followed him out settle in the trees around the horse. He watched until they became black blurs among the green oak and pine, then disappeared in the greyness.

By the time they reached Jaboy's, Cody was in full delirium, and Joseph had a hard time keeping him still. When two of her hired men came to help carry him in, he struggled. The doctor regarded them all coldly, pronounced that he should be in the Cherry County emergency room, or in a medevac on his way to Rapid City, and proceeded upstairs to jury-rig a vacuum pump for the chest wound.

Latta followed, her face wild with worry. Joseph refused to walk upstairs past the ghost shirt that hung in its special glass case, as it had all the years since Jaboy'd bought it from him. At his age, he was finally old enough to be afraid. He wondered how long it would take Cody to be afraid. Maybe never, if he was lucky. Maybe now, if he was luckier.

In the sandhills, there is an unraveling that occurs, voices set loose like dogs at night, howl and run in every direction, dissipate into darkness, rising in bright paths of stars or following the wind grooving the ground itself. The sand is a house, always open, always at home somewhere, small enough to follow you, to enter your skin, perch there, waiting, a tiny voice, a sparrow twitching its tail, preening.

   There are nights here when strange angels come singing, calling us, and there is nothing we can do but try to find them. We lose our voices, and silence opens its doors.

— Caroline
September 5, 1969

*I*t must be snowing, Cody thought when he opened his eyes. Looking down, he saw only a yellow sheet covering his waist, his feet sticking out the bottom. He should be cold but he wasn't. He closed his eyes again, trying to find the howling wind around the logs from before, but it wasn't there either. It was warm in the room, with that humid late summer heat, that prickly thing that happened in the fall.

He opened his eyes and looked around the room. Cabbage-rose wallpaper, the dark carved posts of a bed, a TV. There were oxygen tanks and the familiar contraption beside the bed, a bag of clear liquid hanging from it, the tubing going, where, his left arm. His arm? He looked curiously at it. Up and down the veins were bruised places from the needle. He closed his eyes again, trying to focus. Taking a deep breath that ended when it caught on his ribs, he remembered the beating, then something else, being shot. He'd been shot. He looked at his chest, the upper half in a figure-eight bandage strapping his shoulders stiffly back. He needed to sit up. Being careful not to rip out the needle, he braced his legs and discovered the tenderness in his thigh. Latta's horse. Did he get it back? He must have. He'd tried. But that wasn't the same. What had happened? Was Kya in jail? Attempted murder. But not her. Or was it, at the end there, her voice yelling?

He closed his eyes, trying to even out his breathing, which kept wanting to make him cough. His lungs felt like sandpaper. His throat was so dry suddenly, he didn't think he could stand it another second. Opening his eyes again, he looked around for a glass of water. There it was, with a straw beside him on the little table. He reached, feeling the stab of pain as he raised his right arm an inch too high.

After the water, he looked around again. He'd been here before. He looked out the window, where he recognized the top of the elm tree. He'd woken up here before. Think, he told himself, but all he could recall was something pleasant. This was a good place, and he was so tired and happy to be here. He'd close his eyes for a while, rest, and when he woke up again, he'd figure it out. He let his limbs grow heavy, sinking through the bed itself, his mind flattening out on the cool sheets and drifting off.

The dream was a good, funny one. It began with his mother, Caroline, telling him a story about her childhood, one that made her eyes sparkle, her smile real because it ended in triumph and humor. Then Arthur and Kya and he were children together, stealing ice cream bars from the freezer in the old milk house by the back door. They were so happy together, their fingers sticky with the sweet cool cream and chocolate. When their father found them, he laughed like Santa Claus and gave them candy, fresh frozen Snickers bars because they liked the hard peanuts and caramel. There was a joke too, because the candy turned out to be fake, plastic, and that was even funnier than if it had been real. So they gave him some ice cream, but it was stuck with ants and he pretended to be shocked, but laughed so long he fell to the floor beside them, hugging his three children to his massive chest and fitting them in there like mice, in a special place, as if he were a giant suit coat with a pocket made for each one. It was his own laughing out loud that woke him up the second time.

"Careful," a voice said as Cody tried to pull the sheet up and roll over.

When he opened his eyes, Sharon, his father's old nurse, was standing beside the bed, her serious face almost smiling as she held the IV stand and the needle still in his arm. "Welcome home, stranger."

He was suddenly aware of a draft from below and looked down to see his bare leg sticking out of the sheet. Blushing, he kicked the other leg to cover himself. He was naked. How long had he been like that in front of — "Where am I?"

Sharon smiled and reached for the sheet, which she straightened out neatly from his waist to his feet. "Latta Jaboy's. That Indian brought you here — Joseph Starr. Knows something about medicine. He's around. You should've gone to the hospital, but no one would send you, so they called the doctor and me. You were bad, for a while. Pneumonia. Broken scapula. The chest wound was the worst; it started to go septic. The bone seems to be healing okay, though. You're lucky you were so out of it, missed all the fun and games, trying to keep you in bed and all."

A kind of panic came over him. "How long've I been here?"

"Three weeks. You don't remember anything?" She was watching him closely.

"Three — how come I don't — Jesus." He looked around the room as if he could force information, time, out of the walls, the cherry furniture. "What about the horse? Did Latta, uh, Mrs. Jaboy, get —"

"I don't know anything about that. She'll be in pretty soon. She always comes up after chores and spends the evening. I've been close to putting her to bed too, she's so worn out. But somehow she keeps going. Says the weather doesn't stop, so neither can she. September is —"

"September?"

She nodded, her brown ponytail bouncing on her shoulder.

"But I can't remember anything — what happened —" He was panicked. He hated this. What had he done? What had they done to him?

She patted his arm and smoothed the hair off his forehead. "Just calm down. This happens. You might not ever remember. You were out of your head with fever, and now you're going to be pretty weak for a while. But you're okay. Passed all the crises now, and on the road. Just let it happen."

He liked the cool of her hand, the softness. It reminded him of Caroline when she was pleased with him, rubbing his back and shoulders, combing his fine long hair off his face with her fingers, stroking his skin until he fell asleep at night. He closed his eyes.

"Actually you're pretty lucky. You missed all the bad parts — after the 'accident.' "

He opened his eyes and she stepped back and began to straighten the night table. "Accident?"

"That's what they told the sheriff. Hunting accident. Joseph Starr found you and brought you home. Said you fell off a cliff or something after you got shot by stray bullets from a hunting party." She picked up the IV bag that was nearly flat, looked at it, then made a decision and clipped it off.

"Good." He sighed, not sure whether he meant his sister's safety or the disconnection of the IV. The pull of the needle from his bruised arm made him flinch.

"Why don't you take a nap now, and I'll see about getting

you something to eat, okay? Won't be much to start with —
better than stuff out of a bag, though, right?" She tipped her
head and smiled at him.

She was pretty in a grown-up-woman way he admired. He
trusted her. She'd been through that last night with his father,
and he knew how strong she was. He also sensed how lonely
she must be in the sandhills. The ranchers' wives would use
her for nursing, but she'd never be a part of things. She reminded him of a horse kept alone in a huge pasture, kept so
long that way, you couldn't put another animal in with it. It'd
gotten too used to lingering in the corner, staring off across the
meadows and hills.

What woke him next was hunger. A pure stab of it, as if he'd
never eaten before in his life. This time he managed to prop
himself up a little just as Sharon came through the door with
a tray of steaming food, followed by Latta Jaboy, her face
streaked with dust and sweat, still in her working clothes. He
glanced quickly at his crotch — he was covered. These women
kept coming and going as if he had clothes on. It was embarrassing.

"Here, we'll sit you up. Hold still now." Sharon set the tray
down on the table and went to the other side while Latta
reached under his good arm. Her touch stunned him, as if his
illness had made his skin extra sensitive. Her hands, rough
from ranch work, still made his stomach twist. As the two
women lifted him up, the sheet slipped again and he had to
grab it to keep his lap covered.

Sharon laughed. "We're gonna have to do something about
pajamas, I guess. At least put some underwear on."

Cody looked straight ahead, out the window, wondering if
he had the strength to hurl himself through it. He wasn't used
to grown women standing around looking at him when he was
helpless. It made him feel like a kid again, the way they eyed
him possessively. He could feel his face redden, and he didn't
know what to do with his eyes. Where the hell was his hat?

"Don't worry, we'll figure something out tomorrow," Sharon said with a straight face, and hustled around the bed to the tray. "Right now, I'm going to feed you while this stuff is hot. Get you on your feet again." She pulled the straight chair around and reached for a bowl.

"I'm going to clean up. See you later," Latta said as she left.

"I can feed myself," he protested.

"Okay, but don't be surprised at how weak you feel." Sharon handed him the bowl, which he rested on his stomach. He picked up the spoon and looked in the bowl. Cream of Wheat or grits? The melting pat of butter on top said grits. He got five spoonfuls down before a heavy tiredness overtook him, and he had to lay his head back and close his eyes. He didn't mind; it was such a good feeling to have the warmth in his stomach, his muscles felt exhausted as if he'd worked a fourteen-hour day.

"Cody?" Sharon's voice made him realize he'd dozed again. "Drink some of this chicken soup. Inez made it fresh today." She held the cup to his lips and he tentatively sipped the warm broth, then drank it hungrily. The heat seemed to flood his limbs and he smiled sleepily at her.

"Good?" she asked, and put the cup down. "Just need to take some antibiotics. Then get some more sleep. Let me know if you need the bedpan."

The mention of it suddenly put pressure on his bladder, but he was too embarrassed to nod his head, so he looked away.

"You need to use it now?" She reached under the bed for the stainless carafe. "Don't worry, everyone feels silly about this. I'll go out in the hall."

What he liked about Sharon was how she made him feel okay. He couldn't stand to be very close to someone who'd seen him like this, handed him a thing to pee in, but he could admire the hell out of her, he decided as he put the carafe to use.

· · ·

For the next week, he ate and slept, shaved himself, and sat in an easy chair by the window. He tried to stay awake as long as he could, but found that the raw brightness of the world, the colors and sounds, the tastes and smells, stung him. He'd forgotten how clear and new things could be. Each morning he got up listening to the rising and falling of birdsong. Next he heard the satisfying pop of the back screen door opening and shutting as the house woke and Colin and his sons came and went after discussing the day's work, then Latta's quick sharp boot heels as she thumped solidly down the stairs and hall, and out the door, oblivious of the noisy presence she created. He followed her as if he were listening to music. At night her boots clunked off, one and then the other, in the room next to his, drawers jerked open and slammed shut with protesting creaks, and her body landed heavy and sighing in the bed, pushing the springs from side to side until she was comfortable. Sometimes he'd hear a curse when she spilled a glass of water or misplaced something. He could hear so much, lying there. Everything distinct, lovely. He wondered what her days had been like when he was coming to her in the middle of the night.

He didn't even realize he was falling in love. It was learning her body without its presence that made her blossom in him. He couldn't have said that to himself, but he found her rhythms and followed them, tuning his body to hers, unconsciously. Eating when she did, sleeping the longest at night when she did. Even waking up at three or four in the morning when she couldn't sleep, and he'd hear her go into her little bathroom, run water, walk the halls, sometimes even crack his door and peer in, when he'd close his eyes and pretend he was sleeping. He couldn't have said why, either, but it seemed important that she not find him awake then. As if his senses wanted to watch her without her awareness, as if that were the only way he'd get to know Latta Jaboy. Sometimes he thought he was dreaming her dreams with her, so strange were the places he came to, like nothing he'd ever experienced before.

Often she was in danger, and he tried to rescue her, only sometimes successfully. In the mornings, he thought he should apologize or explain, but he didn't know why.

No one had mentioned the stallion, his brother or sister, the ranch. And for the first time Cody found it easy to push thoughts of them away. He'd always figured he lived a simple life, but this was even simpler. His mind felt cauterized. Somewhere behind the shiny new flesh was his past, but he didn't have to think about it. Thinking about anything for very long seemed impossible, so he just let things slide in and out of focus. Mostly he enjoyed the fact that he was still alive. Food tasted good. The air, even the dusty, sticky spice of fall air, smelled good. The cat meowing, dog barking, horse whinnying, all sounded good. He was grateful, he realized after a week, for almost the first time since he was a child living with his mother, that the world was here and he was part of it. He didn't know whether the feeling could last, but for now he savored it.

When Sharon said goodbye at the end of the week, he was both happy and sorry to see her go. "Call me if you need anything," he told her. "I mean it." She'd been in his life at two key moments now, and he felt strangely attached to her, as if in leaving she were taking some secret with her, some part of his history, and he'd have to know her forever to preserve it. That wasn't a bad feeling, just a new one.

"Thanks," he added, and he kissed her cheek, surprised by the sudden way she pushed away from him. The look in her eyes was confusing — not unfriendly, just guarded, as if to say, That's far enough.

She stuck out her hand and they shook. "Just take it easy a couple more weeks," she advised as he sat down in the easy chair again. She left, the air behind her swirling with thoughts he couldn't sort out. It was easy to take other people's lives for granted, not to have any sort of curiosity about them, to shun and discourage them from talking about themselves. He'd always assumed that was a way to respect them, to let them have their distance. For the first time, though, he was curious about two people, Latta and Sharon. Maybe he should've been curious about everyone else too.

He knew that if you listened to other people in the hills, they'd tell you everything you needed to know — not about themselves, but about one another. Who was sleeping with whom, who was drinking, who was in detox, rehab, getting a divorce, married, miscarried, suicide, crazy, cheating, stealing, backstabbing. He'd never wanted to know that stuff. He'd been the subject of it so long, he didn't want to hear it, with his name deleted because he was in the room, unless someone wanted a fight. Maybe that was it, he realized: he'd had to fight it so often — the things said about Caroline, Heywood, his sister and brother, himself — he'd learned to shut down any mention of another person's life. What difference did it make, he wasn't bothering anyone but Arthur. Kya maybe. Kya. He tried to shove her off the rim of his mind, but she spun back at him.

Had his sister shot him? He couldn't remember the details clearly, but she was there. He thought she'd called out to him, then the gun. Why hadn't she stopped Burch? Why had she stolen the horse? And if she was innocent, why hadn't she called or come to see him? Arthur he could understand. Well, screw both of them.

"Stoney wasn't there when Colin went for it. I called him right after the doctor when Joseph called me, but I guess someone found him first. Maybe the hobbles broke and he took off, but I had people looking all over for him. Hired planes. Nothing. I think someone's got him again. I just hope they know how valuable he is." Latta broke a corner off the banana bread on her plate and put it in her mouth, chewing thoughtfully as she stared at the floor.

Cody didn't want to ask, but he had to know. "Any idea who took him?"

She broke off another corner. "Who'd you go after?"

The food on his tray had long since turned tasteless and he put it on the nightstand, careful not to raise his arms too high where it'd hurt. The bandage was beginning to chafe his skin and he still had weeks to go. Latta stared at him, her face a careful mask of neutrality.

"Hard to remember now. I had a hunch or something — the sheriff find anything?"

"The van driver was in Florida on a job. State police haven't seen a thing. Nobody seems particularly concerned except me. Joseph said, 'Things will turn out the way they should,' and asked for a job. I love it. Fifty thousand dollars and years of planning down the tubes."

"Sorry about screwing it up." He looked at his hands, which seemed so big and useless now.

"I don't think you have to apologize for getting shot, not unless you put the gun in their hands. Who knows, maybe you did." She was smiling, but it wasn't entirely friendly.

"What're you talking about?"

"I talked to Arthur. I told him you should stay here for a while. Your truck's back. Showed up mysteriously one morning. Anyway, he's got the house full of Angus breeders on their annual tour, and he's hired the Dobree brothers to come in and help, plus I'm sending Chris Young over." She leaned back and stretched her legs out in front of her. She hadn't cleaned up from chores, and her jeans were dusty and spotted. There was a little black ring in the fold of her neck.

She wasn't beautiful by any movie standards: she was too short and not petite enough, but she had a rugged handsomeness and strength like in pictures of old-time frontier women. He liked the dirt she felt comfortable wearing. He liked her stubby fingers, ranging in size from thick to tiny, as if her hands had been assembled from leftover parts. They were Latta, full of contrasts. He liked her short muscular legs, the trim ankles and calves rising to sturdy thighs. He closed his eyes and remembered the times they made love, the surprising power of those thighs that squeezed him as if he were a horse being made to obey. And he had.

Was it possible to not like anything about her? He'd been trying to figure that out for the past half hour. She was no willowy girl whose bones he could cut his hips against. Latta's flesh was full of secrets and scars and memories. She was someone he'd maybe never get to know, but the energy coming from her, the intensity and fierceness, made him want to try.

He wasn't aware he had sighed until she looked up at him sharply. "You okay?"

Shrugging was hard, so he shook his head. She got up tiredly and came to the side of the bed. "Your skin's all raw looking. Maybe the bandage needs loosening, now that you're up and around. Want me to try?"

At that moment he would've let her operate just to have her touch him. He nodded his head and she helped him sit up and lean forward.

"It's this fall heat, and you're probably gaining back the weight you lost." Her touch was so delicate he closed his eyes. "Holler if I hurt you." She unwound the padded wrapping holding his shoulders. He felt the rasp on his skin let go, and took a little breath of relief while she rewound the bandage. As she clamped the end in place, she let her fingers linger on the bare skin of his neck, resting on the groove of his collarbone. "I'm so sorry about this," she said quietly.

He reached up slowly, so as not to startle her, like a small bird he meant to capture, and closed his hand over hers. Then he put his hand around her wrist and tugged. She moved fluidly, her eyes half shut already, like a person falling into sleep.

"Don't be afraid," he whispered into her hair as they held each other. He rubbed his nose and mouth in the curls, liking the damp sweat and horse smell of the barn, mixed with the almond shampoo she used. He ran his hands on her bare arms, rubbing the new scar from the branding weekend. She leaned her head lightly on his chest while he let his fingers slide along her rib cage, then up to her breasts. He whispered to her while he touched her there, calming and soothing her like a horse he was gentling. With her strength, men would always try to be on the muscle, but what she needed most of all, he knew, was a tender hand, someone to teach her the difference.

It was her mouth he wanted, but his shoulders kept him from leaning over, so he drew her onto the bed, straddling him, and their lips met. When their tongues touched, and their teeth clicked, it brought tears to his eyes. He wanted to be in her, he wanted her in him, he wished they could be each other as they kissed hard and soft, hard and soft. She was sliding her hands down his belly, rimming the waist of his jeans with her fingers, but not letting them slip below. He reached for her hand and pulled it gently down, whispering her past her hesitation, then covering her hand with his and pressing. A groan caught in his throat.

"You'll have to help me lie flat," he urged her, untangling their arms and legs so he could slide down in the bed and unbutton his jeans. Her face was a mixture of desire and sadness as she stood up, kicked off her boots, undid her jeans, and stripped off her underpants. She didn't cover herself, just lifted her chin as if to say, Take it or leave it, and went to the foot of the bed to pull his jeans off. "Careful," he cautioned when she jarred his shoulder jerking at the pant cuffs.

When they were both naked, she became shy again, sitting on the edge of the bed, rubbing his arm. With the lights on, it was as if those nights before had never happened. He gave her a moment, closing his eyes so he could follow her touch etching his skin. When her hand grew bolder, he put his hand on her back and let it fall to the generous curve of her buttock.

"Latta, come here, honey," he whispered, and when she turned, he could see the tears in her eyes. "No, shhh, it's all right now, shhh." He rubbed her back and shoulders as she folded herself along his side, tucking her head in under his good arm. There was no hurry. Whatever this was would have to work itself through her. He could wait forever if this was the way things could feel. Forever.

They dozed for a while, as if exhausted already by the intensity of each other. When they woke, they moved naturally into each other, keeping their eyes closed, their minds still in that half-sleep place that made things possible. Afterward, she rested half on, half off his body as he sat propped against the headboard. Their movements had started spasms of protest from his back and ribs, but he ignored them. He was wide awake now, afraid of missing a moment that might turn her mood, make her change again. He was running his hands over her body, inspecting her the way he did his horses. He paused at a dark spot on her back and scraped it with his nail.

"Hey." She shook his hand off.

"Thought it was a blackhead or a piece of dirt. Sorry." He laughed and rubbed at the place with his fingers to take the sting away.

"Stop it." She laughed and rolled off him. "Leave my moles alone. What's the matter with you?" She slapped his thigh lightly and covered her front with a pillow.

When he reached for it, she pushed his hand away. "Why can't I look at you?" he asked, and leaned his head back, watching her with half-hooded lids.

"Because. I'm shy, that's why." She turned her eyes to his long muscular legs.

"Not a few minutes ago."

"It's — oh, forget it. Here" — she tossed the pillow off the bed — "okay?" The same defiant look appeared on her face as before when they'd undressed. He didn't understand it, and just kept watching her. She tried to outstare him, but dropped her eyes and reddened. He kept staring. He didn't know what else to do. Sometimes people talked if you waited them out.

She drew tight little interlocking circles on the wrinkled sheet with her forefinger.

"It's just hard to be so naked in front of somebody else. You make me feel naked, Cody. Like my skin is going to fall off after my clothes, and you'll see everything inside me, know all about me. It scares me. What you're doing right now scares me. Will you quit, for chrissakes, staring at me, please." She rubbed her palm stiffly over the imaginary circles on the sheet.

He reached to cover her hand and she shook it off. He covered it anyway, wrapping her small hand in his and squeezing. He wasn't going to let go of her, not unless she told him ño, go away. If he was here, he was here, and she'd have to be too. She'd have to get used to his being close, have to learn to trust him.

"My father was a gentle, quiet man. Lots of times I'd forget he was even in the house. It was my mother who ran things. She knew everything. Treated my father like he was a glass slipper and her feet were too big. Made me hate goodness sometimes." Latta was sitting on the shore next to him and scrolling in the wet sand at their feet with a stick. Behind and above them on the grassy ridge a downy woodpecker knocked patiently at the trunk of a small willow.

"My mother grew up on Rosebud. My father came to the Protestant church there, trying to fight it out with the Catholics once a month. My theory is he saw what he needed — a woman tough enough to take care of him, so he could spend his time reading books and thinking. It wasn't my father you had to be afraid of — it was my mother." Latta laughed.

Behind them, the woodpecker kept up its rhythm, ignoring their talk. A passing speedboat towing a water-skier sent waves puddling around their legs. A few feet away, a tiny frog sat just far enough up the shore that the water edged up its chest. When a boat sent a wave that was too big, it rolled over and then righted itself a few inches farther back.

Cody watched the freckles popping on his arms, the skin turning red as the sun burned down on them. They'd beached the aluminum fishing boat and started walking the eastern perimeter of Merritt Reservoir, talking until they grew tired and found a spot to sit. He had let her talk him into wearing an old pair of her cutoffs, and now his legs stuck out stringy and white in front of him. He wanted to dig them into the sand. The gunshot wound was puckered red and turning purple. His eyes kept going back to it, fascinated that Kya might have been directly involved, although he didn't want to believe it. That was the crazy thing about Kya: anything could happen and somehow he'd have to find it acceptable. She was like keeping a pet rattler. Sooner or later you were going to get bit, so you couldn't very well blame the snake.

"You're getting burned." Latta pressed her fingers into his upper arm and they both watched as the skin turned white, then faded back to dark red.

He pressed her forearm, but it was so deeply browned, the skin didn't react the same. "Indian blood." She grinned and pulled his shirt across his chest and arms. "Don't want you to get too sore." She let her fingers linger on his neck, then trail off his shoulder. He shivered and she laughed. He wanted to pull her down on top of him, but knew it was better to let her build up to it.

"Sometimes I think my father fell out of the sky from another planet. He didn't even know which switch turned on the back yard lights. That doesn't make him a bad person, I know. It just used to make me mad. I swore I'd find someone who could take care of himself. I thought Jaboy was the answer." Her voice had changed, and he looked at her face more closely. The square jaw was tight, the blue vein under her eye jumping.

"God, the water's so blue-green today, actually green. I keep thinking they're putting something in it, but they're not. When I was away all those years with Jaboy, I used to dream about this place. The sandhills. You ever been away?" She stared out across the water, then pointed at a large white bird skimming the air above the water, hunting.

"Only a couple of days at a time." He watched as the bird drifted around the bend. The small bluffs across from them covered with sparse grass, stunted trees, and bushes provided a kind of sanctuary for the river's activity and the perfect hot silence that rested between bursts of noise. "Once Heywood took me to Iowa to meet the man who feedlots our yearlings. It was so — I don't know — every farm was so neat and green, all boxed up. Rivers all straightened out to be efficient. I don't think there's a river left in Iowa. And everybody's so proud of how clean their little place is. Drove me nuts." Another boat sent waves tumbling over their feet. The water was cool but not icy, and felt good on their hot skin.

"Yeah." She stretched out beside him. "I've been all over the world, really all over, and there's nothing like this." She rested her head in her hands and closed her eyes. He could almost feel the beat of her heart, they were so close without touching. He tried willing her to touch him, to rub her hand along the hard ridges of his stomach as he tightened it, but she lay still.

"I feel bad about your mother, Cody." Her voice seemed disembodied, drifting like the bird a few minutes ago.

"Why?" He tried to sound neutral, though the mention of Caroline made him almost dizzy, like it always did.

"I knew she was unhappy. In trouble. I'd see her on the street, pass her, not say a word. It wouldn't have taken much — I know that now. I felt like I was walking such a thin line already. In the community. I didn't think I could talk to her and have anyone talk to me. Now I know better." She laughed harshly. "They had to talk to me because of Jaboy's money, but they always thought I was nothing. Trash. Half-breed. Off the res. My family hadn't been ranching for three or four generations like yours."

"Bennett's," he corrected her. "I'm the bastard Kidwell son, remember." He said it flatly, the way he said it to remind himself, without rancor or self-pity.

"That's right. Arthur's the only Bennett around now, I guess."

"And Kya."

"Kya," she snorted. "I don't count her."

"You should."

She shook her head. "Anyway, your mother seemed so angry and sad all the time. I was half afraid of her, so I stayed out of her way. Now I wish I hadn't; it wouldn't have cost me anything. Soon as Jaboy died, every one of those women stopped being civil to me. The men still talk, but I think half the time they're hoping I'll end up sleeping with them. I don't know —"

"Probably what the women are afraid of too." He brushed at a dark blue dragonfly with cellophane wings trying to land on his cheek.

"I suppose. When do you think we all stop being afraid of each other? I mean, when do we get old enough not to be a threat anymore?"

"Latta?"

"Yeah?"

"You'll always be a threat." He reached up to grab her fist as it swung toward his midriff. "Take it easy, I'm an invalid you know." They laughed and he drew her fingers up to his mouth and gnawed lightly on the knuckles, then kissed them and put her hand back on her chest, letting his fingers trail down across her. The thin scars welting her wrist shone lighter as her arm turned out. He wanted to ask her about them, but didn't want to push her.

"So what was she like?" Latta crossed her legs at the ankles and rubbed her toes up and down her shin. "Caroline — what was she like to live with?"

Cody shrugged and shaded his closed eyes with his hand as if to see into the distance of the past. He wanted to choose the right one among all the images and scenes that jumped by. "Different, I guess you'd say. A lot of stuff pissed her off. Especially once we got the TV and she started watching the news. I don't know. But she *was* funny. You just never knew what would make her laugh. She loved telling stories, especially to Heywood. They'd laugh just mentioning names of people they knew back in Missouri, the military academy he went to, some silly thing they did. Sometimes it was like watching people on TV, the way the audience will laugh so hard at something you don't find funny at all."

"I forgot her birthday and Mother's Day one year. I was a kid, didn't know any better. After that, I never forgot. She called me in, it was Sunday, and told me how disappointed she was in me. It was one time she didn't yell. I guess that's why I never forgot. Somehow that made it worse." He wondered if she could see how the memory made him blush with shame all over again.

"So what'd you do?"

"Went out and picked a big bouquet of flowers out of her garden and brought them in and told her I was sorry. She didn't blink an eye at the columbine I'd pulled up that'd taken her three years to get to bloom. By the time she told Heywood, she was laughing at me. Making a good story. Things I'd done or said, she'd fix up so it sounded a lot more interesting and wilder. I hardly recognized myself sometimes."

Her hand drifted to his head, her fingers finding his hair and following the waves down into the tangle of curls at the bottom where it fell into the sand. "No wonder Heywood was so hard on you," she murmured.

"Maybe. She didn't mean anything. She just wanted to entertain people. She taught me at home, you know. I never went to school, but she was a great teacher. Always making things up and acting them out. I don't know what happened. Her family lost their money in the Depression. Her father got accused of ruining the bank. She loved him more than anything except Heywood, and then he died. I guess her mother and sisters hated her. That's what Heywood said. She was too ashamed to visit them. Because of me, I guess. She died and I hardly knew her. She kept so many secrets. I'd hear Heywood and her whispering and they'd shut up if I knocked on the door or came in the room. Caroline Kidwell — I guess no one knows who she was, least of all me, and I spent fourteen years with her."

It was the most he'd ever said about his mother, and he could feel his chest tighten, his throat close, like when he'd been sick. Put your mind someplace else, he told himself. Smell the air, the light fluid air over the water, the damp hot from the bushes behind them, the sticky buzz of the drying grass and grasshoppers.

"Why'd she send you to Bennett's? You were so young, I felt sorry for you."

Cody tightened against the pity. This was the part he hated about explaining anything personal. Nothing stayed a fact; it got under your skin, stuck and irritated like an invisible cactus spine in your finger. He couldn't answer that question for himself, except to say he failed her, let her down, deserved what he got, and he couldn't say that out loud to anyone. So he shrugged. "She wanted me to grow up." He heard how weird and constrained his voice sounded, almost squeaky, and wanted to take it back. None of your business, he wanted to say.

"You shot that man, what was his name — Axel, John Axel." She said it so matter-of-factly. It wasn't a secret, no point in pretending to himself it was. That was the thing about living in the same place all your life; anything extraordinary you did stayed with you like part of your name: Cody Who Shot John Axel Kidwell. An unarmed man, a man they all knew, caught stealing a turkey, a man they would've given food to. This turned Cody wrong in the community's eyes forever, and he kept wanting to explain for years until he realized it didn't matter. It had become part of his history, so it couldn't be changed. Not now, not ever. It'd die when he did, and no one would care. Joseph had told him that he was just hung up on setting things right, but there was no way that was going to happen. Too much had gone astray already, and no one seemed interested in the historical facts, the so-called truth, so he shouldn't be either. Over the years, he'd learned to ignore anything anyone said or thought about him. It was just so much hissing, so much battering, so much babbling.

"Cody?"

"That I did. Yes." He squinted, trying to remember the scary satisfaction of squeezing the trigger and watching the man fall down. His mother running out of the house, standing on the concrete stoop for a moment, then walking swiftly out to him, slapping him with one hand as the other grabbed the gun, both of them ignoring the man lying there spurting a red arc onto the ground mulled by poultry feet. He was trying to steal Carl the turkey, had tackled the huge bird and was binding his feet together despite the fierce pecking that left cuts on the man's hands. That was the story. The sheriff, knowing better than to arrest anybody, had called Heywood Bennett. "Heywood's your father," she had said, and left him standing in the powdery dust covering his clothes so later, when he flopped tiredly on the top bunk at the Bennett ranch, a thin cloud rose in the dusky light while the other hands ate and he waited, dry-eyed, long since used to Caroline's punishments. It did no good to cry. She wouldn't have him back till she wanted him. He had no clock to her will that worked, only waiting, and his father's Continental like a grey emissary of misfortune arriving to take him away, like the hearse he would see three times after: the funeral for the unknown man he'd killed, the one for his mother, and finally for his father.

"Why'd you shoot him?"

He suddenly wanted to tell Latta. But how to explain, how to tell all the pictures, the images . . .

"I don't know. It doesn't make sense, I guess." The story wasn't right, he wanted to say.

"Tell me," she urged.

"Something about killing takes you to another place, and makes you different for the rest of your life. You can't pretend to enjoy what other people enjoy after that. Nothing is simple, though you try to make it that way. You drink for that time of simplicity, ignoring what comes after, and you hope you can span the bridge over darkness that waits for you every single night of your life." He held his hands up and turned them over.

"What happened that day? Why'd —"

He grimaced and made the words come out the way he'd practiced them. "Heywood taught me to shoot, gave me the gun to protect my mother. Said I was the man of the house. I saw this man at her window — no, in it." He paused, confused by the conflicting pictures. "He was trying to steal the turkey, hitting it with a — a chunk of concrete — smashing its head. There were peck marks on his face. The bird was screaming and I'd been down hunting rabbits. I had to pull the trigger, I had to protect her. They blamed me at first. Then Heywood stepped in. She came outside when she heard the shot. Wrapped in a sheet. I remember the blood on her bare calf, it made a swath like the sweep of a wing. That's all. Blood, dust, and noise. Then it stopped. I was just protecting her. I didn't know him. I didn't know how the blood would look. She never forgave me, I guess."

"It must have been terrible for you," she said softly.

"Yeah." He closed his eyes.

She was quiet for so long he thought she'd fallen asleep, until she slapped at her ankle. "Ow — we better get back before chores." She rose stiffly and offered him a hand.

When she jerked him to his feet easily, he smiled. "You're strong." Putting his arms around her waist, he drew her gently against him.

"You smell like melting adhesive tape," she murmured,

kissing his bare upper arm and brushing the sand lightly off
his back.

"And you smell like — what is that? Sweat and horse piss."
He pushed her away as her hand lifted to swat him. They
laughed and started back along the shore toward the boat.
Cody felt like he should say something else, but he couldn't
think of anything. What he really wanted to do was make love
to her, show her he wasn't to blame. Most of the time lovemaking changed things for a day or only an hour, but that was
enough.

They untied the boat, and Latta steadied it so he could climb
in without jarring his shoulder. The water left icy rings around
his thighs that the sun seemed to burn colder when he sat on
the hot aluminum bench, watching her start the engine.

When they were under way, the front of the boat slowly
slapping the water, sending a fine spray over them, Latta said
in a voice loud enough to be heard over the noise, "I'm glad
you're here." She looked out across the water, as if she were
embarrassed by her words.

LETTERS TO THE EDITOR

Dear Editor,

There is enough expense for a person in any business without finding out that someone had shot 18 holes in a perfectly good stock tank as well as turned on the mill 5 miles from any road. That's destroying property besides trespassing.

I hope they feel proud of themselves.

/s/ Speed A. Settle

— *BABYLON CALLER*

*T*he church where Joseph was staying was three miles from Latta's ranch house. Cody found no evidence of him at the church, though Latta had said she'd hired him to repair the windows and paint what needed painting before winter. The church was hardly ever used in the summer, and in the fall the mice and small animals tried to make their nests in the old wooden structure and had to be driven off. The new windows gleamed smoothly set in the rotting frames. Cody wondered how long it would be before the siding would need replacing.

The ranchers had kept the church intact for the past hundred years, on the Swenson place Jaboy had bought, ever since a man and his wife had come through and left their sick baby with the Swensons while they went on to Babylon looking for work. When the baby died three days later, a neighbor and old man Swenson had ridden twenty miles in the winter cold and snow to find the parents, but they had disappeared. Although wood was scarce, the men had built a tiny cedar coffin somehow, and when spring came, dug a little grave on the hill and put the marker up, *Our Baby*, carved in script on pink marble. Others had joined the baby in the graveyard, surrounded by a wrought-iron fence and a gate with *Eclipse* written in arched letters over it. And soon after, they'd built a church there too, which was used mostly for winter services, especially at Christmas.

Cody edged the old horse down the hill toward the camp he'd spied on the banks of the Dismal River just below the church, weaving in and out of gullies cut in the eroding pastures by recent rains and cattle hooves. As he approached the camp, he noticed the small round structure covered with cedar boughs.

On one of the stunted trees by the river's edge hung a knot of eagle feathers, rawhide, beads, weeds and sticks, and a buckskin bag swinging in the breeze. He rode closer to take a look, but didn't touch it. You never touched something belonging to another person. That was an important rule of living out here, he'd discovered. Too bad Kya didn't believe in it. Stopped, he could hear the faint swish of the water as it curled over the sand and wove through the meadow, the surrounding whir and hum of insects, and the closer crackle and pop of wood burning. Taking a deep breath, he smelled the smoke in the air. "Joseph?" he called softly, and dismounted, dropping the reins so the horse would ground tie.

He walked to the west-facing side, looking for the seam of the door. When a hand pushed out, he stooped down, took off his hat and laid it on the ground and crawled inside. It was so hot it took his breath away. He paused to let his eyes adjust so he could find the empty spot across from Joseph. When he'd settled with his legs crossed awkwardly in front of him, he wished he'd stopped long enough to take off his boots and shirt too. The sweat lodge was built tightly, despite its haphazard appearance. The walls were of stretched hide that gave off a smoky smell of tallow and wild game. Joseph kept the hot coals active from a pile of wood at his side, and the rocks the fire was banked with shimmered with waves of heat.

At first Cody felt the heat turn his skin red and hot; sweat broke out of every pore, soaking his clothes and hair. That was a bearable level. Then it got hotter, and he was panting like a dog in short breaths. Then something happened to his eyes, his head, as if he'd witnessed a lightning strike too close to his face. He felt seared and burned, his head floating watery and ballooned, his lungs burning hot and liquid, even his stomach and kidneys began to burn and liquefy. He told himself he'd leave in a minute. Then he knew it was a lie, because there was no way he'd ever be able to make his muscles firm again, so he let go and allowed the heat to melt him.

He was just giving up when Joseph poured water from a cup onto the rocks for steam and began to sing an old song in Lakota. Cody didn't understand the words, but could feel the intent and found himself singing half a note behind the syllables he stumbled to follow. In the time it took the sounds to circle the hut once, twice, three times, again and again, he forgot about his body and the heat, picturing instead the land around him, the animals rising magically out of the sand, the soil, floating to health again just above the earth. He was still singing when Joseph unfolded himself neatly, pushed open the door, and crawled outside. The fresh air seemed winter cold when it hit Cody's face, whipping him back to the world. Outside, he sat sprawled against the lodge, panting and trying to dry his face with the tail of his soaking-wet shirt.

"Jesus, I forgot how hot they are, yours especially," he said when he could breathe normally again. The old horse was cropping grass peacefully, stepping carefully away from the trailing reins, and Joseph was sitting against the tree that held his medicine bag, his eyes closed. Up the hill the cawing of crows could be heard from the church roof, where they were pacing and flapping.

Joseph looked up toward the crows, then back to the river. "That church is sited over sacred ground," he said casually, as if announcing the weather for the day.

Cody looked up the hill, picturing for the first time the generations that had to lie beneath, native people mixed with whites. "They must find bones when they bury people."

The other man shrugged.

"How'd you find out —"

Joseph shrugged and nodded toward the hill and the crying crows. "They wouldn't leave me alone. Then I remembered something about the grounds here. Dug a little. Now I'm waiting until the time's right. So I sweat and pray, trying to get clean enough." He was dressed in baggy cotton pants with a drawstring waist, hand sewn, and a cotton tunic that was beginning to dry now. His long hair was loose, held off his face by a faded pink strip of cloth. He had been barefoot long enough to form thick yellow calluses on the bottoms of his feet. There was a gauntness about him, as if every extra ounce of flesh had been burned away, stripping him down to essential bone and sinew. His eyes shone oddly bright and flickered between wild and calm. It was hard to judge how old he was; his hair was streaked grey, and his face was a mat of fine lines from years of constant exposure to sun and wind. Plus he had spent more than twenty years trying to drink Vietnam and his early life away.

They sat for a while, letting the sounds of the first migrating geese and ducks take their thoughts in long waves of sound blowing south. A hawk circled lazily up the river valley, catching the drafts, then sinking as it hunted, until it came to rest on the opposite shore a few yards upwind from the camp. It was close enough that they could see the big creamy chest clearly as it waited motionless, balancing on a scrub juniper.

The brown feathers on its wings and back glinted gold and red, and when Cody shifted his position, the bird turned its head slowly and caught them with its eye, but didn't move.

"Thinks he owns the valley." Cody laughed.

"He does." Joseph stood. "Hungry?"

Cody nodded and stood, stretching and flexing. The sweat had loosened the muscles in his shoulders and back that had been tight when he rode up.

Joseph pulled some dried meat from a bag and piled it on a tin pie plate, with a piece of cold Indian fry bread. "Rabbit," he said, and handed Cody the plate.

Cody took a look at the horse to make sure he was still being careful with the reins, then sat down closer to Joseph. The meat was dry and stringy; rabbit was rabbit, no matter what you did. Grease had soaked and congealed on the fry bread, but it was filling. Behind them the crows called, took off, circled the river valley, and returned to the church.

"Don't remember them liking it where there's no trees," Cody commented as he chewed.

"They usually like it over by Merritt Dam and the Snake. They moved."

Cody looked at him, surprised.

Joseph smiled, his lips twisting into their usual ironic shape. "How the hell would I know where the crows like to live?"

Cody laughed. "You always seem to know everything."

"Cause I'm part Indian?" He laughed bitterly, his thin face tightening like a mask. "Growing up, I was 'Tonto.' In the army, Nam, I was 'Tonto.' I get home, we're suddenly 'the people,' hippies trying to move on the res, buying beads, running around in moccasins and loincloths. If it hadn't been so pathetic, it would've been funny." He looked at the younger man. He *had* taken him on when Cody showed up at the ranch, but that was a matter of survival. He hadn't wanted to live with another casualty. He'd seen enough in the war. Educating Cody had been a matter of keeping some peace and quiet.

Cody ate silently, setting the plate down beside him when it was clean. Joseph gestured toward the old army canteen resting in the sand beside the hut. Cody reached for it, offered it, then drank. The water had the clear pure taste of the rock it rose out of, the aquifer, that made this area so valuable.

Joseph pulled a short handmade pipe from his bag, stuffed some tobacco into it, and lit it, letting the smoke ooze out and drift away, thinning into invisibility against the tan and green hills.

"Anthropologists and movie people. They come in, glorify the past for us, then look around at how screwed up and dirty the reservations are now, and hightail it back out. They never mention the dirty Pampers that come flying out the car windows at you, the garbage houses, the abandoned cars and trucks, the twelve people living in two rooms, and children taking care of children. Eighty percent unemployment. Now they want to haul New Jersey solid waste and dump it on Rosebud, and half the people want to let 'em do it because it'll mean not going hungry and cold this winter. We have half of nothing already, and they're taking the rest."

"Having kind of a bad day?" Cody shoveled his boot heels in the sand and stretched his legs out in the two long grooves. The cool beneath the surface felt good.

Joseph laughed again, and this time it had a touch of humor in it. "Self-pity. Sitting out here by yourself, waiting, you get trapped in these head talks, arguments get lopsided. It pisses me off that I'm living on Latta Jaboy's land. Have to fix up their little white Christian church while all the time, this hill, this one, is where my ancestors used to sit and offer smoke to the spirits and have their visions. I'm waiting for my grandfather to send me on. I keep thinking today's the day, but I keep coming back to the same thing. That damn church, the damn crows, and this piss-poor river. It's the Dismal River all right." He laughed and puffed on his pipe, letting the smoke out in little *o*'s. "I'm just impatient now that fall's here."

Cody knew better than to offer any comment. This was the side of Joseph he couldn't approach. He knew his own experience was so small compared to Joseph's, there wasn't any point in saying anything.

They sat watching the hawk watching the valley, and in a moment Cody's eyes drifted shut. Joseph's voice woke him a while later. "How's Mrs. Jaboy getting along?"

He felt a flush come over him. Joseph was asking how they were doing, he knew. As part of the etiquette of the hills, Joseph would never ask a direct personal question if he could help it. Cody glanced quickly at the other man, who was politely staring over his head with only a tiny smile on his lips. "Okay."

"You're almost recovered."

Again, Cody knew the real question was, When are you going home? He nodded, trying to avoid the conversation he really wouldn't mind having, but was too embarrassed to open directly.

"There's a pretty good band in town tonight. At the Buckboard."

"How'd you know?"

Joseph smiled, pleased at the surprise in Cody's voice. "I know everything, remember? 'Sides, Chris and Aubrey came through here yesterday, checking fence. They wouldn't miss a chance at those new schoolteachers from Chadron who've been coming up on weekends. Said Mrs. Jaboy's hardly been off the place in five weeks. Wonder why?"

Cody picked up the canteen and heaved it at Joseph, forgetting the cost to his shoulder until it jabbed sharply. "Shit." He groaned and rubbed it.

Joseph laughed as the canteen rolled to a stop a foot away. "Good aim too. Don't go screwing up all the work I put in bringing your worthless ass back here now." He reached for the canteen, unscrewed the lid, and sipped the water.

"Funny about you two," he said, wiping his mouth with his hand.

"Why?" Cody didn't want to ask.

"Just never thought of it. She's older. Widowed. Especially Jaboy's widow. You never seemed like each other's type. Never would've figured it." Joseph tapped out the dead ashes of his pipe against the tree trunk and buried them. "But then maybe she's grateful to you for going after her horse."

This was the shit he hated most. Was he supposed to defend her honor? himself? What was Joseph trying to do, piss him off? Well, he *was* pissed off. "I never got the horse."

"You almost died trying — that has to count for something." Joseph was grinning.

Cody climbed to his feet awkwardly, since he couldn't brace with his arm. "Just drop it."

"Maybe you just fell in love with your nurse. Guys used to do that all the time in Nam. Or maybe she likes 'em young now."

He kicked a mound of dirt and sand. "It's not like that. She's — different."

"Can't stand to have anyone say her name? You got it bad, Cody. Watch out."

"What's that supposed to mean?" He put his hands in his jeans pockets and stared down at Joseph's relaxed figure. He was afraid to look at his face, so he concentrated on his legs.

"Just take it easy. Give it time. Don't get crazy." His voice was serious.

Cody glanced at his face, which was staring at him now, and he looked quickly away again, to the hands resting in his lap, the pipe lying there peacefully. "What makes you so smart?" He tried to sound tough, but the comment came out like a kid's taunting another kid.

Joseph laughed. "I told you — Indians — we know it all. Besides, I've known the Jaboys and Latta's family for a long time. Just be careful. Doesn't mean you shouldn't take her to the dance, or whatever. Just use a little common sense this time, that's all." The hawk's cry as it took off made him pause.

"You're not a kid anymore. Look what Burch did to you. You're not indestructible. You're on your own now. Arthur isn't on your side. Kya — well, she's Kya. Things are different. If a horse gets stolen, call the sheriff. Or take somebody with you if you decide to play John Wayne. Look around you; some ranchers aren't even using horses anymore. Planes and jeeps and ATVs. More cost effective. Things aren't the same." He closed his eyes as if the subject made him tired.

"What the hell is that woman doing with a horse that costs that much anyway? Things are too valuable now. Somebody *has* to steal them. There's too much at stake all over this country now. Too much here in the sandhills." He shook his head.

"But —"

"Get outta here now. I got work to do." He waved Cody's next words off, rose gracefully, walked back to his hut, and crawled inside.

Cody was left feeling the way he had as a kid. Except this time he was twenty-nine years old and being treated like a kid. He swore softly to himself and walked toward the grazing horse. He'd meant to question Joseph about Latta, and all he'd done was get pissed off.

At any bar nothing happens until it's been dark for a long time. At first the musicians play to an empty dance floor and hall — a siren song like the initial sawing of cicadas that begins at twilight and grows until it silences everything and brings the night to its begging knees. In trucks and cars, from houses where restless petty fights send them out, they arrive. By ten there are enough people so the band doesn't seem to be talking to themselves and the regular grace of the dancers is called out. The drunks drink louder in the corner, afraid to pass the neon barrier of the jukebox guarding the steps. The over-amped music is something you have to push hard against as it rises to drown out the voices of the singers.

Not counting Clark's outside town, there were five bars in

Babylon, all lining the main business area: the two that offered topless dancing, the Liquor 'n' Lunch, the VFW, and the Buckboard, which had recently added the Sweetheart Garden, a bricked patio with picnic tables and a central bar staffed on weekend nights to catch the overflow. The end of the Buckboard's dance floor had been extended, with huge glass doors that could be opened in summer onto the patio. Even in early fall, with cool evenings, the patio was crowded. It was the younger ones who lingered at the dark edges of the dance floor, as if understanding that they belonged outside for a few more years. The older people came as families, father ushering in a string of his older children and wife. They always sat inside, in the special loud, smoky dark of the dance, shouting at each other over drinks and taking the floor with special authority, performing complicated two-steps and cotton-eyed joes, waltzes, tangos, jitterbugs, and bops. They were tough on the bands too, sitting out the numbers that were beyond the musicians' skill. They knew what they wanted.

On the patio the teenagers and unmarried cowboys and women out of high school flitted from table to chair to dance floor, but mostly lingered outside, as if they were so many moths battering against the night glass. Theirs was the more serious construction of desire. Males and females dressed alike in jeans and boots, western-cut shirts. Only the males wore hats, and they danced nervous, tight, all of them, in the gravity of this ritual mating. The cowboys drove sixty, a hundred miles over bad roads to spend the evening on a chance.

Cody and Latta sat stranded on the edges of the crowd at the Buckboard, as if waiting. Time flowed around them in the forms of arriving groups of kids trying to find each other, a slow business that wore its hilarity on the skin only. It was almost eleven o'clock and Cody and Latta hadn't gotten the nerve to dance yet, and for the past half hour they hadn't talked either. They were shifting uneasily on their benches when Aubrey Foster sat down next to Cody.

Dressed in a ruffled pink shirt, big round silver trophy buckle, and his best black boots and hat, Aubrey looked like the pheasant cock that liked to stand on the haystacks in Latta's field. After saying hello, looking over the patio for girls, his eyes lingering on ones he thought particularly available, the cowboy lit up a Camel, flooding the table with smoke before he grinned apologetically and blew it out into the crowd.

"You get rain over at your places?" he asked, his eyes still scanning.

"Some," Cody said, and Latta just nodded.

"Coulda used it a week ago," Aubrey said, drawing on the beer he'd brought with him and signaling the waitress. When she appeared, he drew a circle with his finger indicating a round for the table and she went away again.

"That's the way it is," Cody said, following the other man's eyes to the tables surrounding them. A group of schoolteachers nearby were young and blond and outdoorsy, their skin brushed with red from canoeing the Niobrara all day. Cowboys crawled like ants around their table, fetching them drinks, asking them to dance, and flirting with them. They weren't especially pretty, but it didn't matter. They were new and excited by all the attention from the tall lean men in hats and boots. Probably from Omaha, Cody guessed. They'd marry someone or go back to the city in a year or two when they wore out the possibilities.

"Heard about your accident. You doing okay?" He squinted at Cody through the smoke of his cigarette.

"I'm okay." Cody looked down and sideways at Latta.

"Get that horse back yet?" Aubrey took a deep drag off his cigarette and leaned his head back to release the smoke overhead while he kept his eyes on Latta.

She shook her head.

"Probably on the res. Some Indian using him on every raggity-ass mare in fifty miles." He shook his head and stubbed out the butt on the bottom of his boot. "I'd look on the res."

Latta shrugged. "Haying done?"

"Oh, I coulda put up one more meadow, but decided to try the grazing this winter. My dad never wanted to when he was around, but I might as well, with cattle prices this year. I can afford a little margin. Not like the last few years." The waitress put the drinks in front of them and Aubrey paid her. Cody and Latta lifted theirs to him and nodded, he lifted his, nodded back, and they all drank.

"Yeah," Latta said. "For once I was thinking I should've done more cattle, fewer horses. Can't winter-graze them as well." Latta winked at Cody sitting across from her as they watched Aubrey's eyes, drawn repeatedly to the schoolteachers.

"Why don't you ask them to dance," Cody said.

Aubrey shrugged and said, "Shy?" They all laughed. "Lotta people out tonight. Must be cattle prices they're celebrating." They all laughed again. " 'Sides, my back's been munged up this week. Shoulda stuck to bucking horses. Last two years of rodeoing I was on the bulls. Got bucked away coupla times so bad, my hand hung up, darn things dragged me near to Florida before I got loose." He laughed. "Still got my hand." He lifted it and turned it for them to see. "My back's what took the abuse. That's why I quit. Bull riding's for crazy men. Shoulda stuck to bucking horses. Cody, here, knows what I mean."

"You still rope, don't you?" Latta asked.

Aubrey nodded solemnly. "That's better'n sex most weeks, couldn't give that up. Team roping with my buddy from Mullen, Talbot Taylor?" When they shook their heads, he shrugged. "Good buddy. I didn't have a TV set until last spring when I got a satellite dish. So I didn't even know the war was on for a week until he drove by and told me. Hadn't heard the news in four years." He grinned and lit up another cigarette.

"You didn't miss much," Latta said, taking a small sip of her Jack Daniel's. She was trying to pace herself so she wouldn't get drunk.

"Yeah, I figured that when I heard about it. They don't care about us out here. You know why they put their missiles here? I mean, why not New York City or someplace that's gonna take the first hit. Why here? Because we don't count."

Cody and Latta nodded their heads. It was the same story they heard everywhere.

"Like this Niobrara deal. They're gonna come in and tell us what's good for the river we've lived on and taken care of for a hundred years. Like they know. I went to that meeting — we all yelled at them officials, but it didn't do any good. They don't listen to us. I don't mind people coming out here and seeing how beautiful it is. It's what they take with them where the individual loses his rights." He slugged his beer and raised his finger to the waitress.

Cody was embarrassed that he didn't have any money. Latta had paid for dinner and drinks so far, and now she pulled a ten from the pile of crumpled bills and change on the table. He hadn't been home for cash, and he couldn't very well take money from her for doing nothing. He hadn't even gotten the horse back like he was supposed to. For the past week that idea had been nagging on him, though Latta never mentioned it, for some reason.

As they sipped their new drinks, neither Cody nor Latta doing more than politely touching their lips to the rims of the glasses, Aubrey mashed his cigarette in the ashtray, coughed, and cleared his throat.

"Have this tickle. Know I should quit. Dad had the hay fever so bad, and the smoking just made it worse. You'd think I'd learn." He grinned and pulled out another cigarette, just rolling it between his fingers as if it were an object of comfort.

"Arthur was at the meeting with those fellas from Washington. On their side. Said it would help the economy, have to be forward looking. Everyone yelled at him. He's probably right. Who knows? I just don't think we need a bunch of people coming in and telling us what's what about our land. We take good care of it. We know it better'n they do."

The pitch and beat of the music had been increasing gradually but steadily until the patio was alive with noise and energy. "Mating ritual." Aubrey nodded to the schoolteachers.

"You gonna ask them to dance?" Cody asked again.

"Might. Beer's helping the back. I'm feeling more limber by the drink. Maybe Mrs. Jaboy will dance with me in a few minutes." He looked at her, and she smiled.

"You know" — Aubrey lit the cigarette he was holding, coughed, and stretched his legs out — "I realized this week there's two things I always wanted to know."

"Just two?" Cody asked and smiled.

"Two, I been thinking about it all week." He held up two fingers and they all laughed. "One, if the phone numbers in the men's bathroom really work. And two, if you can really, truly find a date off the '900' numbers on TV."

"That's it?" Cody laughed.

Aubrey nodded and puffed on his cigarette, smiling.

"Yes and no," Latta said, answering Aubrey's questions.

"No and no," Cody said. "Better get to work." He spread his hand out to the crowd around them.

"Mrs. Jaboy?" Aubrey stood up and held out one hand, squeezing the cigarette dead in the ashtray with the other.

Latta stood and followed the big man. He immediately began the endless series of looping twirls and steps the cowboys danced to fast songs, making sure he always kept her hand in his. In the sandhills the man never let go of his partner, not for a second. When the music changed to a slow George Strait song, "If I Know Me," he pulled her tight against his big chest and let his hand wander along her back with a familiarity she didn't like. His shirt stank of smoke and sweat despite the bath she knew he'd had. Once in a while, she stumbled on Aubrey's boots and had to apologize, and the song seemed to go on for an hour. When it finally ended she stepped back, relieved.

"Thanks," he muttered as he followed her back to the table.

Nodding to Cody, he picked up his cigarettes and said, "See ya later," and drifted toward the busy table of schoolteachers.

Latta ignored his retreat, taking a bigger drink of her JD than she had all evening. She was getting loose. She could feel her legs tingle as the band started "Guitars and Cadillacs," but she wasn't going to ask Cody to dance. He had to do *some* of the work. She needed him to make her feel desirable. Though they were sleeping together, she kept ending up feeling like it was all her doing, all her emotion and involvement. This silent-cowboy routine was driving her nuts.

Cody stood up and said, "Want to dance?" She tried not to get up too eagerly, but she couldn't help herself. The music and energy had gotten inside her and was throbbing in her head. On the dance floor, she was surprised by the easy way their bodies flowed in the rock steps, as if they'd danced to-gether for years. She found herself inventing moves she didn't know she had, following his with a grace she'd never pos-sessed. When the music slowed, she stepped naturally into his arms, and put hers around his neck. She felt every inch of her body outlined with his, and as the band played three slow songs in a row, she felt him begin to get hard as they pressed into each other. She hadn't felt that since high school, the way they moved in small rotation as if they were a planet separate from the others, without galaxy, in an orbit mapped only by their desire. She felt her nipples grow hard on his chest, her stomach tense as she danced on tiptoe against him. When the band paused between songs, they kept dancing, as if the music over the amplifiers were just the second sound they were lis-tening to.

It took a minute, after the lights of the hall blazed on and the last call was announced, for them to realize they were in a crowd. They broke away awkwardly and hurried off the floor, like teenagers caught necking in the back seat of a car.

15 ✦ DANGEROUS MEN

*Her funeral's over. All the noses gone home. Hey's afraid he'll ask the
boy if it's true. I told him not to bring Arthur that day. But he had
wanted to see his two sons together, take their picture. His kind of
arrogance grows fat and feathery. Cody ran off to the creek when the
car drove up. Sometimes he doesn't come home till dark and I have to
punish him. If Arthur were mine, I'd whip him. A boy who can't be
trusted. He told his mother, like I knew he would. Marion Bennett
should've trained him better — she'd still be alive.*

— Caroline
April 6, 1966

S o deeply asleep were they the next morning, neither one
heard the front door open and close with a low huff. Nor
did they catch the creaking of the floorboards back and forth
for half an hour, before the sound hesitantly worked its way
up the stairs. What woke Cody was the sense of someone
watching him, which first came in the dream, then pulled him
to the surface. When he opened his eyes, Arthur was standing
in the doorway urgently motioning for him to come downstairs. They stared at each other for a long moment before Cody
quietly slid to the edge of the bed, nodded his head, and
pointed to his boots and pants on the floor. Latta was cocooned
in his shirt she'd pulled on after they'd made love. With her
eyelids twitching, she looked nervous, as if even asleep she
could sense the tension in the room.

Arthur turned and went back downstairs. When he'd been told that the couple were at the Bennett house in town, Arthur had been taken by surprise. He'd never considered her stooping to sleep with someone like Cody. He'd always assumed Latta and he would naturally come together as business partners in marriage. Sex with a person like Cody seemed to belong in the dark stench of the cheapest motel in town, with a sagging bed and stained bathroom tiles. Places Heywood, Cody, and Kya might go to cause trouble. Arthur liked the convenience of his relationship with Latta. She was the present and the future wrapped up in one bundle — every time they got together to talk, he felt like he was paying a premium on an insurance policy, putting money in the bank.

He wasn't a romantic, he was a pragmatist. He'd always secretly approved of arranged marriages. Marriages seemed to last or fail on some mysterious engine of their own design, so being practical didn't seem such a hardhearted thing to do. People could always learn to love each other. Heywood had told him that for years in regard to his brother and sister. He'd always felt like that was a pretty easy thing for his father to say. He didn't have to give up anything for such a grand sentiment. But he'd never fully understood his father, and now it wasn't worth expending the energy. When someone was dead, Arthur figured, that person had locked in his mistakes, his failures and achievements; he'd stopped being mysterious and was simply another tab at the cash register. You looked at the list and saw what you bought and what it cost you.

When Cody entered the living room and sat across from him in the little arrangement to the right of the artificial Christmas tree they never took down, Arthur realized he had to do something about Latta. He handed Cody a six-pack of Pepsi, sweating with cold. "We have a problem." His voice was stripped of feeling. He watched his younger brother pull a can of pop from the plastic ring, flip it open, and drink it in two long drags. He never understood why the kid didn't have coffee or tea, something civilized in the morning. Apparently Caroline Kidwell had never let him have soda pop, so when Cody was sent to Bennett's, he started drinking as much as he could.

Cody opened another can and leaned back in the loveseat; his eyes sought and found his brother's. "What?"

Arthur sighed, looked at his thick hands, and rubbed them together. He was still surprised by his feelings when he saw Latta in bed with Cody. He was always good at controlling himself, then these damn emotions showed up. It pissed him off, it really did.

He closed his eyes and took a deep breath so the anger that was beginning to rise with the tail ends of his greasy café breakfast would sink back down. "We need to talk." He looked at his brother, who grimaced and nodded. Good, they were working on the same plane for the moment. "Sheriff Moon came out to the ranch yesterday looking for Kya. He's pretty sure she stole Latta's horse. I tried to talk him out of it, but he says he can prove it if he can find her."

Cody fingered the white bandage crossing his chest, muttering, "Shit."

Any other man would probably have died from the injuries and bout of pneumonia, Arthur knew. There was a lot of Heywood's physical toughness in his brother. Having watched the punishment his brother took, though, Arthur was just as happy he'd inherited Heywood's intelligence and drive instead.

"Who shot you?"

Cody shrugged and sipped his pop, looking out across the room beyond Arthur.

"Your sister was involved, wasn't she? That's why you didn't go to the sheriff. The sheriff thinks she stole the horse and shot you." Cody's eyes were growing flat yellow and grey. Arthur hurried to stop it. "I've stalled the sheriff, but we can't let it go indefinitely. She called this morning from Mission. The Antelope Motel. I was hoping you could stop her. Get the horse back if they've got it. If Sheriff Moon catches up with them before you do, she'll go to jail. I'm really worried, Cody, I mean it." In fact, Arthur had tried to lead the sheriff to suspect Cody in order to protect Kya, but he couldn't very well tell his brother about the tradeoff.

"You figure she'll listen to me?" Cody shifted his shoulders uncomfortably as if the bandages were chafing.

Arthur wanted to yell at his brother, wanted to stomp around the room, blow him off the sofa with his words, but that wouldn't work. Somehow, he had to stop what was going on in the upstairs bedroom and get everyone back on track. The worst thing he could imagine was Cody with Latta's ranch and a third of Bennett's. After all Arthur had done and been promised, his brother would end up having more. Arthur knew he was the real leader of the family; Heywood had put him in charge of the estate. He was the only one capable of planning for the future. He had to keep control of himself to direct and control them.

"We have to find her before Moon does."

"I already tried this," Cody said. "Maybe you should go."

Arthur leaned forward, clasping his hands together earnestly. "You know the answer to that. She just ignores me."

Cody nodded and sighed.

They were silent as they contemplated the picture of their willful sister, who in some way had always managed to get and do exactly what she wanted.

"So I guess this means I have to go." Cody's voice was cold and flat.

"Look at it this way, Cody. If Kya's got the horse, you can bring it back and keep her out of jail. If she doesn't, well, we've got to protect her, don't we? We don't have much choice here — she hasn't left us any." He spread his hands as if he were a simple man asking for help with a problem he knew he couldn't solve alone. The appeal of it was undeniable.

There was a long silence. Upstairs, the bed creaked as Latta turned over and Cody jerked as if he'd been shot again. He shook his head and rubbed his face. "Shit." He stood up.

"Just hurry. Take my car. Here's some cash and a credit card. We don't have much time. Moon had some things to do this morning, but after that, Kya was his only business. I'll tell Latta you've got a lead on her horse when she wakes up."

Cody shook his head. "I'll leave her a note." No matter what Arthur said, Cody didn't trust him. In the kitchen he found a pencil and scrap paper, but it took him a few minutes to figure out what to say — he'd never written her before. Signing with "Love" was the only part that came naturally. Upstairs, he put the note on the dresser by the door, grabbed another shirt from the closet, and kissed her cheek before he left. She smiled in her sleep.

Cody nodded to Arthur from the hallway as he buttoned his shirt, his face loosening at the prospect of Latta's happiness and relief. He'd put it all right again. Kya too. He'd prove something that way. That felt good. He ignored the feeling of uneasiness about Arthur's goodwill. He liked the idea of redemption so much he hurried, closing the front door with a quick jerk that echoed up the stairs.

Arthur waited until the car was well down the street before he climbed the stairs again. The note was in plain sight, and fit easily into his fist.

Hesitating in the downstairs hallway, Latta looked around her as if unsure where she was, so Arthur saw her before she saw him. When he stepped into view, away from the Christmas tree he'd been examining, concern replaced her uncertainty, and she instinctively tugged on the bottom of Cody's white shirt that covered her underpants. "Arthur —"

"Latta." Arthur smiled and raised his eyebrows.

She wrapped her arms around her chest and stepped into the living room. "Where's — where'd Cody go?" She seemed to sense her own tentativeness, Arthur noticed. She dropped her arms to her sides and moved more confidently to the tree as if curious about the old Bennett ornaments.

"Cody? Oh, well, he said he had work to do. Vacation's over, he wanted me to tell you. You know how cowboys are." By the time his brother got back and called her, she'd be convinced of the story's truth, he figured.

Her hand shook as she reached for a tiny gold trumpet on the tree. The crackled paint looked brittle enough to flake off the glass. Arthur had to stop himself from asking her not to touch it. "He just left?"

Arthur nodded. "A bit ago. Asked me to tell you thanks. Said he feels a lot better now." Her face was so pale, he was afraid she was going to cry. "Do you want to sit down?" He touched her shoulder and she turned to follow him. She sat where Cody had earlier, and when her glance fell on the plastic rings holding three cans of Pepsi, she reached out and touched a sweaty can, rubbing the moisture between her fingers. Arthur tried to keep his expression casual.

When her breathing relaxed, she looked up and smiled at him. "Arthur, please. You should hear yourself. I've spent enough time with Cody to know he's not like that. Just tell me the truth, okay?"

Arthur shrugged. She was just going to make it harder on herself. "I wasn't sure I should tell you, but since you're asking, Sheriff Moon came out to the ranch yesterday looking for Cody." Actually, it was easier than he expected, recasting the story with Cody's name instead of Kya's. Latta was fingering the plastic ring as he concluded: "Moon says he's got some pretty solid evidence against Cody."

Latta looked up quickly, her eyes probing his, but the basis in truth of the sheriff's visit kept Arthur's voice and face innocent.

She shook her head and rubbed her palms on her knees. "I can't believe it."

"Well, I know, but he did take off as soon as I told him Moon was looking for him. That surprised me. Insisted on borrowing my car. Left so fast I didn't get a chance to ask where he was going."

Latta licked her lips, rolled them together in a tight line, and seemed to stop breathing for a moment. "He didn't say anything else about —"

"I'm sorry, Latta." Arthur relaxed, confident that he was in control now. He didn't want to make her suffer. She just had to see that Cody was a mistake.

"Cody just seems to drift into a woman's life, then out again. You're not the first one I've had to tell this to. He can't seem to say goodbye when he's done. His sister and I usually end up with the job." Arthur leaned forward, his forearms on the thighs of his brown lightweight wool pants. He felt like he was telling the truth — even if it was a bit off. Cody had had flings before. One of them, a divorcée from Valentine, had talked to him about his brother at the VFW Christmas dance a couple of years ago. She had been young, skinny, and cheap looking in a way Arthur found himself attracted to, but she'd only wanted sympathy, it turned out. That was when Arthur had decided that when it came to men, women either wanted to be hurt or were stupid. If he were a woman, he'd never trust a man. He'd use his body the right way, not throw it at just anybody. That was why he couldn't understand Latta. She was smart enough to marry Jaboy, but she seemed to be getting dumber as she got older. "I'm afraid Cody uses women sometimes."

Latta pulled a can of Pepsi from the plastic ring, snapped it open, and drank. She was as bad as Cody about that stuff, he decided. Arthur tried to imagine their being married, their ranches joined, the land stretching endlessly in every direction. The picture competed with his dream of living somewhere else, so he could escape feeling trapped by the huge maternal mounds of hills that flowed in and out of valleys, featureless, identical, like some grotesque genetic error. The wind gusted through blowouts, uncovering artifacts from the past, then covering them again just as quickly, as if time, history, were only a moment, a torn narrative, pieces scattered, incomprehensible even when the shards were reassembled: arrowheads his brother collected, dinosaur and mammoth bones Kya brought home, fat old cavalry bullets Heywood had plunked on the dining table at night, shedding their little jackets of sand on the dark polished wood as everyone watched. He never understood the point of collecting that junk. It didn't have anything to do with them.

"That's all?" She leaned forward. "I don't believe you." She smiled and shook her head, folding her arms across her chest and lifting her chin.

It was Arthur's turn to smile as he stood and began pacing, his hands locked behind him, chin tucked as if he were giving closing arguments to a movie jury. "I know he's got some fine qualities, Latta. The way he cares for the animals and protects his sister, for instance. And anything else weak or hurt he can protect. But there are these other aspects as well to consider."

He paused, watching the fear stiffen her face. Arthur looked over her head at the wall where a dark oil portrait of his mother as a young woman hung. "His feelings are erratic. He can turn violent without warning. We used to have a terrible time with him. It cost Heywood thousands of dollars to keep him out of jail after he moved in with us. Stealing, brawling, wrecking things. I'm surprised you never heard the stories, but I guess you were gone so much in those days. He can't help himself. Some people say that John Axel's murder occurred because Cody had stolen Axel's toolbox out of his pickup, parked by the Minnechaduza Creek where he always went fishing. Axel saw him running away with it and followed him. The sheriff found the toolbox behind the house. Moon told me there's plenty of evidence pointing his way as far as your stallion goes. He got shot trying to cheat whoever was buying the horse, they figure. Someone on the res maybe. But Moon

doesn't want it talked around while they're trying to find him."
Arthur looked quickly at Latta. "I'm sorry. I guess he's been
trying to get close to you so you wouldn't be suspicious. He
was there the night the stud was taken, wasn't he?" he asked
gently.

She nodded and watched the floor, hugging herself.

"It's not your fault, Latta. He can't stop himself. He's just
not made the way other people are. Your best hope of getting
your horse back now is to turn it over to the sheriff and me.
We can handle him, and maybe when you've dropped your
connection with him, he'll listen to reason and bring it back
rather than go to jail. I'm truly sorry, Latta. I've been so busy
with the various probate issues and the Holiday Ranches people, I haven't been keeping track of him the way I should."

"I have to go. I appreciate your views on this, Arthur. I'm
not sure I share them, but I will think about it." Latta stood up
and walked out of the room. Arthur could hear her overhead
as she dressed. In a few minutes she was back down, slipping
out the front door.

Arthur smiled and rubbed his damp palms on his thighs.
He had that scary good feeling he used to get when one of his
lies would get someone in trouble — someone he didn't like.
He'd learned early how to turn truth a quarter notch and use
it to settle grudges. His lies usually had some basis in fact —
Cody and Kya were swimming nude in stock tanks at night.
Kya *had* gone out with Jaboy. The point was to make sure
he was in control, kept things moving along just like he'd
planned.

I have eaten a piece of my soul today. It had the stamped ink taste of movie ticket stubs, newspapers. Right now it is expanding, soaking up the good of me, taking me with it. I can feel the fullness in my stomach of old wet paper. I will fall apart in your hands if you try to hold me, touch me. I've become that useless. Something they can aim a gun at — a thin heart. A lethal enough time watching the curtains buzz tight across the blankness I have become, today, my soul eats — I sent Cody to his father an hour ago.

— Caroline
July 17, 1976

*L*atta was working outside when the first of a series of storms hit, but as soon as things let up, she ran from the barn to the house. The lull arrived just before dark, and the hills were caught in a bowl between two storm fronts. Overhead, a rainbow's arc capped the sky, and one end caught in the soft irregular curve of the Dismal River, water lapping the colored edges until it disappeared into the dark leftover of the sunset.

It was the seventh day with no message from Cody. Stripping quickly, she stepped into her shower. "It's time to come clean," she muttered, "come clean. He hasn't called. He's gone. Arthur was right." She picked up the Lava soap and scrubbed her hands with its hard grainy surface. The whole plan she'd made for a life that wouldn't be pointless, erasable, was gone with her horse and Cody. What a stupid thing love had made of her. She rubbed her arms to the elbow, reddening her skin with the soap. She'd wanted him to make her love him. She'd wanted to be taken down. And now she was. Her body felt like a crumpled bag, pieces of rotting meat. She raised welts in big red streaks on her chest and stomach, unaware of how long she was working on single areas.

When the water stopped and Inez pulled her out, wrapping her in a towel, she was shaking so badly she could hardly walk. She was surprised by that. She didn't think people could shake that hard without parts of them starting to fall off. She waited for the joints to loosen from the vibrations, like parts of a motor, but they didn't.

Inez put her to bed like a sick child. "See," Latta whispered over and over, "I'm a failure at everything. I'm nothing anyone could love."

The older woman kept trying to shush her, but the noise of rain pounding on the house got in the way. Latta always figured she had to be of some use to someone. And now she wasn't. She didn't have anyone to work for, any reason. She could lie there for the rest of her life. If she could stand the voices in her head, she could do it. She scrubbed her forehead with a fist and squeezed her eyes shut. Never look outside again. She just wouldn't. Wouldn't anything. If his name came up, she'd unlearn the letters, make them a foreign language.

Inez covered her in a star quilt and lay beside her, humming like a trapped bee until Latta slept. She was too worn out to fight the dreams for once, and kept waking with the sense that Jaboy was alive. They were traveling fast and light through the same landscapes of their early years. Morocco, Casablanca. He told her about being there in the early fifties with the machine guns still in the windows of the hotel from the last raid. Algeria. Lebanon. Syria. Israel. Beirut. Worlds that would soon be gone. Baghdad. Africa. He liked hot, dry places, places where starvation and disease were imminent. Often they skirted the

edges of civil wars, plagues, drought. As if some exotic perfume drifted off the stench of the dead and dying, he found
disaster erotic. Their lovemaking in such places became the
most dramatic thing in her life. It obsessed them both. Later
she would realize that her passion lit his, led him to greater
acts of imagination, until the end, in Mexico, where the world
stopped and she opened her eyes.

Cody. That place was pain. She'd loved him and lost him,
all in one day. It seemed impossible to have luck like that. For
a day or two she thought he'd call or show up at her ranch.
Then she worried he'd been hurt. Yesterday she'd known: he
was gone. He'd left her, like Arthur said. How had she rearranged her geography, her map of herself, so blindly, so stupidly? No wonder boys practiced beating each other up. It was
training.

The door opened, spreading a thin lacquer of yellow hall
light Inez walked into, carrying a tray of food.

Had she ever thanked Inez for Mexico, Latta wondered. For
taking care of her, for saving her life, for helping her get free
of Jaboy? She watched the other woman set the tray down on
the table next to the bed and turn on the antique floor lamp in
the corner. When Jaboy died, Latta had taken the few things
she liked best in the house and moved them into her room. The
lamp was something she'd gotten from her parents when she'd
married. Jaboy had disliked its graceless Victorian design, so it
had stayed in the corner of the back sitting room they didn't use.

Latta found her mind wandering, trying to focus on any object, ignoring Inez, who stood beside her watching. It wouldn't
do any good, Latta wanted to say, it's all over. Instead, they
listened to the quiet rumble of the storm walking across the
hills toward them. Then lightning struck close and the house
shook with the crackle and aftershock, and she jumped and
grabbed the quilt in her fists, gritting her teeth as if the storm
had been aimed at her.

"What did he do? What happened?" Inez sat on the bed

and pulled one of Latta's hands loose, holding it, separating the fingers and stroking the palm. When Latta shrugged and looked away, Inez squeezed it. Latta tried to pull away, but the other woman hung on. "What happened?" Her voice was irresistible.

Latta opened her mouth and tried to say the words, but they were missing when her tongue touched her teeth and her lips tried to shape the sounds. Lightning flashed in the windows again, and the thunder pounded overhead. The air was charged with strangeness now. If the words came, they would fly out into the world, rain down with the rain, and the hills would know. She wouldn't be safe, so she couldn't say. The only place safe was here in her room, her bed, the covers, the dark. "Turn off the light," she whispered, "please."

But Inez shook her head. "Tell me." Her cool hand stroked Latta's forehead, brushing the hair back as if she were a fevered child. Latta felt the fingertips' hypnotic touch pulling the words up her throat and into her mouth, until she'd choke if she didn't say them. "He doesn't love me — he took the horse, my dream, everything is gone —"

The crying was stuck there, crowding, pushing like vomit against the roof of her mouth, up the back of her nose. "It's over," she whispered, and began to sob, curling around the woman seated beside her.

Inez held her fiercely. The rain began pinging and then slashing at the window glass as if it were tiny slivers of metal that could pierce the skin of any living thing. The rush of wind arriving with the rain rose and pushed against the trees and house, heaving its huge body one way and then the other so the wood creaked and groaned like a ship at sea. Latta wondered briefly if the house could float, or if it would sink to the bottom of this upside-down place, falling far beneath the sand to find the water of the true ocean deep within the earth, where sometimes, when she listened closely, she could hear the small cries of its life, inviolate, true, forever.

Inez's muttering and cursing broke through the rhythm of the storm. "We nursed him, treated him as brother, son, lover. I saw my own daughters taken as silly young girls and turned into useless, beaten creatures. By men." Inez's words brought on Latta's tears as she gave in to the old woman's voice.

"Women have to protect each other. No man can do that. I watched my sons grow up. No amount of slapping their faces mattered. And what did prayers do? Nothing. God is another useless male creature. No woman should believe in such nonsense." She wiped Latta's tears with her tough, callused palm.

And the storm battered the house, flickering lights, shaking rafters, sending threads of water under doors. On the stairway, at the turn of the landing, the wind found passage into the house, vibrated the framed ghost shirt until it slid crashing off the wall onto the floor. The pulverized glass sparkled in the dim light like powdered stars on the white and blue paint of the shirt, making the figures seem to shimmer once more with life and power. A few of the larger shards embedded themselves upright in the wood floor around the shirt as if to mark the site sacred. The raw edges of glass glittered savagely in the dark.

Cody tried to call Latta from the Liquor 'n' Lunch, where he'd stopped to wait out the storm. When Inez finally answered, her voice sounded tinny and distant. He was having a hard time making her understand him over the thunder. "Inez, it's me, Cody. I'm on my way. Tell Latta I'll be there soon, as soon as this weather —" When the phone clicked in his ear, he thought that maybe the lines had gotten crossed. But when the dial tone came back on, he couldn't escape the feeling that Inez had hung up on him. Maybe she'd had a hard time hearing him; she always was a little impatient.

He looked out the rain-slashed windows at the water pouring along the gutters outside, then went back to his seat beside the Sykes brothers, who were barely aware of time, let alone weather. Although he'd covered hundreds of miles in the past week — from Rosebud to Pine Ridge to the Black Hills and all the way to Sheridan, Wyoming — he never got close to Kya or the horse. His shoulder and thigh were aching from the long days in the car and the damp, a signal of the future when he'd be hobbling around with arthritis, like Will.

By six-thirty, the weather had lifted enough for him to drive. Inez would have told Latta he called, and she'd be waiting — the idea made him order a pint of whiskey and a six-pack of Bud to go. The rain was warm enough that he'd convince her to come outside with him. They'd go into the hills and lie naked and make love. Ignoring the way the Continental drifted and surged in the water-covered dips of the road, he cracked open a beer and took a long pull. He hoped Latta had noticed how he'd signed his note: Love.

"Love." He said it out loud for the first time in his life, smiled, and drank. Even without the horse, things were good in a way he could never have imagined. He slowed down to straighten the car as it hydroplaned on a large patch of water. A dove paused in the road just ahead, then pushed up and away, making slow progress against the wind. Hawks, as stiff and still as wood, rested on fence posts while the wind furrowed their head and chest feathers. The rain momentarily made them all equal.

The soaked horses stood hunched with their backs to the wind in the paddocks opposite Latta's house. Cody pulled up and jumped out, leaving the engine running. He was going to grab her the minute he saw her.

It took a lot of banging and calling before the door cracked open. Then it was Inez who peered out at him, a large butcher knife in her hand as if he'd interrupted her cooking. Even through the alcoholic glow, he knew something was wrong.

"Where's Latta? Tell her I'm here, Inez. Let me in, okay? It's —"

"Go to hell. You're a bad man. A dog treats its kind better."
She slammed the door.

Cody turned the knob and pushed, but she'd locked it. He heaved his good shoulder against it, but the heavy oak held. He stepped back and kicked it, but only the frame creaked. "Latta, let me in. Latta!" he yelled, shoving the door again and again until his injured shoulder throbbed with pain. He stepped back and looked at the big glass windows. He could smash through one of those. Stooping to pick up one of the ornamental pots of geraniums, he heard a click and a voice behind him.

"Don't, Cody. Just get in your car and go home. You're done here. She doesn't want to see you anymore. It's over."

As Cody rose he saw that Colin was holding his rifle at a safe distance, cocked and ready.

"You're wrong, Colin. Tell her I'm here — Inez has a bug in her ear about something. Ask Latta," Cody pleaded.

"No, buddy boy, I'm afraid you're wrong. Go home now and leave her alone. She doesn't deserve your kind of crap." Colin's eyes held his until the rain seemed to turn cold and drench him sober in the next burst of wind.

Cody looked at the dark windows once more, turned, and walked back to his car. He drank steadily from the bottle while he waited for the defroster to clear the windshield enough to see Colin and Inez standing guard in front of the house. Then he spun the car around and drove away as fast as he could, believing almost all the way home that there had simply been a dumb mistake that a phone call could fix.

Joseph watched the wind blow the water of the Dismal River against itself. Once, his grandfather had told him, the spirits grew angry with the people and shook the earth, reversing the flow of the Mississippi. Such things were simple, but useless except to those few who saw and understood. There was a story to be pieced together, his grandfather told him, there was always a story, and the pieces might be scattered and broken apart, but they were in plain sight too. Like the stars mapping the hills and rivers below.

In the darkness, his grandfather finally spoke. Using the images Joseph would recognize and need, he showed him the things he must put straight. The ghost shirt would come last. There had been so much blood because of it.

The medicine man buried in the hill beneath him suddenly appeared, tall, strong, dressed in native clothes. "There's not much time left now," he warned. "The buffalo is hairless." He disappeared into the flat grey rain.

Then Joseph heard another sound, a keening like a coyote but with hysteria in its sob, like a human's voice. All around him, he saw, there was grief, loneliness, wrong. Not just the Bennetts and Jaboys; it spread across the hills like a flood whose rising waters were drowning the world. People were scattering like ants from their holes in the rain. He too had been running, seeking shelter. Maybe the sandhills were the last refuge, maybe what was happening was inching its way here. He could stop himself from drowning in it, and Cody who was given to him, and Latta who kept his ghost shirt, and a woman on a horse. It was up to him, then. Time to move. Time to act. Yes, he felt his body shiver, and a nausea climb his throat, but he swallowed and huddled down into a ball, wrapping his soaked arms around himself for warmth and closing his eyes, because now he was ready to sleep. His waiting was over.

Arthur heard the branches graze the brick and take the east bedroom windows as the tree fell. Running to Cody's room, he discovered his brother sitting up in bed, staring wildly out the broken windows, ignoring the glass scattered over the floor, the bed, and his legs. He hadn't undressed or even removed his boots, which rested unaccountably on Caroline's quilt. The rain was starting to puddle the floor and follow the settle of the old house to the center of the room. Arthur didn't notice his brother's face at first, not until he left to get bath towels and came back to start damming the water.

"Get up and do something. This'll soak into the dining room and ruin the ceiling. The electricity's out. Help me." Arthur threw the stack of towels on the floor and yelled for John to bring some plastic for the windows. Out of the corner of his eye, he saw the bottle on the nightstand and the glass in Cody's hand. Arthur hollered again for John, and dropped to his knees to mop the water, which was seeping through the floorboards into the dining room ceiling.

John appeared cradling a foot-thick roll of plastic they kept for winterizing and a hammer and nails. Arthur glanced up and said, "Duct tape, dammit."

"I called her and Inez hung up on me," Cody said. "First she cursed me in Spanish. Something about shit and death." He took a long drink, his eyes on the broken windows. His voice sounded far off, abstract, when he spoke again. "I shouldn't have listened to you. Kya wasn't in Mission. No one's seen the horse. But you knew that." He drained the glass and poured in another two inches. The whiskey wasn't changing anything, he noticed, it only made things clearer, sharper. "What did you say to her, Arthur?" Cody looked at his brother, who had stopped his efforts with the towels and was resting on his heels, watching him.

Arthur opened his mouth, then closed it when John came clomping tiredly into the room, holding up a grey roll of tape.

Cody ignored the two men as they struggled in the dark to secure the heavy plastic sheets across the tops of the windows against the gusts of windblown rain, then worked to tape the plastic down the sides and along the bottom. He drank steadily. What he wanted was blankness or anger. He didn't care which. But what he was getting was the loop of scenes with her, which formed a special pain he couldn't seem to escape.

When Arthur and John finished cleaning up, Cody said "You stay" to his brother.

"Check the dining room windows, John," Arthur said, and sat down heavily in the chair he pulled from the corner.

"What did you say to her, Arthur?" Cody's voice dropped, so Arthur had to lean forward to hear him against the storm.

"I don't know." Arthur shrugged. "Just what we agreed." He tried to take a deep breath and realized how tense he was, gripping the arms of the chair. He loosened his hands and twisted his head around to unkink his neck.

"I shouldn't've listened to you."

When lightning flared again and lit up the room, Arthur noticed that his brother's shirt hung open over his bare chest. "You took the bandage off. You're going to —"

"It doesn't matter."

Arthur could feel the palpable distance his brother had traveled from him in the days since their talk. He wasn't going to be able to control him. It was all going to go down the tubes.

"Stop the John Wayne shit, okay? You break that shoulder again and we're going to have to hire another hand. Things are screwed up enough as it is. The bank's frozen the accounts because of probate. Where're we going to get the cash to pay someone to replace you?"

Cody shook his head. "I'm not giving her up, Arthur."

Again Arthur had to strain forward to hear his brother. Why didn't he speak up like a normal person, he thought bitterly. "Well, maybe she doesn't want you, ever think about that?" He shivered. His pajamas had gotten wet from the rain coming in the broken windows, but he knew he shouldn't get up and go change.

There was a long pause during which Arthur watched his brother drink another two inches down the tumbler of whiskey. He wished he could have a drink to warm himself up, but he didn't think he should ask. Instead, he watched the lightning wink through the plastic and illuminate the glass splattering Cody's legs.

"I was trying to think back where I'd heard you sound like this before. Then I remembered, it was that time when we were kids — and that thing with Kya and me." Cody set the glass down on the nightstand and swung his legs off the bed. Ignoring the shower of glass onto the floor, he faced his brother. "What happened?"

Arthur looked away, then realized he'd better keep his eyes on Cody. He shrugged, but felt the truth coming up inside him.

Cody leaned forward. "What, Arthur?" He asked softly, his face a perfectly still mask of dark hollows.

Arthur shook his head. Cody wasn't moving, just watching him. At least he didn't seem upset, Arthur thought, though he knew he couldn't be right about that. There was something about silence he had to fill up. More than anything, Arthur feared what could open up in the quiet between two people. He would fill it with words, even if it meant that language itself became a construction, an architecture that walled them apart rather than together.

"Well?" Cody asked softly, capturing Arthur's eyes.

"I —" Arthur stayed very still, staring into the dark at his brother's pale face.

Cody was too still, but then he rose fluidly, walked across the room, and pulled him out of the chair. The first blow landed with a low grunt of pain from each of them. Arthur's head rocked back, but the punch coming from Cody's weakened right lacked its usual power. Then Cody stepped in, knocking Arthur's breath out with blows to his stomach. Arthur doubled over and gasped, careful to tuck his head and buy time. It took only a few seconds. Cody had stepped back panting, and that was the opening Arthur needed. Balling his fists, Arthur straightened and lunged, catching the side of his brother's face and the weak shoulder. Cody staggered back, bit his lip, shook his head, and plunged toward Arthur, swinging wildly with his left. A fist caught Arthur's ear, tearing and mashing it. The pain was so sharp it made him furious, and he pushed Cody as hard as he could despite the stinging blows to his face. Cody stumbled back against the bed, and would have fallen except that Arthur wrapped his arms around the thinner body, pinning the flailing fists. Locking his hands together, Arthur squeezed. He hoped the goddamned shoulder broke again, and heard a satisfying pop as a joint cracked. Cody moaned but wouldn't stop struggling.

"Enough, okay? Just stop or I *will* hurt you, Cody. You can't win here." Arthur gripped tighter and Cody gasped and nodded.

Arthur couldn't resist one last squeeze, which drained the color from Cody's face as he let him fall back against the bed. Well, he'd been asking for it.

He was gloating when Cody's boot toe caught him in the balls and dropped him gagging to his knees. That was why Arthur didn't hear him get up and go down the hall, into Heywood's room. It wasn't until Cody was entering the room again, arm raised to point the pistol, that Arthur recognized the danger and yelled, "Don't. Stop. It wouldn't have worked — you know that — think —"

Arthur couldn't get up or struggle. It was just as it was in his dreams where he was in horrible danger, trying to run away, but his legs wouldn't work. Cody stood over him with the gun, pushing it into his cheek, cocking it. Arthur could smell the acrid oil of the barrel and his brother's strange sweet sweat. He closed his eyes against the next thing, as he would have pulled the covers over his head when waking to a sound in the night.

"I told her Sheriff Moon thought you had stolen the horse. And that you had a history of being an unfaithful, unreliable lover, a thief, and —" He was panting. "I took the note you left her —"

"Cody? Arthur?" The two men turned involuntarily toward the voice of their sister, who was striding down the hall.

"What the hell are you doing?" she demanded, looking from one brother to the other. When neither man answered, she said, "Put the gun down, for chrissakes. You're not going to blow Arthur's head off now if you waited this long."

She flopped onto the bed and picked up the glass of whiskey on the nightstand and took a sip. "Arthur, go get us a glass, will you?" When Arthur didn't move, she said sternly, exasperation in her voice, "Cody, I *said* put the gun down."

Slowly lowering the pistol, Cody shook his head and whispered "Later" to his brother.

Arthur stood up, staying as far away from his brother as he could, and left the room, hoping he could unlock the gun cabinet and load a rifle in the dark.

"And don't bring any more goddamned guns up here, Arthur. You hear me?" Kya's voice followed him down the hall. "Greta's in the shower, and then she has to get some sleep, so everybody just settle down here. God, what an awful night: I think I wrecked the Blazer. We had to walk two miles in this shitty weather."

Cody took the glass out of her hand, poured more whiskey into it, and drank, watching her face.

"You are so full of shit, Cody. What's this macho crap with the pistol?"

He slapped her so hard her head rocked, but she was on her feet so quickly it didn't seem to matter. When she slapped him back as hard as she could, he was surprised at the way his vision turned black, then red before it cleared.

"Ask Arthur."

"This is more Latta Jaboy shit, isn't it?" Kya took the glass and drank.

"It's not shit. He took my note explaining that I was going away for a few days and told her I stole her horse, and I was through with her."

Kya laughed softly until something in her brother's eyes made her quit. "Really?" She drained the whiskey and sat down again on the bed. "That's sad," she said, and held out the glass. He poured it half full.

Cody couldn't tell whether she was sad about Arthur, Latta, or him. He sat down next to her, his shoulder aching from the fight. He shouldn't have taken off the bandage, but he'd made up his mind that evening that he couldn't keep giving in to the pain. If he was going to heal, he'd have to do what he'd learned with broken bones, wounds, even animals and people: you had to push past the injury, the hurt, make your mind seal over that place, and forget it.

But it was good that his shoulder ached, he thought, sipping whiskey. It reminded him of today. How he couldn't let himself forget this, because Latta was the only person he'd ever loved besides his mother and Kya. What could he say to her now? He'd spent the past few hours trying to think up an excuse, a way to explain, but there wasn't anything to say. If he were Arthur, he'd have the words. But words had always gotten him in trouble.

Cody felt panicky in a way he couldn't remember since he'd been given to Heywood Bennett as a boy. It stung his eyes and nose, his chest and legs, and made him weak. What was he going to do? He felt hands on his shoulders, his back, rubbing, massaging, pulling the aches and bruises to the surface and out of him. He closed his eyes, letting the room rock gently with the whiskey that was finally taking hold. When the hands pulled him back onto the bed, he stiffened, then let go, lifting his legs and straightening the length of his body out. Kya and Latta, his mind spun the names. He noticed how the *a*'s repeated like sighs of pleasure, making the lips part, the throat open before their soft sound. Latta and Kya. His lover who'd just left and his sister who'd helped murder him. Murder.

"Why'd you let Burch shoot me, Kya?" he murmured as he drifted off.

"It was an accident. I didn't know it was you. I love you,

Cody. I'd never hurt you, you know that." She was lying beside him, whispering in his ear.

"But you did —"

"I know, I'm so sorry."

"Bring back horse, then —"

"Can't. We lost him."

"Then I'm lost too."

17 ✧ COWBOY STATE OF MIND

For the Lakota, everything is in pairs of opposites: good and bad, light and dark. Ceremonies help to maintain a balance — you suffer (bad) so your prayers are answered (good). Your purpose on earth is to return to the center, and you walk the Red Road, the balanced life, to get there.

— *from* MITAKUYE OYASIN

At the Home Oil Café, Cody stopped and grabbed a couple of sweet rolls and a large hot tea to go. The place was already full of hunters and cowboys, sitting over greasy eggs and bacon.

"Starting to come down," the woman at the counter said as he handed over a five-dollar bill.

"Early," he said, watching as she fumbled to make change.

"Already got two inches at Gordon this morning. S'posed to be rain. They said it was gonna rain. Now look." They paused and looked out the window at the large wet flakes that were starting to fill the October air.

"Thanks," he said, picking up the tea and rolls.

She waved, calling out, "Have a nice day."

He almost laughed.

By the time Cody reached the road south, the wipers were working hard to push the heavy snow off the windshield, leaving wet streaks he had to try to see through. It was opening day of pheasant hunting. Luckily, the snow was keeping the hunters at bay. They'd wait in warm motel rooms and restaurant booths to see if it stopped. Since his truck heater was broken, he'd be cold all day.

Damn dumb thing to do, though — get drunk when he had to work like this. His head ached dully and his stomach didn't put out much of a welcome for the overly sweet soggy roll he was trying to introduce. Damn dumb thing with that girl too. He hit the steering wheel with his fist. When had he ever started taking it out on women. That was a new low.

Just ahead, the hills he was entering turned grey and blue, the tans muted with the mottled white collecting in them. There was a special silence now, and he cracked his window just to listen. The wind wasn't whirling or howling, just pushing the snow in a long wet veil across the land, hushing it.

In the distance, mist rose off the lakes and ponds in tall smoky columns, and the cattle and horses waited, heads down, rumps to the wind. It would probably quit as quickly as it had started, he realized with a shiver. But the day would be raw for working cattle. He just hoped the old horse was up to it. He'd bring Marcus, the colt, and trade off to teach him some things, even though he wasn't in any shape to give the young horse the patience he needed.

Late as he was, he still slowed and finally stopped when a covey of cock pheasants began to saunter across the road just ahead of him. The first three were brave, walking with the jerky motion he always associated with roosters, looking this way and that like tourists, as if the stopped truck were merely one of the sights around them. One by one, the other three stuck their heads out of the tall grass on one side of the road, peeked around, then slowly brought their whole bodies into view before running across and diving into the cover of grass on the other side. The last stood in the middle of the road, displaying the finely drawn white ring around its neck, the proud colors and droop of its snow-weighted tail, then it too scooted.

Cody shook his head as he drove by them. "You got about two hours to smarten up and hide your butts," he warned the birds.

The Bennett cowboys were an hour late by the time they got to Stannek's, which meant a longer day than normal on a weekend. The cattle were scattered across the hills, eating in small groups the men had to collect. The horses were fresh and hopped sideways every time the snow slid off a post or plant, or a rabbit or quail jumped out. The cattle were cautious and alert, sniffing at the newly wet air and the approach of the men, the cows putting their big bodies between the men and the calves. The cattle had their winter coats now, and the white ones looked dirty and grey already, the black matted and curled. The only way to tell the old or sick ones was by weight and lack of coat.

As the men began to collect and push the cattle, the calves kept breaking away, bucking and spinning, making the young horses snort and quiver with excitement, and even the old horses prick their ears at the sport ahead. Cody tried to keep his back relaxed and ride with the old horse under him as he worked the young animals. A smart cow horse could quickly dump a rider who resisted the motion and didn't pay attention.

They were collecting in a little meadow with pens and gates at each end. The old gelding Cody was riding had begun favoring his left front from time to time, so he was doing the sorting. "There's that cow had the scours so bad this summer." Cody pointed to the ribby Angus that ambled tiredly along, followed by a weak, stunted calf. "Pull her out. She'll ship. Just never got on her feet again, did she?"

Chris separated the cow and drove her away from the others.

"Let's take a look at her calf," Cody called, and watched as the other man roped the calf, got off his horse, tipped the animal over, and tied its legs together so they could examine it without either of them getting hurt. As Cody bent over the calf, he noticed the weepy eyes and snotty nose. Running his hand along the sides, he could feel the thinness of the meat covering the ribs and hips. There was no tag or brand because it had been born too late.

"Should've caught this one earlier, Chris. Ed musta been sleeping on the job. Get the penicillin outta my bag." Cody rubbed the rough hair on the calf's face and patted its bony shoulder. "Mama didn't help you much, did she?" The calf struggled briefly to get up, then collapsed again, its wide pink tongue lolling out.

Some ranchers would cull the herd of any sick calves, but Heywood had taught him that every animal meant dollars if you were just patient enough to do a little more doctoring and handling for the long run. They'd always kept a sick pasture near the ranch buildings, where they stuck convalescing and weak animals in the winter for extra feed and care. It wasn't much more money, and they figured the man-hours were there to be put into something, so it might as well be more work.

They finished with the calf, released it, and drove it into another pen where it immediately began to bawl for its mother. The old cow walked slowly to the shared fence, stared at the calf, then dropped her head to pull at the brown grass. "Probably weaned the thing herself a while ago when she was going downhill. Dried up," Cody remarked.

While other men rounded up more cattle, Cody, Chris, and two others sorted, injected, and branded late calves. Ed rode up and said, "Should put a squeeze chute up here." He was out of breath after his struggle with a yearling held over from the previous year which had kicked him in the belly while he gave it a shot. Cody wanted to remind the man that he was so slow on his feet it was no wonder he was always getting kicked and butted around, but instead he just nodded. By that time more than a hundred calves were bawling for their mothers in the shipping pen, and the mothers were answering with their own noise, though several of them dropped off pretty quickly, interested in eating again. They were already fat with next year's calves.

"Cows look pretty good after all the rain this summer." Ed lifted his hat, pushed his thinning hair back, and screwed the hat back down so it wouldn't fall off. "Piss-ant day."

"I counted ten lame cows, Ed. Plus that old one with the sick calf. What the hell have you been doing up here?" Cody nudged his horse to the fence where the cows milled and waited. "Ever hear of copper deficiency? Look over there at those calves in the sick pen. Ulcers ring a bell? Jesus Christ, you're supposed to be looking after these animals." The other man followed silently as they edged over to the sick pen. "This could've been avoided."

Ed kept his eyes on the ground, his face flushed.

"You're spending the winter with these calves, that's what's gonna happen. I hope the rest of them look better'n this." In disgust, Cody spun the old horse and spurred through the cattle crowding the pen. When the old gelding stumbled and hopped a couple of steps in his trot, Cody cursed and pulled up and jumped off. "Now what?" He lifted the left leg and looked at the hoof. The shoe had come off, tearing away some of the wall with it, leaving ragged holes from the nails. One nail still hung in the hoof, but when Cody tried to pull it out by hand, it wouldn't come. He put the foot down, went to his saddlebags, and pulled a pair of nippers out, then clipped the head of the nail and drew it through the hole. Usually, he'd just tack another shoe on, but the wall was pretty torn up, and the old horse had been limping anyway, so he decided to give it a rest and use Marcus instead.

By the time he was back in the saddle, the last of the cattle were being brought in, and Cody didn't have time to do more than let the colt walk around among the other animals stiff-legged and humpbacked before they started working. "If you throw me, you're gonna die," Cody muttered, and the animal twitched its ears back and forth as if it were actually considering the proposition. He'd have to pitch in or they'd be there all night.

Although he'd started roping off the colt a week ago, Cody uncoiled the rope with some hesitation. When the first loop came whirring overhead, Marcus tensed and locked his legs, flinging his nose up and rolling his eyes. "Easy," Cody murmured, grabbing the horn with his rein hand. "Come on, walk," he urged with a squeeze of his calves, but the horse stood in place and began to shake. "Oh, shit," Cody murmured again in a comforting tone. "Come on, you can do this." He let his wrist keep the rope in motion while he nudged the colt again.

Marcus was taking his first tentative step forward when a calf shot from the herd right in front of him, and a rope came snaking after, landed around its neck, and jerked it to a sprawl at the horse's feet. Cody just had time to drop the rope as the horse exploded, rising off the ground as if dynamite had been set off underneath it, and twisting and kicking out behind as it came down, burying its neck between its front legs and bucking in classic spine-jolting fashion. Cody was off so quickly, he didn't have time to do more than try not to land on his bad shoulder. As it was, he landed on top of the calf, and the two of them went rolling in a tangle of hooves and arms and legs and rope while the horse crow-hopped away and stopped to watch with the rest of the men and cattle. When all the commotion stopped, Cody was lying on the ground with the calf straddling him like a big dog, its eyes wild and a string of saliva connecting its mouth to his face below. The calf lifted its skinny stiff tail and squirted liquid green on his legs, then walked over him and trotted away, dragging the rope.

Cody sat up, wiped the spit off his face, and grimaced at his manure-coated chaps. "Calf revenge," he said, and got up. The men burst out laughing.

"Lucky he didn't have a branding iron, Cody." Will dismounted and turned to pick up the reins of the colt and lead it back. When the colt balked, the man tugged lightly and said, "Come on now, you caused enough trouble for one day." The horse sighed and followed as if it had done this job every day of its life.

Will stopped in front of Cody, who was getting up slowly, brushing at the wet sand and dirt on his clothes and hat, avoiding the manure splashes. "You should know better'n bring a youngster out on a day like this." He spoke quietly but firmly. "Hell, you haven't put near enough time on him yet. Laid up like you been. You look like hell too. Been drinking all night and come out here, you're gonna get someone hurt."

Cody nodded and stared at the ground as he adjusted his hat brim and crown.

"Enough of this mooning around. You need to work so damn hard you don't have time to think about women for a change. Take my horse. Long as you're dirty, might as well put your back in it and do some real work. I'll cull and train the youngster."

Cody nodded again and put his hat on while the old man handed over his reins.

Will always reminded him of Heywood, that same experience and authority Cody found humbling. He would do as he was told; that always worked out best when he got in trouble.

By early afternoon, the colt was letting Will rope calves and was beginning to get the idea of backing up to keep the line taut so the rider could work. He was taking naturally to cutting out the cattle too, keeping them separated from the others so they could be moved from one area to another. Cody had to admire how much better the colt worked for the old man.

Will rode up to where Cody was taking a break while the men finished with the last calf. "Ready to move 'em?" he asked, handing back the authority he'd stripped earlier.

Cody smiled. He didn't have to say thanks — the old man knew he meant it.

"Ed's getting lazier by the week," Will said and stared at the man who was trying to jerk the loop off the calf even though it was tangled around his legs and body. Cody looked at Will and pushed his hat back, so he could rub his forehead where the headache had settled. He was waiting for the old man's verdict.

"You could do better." Will tilted his head in the direction of Latta's cowboy. "That Chris, he's a good hand. Needs some educatin', of course, like some other ones I know." He looked out of the corner of his eye at Cody.

Cody blushed and grinned. "Yeah, well —"

"We're behind. Early winter too. Follows a wet summer sometimes. Birds been flocking early. Frogs gone into mud a week ago. They know what's coming. Better hire more help, get this cowboy carnival on the road." Will reached into his jacket pocket and pulled a tin of Skoal out, offering some to Cody, who took a small piece, then popped a large twist in his mouth. Both men chewed silently for a minute, turning their heads to opposite sides to spit the first juice. When they'd settled the wad comfortably along their molars, they spit again.

"Your daddy was always out here checking on these cattle, making sure a man was doing his job. He usually caught the copper thing when it first cropped up. And the scours. Before it hit four hundred head." Will spoke quietly, keeping his eyes on the hands who were closing the pens and stopping for a rest before they had to drive the separate herds.

Cody kept his eyes on the cattle he'd failed. He knew better than to say anything. There wasn't anything to say.

"Good prices this fall. That should help."

Cody knew he meant it should help make up for the mistakes the younger man had made. The politeness of the exchange was almost unbearable, but the silence that followed was worse.

"Ready? How you wanna do this?" Will finally turned to Cody for the first time and smiled to show he still liked the younger man.

"You think you should take the sick ones to the pen for us to pick up later? You got the colt — and those won't be giving you much trouble. Take Ed and another man. I'll take Chris with me, and two other men, and we'll take the calves and culls. Let the others move the cows to that pasture where the Loop comes through. Then we'll pick them up after we finish with the rest of Ed's, tomorrow or Monday. Okay?" Cody spit again, and decided to drop the tobacco as soon as Will was out of sight.

"You're the boss." Will smiled and spit a long stream, which made the colt sidestep. "Now don't go getting silly on me," he muttered. "This one might be a little *too* smart, Cody. Wouldn't trust him just yet. Course, I know you like 'em that way — women too, I guess." Will touched his hat brim and trotted away.

That was the trouble with these old guys, Cody thought. They had you sized up a hundred years before you were even born. They didn't mind letting you know it either. And they always walked away leaving you with your balls in your hand, trying to figure it out.

Chris cantered by, smiling. "Come on, cowboy." The gate at the other end of the pen was opened, spilling calves and culls down into the meadow. The younger animals bucked and trotted while the older cattle followed, walking with the same slow patience they had practiced for years. Things weren't going to happen any better if you just hurried up, their expressions seemed to say.

As they pushed the cattle through the little space between the hills into the next meadow, Cody thought about moving the bulls down into the front pasture for the winter. Fierce around the females, the bulls were as docile as steers when it was just them. He'd have to ask Will if they should keep the two oldest, who'd had trouble with some of the cows last spring. He'd had to move the cows to other bulls, and that didn't fit with the way Heywood had planned for lines that would produce a long, deep body with excellent meat and little fat. They were always jimmying the lines with their stock, trying to produce the perfect animal. In his day, Heywood had won several national championships with his bulls and cows, which had led buyers and breeders to seek out his stock. But it'd been five years since a Bennett animal had even appeared at one of the stock shows. Cody wondered if it made a difference; maybe he'd ask Arthur about that.

The three pheasants took off almost simultaneously with the booming of the guns. There was a single moment when the entire scene seemed frozen, as if time had ceased, captured finally and held, then everything let out a breath and the cattle exploded in all directions. The guns boomed again, making sure that any animals that had hesitated were going for sure now. The calves ran with their tails up; the older cattle lumbered stiff-legged after them. The horses danced in place, wanting to run with the emotion of cattle, but were held back by their riders. Cody's old horse stood his ground, bored by the scene, which resembled a sack of marbles emptied on a hill.

Another set of booms put Cody into action as cattle disappeared over the surrounding hills. Spurring in the direction of the shots, he yelled as he came so he wouldn't get shot. "You dumb bastards." He pulled up beside the three men in orange and green. "Get the fuck off our land." Two of the men lowered their guns so the barrels hung toward the ground. The third, a husky, red-faced man in his early sixties, kept his waist-high.

"This is state land, Jack," the man said coldly, as if he were used to giving orders and dealing with morons.

"Listen, cocksucker, you just wasted a whole day's work for us, and this is *not* state land, this is private Bennett land. You had to climb the goddamned wire to get here, so get the fuck off."

"Listen cowboy, you better back off. Your boss gave us permission. We just thought we were still on state land — now *you* get the fuck out of here." The red-faced man waved his shotgun toward him while the other two men looked around uncomfortably.

Cody rested his forearms on the saddle horn and leaned forward. He was getting really pissed about the gun in the other man's arms. He slipped his feet out of the stirrups.

"I *am* the boss, *Jack,* and I've never seen you before in my life." He was getting ready to kick the shotgun out of the man's hands. Then he'd kick the shit out of the man. Chris and the other two hands walked their horses toward the little group now, and the other two hunters watched them warily.

"Arthur Bennett owns this ranch, and you're not him." The man jiggled the barrel as if to make his point.

"I'm Cody Kidwell, his brother. Now get the fuck outta here." Chris edged quietly up to the men on the other side and watched them impassively, his rope dangling from relaxed fingers.

The man gave a short laugh and nodded, finally letting the gun tip toward the ground. "Yeah, he said I might run into you. Told me to 'tell Cody to mind his cows and leave you alone.'" The man glanced at his companions for the first time, and they grinned nervously.

Cody sat up and pulled back on the reins so the horse raised its head and opened its mouth, then backed up a few steps. He wanted to kill someone, but he wasn't sure who, the men or his brother. He could ride right over their fat asses, all of them. "Where're you from? Omaha? Denver?"

The husky man let the shotgun droop from his elbow, pulled out a cigarette, and lit it with a small gold lighter. Blowing smoke toward Cody, he smiled and said, "Twin Cities. We're from Holiday Ranches. Your brother's been working with us on a project." The man swept his hand across the meadow and hills, smearing them with a trail of cigarette smoke.

Cody took a deep breath. The day's work was in the toilet; they'd have to start all over, rounding up the cattle, which would be spooky now. It'd be dark by the time they got them to the pens, if they managed to get them that far to begin with. "Fuck you anyway. Get off my land." He pushed his horse forward so quickly the men didn't have time to raise their guns. Chris started doing the same thing, crowding the men, who had to step backwards. Behind them, the other two cowboys rode to join them.

"What, are you crazy?" The spokesman dropped his cigarette and his red face paled as he stumbled backwards again.

Cody didn't speak, simply pressed his horse forward until the three men turned and began to climb the hill they'd come over, struggling with the sandy footing, wet grass, and their guns. Just before the top of the hill, the hunters turned and the husky man shouted, "Fuck you, Jack. Your brother's gonna hear about this — dumb little shit."

"Fine," Cody yelled, and gave them the finger. When the hunters crested the hill and disappeared over the other side, Cody felt a vague disappointment that things hadn't gotten totally out of hand.

When he turned, the cowboys were clumped a few yards away, downcast at the prospect of having to repeat their day's work for nothing. Cody stopped in front of the men and waited, letting his heart calm down, his breathing relax. His body felt a little trembly from the adrenaline rush. He looked at the sky, which threatened to dump more rain or snow on them.

"What time is it? Anybody got a watch?" he asked.

Chris pushed back his jacket sleeve and said, "Three-thirty."

The men were watching Cody intently now. He shook his head and tightened his lips. "Fuck it. Let's go on back. Finish this tomorrow. Have to give the weaned calves time to settle down and learn to eat before they ship next week, so we don't have a choice. Sorry."

As they rode back to their trucks, the disappointment of wasted work seemed to emphasize every ache and chill in their bodies. The men hunched against the cold misty rain that began falling, each one thinking about how much easier it'd be to find a regular job, one that didn't leave you with a tired butt, empty stomach, wet clothes, bruises, rope burns, cuts, and broken bones.

ANNUAL REFUGE BISON / LONGHORN SALE
OCTOBER 2

Valentine — Around 80 head of Plains bison originally from
Nebraska and 120 Texas Longhorns will be sold Oct. 2 at
the Fort Niobrara Wildlife Refuge Complex.
    The sale begins at noon at the refuge corrals.

— *MIDLAND NEWS*

So what was that Hollywood bullshit out there? I can't even
invite guests now without you going off half cocked?"
Arthur tucked his white shirt into the waistband of his tan
gabardine pants and hooked the silver buckle, with his initials
in raised gold tones, on his hand-tooled belt. He hated dressing
up like a cowboy.

"They spooked the cattle, Arthur." Cody was sprawled on
the leather sofa, one long leg hung over the back, the other
resting on the floor. This was the first direct conversation
they'd had since the night of the storm, and it was going as
badly as ever.

"You weren't doing your job, then. Heywood always invited
his friends out here to hunt. There wasn't a problem before."
Arthur put the bolo tie over his head, moved the turquoise
slide up to his collar, and checked himself in the mirror over
the reception table, then slid it halfway down, then up again.

Cody drained the bottle of beer and set the empty down on the rug, letting it slip from his long fingers. "Heywood would've kept them away from our cattle, Arthur. Who were those assholes anyway?" He'd dropped his stained chaps in the mudroom to be cleaned later, but his muddy boots were leaving dirt everywhere he walked. Arthur eyed them and shook his head; cowboy boots killed his achilles tendons. He'd be limping around like an old man for two days after spending the night in his.

"Just some people I met." He looked at his nails critically, pushing the cuticles back. "They'll be out again tomorrow. Why don't you leave them alone this time."

Cody folded his arms over his chest. "We're shipping in a week, and I have to collect those calves again."

"You're not John Wayne."

"Keep 'em out of Stannek's, then." Cody closed his eyes.

"That's where the birds are."

"Birds are everywhere, Arthur. Next time I *will* ride over 'em, they scare my cattle."

"You're an asshole. Just stay out of their way. And be back here in the afternoon to help out; we're having a little rodeo. It's all set. You just show up and work the chutes or pass out the beer."

"Great," Cody mumbled as he settled more deeply into the sofa.

Arthur noticed his brother's chest slowly rising and falling, the mouth going slack as he drifted off to sleep. He'd have to get someone to take the men hunting in another section. Cody was just dumb enough to ruin everything. The rodeo should do the trick. He'd invited all the potential investors to meet with the Holiday people. He'd have his deal by Monday morning, he figured. It was a good one too: he'd end up owning part of their company if things fell apart in a couple of years, and they'd get nothing from the Bennetts.

If only his brother would stay out of things and his sister

wouldn't cause so much trouble. He'd just go to town, pick up the men at their motel, and take them to the house where old man Vullet and John Long were fixing the dinner he'd planned. Maybe, just maybe, with the old man helping, John would manage not to ruin the food. It was a gamble, but the other options were equally risky. At least in his own house, he could get them drunk on good scotch at a reasonable price so they might not notice the food. Then later, he'd take them out dancing so they could see the kind of people who lived here in the hills. Local color, they loved that stuff. That was the whole point. Holiday Ranches: eighteen-hole golf courses, water-skiing, trail rides and cowboys and rodeos, hear the lonesome cattle low — he smiled and walked out the back door.

Cody was dreaming about his father again. The old man was walking around in his pajamas, just like before he died, but he didn't seem angry about anything. In his dream, Cody asked if he was mad at him for stopping the medications. Heywood shook his head and said no, he was ready to die. A feeling of enormous relief washed over Cody, and in his sleep he began to weep. The tears wetting his face woke him.

He was alone in the house and it felt good. What did people do alone in houses at night, he wondered. There was the TV, but he never got the habit. The TV had always been Caroline's domain, and he'd learned not to sit with her. He was too tired to read. He couldn't even imagine getting up for another beer. He half smiled. He was too tired to drink. The image of the girl from last night appeared so fully, completely in his mind, he didn't have time to shut it off. He closed his eyes and covered his mouth with his fingertips. That seemed so stupid — sleeping with her when he loved someone else. He twisted on the sofa, drawing his legs together and rolling to his side.

Maybe his mother had been right: he was evil. When he shot John Axel, she'd pushed Cody away from her, taken the gun, and slapped his face so hard the imprint of her fingers raised red welts that turned black and blue. He'd tried telling her it was a mistake, an accident, but she'd stared at him in a way that made him understand that there just wasn't such a thing. He'd come to understand his own nature over the next years — a person who did wrong, especially when he was angry. A person who must watch his every step, keep on guard against himself. The only time he could let down was when he drank. And that was starting to be when the worst things happened.

A thump and the whirring sound of something rolling across the kitchen floor made him spring from the sofa. He paused. He was alone here. The hands had all gone to town, including Will and his wife. He wasn't used to being spooked. Walking silently across the carpet, he pushed the swinging door open enough so he could peek into the kitchen without being seen.

Joseph Starr was opening a can of soup on the counter next to the stove, and without turning said, "Hungry? I'll open another one."

Cody pushed the door open, letting it slap against the wall, went to the round table in the middle of the room, and sat down. Joseph was covered with burrs and mud and grass, as if he'd just crawled out of a burrow. His homemade clothes hung damply off his thin frame. His hair was braided neatly, but was also tagged with bits of grass and burrs.

"What the hell happened to you?" Cody asked, tilting the chair back and putting his feet on the table.

"Went underground." Joseph dumped the contents of the can into a pan and started opening the second can. "Tomato okay?" He finished circling the top, pulled the lid up, and emptied it into the pan also.

"Yeah, as long as you use milk, not water."

Joseph opened the refrigerator and pulled out a loaf of bread and a block of cheddar cheese which he tossed to Cody, who caught them with a surprised grunt. "Butter?" Cody said, and was ready for the foil-wrapped stick that followed. Joseph set the gallon of milk on the counter and closed the door.

"Grilled cheese, right?" Cody asked. "Got a knife there? Second drawer to your right."

The two men looked at each other and grinned when Joseph picked up the paring knife. He flipped it to the table so it slid into the loaf of bread.

"Thought about you today," Cody remarked, cutting cheese slices and arranging them on the bread in a precise mosaic. "Snow over there?"

"Little. I wasn't paying attention. Been pretty busy." Joseph turned on the heat under the pan, then turned the oven on to broil and pulled out the broiler pan so he could adjust the rack closer to the top. "I'm gonna leave the oven door open till we're ready — didn't realize I got so cold." He squatted down and held his hands in the oven, rubbing them together.

Cody wiped the last of the butter off the knife onto the bread and stood up. "Want me to make you some coffee?"

"Tea. Stir that soup too." He closed his eyes to the waves of heat pulsing from the oven's red coils.

"Want a blanket?" Cody asked his friend, who was resting on the floor, his back against the counters, legs straight out, eyes closed in the red flush of heat on his face. Joseph nodded and Cody went to get him the red plaid throw off the end of the sofa.

Joseph finished the food and sipped at his tea, which had brewed so long it was too dark and bitter. "I knocked, but you were asleep. All the vehicles but yours were gone. Where's your sister these days?"

Cody shrugged and wiped the soup bowl with the last wedge of sandwich and popped it in his mouth. Then he leaned back and picked up his tea mug. He wanted to tell Joseph about Latta and everything, but he didn't know how to begin. He was careful to keep his eyes off the other man, out of politeness but also fear that, as usual, Joseph would see what he'd done, could read it as if he were a piece of printed paper. Joseph had always had that knack, like Caroline had.

"I'm going home for a while," Joseph remarked. "Really need to see Kya before I go, though."

"Home?"

"Rosebud — my cousin's place. My trailer's there."

"You need a place to winter, you're welcome to stay here. Or Latta would —"

Joseph shook his head. "I was sitting out there, that church above me on the hill, crows complaining at me, ancestor voices from inside the hill complaining at me. So much noise, I couldn't think. Decided to go underneath and see what they wanted. Same old complaints. I'm going back to the res for a while. My cousin's. He's political, but he leaves me alone."

Cody hesitated, then asked, "You get your vision?" He was thinking of Heywood's occasional visits.

"Maybe. It's not always like that."

Cody wasn't sure what he believed about visions and religion. It seemed okay for some people. He wasn't like the white people he knew who just laughed at it all, or like others who thought it was all the gospel truth.

"Some days all I saw were car commercials in my head: 'I love what you do for me,' 'The heartbeat of America.' Especially the times Kya came to sweat. Other times, it was other stuff. Have to sort it all out. True dreams and false ones." He smiled and sipped the tea, closing his eyes as the steam rose on his face. "Takes a while. Not like in those movies where you come out of the sweat, grab your tomahawk, and jump on your horse." He paused again and got serious, setting the cup down. "I know one man, thought he got the vision he was supposed to be a medicine man. He did it, but he wasn't any good. Didn't care about the job. Just went through the motions. Nobody ever got helped. He should've waited. Maybe paid more attention to the car commercials. Or Kya."

It took a moment for Cody to laugh. "So Kya was around?"
The older man nodded.

In the silence that followed, Cody gathered his courage. "Seen Latta?" he asked finally.

The other man nodded again.

He's gonna make me work for it, Cody thought. "She say anything?" He found his fists tightening in his lap, his muscles stiffening in his back. He rolled his neck and raised one shoulder, then the other to relieve the tension. Come on, he silently urged.

Joseph shrugged.

"I didn't do anything," Cody protested.

"Inez says you did." Joseph caught his eyes and held them in a flat hard stare like a snake's, unblinking.

"What? What did she say? I didn't do anything." His voice softened as he thought back. Had he? Had he done something — something else he shouldn't have? He'd loved her, then Arthur —

"Said you dumped her, wronged her." Joseph unlocked his eyes and looked at the nearly empty cup, his voice dry and flat as if he were tasting something he'd have to swallow although his first inclination was to spit it right back out.

Cody felt a tremendous rush like a granite slab falling through him, taking everything with it as it plunged. "I what? I *wronged* Latta? Arthur got into it — now she won't see me."

"It's what Inez says. I didn't think it sounded right, but you know women."

"It was Arthur. He took the note I left her explaining how I'd be gone, then he screwed her head up. Told her it was me took her horse." Cody stood up and began pacing the floor. "While I was out trying to find the damn thing."

"What'd you do about it?"

Cody stopped. "Me? I tried to kill the son of a bitch, but Kya stopped me. I don't know . . ." He rubbed a hand through his hair. "I tried to call her. I even went over there, but Inez —"

"Thinks you used her and dumped her, stole her horse too." Joseph's saying it again made him feel stripped, flattened, as if the granite slab had crushed him.

"I didn't mean to hurt Latta," he pleaded. "Arthur sent me on a wild goose chase after Kya. I was just trying to take care of my sister and get the horse back, that's all." He sat down again.

"You keep letting those two turn you around."

"Sort of."

The silence answered him.

"What can I do? Kill him?" Actually that answer seemed so simple, he was surprised he'd discarded it so quickly the other night.

"Can't ignore wrongs. They taint all of us, don't they?"

Cody thought back to how easily convinced he was by Arthur that he should go after Kya, leaving Latta to him that day. What kind of a man did that make him? Then that girl last night, as if the one thing caused another, and another. Now there'd be an endless string of wrong turns, like Caroline had predicted when she threw him out of her house that day fifteen years ago. Evil.

"You're saying I should kill my brother."

Joseph shrugged. "Probably not the best idea. Have to figure out something. In the old days, there'd be punishment, goods to be given in payment, but now" — he shrugged again — "someone has to care when bad things happen. Can't wait for them to go away, out of your life. They don't."

Cody nodded. He was responsible for Latta. He'd made a public statement of being with her and then disappeared for seven days without calling. He'd let his brother have the opening he needed to hurt them both. It hadn't taken much either; he knew how scared Latta was of love. He felt a terrible shame. As if his life, all his assumptions about what was real and not, had suddenly reversed, and he had no idea how he could even go on living, let alone how he would get up, put his hand on a doorknob, and turn it, feeling safe in the knowledge of what lay on the other side.

"I should go see her." Cody stood up.

"See Inez tomorrow. You have to start at the beginning and unravel it slowly."

Cody sat down heavily, sprawling in the chair, stretching his legs across the floor. "It won't do any good." He shook his head. No, there wasn't any way to untangle the knots of family and public wrong. Not without creating more knots in the same places.

Joseph stood up, looking tired.

"You can sleep in my room, bed's got sheets and blankets," Cody offered, knowing he'd be up most of the night thinking. "Kya might show up. Arthur's having a rodeo tomorrow, and she's in and out with that friend of hers, Greta, like a shadow. What do you want with her, anyway?"

"Just something I saw reminded me of her. She came by on and off, asking questions. There's something I thought of that might help her," Joseph said, walking to the kitchen door. "See you in the morning."

Cody waved, staring at the floor. Latta's name came alive in his stomach, made him nauseous. Getting up, he went to the cabinet over the sink where John kept the extra bottles of liquor. Sitting back down with the Jack Daniel's and a glass, he poured some and drank. He was so tired, he couldn't resist the fizzle and flood of relief that it brought, and poured another.

Tomorrow, he promised himself after a few more, tomorrow or the next day at the latest, he'd go and find her, bring her back, marry her. That was it. He'd marry Latta.

19 ✧ A BRIEF HISTORY OF DANCING

Cody wanted to tell Joseph he was acting like an old fool, but Will was helping him buckle on his rodeo chaps and limbering up his rope for him. First Joseph had to try the calf roping, then he was going to get on a saddle bronc, and maybe even a bull. Cody'd suggested the team roping, but Joseph had ignored him.

"Joseph, Joseph, Joseph." The chant rose out of the noise of animals and the crowd. It was Kya, who was making him think he was young enough for this. She sat in the bleachers with Greta, who had barely escaped her father's bullying in the kitchen. When Cody'd come in at noon from working cattle, Kya and Joseph looked up from the breakfast they were sharing from one plate. They wore silly smiles and she was wearing Joseph's eagle claw necklace. Later they gave each other back rubs while Greta and Cody watched. They must've done more than one kind of sweating on the Dismal River last summer, Cody'd decided, not sure how he felt about it.

Aubrey Foster came over, slapped his tender shoulder, and said, "You riding?"

Cody shrugged. "Shoulder's still not right."

"Never stopped you before — you getting old on me?" Aubrey grinned, his pink freckled skin and red stubbled chin blending to give the impression of a pale, oblong pumpkin.

Cody lifted his hat, pushed back his hair, tucked the strands behind his ears, and set it firmly on his head, tugging it into place as he would if he were getting ready to nod the chute open on a bucking horse. "What, you riding?"

"Horses maybe." He shook his head and spit to one side. "Bulls are for younger fellas. Figured it made more sense to run myself over with my pickup than ride them critters. I'll live to a hundred if I stay off them bulls." He spit a brown stream to the side. "You look at them things? S'posed to be resting up for the winter southern circuit, but they don't look a bit tired to me." As if to confirm his words, a meaty shoulder hit the six-foot-high fence, and one of the two-foot-wide posts cracked ominously behind them.

The two men stepped toward the fence and hollered, waving their arms and kicking at the bull to back off.

"See what you mean," Cody said, inspecting the boards and posts to make sure the fence wasn't damaged as the bulls churned again in their small corral.

"Look at that one with the twisted horn, crazy fucker, see his eye?" Aubrey pointed toward one particularly massive black bull who kept pushing his way through the others.

"Yeah, looks like he'd just as soon dump and stick you as eat."

"Look at that loose hide. Like trying to ride a lard-coated barrel. Need some good life insurance for that one."

"Yeah." Cody wasn't paying attention. Arthur was heading in their direction with the three men Cody had encountered in the hills trailing behind. They were dressed straight out of Mustang Western Wear in new stiff jeans, shiny boots, bright shirts with the store creases still in them, bolo ties with ridiculously large slides, and pale grey hats that must have cost them a hundred fifty apiece. They were stepping gingerly around the horse apples strewn on the ground.

Aubrey followed Cody's gaze and spit into the path the men were taking toward them. Arthur Bennett wasn't one of his favorite people. "Look at the catalogue boys. Mustang's musta had a great day." He spit slightly to the side of the first place, trying to draw a wet line across the path.

"Cody." Arthur stopped in front of the two men. A smile tightened his lips as if he were bursting with goodwill, but his flat eyes warned his brother not to mess around. "Aubrey." He nodded at the cowboy, then shifted to let the three men step forward. "This is my half-brother, Cody Kidwell. I think you met yesterday." Arthur paused and glanced at Cody's face, then turned back to the men. "He's got a mean mouth when he's hung over. You caught him on a bad morning, I'm afraid." The three men laughed easily and Cody folded his arms across his chest to keep from hitting someone. "Cody, this is Sid Greenway, Bob Roth, and Marty Castle, from Minneapolis."

None of the men offered their hands, and Marty, the smallest, said, "St. Paul. We're from St. Paul. There really is a difference between the two cities." Sid Greenway glanced at him coldly and the man shut up.

"And this is Aubrey Foster, one of our local cowboys. Does a little ranching on his own too." The men nodded at Aubrey as if he were a local landmark to be noted, but not remembered.

"Who's the chief in the braids?" Bob Roth asked, pointing to Joseph, who was doing knee bends to loosen his joints and stretch the chaps so they didn't feel like they were binding when he jumped off the horse to throw the calf.

"Joseph Starr. Works for us ranchers on and off. You know,

Indian time. Colorful guy. Vietnam vet. Studied to be a medicine man or something like his grandfather, but gave it up when the war came along. Not a bad hand, just a little unreliable when he's on the sauce. A lot of 'em have that problem. Haven't seen him in a while. When did he show up, Cody?" Arthur asked.

Cody ignored Arthur's question. "You offering prizes today?" he asked his brother, knowing Arthur would want to be the big man in front of his business associates.

"Yeah." He looked into the distance seeming to study something, and Aubrey let a stream of tobacco juice land in the sandy dirt between them. The three men held their ground, but their eyes fixed on the darkening splotches that had almost spattered their shiny new boot toes.

"What?" Cody asked, smiling now because he knew he had Arthur, who was famous for his cheapness.

"Buckboard steak dinners, groceries from the Absalom, free movie tickets, and gift certificates from Simon's Hardware and Mustang's." Arthur smiled smugly, folding his arms and throwing his shoulders back.

Cody laughed and shook his head. His brother was something else. Hadn't laid out a penny of his own money. Worked fast too, got all this organized in one evening. Was that possible? No, he had to have been planning for a couple of weeks at least. The realization made him angry.

"Nice of you to include the town," Cody said. "No wonder there's so many people here." He bet Arthur hadn't paid a dime for the barbecue meat either, and Emil Vullet was cooking for free.

"Just wanted to show these folks what a real sandhills welcome is like," Arthur said. "We play hard and work hard. Traditional American values. Backbone of our country, right?" He looked at the three men beside him, who nodded.

Cody noticed that Sid Greenway was the least inclined to this bullshit. His small blue eyes were narrowed, watching him as if to say their business still wasn't finished. Cody stared back, to let him know they could settle it anytime. Aubrey spit again, almost completing the dark line separating the men.

Cody was sitting on his horse watching the roping when Latta's maroon and silver pickup with the fancy gooseneck to match pulled up. As he turned his horse and walked closer so he could see who stepped out of the truck, the sheriff's car pulled up and parked beside Latta's rig. The doors of the truck opened for Chris's brothers and Latta's familiar dark chestnut curls. As the men drifted toward the arena and the other cowboys, Latta looked around uncertainly, shading her eyes with a hand. Cody felt her catch sight of him.

He didn't know whether to walk over to her and have it out or wait. He didn't want to crowd. Maybe she didn't care. Maybe he'd screwed it up too badly. At least Inez wasn't there to yell at him again.

He remembered the girl two nights ago, and the lost horse, and a spasm of pain split his face under his left eye. He'd been getting that ever since the beating Burch had given him, whenever he was nervous or tired, or when the weather changed. The fight with Arthur hadn't helped either. He didn't have any right to talk to Latta now. He'd still failed to get the stallion back, hadn't even questioned Kya a while ago in the kitchen.

He turned his horse and walked around the back end of the arena where Joseph was still listening for the calf-roping results. When he was announced in second place, he grunted and smiled. "Not bad for an old Indian," he said as Cody stopped beside him. "Saddle bronc next." His voice was neutral, as if riding with the younger men was the normal course of affairs.

Cody's whole body was stiff with the feeling of Latta close by, and his throat was so tight he was afraid to speak, but he had to shake it off. "How long has it been since you rode bucking horses, Joseph? You think this is a good idea?" He was annoyed with him, almost as much as he was with Latta for coming here.

"Joseph, ride 'em cowboy!" Kya could be heard hollering and laughing. The other cowboys looked at the Indian and smiled. Cody wondered if he was going to have to take all of them on.

"Good day to die," Joseph said, nudging his horse against Cody's, squeezing the younger man's leg between the two animals.

"Watch it. Good day for *you* to die, maybe, but don't include me." Cody moved his horse a few steps to the side.

"You should ride too. It's a good day. I can feel it." Joseph tapped his chest, grinning broadly.

"Don't give me this Indian crap. My sister's making you act like an asshole."

"A little harsh, my friend. You shouldn't judge what you don't know anything about. I can beat you at bucking horses. Always have, always will. You're just not as good as you think you are. Don't have the concentration yet. Still too young." Joseph wasn't smiling anymore, just leaning his forearm on the saddle horn and watching the men get the saddles ready for the bucking horses.

Out of the corner of his eye, Cody saw Latta standing with Arthur and the three yahoos from Minneapolis, whose clothes glittered in the sunlight. One of them took her elbow and the sheriff joined them. "Fuck it. You're on. Bet?"

"A horse."

"You don't have a horse." Cody lifted the reins and drew them back while he nudged the horse, who stepped back in response.

"The bet is a horse, whoever beats the other — in points — that's the bet. My problem where I get it."

Cody nodded. "I'll see you at the funeral."

"*Yahta —*"

Cody waved him off and went to get his equipment. Maybe

it was a good thing that he was riding — kept his mind off Latta, he decided as he loped to the house.

"Come on, you cowboys." O. K. Luther, from Liquor 'n' Lunch, began the spiel that would last till the end of the rodeo. "We got the old guys lining up here to beat the boots off you young-uns. Joseph Starr, Ash Blake from Gospel Cowboys just signed up, and Colin Young. These boys were rodeoing before any of you were born. Their hide's so tough we could shoe horses with it. Colin says his boys are gonna do chores for the winter if he beats 'em, and it's gonna cost Cody Kidwell his best horse if Joseph outrides him. You know, folks, I was down at the Old Timers' Rodeo in Hyannis a while ago, and I saw some rough stock there, bucking the tar off the roofs, couldn't get these old boys loose. Rode 'em to a standstill, some of 'em. Course, they knew if they went off, they'd break every bone in their bodies. So they got a lot of incentive. Who else is gonna go here in the saddle bronc? We got the senior men versus the junior. Dallas, you gonna ride? Come on, show that boy of yours what you can do. Nope, Dallas doesn't want to em- barrass his son, figures it'd be unfair advantage. Oh, no, here he comes, okayyy, Dallas is gonna ride too. Put up a crisp little old twenty-dollar bill against anyone wants to take his bet too. What about it, rodeo cowboys, think you're tough enough?"

Cody slipped in and out of the mudroom without being detected by the little group congregating in the living room. He could hear his brother's voice and the slower, stubborn one of the sheriff. Latta he couldn't hear at all. Kya was flirting with the three stooges in the yard, dipping her fingers into the barbecue sauce and licking them, offering some to the big- mouth prick he'd had the run-in with yesterday. That girl had an education coming. And Joseph had seen enough to know better. He'd been around for most of Kya's crap; it didn't make sense that he'd fall for it now.

As he sorted through his old gear for his gloves and bucking strap, he wanted to peek around the corner of the kitchen, catch a glimpse of Latta, make sure she was okay, but he didn't want to get into it with the sheriff. That goddamned horse again. When hadn't it been for the past six months? Probably end up killing one of them. It'd almost been him, still could be. He slipped out the back door.

More trucks and cars were pulling in, and the bleachers filled as O. K. Luther continued his spiel on the microphone. The Sykes boys were lacing strings around the wrists of their bucking gloves when Cody stepped down from his horse in back of the chutes. Standing with the three of them, Cody could smell the recent booze, but they seemed fairly sober. At least they were standing on both feet without swaying, and their wrist wraps looked pretty straight and even.

"Hey Cody, where's this stock from?" Curt asked, reaching behind him to stretch his shoulders and arms, then over his head.

"Tousley. Says he's giving 'em a rest." Cody turned his arms slowly in circles to loosen his shoulders. Every rotation, he could hear the pop and grind from the break. He just hoped he didn't break it again.

A horse squealed and kicked the boards in the first chute, and tried to rear up and lock its front legs over the top board. Men scattered and hollered, waving their arms from above.

"More like giving 'em a tune-up." Curt grunted, doing his knee bends and then squatting to slowly send one leg, then the other out in front of him.

Cody could remember when Curt was so limber he could leap straight up in the air from that squat, come down bouncing, and kick out like a place kicker. Now he was huffing and puffing, red in the face, having to hold on to the side of the fence to keep from toppling. He hadn't ballooned like Ty was starting to, but he'd lost some of his coordination. It could get bloody out there, Cody realized as his eyes caught Ty and Haney Sykes furtively nipping from a pint of Cabin Still. He hated to see that; shouldn't drink and ride.

"Thought you gave this up." Aubrey grinned at him and rolled his eyes in the direction of the Sykes boys. "Not using liquid courage, are you?"

Cody smiled and said no.

"Need anything?" Aubrey asked Cody, who shook his head. "You got number five. Real sweet-tempered horse." He nodded toward a big heavy buckskin mare who was being driven up the alley into her chute, kicking out and stopping to lunge and bite at the men leaning over the top boards. "Pleasant animal. Just don't get bucked off — she looks hungry. Asked one of Tousley's crew about her, said they used to run her in the bull riding."

Cody grinned and shook his head. "Thanks."

"Say, you get that lady fortuneteller to talk to you yet?" Aubrey pointed toward the stands, where Rosalie Crater was talking to a small circle of women.

"Nope." Cody bent down to make sure his spurs were resting in the right place, refastened the buckles, and stood up.

Aubrey was still watching the stands. "I been thinking about it. Heard she could tell your future real good. I just wanna know if I'm ever gonna get laid again." He grinned and clapped Cody on his sore shoulder. "You probably want to ask her something else. That little girl put out pretty good the other night at Clark's? I been thinking 'bout —"

"Don't," Cody said.

Aubrey held up both hands and took a half step back. "Okay, relax."

"I'm getting married." The words slid out so quickly, Cody didn't have time to consider the wisdom of his announcement.

Aubrey widened his eyes in surprise, opened his mouth to say something, shut it, then opened it again. "Sure you wanna do that? I mean, I thought —"

"Don't talk it around." Cody tugged his hat down hard over his ears in preparation for the ride. "Haven't exactly told her yet."

Aubrey laughed. "Typical Cody Kidwell. What if she says no?"

Cody looked at him in surprise, then shrugged.

"Think you better see that fortuneteller with me, Cody."

"I gotta ride. See if Joseph needs anything, will ya?" He nodded in the direction of the older man, who was trying to fasten a stubborn buckle on his spur, and walked away toward the chute.

"Okay, rodeo fans," O. K. Luther announced, "here comes the first horse in chute one. Tousley tells me he just picked this gelding up from a little old lady in Iowa, only drove him on Sundays to church — till he killed the preacher. Now he could pull Christ off the cross. Ladies and gentlemen, a horse called Saddam Hussein, with Ash Blake riding, one of our old-timers, sixty-five years young today."

There was a loud clatter as the chute opened and the horse fought to get out, then cheers as the horse spun and bucked, sending the rider spilling out behind it. Ash landed on his butt and was slow to get up, rubbing the small of his back and hopping as he walked back to the chutes. One of the other cowboys retrieved his hat, dusted it off, and handed it to him.

"Well, it's horses one and riders none, folks, but let's give a big round of applause to the old cowboy for a good try. He'll need it tonight." Ash grinned and put his hat on, climbing the chute to help load the next rider on his bronc.

Chris Young rode a hard bucker to the whistle and did a flying dismount into the dirt, pulling a good score of 80 the others had to chase. Two more cowboys got bucked off, and Tousley was grinning from the judging booth at the quality of his new stock.

Cody braced himself on the boards above the saddle while the man behind him tightened the bucking strap and two men in front held ropes on the mare's head so she couldn't turn and get a bite of either one. She grabbed the top board in her teeth and shook it, her eyes rolling wildly.

"Ready?" Aubrey asked, and Cody lowered himself into the saddle, wrapping the rein once around his hand, checking the rein length again, and positioning himself so when the chute opened he'd have the spurs in her shoulders.

"Ready?" the gate man asked. Cody nodded and the mare exploded into the arena.

Each jolt sent his spine through the top of his head as he tried to keep to the rhythm — jump, kick, spur, jump, kick, spur — the bucks threatening to send him too tall in the saddle, then up and out. He fought to keep his toes turned out, spurring along her shoulders. His feet kept wanting to drop back, his legs swing out, and he had to struggle to keep himself in position as she twisted to the left, away from his hand, and he tilted. Where the hell was the whistle? The next buck kicked him loose and he was starting to go as the whistle blew. Land left, land left, he told himself, ignoring the mare, who tried to kick him in the head as she unloaded him and plunged past.

The wind left his lungs when he thunked on his back. He fought the panic and rolled to his good side. His shoulders were fine. He concentrated on that, and took shallow breaths until he could take a big one again. Slowly standing, he picked up his hat and walked back to the chutes, only then becoming aware of the announcer's voice.

"Good ride, scored seventy-eight, second behind Chris Young. But we still got a lot to go here today. Some good old-timers too, used to ride the fur off a buffalo when they had to. We'll see if they still can."

"Let's see, our last cowboy just made the whistle. We'll see if our next contestant, Ty Sykes, can beat him. Sykes boys used to win big on the high school rodeo circuit, if you remember. Went to the nationals a couple a times too. Tousley tells me this is another young horse, outta Minnesota — don't hear of many from there. Says this horse shows real talent, could be a top one. And nobody's rode him yet. Here's Ty Sykes on Kickstart. Uh-oh, this boy's in trouble. Hat goes flying, cowboy usually follows. See there, bucking rein's too short, he's hitting the dashboard, up and out, over the head."

The ring went silent as Ty lay too still, while the pickup men cornered the bronc, unhooked the bucking strap, and picked up the rope to lead the horse back to the corral. Everyone waited a minute to give the cowboy a chance to get up on his own, then his brothers ran out to check on him. By the time three others joined, including Sharon, the registered nurse, Ty was smiling happily, snoring away, each exhalation loaded with the smell of liquor. "He's drunk, is all." O. K. Luther said. Haney Sykes giggled and lifted one arm, Curt the other, and the two brothers dragged Ty away to sleep it off.

"Drinking and driving, folks, just say no." A round of relieved laughter followed O. K. Luther's joke. Everyone knew where the Sykes boys spent their days. "Now we have another old-timer, says he's fifty years young, straight off the res to give these cowboys a taste of good old Indian medicine, Joseph Starr. He'll be riding one of the top horses in Tousley's string, one of the top horses in the country last year. In fact, only two people rode him all of last year, and they wished they hadn't. They're just getting around without crutches now. Here's Joseph Starr on Black Magic."

The horse and rider burst from the chute in a spin of color, legs, and arms. "This is a good ride, good spurring stroke, he's sitting tight, this horse can duck too, notice those quick turns left then right, that's how he gets rid of most of them, but this old Indian is riding him, yes, there's the whistle, he's waiting for the pickup man, there they go, good ride. Very good ride. Eighty-three points. Puts him in first place. Now these youngsters got something to shoot for."

Cody and Joseph stayed away from each other while they waited, and helped the other men with their horses. Curt Sykes was the last to go. Haney, who'd been bucked off and stomped on a little, was sleeping it off with Ty.

Curt's horse turned out to be the wildest bucker of the

saddle broncs, spinning and twisting, then jumping and kicking in classic style. Curt, sober for the first time in months, found the rhythm and rode the horse as if he were six years younger, keeping his position, his right hand held high, watching the body of the horse for direction, spurring in long sweeps without letting his legs fly out. When the whistle blew, he wasn't even aware of it, he was so far into the world of their bodies whirling and leaping, and it took the pickup men riding up and grabbing at his waist to remind him to let go of the bucking rein and slide off.

"That was a truly great ride, folks. Judges give it an eight-six and Curtie Sykes wins the saddle bronc and a pair of Justin boots at Mustang's. Congratulations, Curt. Glad to see you back." Another round of applause went up for the cowboy, who was puking behind the chutes from the effects of the ride and alcohol withdrawal.

"Where's my horse?" Joseph Starr came up beside Cody behind the chute.

"It's not over yet. Still got bareback to go. And you only got what, second? I can beat that."

"Maybe, but it was only for this contest. You owe me a horse. I've got witnesses."

Cody stared at Joseph in surprise. "Witnesses? Since when do we need —"

"Since you won't pay your bets. You ought to be ashamed, trying to cheat a poor old Indian off the res when you have so many horses already." Joseph kept a straight face, but Cody could tell his eyes were laughing at him.

"Okay, okay. Take a horse. You win. I'll tell Arthur."

The crowd took a food and drink break while Tousley's men moved stock around the small corrals and chutes for the next contests. Cody's attention was drawn by the girl he'd slept with at Clark's, who was on the arm of Burch Winants. Kya joined them, and Burch swaggered toward the food tables with a girl on each arm.

"That son of a bitch."

Joseph put a hand on his arm. "Not today, they're guests. You do your business another time." He spoke quietly, in a firm voice.

Cody jerked away and turned on Joseph. "I don't need you to tell me what to do all the time. You're not my father — he's dead — I do what I want now." He felt a hint of hollowness in his tone when he saw the flick of something in Joseph's eyes. But the older man was careful to keep his face blank.

"Whatever. Seems to me you have a whole list of people you have to beat up here today. Why don't you try something besides beating up on yourself and everyone else. You're going to get too old for that one of these days, and someone is going to hurt you permanently. And leave Kya out of this — she's a grown woman, Cody, with a nature you don't even begin to understand."

Cody kicked at a pile of horse manure, sending pieces flying at a cowboy walking past, who stopped, looked at the angry face, and kept going, shaking his head and muttering "Crazy bastard."

"Going to kill him too?" Joseph asked.

Cody avoided looking at him now, knowing that Joseph's eyes would be laughing at him. In fact, there *was* a whole list of people, Joseph was right. "I owe Burch. He knows it too. Can't be any other way."

"You're not living in the Wild West anymore, Cody. Sure, maybe you can get away with it — taking him to the badlands, help him disappear. But there's too many people now. Revenge doesn't work anymore." Joseph paused and watched Kya and Greta with their heads bent together, laughing. "It's just lucky you've been here in the hills where there's all this room, but even the hills are changing. You can't stay out here alone; you don't even want to. You want your sister to stay a little girl, a playmate. She keeps trying to find something else, a way to grow up maybe, but you don't want her to."

"Now wait a minute, you're not going to blame me for Kya." Cody stiffened his body, leaning against the corral fence, arms folded across his chest so he could keep an eye on everything he hated at the same time.

"You boys should leave her alone. Let her find her own way. And you should get out of Arthur's way too."

Cody shook his head. "I thought you were so damn smart. Can't you see what he is — what he wants to do?"

Joseph nodded. "Sure. But look at what you're doing. Drinking yourself to death, getting into one bad thing after another because you're pissed at Arthur, and Heywood, and Burch, and everyone else. I saw plenty of guys like you in Nam. They didn't last. You're just lucky you're here. What are you going to be in ten years? Half dead from alcohol, pushing cattle, pretty looks gone, alone."

"What's wrong with that if I choose it? It's mine. I'm not hurting anyone."

"What about Latta? Kya? And even Arthur, who could use a brother, not a liability. But you know, it's *you* you have to come to terms with." Joseph paused again, looking out over the growing crowds. "Your father was no dummy. He knew leaving the ranch that way in his will would force all of you into a corner, where you'd have to figure it out. He was hoping for the best. He knew he'd done some good things, and some bad. But he was honest with himself. And that's where it counts the most, because it's the lies we tell ourselves that finally end up screwing things up."

Cody shook his head. "Heywood was a selfish old fart who made my mother crazy, and me a bastard. He gave me a brother who's hated me since the day I walked into his life, and I don't blame him for it. And a sister who — never mind. I'm just who I am, Joseph. I just go along, clean up, make sure everything works. As far as the rest goes, I know I fucked up with Latta and —" He stopped and rubbed his face hard with both hands. "What do you want me to do, Joseph?"

"Don't give up," Joseph said, smiling slightly.

"On what?"

"I don't know. I'm not some goddamned oracle, Cody. It was just the first thing came to my mind."

"A slogan?"

"Life isn't perfect, neither is Joseph Starr." Joseph looked over at the younger man walking beside him, his hands thrust in his pockets, shoulders hunched in thought. "Let's draw our numbers and take a look at the stock."

"I'm going to marry her."

Cody's voice was so quiet, Joseph had to stop and ask, "What?"

"Marry Latta."

"Why?"

"I have to."

Joseph turned toward the crowd, his eyes seeking and finding Latta. "She know?"

Cody shrugged.

"Well, does she?"

"No, but I just have to — it's the right thing to do."

"Why?"

"I think I love her — has to be love. Isn't like any other kind of craziness I've ever felt."

They began walking again toward the horse trailer that was serving as an office for registering and drawing rides.

"She's a grown woman, Cody. She needs a grown man. Not a kid who's still getting in bar fights."

Cody was about to answer when he was interrupted by loud voices at the table where Esther Mervin sat, taking care of entries. Curt was fighting about Ty and Haney's right to ride. Joseph and Cody stepped up, one on each side of him.

"Let 'em sleep it off, Curt," Joseph said. "You're doing fine without them. Just give it a rest." He put his hand on Curt's shoulder, but he shook it off.

"Everyone thinks —"

"We're just trying to protect them, Curt," Esther said. "Just forget it. Look, here's your entry money back." She rolled her eyes, her thin lips pursed tightly as she tried to sound accommodating.

"They're my brothers," he insisted. "We do everything together. If they can't ride, I can't."

"Come on, buddy." Cody slung an arm around Curt's neck. Curt's face was flushed, his shirt damp with sweat, and a sour smell was coming off him. His eyes were a little unfocused as he looked at Esther, then Joseph and Cody.

"I need — little nap," he muttered, and stumbled away toward the shadow of the nearby trees.

"Darn drunks." Esther's lips curled and she looked like she could spit.

"He's not drunk, he's sick," Joseph said, and put his name on the form. Esther looked at him as if he were just another one of the same bunch of ne'er-do-wells — drunks, cowboys and Indians. Esther always volunteered for rodeos and 4-H events, spreading her sour attitude everywhere. It was a joke among the cowboys that you could tell how well you were going to do by how mean Esther Mervin was when you signed up.

"Gimme Curt's horse too," Cody said, sticking his hand out so he could draw.

"He's not riding. He's drunk." Esther kept the hat firmly planted on the table, leaning over it as if Cody might try to rip it away.

"He's not drunk, Esther, he's sick. Now give me his darned number. This is my ranch, I say who rides and who doesn't." Cody surprised Esther so much, she pushed the hat toward him and he drew the two numbers. "Eight for me, ten for Curt. Write it down. Joseph, here, gets what? Four." He tipped his hat and smiled. "Thank you, Esther."

"Damn Kidwell brat."

They could hear her muttering as they walked back to the chutes, which were being loaded with the bareback stock.

While Joseph concentrated on getting his glove on and his spurs adjusted, Cody watched the crowd begin to move toward the stands and chutes. Where was Latta? It took him a few minutes to sort out Arthur and his cronies, who were sitting down in the front center of the stands, holding their drinks up to keep them from spilling as people pushed by. Latta, Latta . . . He sorted faces and bodies. There she was, impossibly, sitting at a picnic table among the willows behind the elms, leaning forward, talking intently to Burch Winants. Cody's stomach twisted. He felt furious and nauseated at the same time.

"They're starting. Gonna help me here?" Joseph followed his eyes and looked away quickly. "Come on." He pulled Cody's arm, leading him toward the horses waiting in their chutes.

It was the middle of the afternoon, and the crows were beginning to flock back to the trees in long, hesitant clots of broken black. Their cawing blended with the neighing and squealing of horses, grunting and thudding of bulls, laughing and hollering of people, and sent the music high overhead into the surrounding hills and sky, which sent it back, echoing and ringing against the ear like a phone off the hook.

The first three horses kicked real well and blew their riders out with little trouble. Joseph's horse was a moderate bucker with a good spin, but not lively enough for a top score. He kept his position, leaning back and spurring well, but just didn't get the bucks. Curt fared better, except his legs started bouncing and he lost his position, got pulled upright, and didn't get set down good. Ash Blake had a fine ride this time, leaning way back, decent grip on the rigging, spurs on the shoulders the whole time. He pulled a top score. Cody was doing okay until he got on the tilt again. His left leg got straight and pulled him out of position, bringing both legs back to the horse's belly and bouncing him up and off before the whistle. He could've sworn the pinto turned and laughed as he went tumbling off.

"Chokin' for the money, Cody. Two horses." Joseph grinned at him as he climbed the chute out of the arena.

"Bulls, then."

"Sure you're up for bulls? They're a lot harder than the horses, and you're not doing real good as it is."

"You in or out? I'm riding one way or the other." Cody climbed down to go get his bull number.

"In." Joseph climbed down after him.

"Your brother said no bulls." Esther held the hat against her chest this time.

"Give me the goddamned hat." Cody reached for it. "Now."

She handed it over and he drew his number.

"I'll have to tell him," she snapped.

"Fine." He turned on his heel and walked away, his back and shoulder stiff with anger.

"Number two — that brindle over there. White around the eye. Big sucker. That's yours. I got number eleven — brown thing with horns." Joseph was leading him through the fences, telling him what Tousley's men were saying about the bulls, but Cody wasn't listening.

He climbed the chute and braced over the bull's back while wrapping his glove one more time. Then he sat down, putting his hand in the grip, wrapping the rope around it. The bull beneath him snorted and twisted its head, swinging the horns to gore anything he could, humping his back up and sucking in air as Cody dug his spurs into its sides and tried to grip the loose skin to keep from sliding off.

"This here is Bojangles, new young bull outta Texas," O. K. Luther announced. "Ain't been rode yet. He'll smoke a rider if he gets the spin on — watch, here he comes."

The chute door opened and the bull plunged out, bucking and turning left, left, right, pushing back when he turned so Cody felt his feet trying to come up and away.

"He's bucking good there. Notice how he keeps dragging his head down, trying to pull the cowboy off."

Cody could hear every word distinctly in slow motion, as well as the other voice telling him calmly, "Toes out, spurs in, keep your back supple, follow the motion, keep your focus, focus, ignore the whip that's cracking your shoulder in half, feel his muscles, feel him, slide with him, turn with him." The bull was getting madder and madder with the rider who wouldn't be dumped. When the whistle finally came, followed by a huge burst of applause, Cody loosened the hand grip and baled out, hit the ground with a stumbling run, and quickly headed for the chutes before the bull could reverse and gore him.

"Great ride, something for the rest of them to chase now. Gonna take a heck of a ride to beat that one. Good to see you back riding, Cody. That bull did everything but pull a knife to get you off."

Joseph's bull stuck his horn through a board in the chute while they were getting him ready. "Watch him," one of Tousley's men warned. "Thinks his business is fighting, not bucking. Just as soon stop and hook someone as buck." The bull swung his huge ivory horns tipped in black, and cleared the rails above the chute.

"Score is bulls seven, cowboys three. Let's welcome another old-timer who's riding pretty good today, Joseph Starr, on one of the meanest bulls in the new crop, Tousley says, Diablo Dan. The gate opens, uh-oh, the bull scatters, going every direction, there he starts bucking away from the cowboy's hand. He's spinning, that centrifugal force pulls you right down in the well. Uh-oh, legs coming up, he's tilting, oh no, hand's caught and that bull is mad."

Everyone went silent watching Joseph being dragged by his hand beside the bull, who was still bucking, trying to turn his horns far enough around to stick the man at his side. The pickup men attempted to get close enough to pull the bucking strap loose and corner the bull so the rider could unhook his hand. Then Joseph managed to reach up, unfasten the glove, and drop.

Just as he was getting to his feet, the bull turned and zeroed in on him. Joseph barely had time to fall and curl and put his hands around his head as the bull tried to gore him and pounded over him with his hooves. Kya ran to the fence and yelled "No!" Just beyond the fallen man, the bull stopped and stared at her. When Cody came running across the arena, the bull spotted him. Kya yelled again, but the bull snorted, lowered its head, and ran toward Cody, who was picking Joseph up. Cody dropped the man, took his hat off, and flung it at the bull, momentarily throwing its attention so the pickup men could move in again. By that time, Curt was on the other side of Joseph, helping him stagger quickly toward the chutes.

The men above hauled up the dazed man, and Cody and Curt scrambled out of the way just as the bull's horns came crashing against the boards below them.

"Helluva way to earn a living," Joseph muttered, and spit some dirt out of his mouth. "Thanks. I was just starting to get mad out there. Who knows what I woulda done to that bull." He took a deep breath and winced. "Damn thing thought I was a piece a carpet." He winked at Kya standing a few yards away, and she smiled and shook her head. Her eyes filled with tears she was ignoring.

"Looks like you'll need a new hat, Cody." Curt laughed and nodded toward the arena. "Bull's wearing your old one."

The bull had speared the hat and was trotting around the arena, ignoring the men on horses trying to shoo it back to the corrals, and shaking its head angrily.

"Looks better on him anyway," Cody said. "You owe me a horse, old man." He looked at Joseph.

"Yup. And you owe me two horses."

Proverbs:
— *A cat will eat until its brain bursts.*
— *A man too full of himself bursts into flames.*
— *This journey is about grief.*
— *Prepare for the blood river, the round lake, the clouds of fire.*

— Caroline
May 31, 1979

Tapping his beer bottle on the picnic table to the Dwight Yoakam music blaring from the speakers in the upstairs windows, Cody looked around for Joseph or Kya, but no one in the whole yard seemed familiar. He'd been concentrating so hard on drinking, he'd forgotten about other people. He thought he saw Latta under the string of lights by the food table with Sid Greenway, the fat dickhead who'd wanted to shoot him. He stood up. Maybe it was time to do something about him.

"Sit down, Cody." Arthur put a meaty hand on his bad shoulder and pressed.

"Ow." Cody rubbed the sore place and sat down. He was tired anyway.

"Listen, I have a favor to ask you." Arthur sat across from him.

Cody stared at him and drank.

"I'd like you to leave those men alone. I know they're shits, they think we're a bunch of hillbillies, but I'm trying to get something done here, and I need them for now. They're leaving tomorrow; you won't have to see much more of them. Big relief to me too, let me tell you. I had to do everything but suck the pee outta their dicks for this money. In six months or a year, if they show up and hassle you, you have my blessing — beat the living crap out of them. Okay? Just not tonight. No trouble?" He spread his palms, but there was nothing there, only the glistening sparkle of sweat.

"Not even Burch Winants?" Cody cocked the bottle at his brother, leaning forward and resting his elbows on the table.

Arthur just watched him.

Cody sighed. "Fine. I'll just get drunk. Only keep that fat fuck off Latta."

"You still in love with her?"

"You sorta fixed that, Arthur." Cody drained the last of the beer, set the bottle down, and picked up another from the row.

"Yeah." Arthur shook his head. "That was a mistake, a big one."

Cody looked closely at his brother's eyes to see if he was mocking him, but his expression seemed genuine. Cody glimpsed the top slice of the big orange moon that was just rising over the house and pointed his beer bottle at it.

Arthur turned and stared, nodding. Glancing up at the lights in the trees overhead, he said, "As long as I can remember, Bennett barbecues have meant hauling out those damn lights and stringing their sorry little yellow and red bulbs across the yard, around the porch, and tying them to this elm. How did we ever decide on that?" Arthur sipped at his beer.

Cody looked up. "Same way we decided to do anything, probably. Gotta fill time somehow."

"Intentionality isn't your strong suit." Arthur chuckled. "Don't get me wrong, I'm not making fun of you. I know you intend to do the things you do. You just operate on instinct a lot more than I do."

"You know, Arthur, half the time I don't have a clue what you're talking about. Isn't anything just simple?"

Arthur turned the beer bottle in his hands. "I don't see a lot of simple things, if that's what you mean. You and Kya, you can just sit on the outside of the world and not get drawn in, not get involved in the complications. I'm always in the middle of them, it seems. Makes it harder."

The earnestness of his brother's voice made Cody try to consider seriously what he was saying, but the alcohol and the feelings tangling with the words kept making them flat and meaningless. He nodded anyway. Do what people expect you to do sometimes, Joseph had told him.

"What're we gonna do about Kya?" Cody leaned toward his brother as if this were a matter of urgent secrecy.

Arthur leaned back, looking around. "It's funny," he said, looking at Kya, who was dancing with Greta and Joseph to the music, ignoring the frowns and whispers of some of the older women. The men just looked on with interest in their eyes.

"What?"

"She asked me the same thing about you tonight. I was wondering, do you ask each other what you're going to do with me?" Arthur leaned back, cradling his head with his hands and crossing his legs awkwardly in the tight space between the bench and table.

"No. You always seem to be in charge of things. There doesn't seem to be any reason to worry about you, I guess." Cody twisted again, lifting his hat, pushing back his hair, and resettling it.

"Oh." Arthur's face flickered with something Cody couldn't figure out. They both watched Kya draw Sid Greenway into her dancing circle. At first the man moved clumsily, self-consciously lifting one leg, then the other, but Kya was clearly laughing at him, pushing him, until finally he laughed and began to find the rhythm and motion of the dance.

"You know, there's one thing," Arthur said. "I always did want a brother, all my life. I just didn't want to see my mother hurt. It was so lonely growing up. You wouldn't believe it." He looked up at Cody's face. "But then maybe you would."

"Lonely?" Cody picked at the peeling label on the beer bottle.

"Out here, yeah. I can't stand it most days. The best thing we ever did was buy that house in town."

"Why do you stay out here, then?"

Arthur looked at him for a long moment, chewing his bottom lip, pressing the inside of it against his teeth with his thumb. "First there was Heywood. Only man in the county who could make his kids stay on the ranch when they grew up. Point of pride. Now it's the will. You two couldn't handle this place alone. You'd kill yourself for sure, and Kya just doesn't care."

Cody looked at him. "Taking a lot on yourself, aren't you?"

"Haven't you figured it out? The old man gave each of us a role. Like we were a bunch of actors he hired to play his kids. The only way it worked was if we did our jobs, stayed in character. It just seems easier to keep doing what we were doing, I guess."

"What's this resort shit, then?"

Arthur waved a hand, as if pushing the question and its underlying worry away. "That's nothing. I'm just diversifying. Heywood started working on this before he died. Wanted to start getting out of a cattle-dependent financial picture. I wouldn't do business with these assholes if it were up to me."

Cody picked up the empty bottle and threw it into the darkness behind Arthur. "Then why the hell don't you stop it? He's dead, Arthur. The will may force us to keep the ranch together, but it doesn't mean you have to screw this up just because *he* wanted to."

"Easy for you to say. You're still doing just what he planned for you, you know. He liked how you'd work yourself to death for him. You ever wonder why he didn't just give you or your mother some money of your own if you were his kid?" Arthur handed him his empty bottle. "Here, throw this one for me."

Cody looked at it, half tempted to break it over his brother's head, then heaved it into the darkness too. Now scanning the crowd, he noticed Kya, Joseph, and Latta talking together, sitting in chairs near the fire. He couldn't tell the tone of the conversation, or the words; at this distance he could just see their lips moving when the dark hollow of their mouths opened in their faces. The fire and the conversation held the three of them together for that moment, washing them in the red glow of flames, sending hot curves up the bends and shadows of flesh and bone, welding their clothes to them like molten bronze. He wanted to get up and walk over to that group and ask what they were talking about, but he couldn't. That distance was his. He owned it. He'd made it, or it had been made for him, he couldn't tell for sure which, but he knew the distance, as familiar as his mother's breath, musty with cigarettes and acid from coffee.

"Wonder what they're talking about?" Arthur said. Then he pointed to another figure sitting with her chair placed so the other three actually faced her. "Who's that?"

How had he missed her, Cody wondered. "That psychic lady, Rosalie Crater, I think. Kya's all into it. That's where she met Greta, remember?"

"You believe in that crap about psychics?"

They watched as Burch brought Sid Greenway and the other two men over to the fire, laughing and pointing at Rosalie.

"That bastard." Cody started to get up.

"Let it go, Cody, please." Arthur looked at the muscles cording his brother's neck.

Joseph stood up and Burch took his place in the chair, slouching, cigarette dangling from his lips, tucking his hands into his side pockets. Burch sat between Kya and Latta. It made Cody crazy to see it. He took the empty in front of him and tried to squeeze the glass hard enough between his hands to shatter it, but nothing happened. He was still squeezing when Arthur left and brought back a couple more cold ones.

Setting them down, he glanced at his brother's bowed head concentrating on the bottle in front of him, knuckles white, and said, "I'm going over and check that psychic out. What'd you say her name was, Rosaline Carter?"

"Rosalie Crater." Cody let go of the bottle so suddenly it tipped and rolled off the table. He picked up the fresh one.

"Yeah. Wanna make sure she doesn't screw up Sid's head over there." Arthur tilted his head toward the group by the fire, where the men had taken over the chairs, with the shortest one sitting on the ground. Rosalie was pointing at Burch, who was smoking nonchalantly.

"I'll keep an eye on that little Winants shit too. Don't worry." Arthur started to pat his brother's shoulder, then stopped. In that mood, Cody took every touch as provocation. Like trying to pet a bobcat.

"Oh I'm not worried, not at all. Nope. Not. At. All." Cody put the bottle to his lips again and let the cold beer slide down his throat without making the effort to swallow. He shouldn't have switched to beer; it took too much to get drunk. "Yeah, that's the problem." He stared at the bottle.

"What's the problem?" Joseph slid in across from him.

He waved Joseph off, lifted the second bottle, and drank.

"Gonna get drunk."

"Yeah, drunk and sick," Joseph said. "So when do I get my horses?"

"When do I get mine?"

"Soon's you finish shipping calves."

"What's that have to do with anything?"

"Come see me. I'll be at my cousin's outside Mission."

"I suppose you want me to deliver your two there."

Joseph shrugged and nodded. "Good idea. I'll choose 'em tomorrow. You can feed 'em another week or two for me." He smiled.

"Do you have the horse you owe me, or am I just going to get back one of my own?" He studied the older man's face, trying to penetrate the amusement in its expression. He wasn't in the mood to be tricked.

"In a manner of speaking." Joseph looked up at the bare tree limbs as if he'd left something there, cocking his head one way and then the other.

"What manner of speaking is that?"

"Ever notice" — Joseph twisted on the bench — "that if you concentrate on the spaces between limbs, not the limbs themselves, everything looks different?"

"Indian lore?" Cody drank again.

"Nope. Just something I noticed one day sitting in Nam. Got sick of looking for enemy soldiers we couldn't see anyway, so I stopped looking at things. Tried to look at not-things. Spaces that were empty instead of full of something."

"No wonder we lost the war."

"I was doing it on the hill this summer too, trying to figure out what to do about the holy man buried there, the church and all."

"You figure anything out?"

"I'm working on it." Joseph looked at the sweaty bottle, staring a little too long, as if it were a kind of food he was hungry for and couldn't afford.

Cody put the bottle down, sliding it over the rough board surface a ways from them. He suddenly felt he'd been discourteous, drinking in front of Joseph. "Latta's still here."

Joseph nodded, pulling the red kerchief from around his neck and spreading it on the table. Refolding it and twisting it in a long tube, he tied it around his head, flattening the greying hair back of his ears. "Darn hair keeps getting loose, even in braids."

"She say anything?" Cody rolled his lips tight.

Joseph looked at him, keeping his face neutral. "Why don't you talk to her?"

"Don't know where she is."

"She's around." Joseph nodded toward the crowd.

"I better not get up yet. Gotta stay outta trouble, I promised."

Joseph laughed, rubbing his neck under his chin. "First for you, huh? Okay, I'll look for her."

"She doesn't want to talk to me."

"Maybe." Joseph stood up. "Just don't pass out before I find her."

Cody waved him off. What he needed now was a place to sleep or another beer, he decided. If there was a hell, it was something like this, trapped at a picnic table, surrounded by people he wanted to punch, listening to the same beat-up songs over and over. But in hell there'd be no mercy, no alcohol.

Caroline had taught him that. Cody remembered one morning when he'd woken up at dawn to find that the shade of the draw-down overhead lamp in the kitchen had broken somehow, leaving sharp white plastic shards on the floor, and Caroline walking through them in her bare feet as she made breakfast. It took a year for some of the pieces to work their way out of her feet. And every night he'd sit her down, with a bowl of hot water and Epsom salts, to help her soak and draw out the shards. He'd made a pad out of cardboard with a hole in it when a piece of plastic started poking through; he'd tape the cardboard on so she could walk without driving it back up. He couldn't tell for sure if she was in constant pain. She never complained about her feet as she limped around.

Some nights Cody dreamed she was still alive. She wanted her house back. She wanted her lover back. She didn't seem to want her son, though. That always seemed clear. She wanted her things back too, her letters and scribblings, her books and clothes. And Cody didn't know where they were. He'd never asked. Things, the house itself, seemed to vanish after her death. He'd simply assumed Heywood had taken care of it all. Had he burned everything? Cody had never gone back to the house. Maybe he should, maybe this winter when things got slow again, he'd go back. Maybe everything would be there just the way she'd left it. He didn't think so, but he wasn't sure he wanted it that way anyway.

"Cody — Latta. Latta — Cody. You two know each other, right?" Joseph sat down across from Cody, slightly out of breath, and Latta sat down beside Joseph. Then he moved down, pulling Latta after him so she was directly across from Cody. Joseph was grinning, until he noticed the two empties on the table.

Cody was afraid to look at her when she was sitting this close. Then he decided to try just a piece of her — her arm: same tanned skin, muscled, sturdy, neat, that place where it met the shoulder he could see from the opening in her collar, where he'd kiss her and she'd writhe so he'd bite along the whole ridge, feeling her go limp and press back into him. It didn't do any good to look at her this way. He glanced at her face quickly, hoping she couldn't sense the stirring in his body. Even in the dark, her brown eyes had a shield, a barrier in them. Don't come any closer, they said, stretching their hands out against him. He looked at her mouth, her crooked nose, her strong cheekbones, as if this would be the last time and he had to memorize it all.

"Here you go, bro, you're gonna need this." Kya put a fresh beer in front of him and ran off laughing.

Latta just looked at him, disgusted.

Well fuck it, he thought, and picked up the bottle, taking a longer pull than he wanted.

"Joseph said you needed to talk to me about something." Latta sat stiffly, her head thrown back, looking down at him. Her voice was formal, the way it used to be.

"I —" He tried staring at the tree trunk behind her. What

had Joseph said about spaces between things? "How are you? I mean, how've you been?" He let himself look at her face again. No flicker of anything.

"How do you think?" Now there was a flicker, her expression grew harder.

He shrugged. "I tried to —"

She folded her arms and turned her head toward the crowd.

"I'm sorry, Latta." It was the only thing he could think of, especially with Joseph sitting there.

"Yeah, well, that doesn't do a hell of a lot." She turned her fierce eyes on him. This time they were full of anger and hatred.

He picked up the bottle quickly, trying to keep his hand steady as he put it to his lips and drank.

"And if that's all you have to say —" She started to get up. Joseph touched her arm.

"What do you want outta me? It was Arthur who started this, not me. And you're talking to him, I notice. All I ever did was —"

"Run away at the first problem. Not to mention stealing my horse, or help whoever *did* steal it." She looked like she wanted to hit him. Not slap him, hit him, he realized, and shrank back. "How can I trust you now? When something bigger comes along —"

"I tried to see you, but Inez —"

"Yeah, I know, Joseph told me. So what? Why didn't you force your way through the goddamn door — you're Mr. Macho all over the place. If it'd been your sister on the other side of that door, hell or high water wouldn't have stopped you, and you know it. But not for me. No, you let my seventy-year-old housekeeper turn you away like you were twelve years old. No, you sat around feeling sorry for yourself when I was the one in pain. I was the one needed comforting and convincing." She was yelling loud enough that people nearby stopped and looked over, then turned their backs so they could listen without appearing to. Someone had turned the music up another notch, so the bass distorted and the music was wailing out a bit louder than her voice.

"Look." He slammed the beer bottle down. "I tried, god-damn it. I thought you hated me. I didn't steal your horse. And how was I supposed to know you wanted me to break the goddamned door down — with Colin holding a gun on me?"

A terrible smile appeared on her lips. He wanted to wipe it away, but it was too frightening. "You let it happen, Cody. You left me there with Arthur. You let him talk you out of me, didn't you? You didn't stand up for me. You disappeared for a week. No letter or phone call. And some bullshit about a stolen note. I'll never forgive you for that. You hear me? *Never*, no matter what else."

He bowed his head, and she knocked his hat off. He felt such a burst of anger, he didn't even know it was inside him until he was standing, pushing her back against the tree, her blouse in his hands, Joseph at his side, pulling on his arm, but Cody was ignoring that, he wanted to stare down into those terrible angry eyes, he wanted —

"You make me sick," she said between gritted teeth. "You're just another goddamned cowboy. If I had a gun right now, I'd shoot you myself. You hear?"

He dropped his hands, staring at her as she pulled her shirt down, brushing the front of it off as if he'd left dirt on her. She moved deliberately, not letting herself be hurried by him. Then she bent and picked up his hat and threw it on the table.

"Stay off my land or I'll call the sheriff," she said, and dis-appeared into the darkness beyond the overhead lights.

His nerves were strung up with claws; if he moved, he knew the points would sink into him permanently. He closed his eyes. This was worse than losing Caroline, as bad as the day he'd shot that man. No, worse, because he knew that Latta was the woman he loved, would love, might have always loved.

He looked at his hat, afraid to touch it again. Then he was moving, sitting down, putting it slowly on his head, waiting.

Her words were a loop playing in his mind, just behind his eyes, so everywhere he looked they were there, accusing him, confirming his suspicions that really he was not a good man, that no matter how hard he tried, he couldn't take care of anyone; no woman was safe with him as her protector.

Cody chose the old stud because he was big enough to carry both of them. Tying the stud to a post, he avoided the teeth that would grab him if they could. Just playfulness, but he didn't want to have to slap the horse. He didn't want to have to hurt anything. He moved dreamily to the nail where a bridle hung, and slipped it on over the halter so he'd have the rope too. The distance he'd felt in the yard had followed him, and he swam in its waves, feeling weightless as he led the stud, holding tightly to the offside rein to keep the horse's head turned away from his body. When the stud tried to cow kick to the side and front, he only had to step away and ignore it.

Kya was standing in the moonlight of the doorway. She was barefoot, for some reason, but he noted it only because it seemed another part of an odd, shimmering world. She sprang onto the horse first, grabbing the reins while he knotted the rope around the stud's neck. Then he steadied a hand on her thigh and swung up lightly behind her, holding her hips as the stud grunted and rounded his back. Kya bent forward, sliding her hand along his neck, whispering while she pressed her heels into the heavy sides. The horse stepped out, walking quickly and breaking into a trot. In a moment, he flowed into his long lope, aiming for the nearest hill, head down as if he were grabbing the ground between his teeth to pull it faster and faster toward him. At the top of the hill they paused and then plunged, the riders leaning back to avoid sliding over the horse's head or tumbling forward if he stumbled. But he didn't. The hooves found only smooth sand and dirt, weaving their way through the thickets of soapweed and tall thistles, galloping flat out as they raced across a meadow, the two riders hugging his back, becoming all one animal.

When the horse was breathing in great heaving wheezes, body trembling, steam rising from his hide, thick sudsy foam between his hind legs, flecking his chest, long white skids on his neck from the reins, they stopped and threw themselves on the ground. With their arms and legs spread out as if they'd dropped from a great height, and with eyes closed, they were breathing as hard as the horse.

Kya was the first to open her eyes, because there was something wrong. The horse's breathing had calmed, but Cody was too quiet. His breath kept catching as if he were trying not to be heard. She rose on one elbow and looked at him. His eyes were closed, but thin silver streaks marked his face.

They lay like that for a long time, Cody crying the way he had when they were younger, silently, when to do such a thing he had to give himself up to it. Kya never cried like this. Her tears came in brief, violent storms and disappeared quickly, but she knew better than to try to touch or talk to him.

After he'd been silent for a while, she crawled to her brother and climbed on top of him, lying along his length, her hands capturing his and pressing them into the sand. When he opened his eyes, she bent to kiss him and he turned his head. "Don't."

She smiled. "I wasn't going to. Just checking to see if you were back yet."

He wiggled uncomfortably. "Get off."

She shook her head. "Got something to tell you."

"No, come on. I can't do any more of this tonight. Just get off. I have to walk the horse out before he ties up."

"Look, personally I think she's a stupid bitch, but you've decided to ruin your life for her, so I have to say something."

He closed his eyes, took a deep breath, and relaxed. "Okay, what?"

"She's pregnant."

Cody opened his eyes. Then he heaved, trying to dislodge her again. "Latta? Latta's pregnant?" He panted.

Kya pressed her dead weight down and held him, her face a few inches above his. "Yes. Latta's pregnant. She told Arthur, says it has to be yours. The psychic says it's yours. *I* say it's yours. Inez's looking for you with a carving knife. She thinks you raped Latta, *and* got her pregnant. I guess she didn't tell you, huh?"

Cody shook his head. The back of his nose was filling again, and he could taste the salt on the roof of his mouth.

"What're you gonna do?"

He just lay there, unable to think of a single thing. Overhead, the stars blinked distant and cool; they seemed to be sending messages somewhere, but not to him. He'd noticed that the fall and winter skies were like that, as if the weather sent them farther away, to give the snow and wind and cold more room to howl and clatter against the world below. It was hard to imagine anything good up there, like heaven, but not so difficult to see a kind of hell down here. Maybe those old people who wrote the Bible just got it messed up. Maybe they had to believe in their heart of hearts that something better existed someplace else, because it sure wasn't here.

After a while a star burned across the sky, and he remembered Caroline holding him on the porch at night, waiting to get sleepy. "Strange angels," she used to say, stars shooting to earth to live with humans. "You're one," she had told him. "Maybe we're all strange angels, skating through the night sky toward some distant home."

"Strange angels," he whispered out loud. Latta. His baby.

21 ✧ CEREMONIES

Aerial views of the rocky outcrop called Slate Prairie in the Black Hills and named "Tayamni" in Lakota resemble the constellation of the same name. The symbol for the earth sites is ▽, and the symbol for the stars is △. These shapes are not flat triangles, but cones, vortices of light. The inner shape of a star is an inverted tipi. When earth sites and stars are combined, the image looks like this: ⧓. Thus, what is above is like what is below. What is below is like what is above.

— from LAKOTA STAR KNOWLEDGE

A barbed-wire fence that enclosed the small graveyard kept out the cattle and horses inside the Rosebud Timber Reserve, and another fence, of woven hog wire, separated the tallest marker, over which waved a tattered American flag from an old lodgepole.

"Iron Shell's grave," Joseph explained as they approached. "Tobacco offerings." He nodded toward the garlands of knotted cloth tied at regular intervals on thread. "Colors mean different things. Prayers, thanks, healings. He was a powerful man."

Kya picked up a feather hanging from the fence by a strip of yellow cloth. "Eagle — must of wanted something big." The day was quiet and cold. She shivered in her jeans jacket and stuffed her hands in her pockets. The stars and stripes on the flag were so faded they seemed to be bleeding away, as if the cloth were reclaiming itself.

"Lots of people must come here." Greta gestured toward the dozens of tobacco ties and cloth strips. The girl's chopped blond hair clung flat to her head as she bent to examine the marker.

"He was a good man with strong medicine. His wife's over there." Joseph pointed out the other group of graves with much smaller headstones, also garlanded with cloth strips and knotted tobacco offerings. At their bases leaned coffee cans and glass jars of dead flowers and clumps of faded plastic flowers stuck directly in the ground.

Kya paced the tiny graveyard, uncertain why he'd brought them up here. She'd asked him to help her find information about her mother, not take them on a goddamned tour. Greta kept asking questions, which slowed them down too. Maybe it hadn't been such a great idea bringing her along.

"Let's go," Kya said, and walked quickly back to the Blazer. What she wanted wasn't here. When she'd agreed to drive Joseph to a few places he needed to see, she hadn't counted on graveyards and scenery; she hated scenery.

"The birds aren't even chirping up here. Where have all the animals gone?" Greta asked.

"It's always quiet up here," Joseph said, climbing in as the truck rolled forward.

"Look back," Kya said. Behind them a flock of turkeys was pouring across the road and up the hill to their right. With their long legs and big feet, their bodies looked like big glittery puffballs floating black and gold over the ground.

"My cousin'd like one of those for dinner," Joseph said.

"I bet." Kya stepped on the gas.

Several miles farther down the highway, they turned in again. The poles of the Sun Dance ground rose with a stark symmetrical beauty on the hill above them. The morning had been cloudy until the moment they arrived, then the sun broke through and caught the fresh yellow gleam of the ends of the tepee poles resting in a pile to the left of the ceremonial grounds. The domes of willow ribs for the sweat lodges shone dull white like bone.

Kya stepped to the edge of the ridge and looked out across a huge valley to the distant, rolling, juniper-covered hills. "I have to admit this is pretty amazing," she said to Joseph beside her.

"Not bad." He tilted his head and squinted.

"I wish Cody were here."

"Change of scenery'd do him good, I s'pose." Joseph put his hand on her shoulder, which stood level with his.

"Take his mind off Latta Jaboy or whatever's making him so damn dark." She felt the calm from Joseph's hand spread down her back and chest like a shawl.

"He's pretty wrapped up in his own pain these days."

Kya shook her head and grimaced. "I'm supposed to be looking out for both my brothers, according to Miss Rosalie. But Arthur doesn't spend a dime or a minute that can't give him a return. And Cody won't crawl out of the hole he's dug for himself to notice anyone else. I just don't get it." She shrugged off Joseph's hand and walked impatiently to the open-sided shelter roofed with cedar boughs where observers sat during the Sun Dance ceremony. Greta was mousing around with her arms folded across her chest, hands stuck in her armpits as if she were afraid of air. Kya wanted to set off a firecracker under her to get her going, put some life in her. Joseph dropped to his hands and knees, poking at something on the ground.

Kya kicked at a torn piece of bright blue plastic caught with an empty potato chip bag and a Coke can in the weeds. "Look at this crap." She spun around. "Can we get going?"

Joseph stood and walked slowly past her around the outside of the ceremonial circle. "This is the east gate. During the actual ceremony, it's forbidden to cross the path of the sun through the eastern gate."

"*How* forbidden?" Kya paused right in the middle of the gate, smiling.

Joseph looked at her from the far side of the perimeter, enclosed by posts and rafter logs at regular intervals. "You'd get in a lot more trouble than you'd like." He continued walking slowly. Kya watched him. He was just enough of a mystery to interest her. And he knew enough to keep walking away. She liked that. If Greta weren't there, she'd try to tease him into making love right here in the eastern gate.

"Doesn't it feel spooky?" Greta spoke a little breathlessly beside her.

Kya looked down at the small face, struck by just the kind of dumb awe that made her impatient. "Not really." Greta looked like she'd been slapped, and she dropped her eyes the way Cody did when he'd been hurt.

"I'm sorry, I'm just tired and hungry. This standing around — let's just get going. Maybe we can find someplace to eat in St. Francis."

On the road out to the highway, Joseph pointed to the sweat lodge half buried in trees behind the medicine man's small square house guarding the entrance. "That's the women's sweat. Theirs are always a little ways off. Women pierce their upper arms." He pinched the top of Kya's arm, making her twist away. "They dance right alongside the men with their pierced chests. The tree's gone — they take it down after the ceremony."

"I'd like to do that," Kya said, turning onto the blacktop toward St. Francis, ten miles away.

"Maybe. It's not a macho thing. You have to do it for the people, for the whole community. If you do it for yourself it can backfire, make things worse, or you won't be able to take the pain, have to drop out. Sacrifice is the key." Joseph looked out the window.

"I could probably do it," Kya muttered uncertainly, pouting so she didn't notice Joseph's lips curve into a smile. "Pain doesn't scare me."

"I couldn't do it," Greta sighed from the back seat. "I hate blood and I hate to be hurt."

Kya glanced at her in the rearview mirror. "You'd help me, though, wouldn't you? If I needed moral support."

Greta laughed. "Sure, with my eyes closed. I don't even want to imagine a ceremony like that."

"You're braver than you think," Joseph said.

Kya glanced at him. He'd never addressed Greta directly before.

"When you get to the second street, turn left," Joseph said when they passed the St. Francis town line. "The mission and school are up ahead, but I want to check this place out first."

They turned onto a rundown street of houses and stunted trees. Native men walking or standing along the pavement stared at them openly. They were three blocks from the eastern edge of town when Joseph said, "Here it is. Turn here, 10–70 Street. They call it 10–70 for the police emergency code that gets used so often."

Kya was driving so slowly, Greta was afraid she'd stop. Joseph peered out the open window. Dumpsters stood haphazardly on the street, their maws open, erupting garbage. The ground was cluttered with soiled diapers, beer cans, bottles, milk cartons, every form of human trash, which made its way up the dirt and weeds and collected with broken chairs, torn clothing, and old appliances around the foundations of the houses. With no attempt to do more than batter what was already ruined, rusted abandoned cars and trucks, engines, bumpers, and other parts decayed in the yards. For two blocks there wasn't an unbroken piece of glass. Every window was a patchwork of cardboard, cloth, duct tape, aluminum foil, wood. No lights were on. No people could be seen, though it was late afternoon. Nothing grew, as if the desperation of abuse here were too powerful. Dogs were the only things moving on this landscape — skinny, cringing adult dogs and small fluffy puppies.

"Slow down here. I think this is where my niece lives. She might know something. My cousin said she'd moved in with Buster Steps Aside Crow." Joseph got out of the truck and stood for a moment so the inhabitants could get a good look at him. A light went on inside the house, but the door remained shut. Then the light went out again, and stayed out. Joseph walked to the door, knocked, and waited. He did that for ten minutes, calling her name softly, then gave up and went back to stand by the truck. "They're afraid," he said over his shoulder.

"I guess they're not coming out," he said finally, and climbed back in. At the end of the last block, where the street met another at a T-junction, he pointed to a house on the left that was every bit as dilapidated as the rest. The only difference was that the windows and doors were covered with sheets of plywood on which had been sprayed in black paint, *Please, this is not your house.* "That's where you were born, Kya. That was your mother's place."

Kya flinched as if she'd been hit. She stared at its hard outline in the failing light, and for the first time something that might be called fear appeared in her face, but only for a moment. Then she sighed and stepped on the gas. "Let's get outta here before someone mistakes us for Indians."

"This is the low-income-housing area." Joseph pointed to their right as they cruised slowly down another street back to the highway. The houses were a definite improvement on 10–70 Street, though their paint was chipping and their square, boxy shapes were only slightly larger and better kept. "Sioux 400's — that's what they're called. The government gives them model names and numbers like that."

Kya looked back and saw that most of them had their lights

on and whole panes of glass in the windows. She tried to fit words to what she'd just seen, but couldn't. In Babylon white people hated the Indians off the reservation even more than the few blacks who lived in the hills. Had they ever seen the way these people had to live, she wondered. Did they have any idea what was going on here?

"This is a lot worse than the pictures of big-city poverty they show on TV. As bad as the famines and squalor in foreign places," Greta murmured.

Kya wanted to roll down the window and yell something. No wonder her mother was lost, never to be found. Just outside of town, they slowed and then stopped because a car was standing just ahead of them in their lane. A man stood with his back to them, hands resting on the trunk, leaning forward with his head down. There were other heads in the car, outlined by Kya's lights.

"Should we stop and see if he needs help?" Kya asked. They could see the smoky exhaust rising in the beams of the head-lights.

The man straightened and Joseph said, "No, pull around." The headlights caught the clear puddle at the man's feet and the look of sweaty anguish as he turned to walk back to the driver's seat. Passing the car, Greta had seen how serious the faces of the family waiting inside were. "Drunk or sick," Joseph said.

At least they have a car, Kya reminded herself. At least they could get out of 10–70; they weren't stuck there. It'd been a newer car too, not too rusty or anything. Packed full of family. At least he had family. She tried to imagine her mother some-where in the world without her, but couldn't picture anything. Instead she saw Cody, alone, with no one in the truck waiting for him, too drunk to take care of himself, and she felt afraid again.

"My mother's gone, you don't know where she is," Kya said

quietly. She drove with caution, as if any small accident could ruin her life forever — sending her back to that terrible place, 10–70 Street.

"Just the house. Thought you'd want to see it," Joseph said. "Your mother left you in Heywood's truck one night at Clark's. He never saw her again. You were asleep with a note pinned to your dress. Lucky it was warm out, I guess. You're lucky. You'd been living on Coca-Cola and soda crackers before he brought the two of you to Clark's. He paid old lady Clark to feed you. Mrs. Bennett's death was lucky for you. He could bring you home. Anyway, nobody's heard from your mother since then."

Kya didn't feel angry or hurt. That surprised her. Not numb or indifferent either. Just lucky. Maybe lucky.

They were almost to Joseph's cousin's place, driving swiftly through the dark, lonely countryside, when Joseph reached across the seat and took her hand. Opening it, he placed a tiny buckskin pouch in her palm. He spoke quietly so as not to wake Greta, asleep in the back seat. "I found the one I was looking for at the Sun Dance grounds — right by an old anthill. It's extra good to find a stone the ants bring up from underneath. It hasn't been tainted by life up here yet. Pin it inside your shirt or keep it in a pocket. It's your *tunkan*. My grandfather gave me mine. It's your guardian spirit. Address it as *Tunkasila* when you pray."

Kya closed her fingers around the inch-square pouch. Everything was becoming different now, as if someone just outside the world had changed the volume of light in the eye, refocused the tension of air on the skin, fretted the sound in the ear.

"If it doesn't work, throw it away and start over." Joseph smiled. "Maybe the ants just tossed it out because it was trash."

All of Arthur's deals were in good shape. Holiday Ranches was a go-ahead, according to Sid Greenway the day after the visit.

Arthur had convinced local investors to put up most of the money. Even Latta Jaboy had gone along when he'd explained his cash flow and given her shares in the new company instead of repaying the farm loan. If Sid's end failed, Arthur had fixed it so they'd all come out ahead. In fact, that part of the deal was so good, he half hoped the thing would collapse. Good local PR. The laundromat–bowling alley in Ainsworth would be his in a month, provided he could get the bait shop moved out. The restaurant he was starting in the old bakery with Emil Vullet would open in time for the holiday season. Rosalie Crater hadn't given him any trouble when he'd made her leave. Cattle prices were high, and Bennett stock was bringing top dollar. The farm south of Broken Bow proved to be a good investment for fattening the stock they were carrying over. The sorghum had come in better than expected. Kya wasn't around causing trouble. See, he wanted to tell his family, if you just leave things to me, we'll get rich.

Right now he had only one problem, and he was in the attic fixing that: finding the other will, so he could free up enough money to move forward. His mind kept wandering along these lines as he scanned the individual scraps of paper in Caroline Kidwell's boxes. The diaries, as illuminating as they were, weren't yielding any evidence he could use. That Caroline had an affair besides the one with Heywood was clear, but so far there was nothing to prove that Cody was fathered by anyone else, although Arthur would've bet his life on it.

Against his better judgment, he'd started over again with the documents from her early years. He had to be systematic. Opal Treat wasn't helping much, except to say that the Kidwells were an old, respected Southern Methodist family whose ancestors were divided during the Civil War. At the end of the war, one family had to flee Camden County for being "Black Republicans." They'd had money and lost it, but the only disreputable thing about the family was their strange daughter, Caroline. "Like that's news," Arthur had muttered.

He was trying to let the state of his business affairs buoy his spirits as he searched, but it was hard. The attic was almost colder than outside. His shoulders and back ached from sitting on the floor and bending over, and his eyes were starting to burn from the dim light of the bare overhead bulb. He was thinking he should go down and bring up a lamp when he lifted the last paper in the bottom of the box. It was a yellowed, official paper with the embossed county registrar's seal in jagged lace over the signature.

He had to read it several times, because his eyes wouldn't accept what it said. A marriage license, the two of them underage, sneaking off to Arkansas. Another paper, an annulment petition filed by her parents. Rejected. Same state. "But wait," Arthur's lips formed the words, "wait."

He carefully repacked and stacked all the boxes as they'd rested before, being gentle, respectful, the way you're supposed to with the dead you disturb, because the last thing you find out is that you really don't want to call them back. After all is said and done, you really need them to stay there, dead. He moved deliberately, like a child who has opened a parent's dresser and found things that have shocked him and must now return everything to its previous order, despite his own desperate urge to run, avert his eyes and his innocence from the knowledge that was waiting, grown-up and dark, in the tall dresser drawers.

It wasn't until Arthur was downstairs again that he realized he was still clutching the marriage license and a packet of brittle letters tied with a faded blue ribbon whose looped edges were frayed and brown. He dropped them on the kitchen table and stared at them as if they were the weapon he had just used to kill himself.

The documents on the table behind him seemed to stare accusingly. He was strong, he could take it, he answered the imaginary dialogue. He wasn't going to tell Cody anything. Not in a hundred thousand years. Let the little shit think what he wanted, who cared. *His* mother, Marion Howe Bennett, was the one with the name publicly bestowed. She was the wife Heywood Bennett chose to acknowledge, and even in his screwed-up way, that said something more important than an adolescent wet dream back in the Ozarks with some hillbilly nut case. It just wasn't the same thing. Two marriages, but only one counted, the one he told people about. The man hadn't even bothered to acknowledge Caroline or Cody after Marion died. Hadn't wanted it known. Probably didn't even realize his marriage wasn't annulled. Or he hadn't cared enough about anyone or anything.

That bastard Heywood had made bastards of them all. Arthur pounded the table so hard the dice-shaped salt-and-pepper shakers jumped and spilled. He'd be goddamned if he'd tell Cody or Kya or Selden Monk or anyone. No wonder there wasn't another will. Just another big lie. Heywood Bennett had lied to them all, screwed them all. When it came down to it, all he cared about was one person, Heywood Bennett. And maybe Caroline Kidwell. The children were mere accidents of his nature. And there just wasn't any way to feel now but bitter — as bitter as a mouthful of salt a thousand miles from water.

While Greta slept on the floor at the opposite end of the trailer, Joseph and Kya made love in his small bed. With each thrust of their hips, she felt a part of herself open and give, like a pile of rocks he was slowly dismantling. Afterward he pulled the star quilt his grandmother had made over them, tucking in the edges so the points fixed the geography of their joined bodies. Kya felt so light now, she was glad for his weight holding her.

"Tomorrow my cousin's having a healing," Joseph whispered in her ear. "I asked him if we could come."

"I don't know, Joseph. This Indian thing — what good did it do my mother?" She was sleepy and didn't want to think about anything.

"Couldn't hurt. Maybe you'll stop listening to all those *Hey-oka* clown spirits that's got you thinking backwards."

"Yeah? I'm thinking something pretty straightforward now, aren't I?" She reached between their legs and touched him.

He groaned. "There's free food afterwards. Some of these women are good cooks too. You won't have to eat the dog — it's just that old shepherd mix of my cousin's — ow — stop — where was I? Oh, careful. Just remember to say '*Mitakuye oya'in*,' which means 'all my relatives,' before and after prayers and food." Kya rolled her hips and he stiffened in resistance. "And if you're touched by anything like a hand, a rattle, or a paw, it's a healing and a blessing. You say 'Thank you, Grandfather,' '*Pilamaya Tunkasila*.' Oh, Kya . . ."

"Thank you, Grandfather," she whispered as she drifted to sleep with a smile on her face that Joseph watched for a long time. He wasn't certain that this was a part of the vision, but he couldn't be sure it wasn't either. Tomorrow he'd take the two women to see the vision hill on the buffalo preserve. He was working by instinct and prayer now. That's all he had left anyway.

At dawn Kya dreamt that she was trying to get someplace a great distance away. She was going to take a train, but once she boarded, she discovered she was inside a giant centipede. She recognized the light orangy tan and the odd interior. She thought of escape, but the side that had been open for passengers shut and locked in notches like a zipper. They were moving quickly, the segments of its long body reticulated like snake jaws from one to another as the centipede moved over the rough hilly terrain.

When she woke up, Kya knew what it meant. She was changing. Things were changing. If anything was to change in their family, if they were ever going to help each other instead of taking each other apart, she would have to make it happen. Rosalie Crater, for all her dowdy clothes and makeup, had been right. The flow of events in the past week that had brought her here with Joseph seemed natural, inevitable. Either that or she was getting too old to resist anymore, and for the first time in her life, she realized that that might be okay too.

When she felt Joseph stir beside her, she rolled over and put her head in the hollow of his arm. "You awake?" she whispered.

"Um."

"I feel like I've kind of messed things up."

"Uh-huh."

She kept her eyes closed so she wouldn't be distracted. "Do you think it's my fault Cody got hurt?" She held her breath while she waited for his answer. She'd never asked anyone to judge her before.

"You know the answer to that, Kya."

She exhaled and opened her eyes to the morning light cracking the dark room.

It was an accident, but she was responsible, wasn't she? Even though her brother forgave her, she had to make up for it. It was only fair. Feeling strangely relieved, she fell asleep again, this time imagining she heard the grey stallion's high whinny calling his mares in the pasture right outside the trailer's window.

The *yuwipi* stones talk. They tell me what the illness is, if a person has been shot with something, and what medicine to get. I don't know myself. The stones say. They tell me what [the nature of] the illness is and what to do. Like ghosts. A dead boy or girl may hang around the house, annoying. It is because the ghost wants to say something to them [the parents]. I can do that, and tell the parents what the child wants to say.

— *from* THE MEDICINE MEN

*T*he horses were silly about being in the fall woods, with a late afternoon chill layering the air in a cold stillness that carried and magnified every sound. To the west, the blue line of weather hung on the mountains, as it did most days, so Latta ignored it, figuring she'd make it to Joseph's cabin before night.

"Good girl." Latta patted the bay mare's neck. She was a sturdy horse, and would be part of her foundation stock if she ever got the stallion back.

Since the rodeo at Bennett's a week ago, she'd decided that if anything was going to be done, it would be up to her. Cody was unreliable, a drunk. She used to think he was so sensitive. She remembered once, while they were walking, he'd stepped into a bush filled with fritillaries and let them rise in a cloud and gradually take him in as part of their orbit, hovering about his hands and arms as if he were just more bush. He'd told her to lean into the bush for the sharp scent, and smeared a twisted leaf on her cheek, and laughed as the butterflies fluttered up to her eyelids and lips. But it turned out he couldn't be trusted.

"Look for the stream," Joseph had told her. But she couldn't see or hear any water. She wondered if, in her haste, she'd packed a compass. She was a damn fool who deserved to get lost if she hadn't. She was a damn fool anyway, waiting all summer for someone else to take care of her business. Had falling in love with that man made her so helpless? She leaned forward, shifting her weight to the front of the saddle so the mare could dig in and climb more easily. She was sure-footed, just needed some seasoning. Latta had brought the older, more reliable mare to pack, though even that one was snorting the brisk air, looking to the west and perking her ears.

The light failed immediately at this time of year, the orange sun fading and shrinking as if it would disappear forever, then simply stopping, overtaken by the sheath of thin clouds that waited for it every night along the horizon. Latta decided to stop while she could still see a few yards around her, rather than pushing on and perhaps missing the cabin in the dark. When the special darkness clamped down, there would be nothing unless the moon rose, and she hadn't paid attention to the moon in weeks.

She'd started getting sick right away, and all day, every day, she would vomit at a smell, a sound, a motion, an idea. Being pregnant had forced all her attention to her body, to the gradations of nausea, to the small pucker of flesh around her middle she was convinced she saw, though she'd actually been losing weight. Her face felt drawn and old as she looked in the mirror for the answer about having an abortion. By now the whole county would know, must know — and she'd put the decision off another day.

She'd learned that she just couldn't breathe too deeply. Take little shallow pants when the nausea came, then the body got fooled. She didn't know whether the sickness was the baby trying to rule her already or whether it was her body telling her she was too old to be considering a baby. Three doctors had told her she was too damaged to conceive again, so she'd stopped wishing for a child years ago. Now she didn't want it to be anybody else's. Just hers. If she could guarantee that, she'd have it.

She was going to go crazy if she didn't stop thinking about it, she decided as she stripped and hobbled the horses. She gave each of them several of the whole cobs of corn she'd packed, and built a fire for herself in the clearing beneath a small hill. She didn't really need a fire, she reminded herself: even the coyotes stayed away during hunting season. They were smart like the deer and stayed well hidden from the gun-happy hunters. She hadn't seen a deer the whole time she'd been in the woods. In the summer she would've come across at least a couple, fawns even, lying in their hollows, gazing around themselves with wide dark eyes, surprised at every little thing. She'd always wanted to rub their spotted coats that looked like expensive plush. Cody'd told her he had walked a foot from one more than once, but hadn't wanted to put his scent on the baby and drive the mother off.

She pulled a doughnut from her pack and made some tea. Lately, all she could stand to eat were these greasy, heavy doughnuts Inez fried in lard and dragged through sugar. For some reason, they settled her stomach.

Overhead, the last of the crows were flapping into the pines and cawing. All afternoon the woods had been silent except for the small twittering squeaks of sparrows, but at dusk the crows started to collect, as they did every night all winter long. She liked having them there, behind her, perhaps watching out for her. She'd read that they were highly intelligent, like parrots, with the IQ of a five-year-old human. Since then, she'd been observing them with a new respect. She just couldn't see what made them smart. The configuration of their brain was different from that of the human brain, the article had said.

She looked at the dark blot of a crow's head and wondered how big its brain could be. As large as a quarter? a fifty-cent piece? But was size everything? A human brain was lots larger, but humans used only a tiny part of it, a quarter, a fifty-cent piece . . .

She laughed for the first time in weeks, and liked how it made her belly relax. She really was better off out here, snuggling down by the fire in the little nest she'd built out of a ground cloth, her sleeping bag, and a tarp she'd staked to cover her head.

The dark came to rest quietly, stilling the crows, until only the chewing of the horses as they pulled the grass and the hiss and crack of the pine fire were left. Stars hung above, but clouds moving in from the west gradually blotted them out. In a few hours there would be nothing to see. Latta shivered. She wasn't cold or afraid; it was something else. All her adult life she'd been trying so hard to become a person who was consistent, solid. Now she saw that there were pockets of secret desires perforating her.

Jaboy must have had something inside him that made him so spoiled, so bent on spoiling life for himself and everything around him. His kind of desperation frightened her at the end — and should have at the beginning, only she'd been determined to escape her parents, her youthful misery. It had taken her a few years with Jaboy to learn what misery could really be. Yet she'd forgiven him when he died. She'd kissed his coffin and said goodbye, feeling like someone in a Dracula movie, praying the stake was still in his heart, that the motion into the ground wouldn't jiggle it loose so he could rise again, track her down, and start all over.

She wasn't tired, but she was thirsty. Rummaging in her packs, she found the herbal tea in the plastic bag Inez had sent along. The old woman was always burning herbs and mixing concoctions of stinky weeds for cures and purgatives. More than once, Latta had found groupings of sticks and pebbles, feathers and beads, and other things around the house and yard. Once there'd been a small clipping of Elvis from a magazine, another time the faces of men with the backdrop of the Crazy Horse Monument and Mount Rushmore superimposed in a corner. She resisted asking Inez about her altars. This tea was supposed to bring sleep naturally, uninterrupted, unimpeded. Anonymous sleep. That's all she wanted, to sleep without knowing it again — the way she had before she'd met Cody, before she'd lost her horse and gotten pregnant.

While the tea cooled, she put a few more small limbs on the coals so she could fall asleep with the warmth and light on her face. The drink was a little bitter and smoky, as if it had drawn its flavor from the ashes of the fire. She closed her eyes, smiling at how relaxed she felt, yet aware of another voice inside saying, Come and get me, as her waiting dreams were beckoning her. The last thing she remembered was watching the coals of the fire blink out one by one.

It was Cody who came. Cody, the way he smiled shyly, pressing his wide lips in boyish happiness, dropping his eyes in sadness at certain thoughts. The bareness of his shoulder, the small round knuckle of bone that sat there, the lean ropy muscles of his arms, the naked thrust of his long wrists, the ridges of muscle on his stomach. She'd wanted nightmares, something she could battle. Not this loving. Not this man she had no defense against. Not this longing.

Then there was the long line of his torso, his arms stretched along the top of the headboard. He wore a pale grey Stetson she'd bought for him, dipped down on his forehead so his eyes shone pale yellow and sexy, watching her as she bent over his naked groin. Watching her from a distance, as if he were saying, Can you do it? Can you make me? Can you move me?

She shook her head and backed away. There was a baby she had to get help for. It was in a net bag, naked like a piece of suet, and it was winter. She had to take it to the doctor on an old horse, an old swaybacked white horse as short as a pony.

She didn't have a winter coat, she was already getting cold, what about the baby? Naked in a net bag tied to the saddle horn? She had to wrap it up, she suddenly realized, and opened the bag. It was cold and rubbery. It's dead, she yelled. But it opened its eyes, beautiful green eyes, and she knew it was still alive, not even shaking in the cold. It wasn't even sick, it was healthy and pink. But a man had given it to her dead, she thought. He thought it was dead, didn't he? He'd been trying to trick her with a dead baby.

Although her watch said 5 A.M. when she woke up, the crows were cawing and swinging in great circles over the clearing, venturing out and back as if they were negotiating directions among themselves. She blinked at the cold fire. She'd been crying in her sleep. Her eyes still felt grainy, wet, sad. There was a catch in her breathing, and she discovered that she had the hiccups and couldn't stop, as if the last sob had gotten caught there and couldn't get out. She tried willing herself silent, telling her chest to stop heaving, stop thrusting up to the catch, but it wasn't working. She struggled out of the sleeping bag and stood up.

Her horses were lying down a few yards away. She made herself ignore the hiccups of trapped sadness as she dug out another doughnut. She was way past crying, she realized. Losing this man was like losing a part of herself. If Cody cared, he would have come for her. If he cared, he wouldn't have left her that day or stolen her horse. If he cared, he'd be here now. But this wasn't about him, was it, she reasoned, trying to stuff a bite of the doughnut into her mouth between hiccups, only to spit it out again when it wouldn't go down her throat.

She was the one in trouble here, not him. She was the one who couldn't catch her breath for the memory of their last night together trapped in her chest, trying to cry out her need. The oval silver of his belt buckle flashed at her and she stumbled as she dragged wood for her fire. He'd won the belt that day he'd broken his collarbone, and she'd yelled at Heywood. The hiccups grew as she remembered the flap of leather tongue that hung off his slender hips. She'd never, never wanted a man like this. She threw the matches down, dropped to her knees beside the cold fire, and tried weeping.

She plunged her hands into the barely warm ashes and smeared them on her cheeks, down her shirt, the front of her jeans. She grabbed more and rubbed them in her hair. She threw back her head and howled, long and loud. The sound, full of her loneliness and grief, pushed her voice up the hill, past the treetops, into the sky.

By the time she fell asleep again in the flat grey morning light, big sticky flakes of snow were starting to blot out the woods and horses.

By twilight Marcus was staggering with exhaustion from going all day in the storm. Cody was just getting ready to stop and rest again when they slipped and went tumbling into the creek. The snow had swollen its waters, so he was waist deep before he could step out, pulling the struggling horse with him. With the approach of night, the snowflakes were getting bigger and thicker. Sometimes that meant the end of a storm, but Joseph had promised a blizzard when Cody had called about bringing the two horses he owed, then called again to find out where Latta had gone after Inez had called him. Kya and Joseph said they couldn't start for a few hours, so he'd left the second horse in the trailer parked beside Latta's. The temperature had been dropping all day, but Cody hadn't really noticed until he stepped out of the creek and felt the immediate frigid bite on his legs, the icy water sloshing in his boots.

He was trying to lead Marcus to level ground where he could remount safely, but the horse stopped after every step and put his ears up. Finally he let out the little questioning whinny he'd been using all afternoon. This time there was an answering neigh. Marcus puffed his body up, shook his head, and raised his tail, spinning one direction, then the other as he bellowed loudly. Cody stood still, listening, but the storm muffled the direction of the sounds, so he couldn't tell which way they were coming from.

"I hope you know where you're going." Cody patted the horse as he climbed on again. "Let's go." He nudged Marcus, giving him his head. The horse stayed with the creek, climbing the hill faster in the blue twilight than he had all day, whinnying and grunting every few minutes, listening with his ears pricked for answers.

It was only a few minutes before he came to the little sheltered lee by the creek where two snow-covered horses watched them as if frozen in place. Marcus whinnied again and the two came to life, trotting through the drifts, snorting loudly and trembling. Cody looked around for Latta, but all he could see were mounds of snow. He dismounted and struggled down the low hill where he could see better. Then he spotted the one black edge of the tarp that was still staked up and ran toward it, calling "Latta?" His legs and feet were so ice-encased he could hardly lift them, but it didn't matter now.

23 ✦ *WHITEOUT*

The blizzard caught Emerald Smith and Colin Young in North Platte having a Chinese dinner after their annual checkups. Hiram Green hooked up an old sled to his roping horse and pulled feed to his cows, saying it was the best time he's had in years. Bode and Liz Hewitt have returned home from their travels in warmer places. They report the Mirage Hotel and Casino in Las Vegas is fabulous. There they saw the white tigers, the two baby dolphins born in the indoor pool — the baby boy dolphin has since died — and the erupting volcano that turned the waterfall red.

— *BABYLON CALLER*

*I*t doesn't take much to get lost in a storm like this," Greta said as they packed the Blazer with sleeping bags, spare blankets, and food.

Kya didn't pause as she stuffed the stack of newspapers into a corner. "If you're so worried, stay here. Joseph's cousin will take care of you. I'll come back when we find them."

Greta shook her head, and the snow accumulating on her hair slid off. "You might need another pair of hands." She didn't add that she couldn't trust Kya to come back for her. The only way to keep up with Kya was to stick with her. She didn't like it, but Kya was the closest thing she'd had to a friend in years.

"Better put these on." Kya tossed her a pair of Joseph's cousin's chaps. "Least they'll keep the cold out for a while. Even wet, they'll be some protection."

Greta held up the pieces of leather and shook her head. "You'll need these — I'll be riding behind you. I have two pairs of jeans on." She tossed them back to Kya, who shrugged and strapped them around her waist, then bent to fasten the sides around her legs.

"You women packed?" Joseph said. "I got the horse loaded. My cousin Ray says his truck is a bull in this snow, even with the missing headlights. It's got the CB too, so we can call for help if we have to." Joseph was wearing a greasy, torn tan jumpsuit over his jeans and flannel shirts. He grinned as Kya looked him up and down.

"That's got more holes than cloth, Joseph." She slammed the back gate of the Blazer and turned the key in the lock to raise the window.

"What's left is waterproof."

"Ready to roll?" Kya walked to the driver's side and pulled the door open. "I'll lead. Honk your horn if you get in trouble." She stood on the running board, looking back at the beat-up truck and the rusty stock trailer it was pulling. The horse inside kicked and stamped, shaking the rig from side to side. Even above the wind and snow, they could hear the creak and whine of the tired metal joints. "That thing gonna make it?"

Joseph nodded. "Sure. Only looks bad. Our vehicles have to look like this or they think we stole 'em."

"Just wish you'd talked your cousin out of another horse. This riding double is crazy."

"He's a strong horse. Could probably carry all three of us."

"Let's go. Storm's only getting worse." Kya climbed in and settled beside Greta, who sat shivering on the passenger's side. "Heat in a minute, girl." She started the engine, revved it a couple of times, and peered through the windshield, which kept crusting up with snow despite the wipers. She could see only a few yards ahead before the road swirled out of sight. "This is gonna be one bitch of a deal. Goddamn Latta. She has to kill herself and take my brother with her. You keep your eyes on that red cloth on Joseph's antenna, okay? If there's too long a time when you last saw him, holler and I'll slow down. Just remember, he won't be able to stop very fast on this stuff, and I don't want him climbing up our ass with that rig. Who knows if the brakes work."

Kya let out the brake and they eased forward down the road toward the highway. They'd have to go across the most desolate area of the Rosebud Reservation, with no houses or ranches visible from the pavement, before they could cut down into Nebraska and reach the area where Joseph's cabin was. The roads would be drifted and slippery.

"Wouldn't it make sense to go back down across the border where there'd be more traffic?" Greta asked.

"Don't have time. Just hang on. Keep your seat belt fastened. And watch Joseph. We're screwed if we lose him." Kya pressed the truck up to thirty, then forty, ignoring the way the snow ruts wanted to catch and twist the wheels. She kept the steering wheel firmly in her grip, making it behave, muttering curses to herself without looking back.

The red flag behind them was gone for several minutes before Greta groaned. "Oh no, it's a whiteout — I can't see behind us. Slow down, Kya."

"Shit." She applied the brakes a tiny bit at a time, letting the easing on the gas pedal do most of the slowing. "See him now?"

"No." Greta had a terrible feeling she'd lost him for good. She hadn't been paying attention.

"Now?"

"No."

"I can't just stop, Greta, he'll rear-end us. You have to watch carefully."

"Wait — wait — okay, yeah, there's the red thing, just go a little slower. He's creeping along back there." Greta heaved a big sigh.

"Jesus, Greta, we have to get there before dark or we can kiss all our asses goodbye."

"Just be careful, Kya. How're we gonna know where to turn off? Everything looks the same in the snow, the way it's coming down." Greta looked at the disappearing land around them.

"Joseph described the place. Should look like a goddamned parking lot by now if Cody and Latta found it too." Kya drove with a confidence Greta would never feel about anything. She couldn't imagine Kya as old, she realized as she watched the unlined face staring into the white ahead of them. Even if the skin failed, and the bones, Kya would never follow that disintegration.

Some women were old at twenty or thirty — little mamas and grandmas, even as children. Others seemed to take a while longer, until something broke them, like a horse to saddle, and they quit caring so much. They plodded heavily into the stores, bought their little items, plodded heavily back home.

Then there were a few women who were always the wild ones, loose, tramps, town sluts. They were the first to do anything: smoke, drink, try drugs and sex, drive too fast, shoplift, have babies out of wedlock and abandon them, anything and everything. They died early, turned into drunks or nut cases, or fell into a man's hands and got beaten so regularly they couldn't get off their knees again. Only once in a while did this kind of woman survive and remain wild, as if she couldn't be caught, and there wasn't any pen or fence she could be trusted in. That was Kya. She escaped, no matter what she did. It was worth it just to have a Kya around, like the last uncaught, untamed horse. They needed that kind of woman; she made the rest of them brave once in a while, Greta decided.

"Watch out," Kya said, and pulled hard against the steering wheel as the truck tried to swerve and slide, plowing through a drift in the road. When they'd straightened out again, Kya glanced over. "You okay?"

Greta laughed. "I'm fine. Perfectly fine." She put her mittened hand over Kya's bare one on the wheel, then pulled her hand back.

"Some fun, huh?" Kya smiled, her green eyes lighting up.

"The best," Greta said. She meant it too. She was glad to be here, listening to the *thump thump* of the slushy ice as it splashed up against the undercarriage, breathing the stale hot air of the truck mixed with the light mildew of the blankets and the musty ink of the newspapers, and seeing the blankness beyond the snow just ahead. She wouldn't have ever had the courage to come this far alone. She'd still be in that bathtub, soaking off the smoky grease of Wanita's Sweete Shoppe and killing time until she had to go for Emil. Now she'd never go back. She wouldn't have to anyway, not now. Emil was hooked up with Arthur and John. He hadn't been to the Senior Citizens Center in a week. And he didn't seem concerned where his daughter was.

That was almost the best part. She was the only one who knew where she was. No one was keeping track. No one told her not to get into Kya Bennett's Blazer and head out in the middle of a blizzard to rescue a pregnant widow and her handsome cowboy lover. For the first time, everything seemed clear and understandable and complete. And she wasn't afraid of anything.

It happened as they were heading west toward Chadron on Route 20. And it happened slowly, as bad things often do. First they left the road, and the windshield went white. The Blazer tried to grip something, but there were only the mountains of snow, spinning and spinning toward them, a thump and crackle from behind that sent them one way, then another, the Blazer airborne, flying with the snow, Kya gripping the wheel terribly, Greta silent as they flipped and landed upside down.

When everything stopped, there was silence except for the wind blowing flakes through the smashed windows, sprinkling the extra blankets and food. Kya loosened her grip on the useless steering wheel and shook her head. There were a few small cuts on her face and hands, but she was fine otherwise. She looked around in wonder, then realized she was hanging in her seat by the belt. She was trying to release it when Greta moaned, and Kya looked over as if just remembering about the other woman. Blood began to seep from a cut on Greta's forehead, and her face was too white.

"Greta?" Kya called softly, waiting for her to open her eyes. "Greta? Wake up. We're okay."

The eyelids fluttered, then opened, and she began to struggle wildly.

"Stop. We had an accident. We're okay."

Greta looked at Kya, then slowly smiled. "I was having the best dream. Are we dead?"

Kya frowned. "Don't be stupid. Now, help me get outta this, and I'll help you, then we have to see where Joseph ended up. I knew he was going to hit us — I could feel it for the past fifteen minutes. Shoulda listened to myself." She fumbled with the belt until Greta released her, and she pushed the door open and climbed out, letting in a huge swirl of snow.

"Hey," Greta yelled.

Kya turned around and, hanging over the edge of the truck, leaned in and pulled Greta out.

A moment later Joseph appeared, leading Latta's stallion, his sleeve pulled up to expose a cut that was oozing pink through the snow he'd packed on it. "You son of a bitch. You had him all along!" Kya yelled, grabbing the lead rope.

"Winants boys never could hang on to anything," Joseph

said. "Anyway, I ended up in the ditch on the other side. We're not gonna git that rig out today, though, I can tell you that. Lucky we only jackknifed and slid after we banged into you." He wrapped his dirty handkerchief around his arm, hunching over with his back to the wind.

"I can't believe you have Latta's stallion," Kya was saying over and over, as if the accident had jarred something loose in her voice box.

"Ray found him for me."

The stallion licked Kya's fingers and nuzzled her hair in recognition. She blew in his nose and he blew back, then flung his head up and shook off the snow collecting on his mane.

"What're we gonna do now?" Greta asked, hugging herself and blinking away the pelting snow.

"Well, we still have to go after Cody and Latta." Kya looked down the highway. The snow dissipated for the moment, and they could see farther than they'd been able to the whole trip. They weren't far from the turnoff, but it was probably too far to walk. They needed the horse.

"What we could do, the two of us ride the stud in. We're close enough. Just have to leave one of us here." Joseph and Kya both glanced at Greta, then at the hills that were beginning to mount around them, with the straggles of pines and cedar that indicated they were nearing Chadron.

"But what'll I do?" Greta whispered.

"My truck's okay, just stuck. You wait in the cab with the CB, keep trying to raise someone to come and get you. I tried but nothing came up. We'll leave blankets and coffee and food. You shouldn't be here long. This storm won't keep everyone off the roads. There's always more fools like us around." Joseph went to the back of the Blazer to pull supplies out, as if it were already decided.

"Kya?" Greta asked in a small voice.

"It'll be okay. He's right. Of the three of us, you're the one who should stay. I'm stronger and can ride better, babe. That's just the plain fact of it. Soon as I get my brother, I'll be back and make sure you got out, but I *know* you won't be here that long. Even if you have to spend the night, you'll be warm enough. Run the heater once in a while, but don't forget to crack the window. If the temperature drops some more, you'll be okay, long as you stay with the truck. Nobody could miss the mess we got here — someone'll probably come along ten minutes after we leave. You'll be someplace warm, drinking hot whiskey, and I'll be out there freezing my butt off."

She moved to the back of the Blazer and helped Joseph unpack and carry stuff across the road to the truck while Greta held the stallion's lead rope. When he tried to nuzzle her hair, he found the blood and stepped away. After that, he stood a respectful distance from her without trying to tug on the rope.

"Here." Kya dug some bills and a credit card out of her jeans and handed them to Greta. "Call Arthur, tell him what's going on. Then hole up in a motel in Chadron. We'll be there in a day or two. Have a drink on me, okay?" They hugged for the first time, which surprised and pleased Greta.

The cab of Ray's truck wasn't as luxurious as the Blazer, and it smelled of years of exhaust and sweat. Greta sat with a blanket around her shoulders, another around her legs. The newspapers for insulation rested on the seat beside her. She'd wait to wrap those around herself. Through the windshield — which was starting to ice up, so she had to keep scraping at it with her fingernails — she watched Kya and Joseph saddle the stallion and tie bags, blankets, and sleeping bags on themselves and then mount, Kya in front, Joseph behind. With a last wave they were gone, leaving the truck in white, icy silence.

She watched her breath for a while, puffing out in little clouds, then disappearing onto the windows, which were soon sheeted with an opacity it took her nails longer and longer to dig through. She thought the temperature was falling, but decided she was probably just cold from sitting still. As the afternoon light began to fail, she experienced a small panic, struggling with blankets, steering wheel, newspapers, food they'd given her, as if everything were working against her. Then she remembered to turn on the CB and broadcast, but she couldn't think of anything to say except, "Help, I'm off Twenty, our trucks slid off." Then added, "Near Chadron," and flipped the dial off. She didn't want to suck the battery dry; the CB was so staticy already. When she couldn't stand the cold or the silence anymore, she turned the ignition and flipped the heater switch, letting the ping and grinding whip of the motor comfort her for a few minutes, then turned it off again.

Her head had begun to ache, as if her brain were swelling, or the blood that had seeped outward at first were spilling inside. She was so cold, she reasoned, that was the real problem. Her head wouldn't hurt so much if she weren't so cold. She looked at the newspapers on the seat, then swept them off onto the floor. She wasn't going to wrap up in old newspapers. The whole thing was too ridiculous. She'd just turn the heater on and leave it on. Joseph had said there were two huge gas tanks that would get her through the night if necessary. And she'd keep trying the CB and someone would find her.

The heat felt good, even if it was a little smelly from the dusty old ducts, and she liked having the windshield defrosted and the side windows melted off, even though she couldn't see anything but the eerie dark blue and grey of the snow falling. She liked how cozy the truck was becoming, how the defroster blew the round beaded dream catcher hanging from the rearview mirror, making the feathers dance lightly. It looked like an irregular spider web, everything spinning off the circle toward the center in jiggly lines. Maybe it was supposed to hypnotize you, put you to sleep, she thought as her eyelids drooped. Not while you're driving, she argued, shush, she said, it's so nice here, so warm, so familiar, Kya, Kya — she smiled and held her arms out for the figure walking toward her. I'm glad you're back, she murmured in her mind, I missed you.

There was something else, something Kya was trying to tell

her. "What?" She tried lifting her lids, but it was too hard, so she decided to just look through them. Something about the window, oh, she'd forgotten to leave the window cracked. Had she? No, it was too cold, that was why, the snow kept trying to get in the truck. "It doesn't matter," she murmured to the other woman. "Let's just stay here and sleep. I did the brave thing, didn't I, Kya? I did it." She smiled.

There was a small jerk in the muscles of the figure stretched out on the seat, then a letting go, as intention flowed outward. Hours later, the battery failed and the engine stopped, sealed in the snow that had clogged the tailpipe.

"Watch it, don't — Jesus, am I rescuing you or you rescuing me?" Cody was shaking so hard he couldn't unfasten his iced jeans. Latta had already pulled his boots off, but he hadn't let her touch the ice-stiff socks yet. His feet hurt too bad. It turned out that Joseph's cabin was just on top of the next hill from where Latta had camped, and it hadn't taken them long to move up there and force the door open after digging the drift away with their hands. The horses were safe, waiting out the storm in the little corral Cody'd rigged with rope under the shelter of the pines. The animals had forgone the usual getting-to-know-you period of adjustment and bunched together immediately when he'd turned them loose.

"Just get the fire going, let me do this." He waved her hands off, struggling again to unbutton his jeans.

Latta stood and looked around for paper or kindling, then spied the books on the corner table and the wood by the door. Except for the evidence of a deer hunter or two, who'd left the place relatively neat, no one had lived here since Joseph had brought Cody out. She chose an anthology of English literature over the native-medicine book, because its pages were tissue thin and would catch better, she decided. She hoped it wasn't one of Joseph's favorites. In a few minutes the crackling and popping of the juniper, with the first smoky puffs that refused the cold chimney and entered the room instead, made them feel more comfortable, safe. Methodically piling logs on, Latta was aware that after the sleep in the snow, her body felt better than it had in three months. When Cody had woken her, the nausea was gone for the first time, and she was hungry, ravenous in fact.

Without looking directly at Cody, she threw her coat on him and took his wet clothes to the fireplace to dry. "Blankets on that shelf over your head," she said. "I'll fix us something to eat."

"There's soup in those bags on my saddle," he said through chattering teeth. While she was looking for food, she found a sweatshirt she'd packed and tossed that in his direction. "Thanks," he murmured.

She found the soup, but no can opener. Just like a man. She went through the rest of his things, found his big knife, and with the thick blade punctured the soup can and jacked it open, nicking her finger on the ragged edge of the lid. She took down Joseph's two pans hanging by the fireplace and poured the soup in one before realizing she'd have to go outside for snow to make the water necessary for it. Glancing at Cody, curled on his side, knees drawn up and snoring lightly, she hoped he wasn't suffering from hypothermia.

It took her a few minutes to push open the door that a snowdrift had shut again, and when she did, she gathered enough snow in the pan and coffeepot to melt for drinking and cooking. The storm was building, and she wondered if she could make it out to the woodpile and back without getting lost. Joseph had left a small amount of wood inside that they'd go through before long.

Here she was, taking care of him again. Every time he tried to take care of her, he nearly got himself killed, it seemed. She would've been fine — well, she couldn't say that for sure. What if she'd just kept sleeping and her body got too cold? Maybe if he hadn't come for her — but she'd never know, would she.

Squatting in front of the fire, she felt her belly, beginning to swell against her pants. She touched it hesitantly, not certain that she wanted to make friends with it. What if it came out looking just like Cody and she had to face that the rest of her life? What if it looked and acted just as messed up as him, or Kya, or Bennetts in general? Or what if it was like her mother, dark as a reservation Indian? What if all the Indian came through, and it was treated like an Indian all its life? What if it hated her for the white blood? A child could be taught to hate anything.

Unconsciously, she tapped the small swelling as if to say, You just behave in there. Don't give me any of your father's shit, hear? Then she put her palm on it and rubbed back and forth. The soup was beginning to boil on the fire, and it smelled delicious. The water in the pot had begun to steam too, and she stood reaching down two mugs off the shelf that held the few dishes. She shook out the insect carcasses dotting the bottoms, dropped in tea bags, and poured each full of hot water. She found two spoons and a single bowl and poured half the soup into that, her mouth watering over the little pieces of vegetables and pasta letters floating in the thin red broth.

She left the pan with her soup in it beside the fire to stay warm and went to the bed with Cody's. There was a moment as she kneeled beside the cot, a moment when she saw the pulse caught blue in the curve of his neck, fluttering against the skin, that she remembered what it had been like to rest herself on such a fine strength as the bones and muscles of his body. She shook his shoulder. "Wake up — eat some soup."

He took a long time to come back from his sleep, and when his eyes opened he just stared at her, and she could see how far and long he'd been away. They were a calm blue, watching her as quietly as if he were still asleep, and she couldn't look away either, they'd caught her. They didn't seem to be him, not the him she was angry with, not the him who had let her down.

It was the him she took a chance with, the only man she could ever stand to let look that long into her eyes.

When he lifted his fingers to touch her face, she pulled back and held the soup out. "Here."

He let her hold it that way for a long moment, then swung his legs up and crossed them, sitting up, being careful to use the blankets to cover himself. She went back to the hearth for the pan and a spoon for herself. She was going to squat there and eat, but decided to join him — to make sure he ate, she told herself.

"I haven't had alphabet soup since I was a kid," she commented between mouthfuls. "Still tastes good."

"Hm." He spooned the soup in so quickly, she wondered how long it'd been since he'd eaten. He didn't smell like liquor at least, so he hadn't been out honky-tonking, though she had found his quart of whiskey in his pack. Who the hell would pack that weight in?

"You okay, Latta?"

She stopped, letting the spoon clang back into the remnant of the soup at the bottom. "Want more?"

He looked down, then at the wall opposite, letting his eyes follow the logs to the fireplace and sweep back around. He shook his head. "I'm fine. Thanks."

"There's tea."

She handed him the mug and took the bowl in return. On the bottom he had saved as many letters as he could, and written, I LV U. She turned away so he couldn't see her face. Then she turned back, taking the spoon and mashing the macaroni into a whitish pulp.

"It's a little late for that, don't you think?" she demanded.

He ducked his head and she wanted to pummel him. What right did he have to make her feel sorry for him? As if she'd screwed *him* over. She went back to the fireplace and scraped the remains of the macaroni into the fire, liking the searing odor that flooded the room for a moment.

He moved so quietly, it was only the swirl of the blanket he'd wrapped around his waist that she caught in the corner of her eye that told her he was up, moving toward the door. She whirled, thinking at first that he meant to leave, but he stopped by the spill of their things and began searching. He stood up, a comic figure in a dark green army blanket skirt, red sweatshirt so small it looked like a child's, and rumpled hair that lay in wild peaks and plains on his head. In his hand he held the quart of Irish whiskey, his eyes muddied brown and black.

"Cody, don't —" Latta started to get up.

"Screw you, Latta." His voice was cold and she shrugged and turned her back. Behind her she could hear him uncapping the bottle and putting it to his lips, letting the long gurgle slide down his throat, unimpeded until he stopped for a moment, gasping for breath and hiccuping as if the whiskey wanted to come back up.

It scared her. If he got drunk and did something, she wouldn't be able to stop him. She got up slowly, unconsciously holding her right hand over her belly as if to balance and protect it, as she would in the months to come.

"We're going to need more wood pretty soon," she said, looking around the cabin. The only chair was a handmade wooden straight-back, hanging from a peg on the wall. She went over, reached it down, and set it a few feet from the cot, facing Cody, who was propped against the wall, sitting cross-legged, blanket over his shoulders, the bottle cradled in his lap.

"Go get it," he said, tipping the bottle to his mouth again and drinking. His eyes watered a little from the explosion in his chest and stomach, but he sniffed and ignored it, keeping his eyes on her.

"Why don't you grow up, Cody. Just grow up." She crossed her arms and dug her fingernails into the flesh along her ribs, pinching.

He laughed harshly and deliberately put the bottle to his

lips again, keeping the liquid pouring down his throat even longer than before, without taking his eyes off her. When he pulled it away, she saw that he'd already drunk a third.

"What do you want, Latta? Just what the hell do you want from me?" His voice was already starting to slur, losing the metallic edge it'd had a moment ago. He drank again, and this time it seemed automatic, as if he might forget to stop. She almost stood up and took the bottle before he choked and stopped.

"I loved you," he accused.

She felt herself softening, but it was the whiskey talking now and that made her mad. "Didn't last long, did it? First chance you got, you stole my horse and left me, you son of a bitch. You know the only thing I hate about being pregnant?" She paused, letting the fear and uncertainty fill his eyes. He put the bottle to his lips, then stopped and lowered it. "I hate that it has to be half yours." Her mouth went twisted and ugly, as if she were spitting out the foulest thing she'd ever tasted.

She liked how it shook him, how he turned his head as if she'd hit him. He put his hand over his mouth, either to stop himself from vomiting or speaking. The wind outside bodied up against the cabin, pushing on the walls until they creaked, and little pelts of icy snow spattered the window in gusty bursts.

"You don't give an inch, do you Latta? Nobody can ever make a mistake around you. Like you're so perfect or something." He waved off her opening mouth. "What did I ever do to you, just tell me that. Is it Kya? Because I care about my sister, won't let you drive her away because she was young and your husband took advantage of that?" He waved her off again and drank quickly.

"I feel sorry for you. I really do feel sorry for you — makes you crazy to hear that, doesn't it? Little half-breed Indian girl married to a jaded old fart for the money. She never has to lift a finger unless she wants to, then he fucks some other little girls and doesn't want her anymore, over the hill at thirty, yeah, that was a raw deal, so fucking what, Latta?" He held up his palm while he took another drink.

"Then the old bastard dies and you're scot-free. You get money and land, you can do anything you want. You did too. Next you start fucking around with me. And I almost get killed trying to take care of you and your horse. Okay, we fall in love — don't say anything, Latta. That did happen. *We fell in love.*" He stopped and drank slowly for the first time, letting himself taste the whiskey.

"Things are good — so I think. But I'm wrong, aren't I? Things are still fucked up, because you, Latta, you haven't really made up your mind about me or the whole goddamned world you think owes you something. For what — a lost horse, a husband, a life you didn't get?" He took a deep breath. "Yeah, you wanna know the truth, Latta? When I left that day, I thought I'd fix everything. Find the horse again and ask you to marry me. Pretty fucking stupid, I guess." He slowly lifted the bottle and drank as if he were drifting off into another place.

"But you know what?" He waited for her to shake her head. "The baby's mine. I still want to marry you. I want to raise the kid. There's been way too many kids with only one parent in my family. This one is gonna have a mom *and* a dad. I decided." He lifted the bottle, then put it back down, watching her hopefully.

"I don't know what land of Oz you live in, Cody, but nobody tells me what to do. Especially about getting married. Where were you the past weeks when I was puking my guts out all day long? Why do you think we're out here in the middle of a blizzard like this? You think coming after me and having me drag you up here before hypothermia kills you makes up for everything? I'm gonna have one kid, I don't need two. Now give me a drink of that."

She reached over for the bottle, half rising from the chair, but he held it against his chest and shook his head.

"Cody —"

He squinted at the label. "'Could cause harm to unborn children —'" He grinned and took another long pull off the bottle. He was at the stage where he was getting drunk and didn't know it yet. She didn't want him any further along than that.

"Just one little one, to warm up," she said in a soft low voice, enjoying the flicker in his eyes when he caught her sensuality.

"Come here, then," he said in a muffled voice, protecting the bottle in the crook of his arm.

She hesitated, then shrugged. He opened his legs and she slipped across his lap, letting her legs hang over his and leaning back against his arm. "Here, I'll hold it." He tipped the bottle to her lips and yanked it away so quickly, after a thin trickle, that it bumped her front teeth.

"Ow, watch it." She punched him in the chest harder than she intended and he caught her hand, squeezing it until she opened her fist. Taking a quick drink while keeping his eyes on her, he started to put the bottle to her lips again. As she tipped her head back, he leaned down and kissed her instead, letting a tiny spill of whiskey roll from his tongue onto hers. It sent such a warmth through her, she shivered, trying to resist the heat and weight of his body, the soft throb between her legs. Get mad, she urged herself, but the looseness already in his muscles seemed to seep into hers. You slut, she accused herself. But she felt like she hadn't eaten in months, years, and here he was, so rich and sweet, she snuggled against him, pretended to resist, and he kissed her deeper.

When his fingers tentatively stroked her swollen and tender breasts, she almost tore her shirt off for him. She reached under the blanket and put her hand on the hardness between his legs. She wanted him to hurry. She felt her personality disappearing. She didn't think anymore, she just wanted, wanted him, wanted to keep her eyes closed and be two animals, tearing each other slowly to bits.

She woke up first. He hadn't lost his power to move her, she thought. It came on gradually, like the clothes she was dressing in: that was why she should hate him. The very reason — his power to touch and move her, to make her forget and forgive. Jaboy had done that to her until she hated herself and then him so much she wanted to die. She wasn't going to get herself in that fix again. She wasn't going to give herself over to her body like that. She couldn't trust herself or him.

She walked to the fire and stared back at the corner where Cody lay sprawled, snoring in little snorkely breaths, spewing the dead smell of alcohol and sex into the room. Make him ugly, she demanded of herself. Find every ugly little thing about him. She shook her head and hugged herself. The stroke of his fingers was too new on her body, she could still feel them between her legs, doing what he'd learned to do to make her come, patiently, just the right rhythm and pressure. She hated that she'd taught him that. That he'd walk around the world every day knowing that he could slip his fingers down there and do that anytime he wanted. She must've been crazy. She stood for a long time, watching the fire without realizing it was dying out.

He slipped up behind her, wrapping his arms around her and pressing his naked body against her back before she could stop him, enclosing them in the blanket he wore around his shoulders. She let him stand like that for a few minutes, until he slid his hands down, resting them possessively on the small mound of her belly. She ducked out of his arms and turned. "We need more wood."

He stared at the fire and the blanket dropped off his shoulders. His hair hung damply on his bare shoulders, and as the light flickered up and down his long muscled limbs, the purple scars were dark holes. "I'll go," he said quietly. He pulled his drying jeans from the little hooks to the side of the fireplace. He dressed tiredly, as if everything in his life were just another chore that had to be done now.

He looked at her once before he shoved the door open against the drifts. In his eyes was something she couldn't read because of the shadows and because, after all, she didn't want to.

He was gone so long, she worried he'd gotten lost or left her. But she wouldn't let herself go anyplace with the idea. She made herself sit in that cold center she'd found, the place that numbed her, that made the wet draining between her legs onto her underpants just another way she betrayed herself.

When the door finally started to unwedge again, she went and pushed at it to help. Cody's figure was covered with white, as if he'd painted himself, down to his eyelashes and eyebrows. His face was burned red. He dropped the armload of wood on the floor and stamped the snow off his boots. Pulling his gloves off, he stood in front of the fire, holding his hands out to the flame, turning them over as if he were trying to toast them. "Wood's dry. I dug through the top levels. More outside the door so we don't have to go far. That's what took me so long," he added, as if she'd asked. Puddles of water formed around each foot in front of the fire. "Checked the horses. They're okay. Storm's made 'em goosy." He chuckled at some private image and unbuttoned his coat, then untied the scarf holding his hat on.

"Almost stopped snowing, but the wind's come up so bad, we wouldn't make it out anyway." He turned to warm his back and wiped his face with the tag end of the damp scarf. The front of his jeans was splotched dark with melted snow. He figured if he stood in front of the fire long enough, maybe his clothes would dry on him. A little more whiskey would help too.

After he'd piled three big logs on the fire, he hung up his

coat and put the straight-back chair in front of the fire so he could drink in comfort. He was just uncapping the bottle when Latta went over to the cot and lay down. The room was silent for a long time except for the fire bursting a pocket of resin or the wind outside finding something loose and banging it off or whistling around the sharp edges of the cabin. It had been built so tightly, there wasn't much to resist the wind except the edges.

Drinking, he was able to forget the angry face behind him and to let his mind choose other ideas. He found himself thinking about the baby, how he'd teach her to ride and hunt and work cattle. He knew it'd be a girl. But he wouldn't let her be useless, not like Kya was made by Heywood. She'd be more like Latta, able to do things, take care of herself, but she wouldn't be afraid like Latta. She'd be strong enough to love. He felt a little jealousy rise up in him. He'd have to stop himself from wanting to make her love only him — like Caroline had done. Even when he was too big, his mother had brought him into her bed on nights Heywood wasn't there, holding him and crooning, "You're my man, my little man, you're the only man I love." He'd felt proud and ashamed at the same time, pushing away from her and walking the cold floor back to his bed, where the sheets had chilled and he'd have to slide in and warm them up all over again.

He wouldn't do that to his child. If Latta gave him a chance, he'd be a good father. This was something he would know how to do — and if he didn't, he'd learn. He didn't know why he thought this, but he did. It came from his gut. It was like herding cattle, breaking horses, making love. Loving a child. That he could do. That he could.

In deer-hunting season the streets of Babylon are lined with cars and trucks with the dead displayed on them. Gutted and splayed, the insides bloody to the sky, they spread their legs in obscene gynecological display. There's this odd disrespect about it. They aren't even accorded the care given household objects, rolled rugs and Formica-topped kitchen tables. Inside the bars hunters drink and laugh in bloody clothes, newly sprouted whiskers and sour breath, while the kill waits, a bundle of fur and flesh, dogs sniffing hungrily at the long pink tongues, the gelid staring eyes, the black nose dripping frozen snot.

— Caroline
October 30, 1977

*H*e was smiling happily to himself, eyes half closed with the images of his future life with his child. It was hard to keep creating the pictures without a name he could call her, so they could talk. She'd be the first person he could really talk to. He'd take her for long rides, even when she was tiny, perched in front of the saddle, and explain the land to her. He could hardly wait until she saw the pelicans fishing in their long curved rows, sailing across the lake, and the avocets, with their long bills and thin mincing legs. She'd like that. She'd like everything he could name and give to her. She'd call him Daddy. He smiled foolishly at the idea, liking the way her pretty lips said it. She'd have his mouth maybe, or Latta's, it didn't matter;

they'd be pretty lips because they were hers. But she needed a name.

"Caroline, Carrie," he said softly.

"What?" Latta's voice startled him. He'd forgotten about her.

"The baby — maybe we could name her Caroline, or Carrie. What do you think?" He tipped the chair on its rear legs and leaned his head back so he could see her upside down. What he saw was the rush of her body as it hurtled off the cot and caught the chair, yanking it all the way over.

"Latta! Ow, goddamn it!" He untangled himself, looking around the floor for the bottle before all the liquid spilled out. When he couldn't find it, he looked up her legs to where it sat cradled in her hands. The glass was lying on its side a few feet away where it'd rolled, the last of the whiskey trickling onto the floorboards.

He stood up warily in case she was going to come after him again. "Latta —" He held his hand out.

"Is this what you want? Is this it?" She held the bottle out, and as he reached for it she hurled it so hard at his head he had to duck. It shattered against the wall behind him, spraying chunks of glass and whiskey across the room.

"You dumb —" He started for her, a little unsteady on his feet, and she kept her hands up, ready to fight him if she had to.

"Dumb what?" she taunted. "Bitch, cunt, whore — which is it? Your whiskey's so important? We're stuck here and I get to watch you get drunk. Just for once I'd like a man to stay sober and talk to me, to have a conversation that made sense from beginning to end. We have to settle this, Cody, and you're loaded again, naming a child you've decided for God knows what reason is going to be born, and for God knows what reason is a girl. You think I'd name a kid of mine after that crazy woman? You got another thing coming."

His slap caught her with her mouth open, and she bit her

tongue enough that blood started right away. She slugged him with her closed fist and he staggered backwards, holding both hands over his nose, head down like he was going to vomit. She watched him take the few steps to the door, push it open, and walk out, leaving the snow to swirl in behind him. She could hear his retching above the wind. When he stumbled back in, pulling the door closed, he was holding a ball of snow against his nose as it stained the white pink, then deepened to red. She took a step toward him. She hadn't meant to do this much damage, though she was holding a piece of her shirt against her mouth and trying to swallow blood herself.

"Cody, I'm sorry."

He waved his hand at her, but wouldn't raise his eyes.

She'd done the thing no one else had ever managed: she'd broken his nose. He could feel it the minute the blow landed, the crack and crunch of cartilage and bone. He hadn't meant to hit her. He hadn't meant anything to come between them again. He picked up the chair and sat down in it, leaning his head back with the snow against his face, though his fingers were getting numb and the blood was dripping through, darkening the front of his flannel shirt in the steady melting red stream. He didn't care.

"Wait." Stepping through the broken glass, she rummaged in her pack and pulled out a towel, got more snow from just outside the door, folded it in the towel, and gave it to him. He let what was left of the bloody snowball drop to the floor.

"Thanks," he said, voice muffled by the bath towel.

"Is it —" She leaned against the wall beside the fireplace, watching him, her arms hugging herself.

"Broken."

They listened to the wind try to crack the log walls open, slamming at them suddenly with a tree limb. The fire was working its way through the wood, melting it red and yellow. It seemed to turn the logs hollow and liquid first, then break them into little chunks, and finally grey flakes and crumbs.

"How's your mouth?" he asked, pulling the bloody towel away for a moment to let his face warm up.

She touched her tongue with her fingers. "Okay. Tongue's sore. Can't do anything about that, though."

"I'm sorry." He kept his gaze on her mouth so he wouldn't catch her eye.

"It's okay. Jesus, look what I did. Isn't there anything —" She took a step toward him.

Stay back, he wanted to say. Just stay back now.

He hated the next part, but he'd seen what could happen to a nose if a person didn't do it, so he nodded. "Got any tape in your first-aid kit? And gauze or cotton?"

She seemed relieved to be doing something as she pulled out the things he asked for and held them up.

"You might have to help me." He closed his eyes and took a deep breath, exhaling slowly the way he did before he'd settle on the back of a horse or bull. "Have to tape my nose straight and stuff some gauze up there to hold it and stop the bleeding." He wanted to add that a stiff shot of whiskey would really help about now. But he'd have to suck it up. Be a real cowboy. He grimaced and touched the nose, trying to see how it wanted to shift with the broken bone, so he could tape it right. Finally he said, "You're gonna have to tape it."

Her hands were shaking as she cut two strips and held the first one over his nose, then let it drop. "I can't. What if I get it wrong and you have to walk around with a crooked nose the rest of your life? You'll never forgive me."

He just closed his eyes and waited.

She held the tape up again, stretched delicately between the tips of her fingers. "I don't want to hurt you."

He looked in her eyes. "Little late for that, isn't it? Just tape the goddamned thing, will you, Latta?"

She squinted and tried to see his face as a problem of geometry, divided into quadrants. There was a grinding sound as she moved the nose into place and snapped the piece of tape on to hold it. He groaned and almost threw up on her. When he settled back again, he nodded slightly for her to stuff the gauze up the nostrils. This time he did vomit, and when he stopped he closed his eyes so he wouldn't see the few remaining bits of alphabet soup mixed with the whiskey-flavored yellow bile on the floor between his feet.

"Cody? Don't pass out."

He lifted his head. "I'm okay." He looked around at the broken glass and the vomit. "Stay out of the way, I gotta clean this up." When she opened her mouth to protest, he said, "Just go over there to the cot and sit. It's my mess, and I always clean up after myself."

She shook her head and walked to the cot, keeping an eye out for stray glass, and sat down on the edge, then thought better of it and pulled her legs up and wrapped one of the mouse-eaten blankets around her shoulders.

"Cody."

"What." He found the broom in the dark corner opposite the cot.

"I really am sorry. Does it hurt?" Latta's voice was timid, like a child's. Like Caroline's was sometimes, he remembered, after she'd done things she shouldn't.

"It's okay." Actually, it hurt like a son of a bitch, throbbing in big sickening waves that made him feel like his whole face was swelling. Sweeping, bending, any physical motion made the blood rush to his nose, pushing against what felt like the jagged edge of bone, producing surges of dizziness. Now he understood why breaking a person's nose shut him down so quickly in a fight.

"Why does it always end up like this with us?" she asked. He looked at her. She was leaning against the wall, her hands resting naturally on her stomach.

"I mean, we either fuck or fight."

He squatted to pick up the larger pieces of bottle glass and put them in the pan he was using.

"It's crazy, don't you think? I mean, if anything was ever there, you know, don't you think we wouldn't be at each other all the time?"

She didn't need him in the conversation, he could tell. She was off and running by herself. He'd just clean up the glass; if she hit him again, he'd probably pass out anyway. But there was no way, no way in hell he was ever going to hit her again. He'd held back his blow, instinctively, but she hadn't. She never would. And someday, if he didn't stop now, he'd hurt her because of all the passion between them.

When he'd swept up all the splinters of glass, collecting them on the end leaf he'd torn out of a book, he went outside and put the glass in a little pile to the north of the cabin, out of the way of traffic and animals. He thought about it, and went back and pulled two logs from the pile by the door and positioned them over the glass so nothing would accidentally cut itself. His body, without a jacket or gloves, was numbing quickly in the bitter wind and blowing snow, but he was tempted to stay out there in the relative safety of the storm rather than face the litany of Latta's voice, which hadn't stopped even when he went outside.

He peered in one of the remaining clear patches on the window. Latta was gesturing with one hand, rubbing the inverted bowl of her belly with the other. What was she telling their child, he wondered. He didn't want her to grow up hating men because they were bad to her, having the same crummy times her mother had.

Then it struck him. What the hell was he thinking? Christ. Latta was forty — she probably didn't even want this child. He watched her reposition herself, lying down with her knees up as if to relieve pain in her lower back. Her hands seeking and finding the comfort of the baby's place in her body. Her eyes searching the ceiling as she spoke. Maybe she hadn't even realized he was gone. Maybe this was the way she always was, alone. He realized how much he loved her. He loved her crooked, thick little fingers, the little gap between her front teeth he'd run his tongue up and down when they kissed.

The wind shook the tree he was standing under, and dotted his hair with icy confetti. He shivered — time to go in. Go in and take it, whatever she had to say, whatever she needed from him, because that's just the way it had to be.

"Hush, little darling —" She was singing in her little out-of-tune voice. She stopped when he pulled the door tight, stamped the snow off his boots. He put another log on the fire and stood there trying to warm up again, waiting for her to begin talking.

"What do you want, Cody?" The distance and quiet in her voice was unnerving. "I mean, here we are. Maybe it's time to put it all out on the table. What do you want from me? I'm too old for you. So what is it — my land? my horses? my what? Just tell me that. What is it?"

Cody turned, holding his hands behind him to keep them warming. "You. I want to marry you and raise our child. Be a good father, a good husband. Take care of you. I don't know, whatever you want or need —" He could feel his words failing, as if they were trying to swim for a shore that was simply, fatalistically, too far away.

Latta shook her head. "It won't work. You think that now, sure, move in with Latta, no more problems. I can see that. For now, it might work. Then it would go to pieces. The kid would keep you up one night too many crying, or things wouldn't go well with the horses or cattle, you'd get restless. Look at now — we're here one evening and you get drunk. After the newness wore off, it'd be the same. You'd be in the bottom of a bottle every night after a while."

"Is that it? The drinking? Fine, I stop drinking. Won't touch a drop, if that's what it takes. I don't have to drink. I can stop — I don't even know why I do it." He shrugged as if he'd just found out his fatal disease could be cured with aspirin.

"See, that's the problem — you don't know why you do

anything. And I think about everything, every single thing, because I've learned you have to spend time looking at yourself, your life. Every time I try to ignore it, try to slide by, look what happens — Jaboy, and now you."

"That isn't fair. I messed up, but I'm not like Jaboy. I love you, dammit. What do I have to do to make you see that?" He started across the room, but she held up both hands.

"Don't. We have to talk this out, and I can't do it if you're close. We proved that. Just get the chair. Bring it over here or something, but not on the cot, I don't want you here." She tugged at the corners of the blanket she was sitting on and tucked them more securely around her legs.

"Latta, look —" He set the chair down and sat close enough that his knees were touching the cot's edge. He leaned forward, but kept his palms together so he wouldn't be tempted to reach out and touch her.

"Move the chair back. I feel like you're, I don't know, trying to suffocate me, for chrissakes. Just give me some room."

He moved back a foot, feeling as if her dark eyes were pushing him away. He knew he had to hold some kind of ground or she'd have him at the wall in no time.

"I don't know why you have to make this thing so complicated. I love you. I think you love me. So what's the problem? We have our baby, we raise it, try to give it the kind of things we didn't get. Maybe everyone does that, but we try harder. We stay together and stuff. She has a mother and a father. We work, we make each other happy, and in twenty years —"

A look crossed her face and she burst in. "In twenty years you look at me and I'm an old woman and you're still a young man, and you'll hate me for the trick of love. I know how it goes. It's my whole story." She looked at him defiantly, her dark eyes glittery with truth and anger.

He was shaking his head slowly. "No."

She nodded, raising her eyebrows and smiling a bitter little smile that stretched her mouth into a line as thin as a pie plate.

"Most people only have one story in their life, one version of things that comes to them and makes them live. This is mine. I'm just better off recognizing what it is, and at least" — she looked at her hands, still tugging the corners of the blanket, which wouldn't budge because her body was holding it down — "I can spare you the story becoming yours. You're someone whose story isn't decided yet. Anything could happen for you, anything's possible. That's one of the best things about you." She looked at him, her eyes soft brown again.

"I just don't want to be the one to ruin it for you," she said. "I'm not going to spend the rest of my life being Jaboy to you." She looked toward the fire, her voice getting slow and dreamy, as if it were no longer important that he was there. "I've thought about having an abortion. I really have. I made the appointment even, then I got up that morning, and I was on my way out the door. It was funny, I kept delaying it. Kept running later and later, until finally I couldn't make myself go out and get in the truck and drive to North Platte and do it. I went back upstairs and slept for the next twenty-four hours straight. It wasn't going to be like Mexico again. I couldn't go through that again. Maybe I'm nuts, but this baby — it's something. Even more than Stoney."

Cody couldn't get past her. He couldn't put it into words. But for him it was there, that feeling that made every one of her imperfections, even the few grey hairs, something of value. He would lie down, mingling his body with hers, if she would let him.

"What happened in Mexico? Tell me."

She shivered and tucked her chin into the hollow of the blanket around her chest. He wanted to go to her, but knew he shouldn't.

"Mexico. Oh yes." Her voice was too bright and too lightweight, like a new cheap knife.

He waited. Her breathing went shallow.

"I'd gotten pregnant. He didn't want children. He wasn't

sleeping with me anymore — aside from the few times he was drunk and couldn't find anything else to stick it in. That was how I got pregnant. Anyway, he told me he'd throw me out on my ear without a dime, shame my parents. My father was still trying to preach, even though his church had dwindled to nothing. It would've killed him."

Her face was very pale now, as if the telling of the story were draining all the life she had stored. It was painful to listen to her flat voice explaining how Jaboy had taken her to Mexico after she discovered him with Kya. She pulled at the blanket and rolled onto her back again, raising her knees and squeezing her legs together, with her feet layered on top of each other to keep warm. "I had morning sickness so bad I was throwing up all day long. Jaboy laughed and gave me some drugs he said would help. I don't know why I took them, because the next thing I knew we were in this terrible place. Dirty, dark. Pigs in the next room. Pigs! I'll never forget that smell."

She closed her eyes, then opened them again, running the tip of her tongue around the outline of her lips.

"I was so out of it, it took me a while to realize that Jaboy'd brought me there to get an abortion." For the first time she faltered and took a deep breath. "I didn't even try to stop him, really. Somehow it made sense, seemed the right thing to do. The drugs made it easier."

She sat up, pulling the blanket around her and curling into a ball in the corner, pressing her back against the log wall as if she were trying to make herself small. "Sometime during the night I began to bleed too much. I didn't care, I'd allowed him to kill my baby, what use was I to anyone? So I took his razor and tried to hack open my veins, tried to kill myself before I passed out." She shook her head as if disgusted by her continued existence. "Jaboy found me all covered with blood. He got me to a doctor who got Inez to come take care of me. After that I was just another useless household appliance, an ironing board, something that meant virtually nothing to him. I stayed because it didn't matter anymore. It took me a long time to let someone touch me. When I did, I wanted it to hook up with the pain again. You never want to do something yourself that you can get someone else to dirty their hands with."

Cody leaned forward and held out his hand, but she shrank tighter into her corner, shaking her head.

"Don't," he said, not wanting the next part, but she kept going.

She laughed in a high, hysterical way that wobbled. Cody got up and sat down on the cot, started to touch her, then let his hands fall. "Latta —" She just looked at him, laughing until tears streamed down her face, then laughing more, until he began to back away from her, groping behind him for the chair again.

"You're the one screwed it all up." She gasped for air.

"What do you mean?"

"You were more helpless than me, even more fucked up."

He started to shake his head, to argue with her, but she just laughed. He didn't know what to do or say.

She wiped at her eyes, but the tears kept coming, though she stopped laughing. She hiccuped. "I didn't think love would show up. I didn't think I could feel anything again. I couldn't remember if I ever did love Jaboy."

"You can't give up —" He said it sternly.

"You don't know — anything."

"I'm sorry — I —" He reached out for her again, but again he didn't touch her.

"Can't do it, can you? You're afraid of me. All this time I was afraid of you, your looks and your silence. How you could move me. But it wasn't you, it was me I was really afraid of. And now you are too."

25 ❖ DOING THE WHEEL

Traditional Lakotas believe that when you die, your spirit goes to the Milky Way, and travels south until you meet an old woman who sits at a fork and judges how you lived your life. If you followed Lakota virtues — helped others, lived in harmony, walked the Red Road — you take the left road which leads you back to the center. If you walked the Black Road — being greedy or selfish — she takes you down a short path on the right and pushes you off. You're reborn and get a chance to try again to live in harmony.

— from MITAKUYE OYASIN

When the phone call came from the Chadron sheriff's office saying they'd found a woman's body, a part of Arthur detached itself and floated loose, like a small but significant bone, without which entire joints and pieces of him could not function. He had been trying out the buttons on his new remote phone when the ringing startled him. Then he'd had that moment of proudness and walked with the cordless receiver into the dining room, and sat down at one of the big mahogany carved chairs he'd found in Omaha and had shipped out with the huge table. As he noted the clarity of the reception and made himself comfortable, the deputy had gone through the rigmarole of identifying who he was and making certain he had a family member. Arthur assumed it was about

Cody, but since nothing fatal ever really hurt his brother, he figured it was just another accident he'd be paying for.

Now the almond-colored receiver stood on the table in front of him, a red light blinking mysteriously like a warning of things to come. It's too late, he wanted to tell it. You should've said something earlier.

He felt a strange salty tickle in the back of his nose, an alien heat in his eyes, a swelling in his throat, and water blurred his eye and spilled. Kya. He couldn't bring the sound of her name heaving up his chest. It came trickling out like the most horrible of crimes, the secret of the real love he had for his sister, so real and secret even he was surprised by its power. He tried to picture her as the deputy had described it, lying in the front seat. The smile was the only part that could be true.

That her death could be so small was the worst part. He wondered if she were disappointed with it. Kya loved bigness: at the county fair, she'd always dragged him to see the biggest bulls, the biggest hogs, the biggest squash and watermelons, the biggest dahlia blossoms, sunflowers, ears of corn. Even the big stallion she'd stolen from Latta Jaboy — that it was the tallest horse in Cherry County would make Kya want it. Arthur could see that. It was so obvious. He could've bought her a big horse and avoided all the hassle. Why hadn't he done that? He'd made her ride what was on the ranch, the small efficient quarter horses and crossbreeds. Why wouldn't he buy her a big horse? It seemed so simple a thing now. Why had he held back the money? He couldn't even remember, there had been so many times he'd done it. Because — that's what he'd told her — because she couldn't have everything she wanted. Why not, she'd ask, and cock her head at him, truly puzzled. Because, he'd say, just like Heywood when they'd ask the same question, as if *because* were its own economy.

Over the past year particularly, Arthur had tried to control her. As if all the burden of Heywood Bennett, the Bennett generations behind him, had come to be his, his alone, because he was the only true son. True son, bastard son. What difference did it make now? He'd driven her off, put her in that truck with some nameless reservation Indian, looking for her family, her true one, because he'd always insisted both she and Cody were the bastards. And then he'd kept her close enough to remind her of it. Kept her powerless in the most important ways. But she'd won, and now nothing could change. What he'd done was his forever, because she'd escaped the consequences, the smallness of his imagination.

They were sending the body back to Babylon, the deputy had said. He could pick her up, but he couldn't remember the rest. He'd have to call the sheriff.

How did you take care of the details when your sister died? With his mother, his father had done it all. He remembered looking into a coffin where a woman in a dress they said was his mother lay. He thought they'd made a mistake, and he tugged at his father's jacket to tell him they were in the wrong place, but he'd been shushed. He'd pushed a chair up close and gripped the edge of the sky-blue coffin for balance, trying not to breathe in the sweet flower and medicine smell, trying to see if there was anything he could recognize. Even her thin mouth had been too full, the cupid's bow of her upper lip gone in a straight red line. If she'd only open her eyes, he'd thought desperately, he'd know by the color. Hers were grey-violet. Even his father had loved her eyes, the color of sage in late summer. But she wouldn't open them. He'd known with certainty, though, that they wouldn't be the right color. After that, he'd slipped quietly to his father's side, and watched.

When Heywood died, he'd done his duty. But the rules of their relationship were so well ordered, there hadn't been anything left over. No, when he buried Heywood, Arthur knew exactly who was in the box and where it went. He'd felt almost lighthearted the next day.

Kya was dead. How would he bury a sister? How would he make a phone call, pick out a dress — would she need underpants, shoes, lipstick? Headstone? A piece of rock to hold her down? Impossible. Our dear, my beloved, how to begin, to end, my sister? Had he wished his sister dead so he could get her share? Because his sister loved Cody more than him? She'd protected Cody all their lives. Like a twin or a little wife, she'd watched out for him. That was why Arthur had told on the two of them swimming nude in the stock tank that summer night. That was why Cody got the whipping and Arthur had gone away.

Now it didn't matter. Arthur got to his feet, unsure whether his leg was asleep or a permanent numbness was beginning to set in, one that would gradually cripple him. He'd walk with a cane and people would say, "It happened the day his sister died. He's been like that ever since." He would gain a sandhills reputation, the kind that came with a sort of miracle, an unexplained mystery, a sign of the power of things to happen. The reverse of the healings that evangelical preachers claimed. His would be the striking down sort of thing, not the raising up. He would ask for more, he decided; he would pray to God, if he could find one, to make him suffer more. If he wasn't going to die from this, he wanted to hurt.

The phone was ringing again. "Arthur —" Sheriff Moon drew his name out as if he were relieved.

"I know. Is she there?" Arthur found an efficient place and slid into its administrative voice, grateful that something was left.

"Can you find Emil Vullet? I haven't been able to get a hold of him. Is he still staying with you?"

Arthur rubbed his hand through his short thin hair as he tried to remember where Emil said he was going to be when they'd talked last night. "I don't know. Is this important? I can just come down by myself."

"Emil needs to be here too."

"Just a minute." Arthur put the phone down and went to the kitchen. He'd heard voices and someone trying to open the back door. By the time he got there, Emil and John were standing just inside, trying to shove the door shut while kicking the snow out of the way.

"Something's happened to Kya," Arthur said when the two men looked at him, sobering as they noticed his pale face and red eyes. "Sheriff wants us to go identify —" He couldn't say the words out loud and was relieved when the two men nodded and looked away.

As they pulled into the big paved parking lot, twice the size of the one for the Absalom Food Center in town, Arthur wondered who the hell they were expecting to bury, the president? Nobody ever died who needed space for this many cars. And now the only other cars belonged to the sheriff and Dayle Gardner, the funeral director. The new mortuary was situated on a flat piece of land that took the blowing wind from every direction. A few struggling cottonwoods, choked with snow, were planted around the long, low ranch-style building, designed to look like a house you'd be comfortable living in.

Inside the entryway, there were placards of polished wood and bronze pointing in various directions: the glass door for the flower shop, which sold mostly plastic and silk arrangements, with a few huge sprays of real flowers in case a family wanted to splurge; the reception room; the casket room; and the visitation rooms with various themes, all horrifyingly tasteful. The furniture was mostly brocade-covered armchairs and sofas. The off-white walls were decorated with prints of wildlife or soft misty flowers. Everything was aimed at neutralizing death, as if it were yet another social occasion that could be dealt with appropriately with a kind of know-how, manners, and pastel tones. Like a women's bathroom, there was a certain amount of matching calico and ruffles, including the tasteful Kleenex containers that sprouted discreetly on the end tables beside the small vases of dried flowers. Death needed a lot of flowers.

It grated him that his sister was here. Death should never be nice. It should be as raw as he felt. The place where you took the dead should be as stained and battered and used up, as patched together, as jury-rigged as life itself.

Once inside the cool of the refrigerated room where they kept the bodies for embalming, Arthur realized he had been hurrying toward death, and he should have been going the other direction. He kept glancing at Emil, Dayle, and the sheriff, hoping they could tell him this was all a joke, but their grim faces never smiled. On the table, the body looked shrunken, as if death had made Kya small. She was covered in green plastic like a giant trash bag.

As if some deference to the dead were required, like glancing at the crucifix as you passed the nave of the church and crossed yourself, Sheriff Moon and Dayle Gardner paused before stepping forward. As he watched, Arthur knew he'd remember every single gesture, every tiny tick of the dripping stainless steel sink in the corner, every possible variation of the hum of the overhead fluorescent light. He was glad the floor and walls were concrete, plain grey, everything stone and metal here. He wanted to warn away the hand reaching for her, as if when it opened the bag, a blizzard of bees and wasps, stinging, flying, brutal things, would come rushing out, drive their eyes back inside their skulls. But the fingers pulled and the zipper roared and the sigh of the plastic made them all start, as it breathed out with a hiss and collapsed around her arm, her shoulder, her blond hair, her pink face, made perfect now as the flesh had sunk from the round cheeks and she achieved cheekbones. She was as lovely as she would ever be.

Arthur felt a thump in his chest, a breathlessness that let out only the single word "Greta," before the tears began to fill his eyes. He could not explain why he was so terribly moved by this dead woman whom he hardly knew. It wasn't only relief because it meant Kya was alive. It was something else: it was for anyone, anything that had died, and would, and was. It was for life itself he had tears now, blurring the human distinctions so personal and small and absurd.

Emil approached the girl on the table hesitantly, touching her arm first, as if he couldn't feel the cold stiffness, smoothing her short-cropped bangs off her forehead as if she were a sleeping child again. He leaned down to kiss the hard white skin, to wish her goodnight, sweet dreams, and pulled the green plastic back up under her chin, tucking it in around her small shoulders, as if there were nothing unusual about his daughter's sleeping in front of these strangers. It seemed to the men in the room that the little smile lingering on her lips was the result of a dream still playing itself out in her mind before she entered some greater darkness.

You always end up regretting August.
November is judgment time.
December — that's what kids know.
Lent is pretty useless.
Kids aren't afraid enough in spring.

— Caroline
March 12, 1970

The first thing that woke Cody and Latta was the saddles thumping on the floor, followed by a spray of windy snow that made them shiver. The fire had died down, but the cabin had remained snug until the door opened.

Kya shucked her outer clothes and shook like a dog, spraying wet from her pants and hair in a small circle around her. Joseph reached for a towel from the packs spewing clothes on the floor, and rubbed at his face and hair. His long grey braids were balled with snow he tried to pull off until he discovered strands of hair coming with them. Cody squatted in front of the fire, poking its brightness up another notch, keeping his face turned from his sister. Latta struggled to open more cans of soup, but then Joseph took over, wordless, quickly jacking the knife around the top and dumping the contents into the saucepan at his feet.

"Cody —" Kya stooped beside her brother, putting her arm

around his shoulder. When he turned to hug her, he tried to do it so fast she wouldn't notice his face at first, but she pulled back and stared. "What the hell happened this time?"

He shrugged, avoiding her eyes. "Broke my nose."

"Jesus Christ. How'd you do that?" He wasn't grinning, and she could sense something was off. She looked around the room as if the answer would be somewhere obvious, until she caught Latta looking at her with a swollen upper lip.

"Just let it go." Cody put his hand on her arm, and when she started to rise, squeezed it hard enough to keep her down. "It's no big deal."

"Cody, you are such a jerk." Kya pulled her arm away and stood up, circling the room slowly, as if she could reconstruct the past hours by scent.

"Come here and take off your boots, they're soaked," Cody said to his sister. "Sit down on my bedroll and take 'em off."

He was grateful when she complied, and he got up, moving hesitantly because his eyes were black and his whole face throbbed.

After breakfast, the four of them sat on the blankets on the floor, resting. There was a full, uncomfortable silence that no one could successfully break until they all drifted to sleep for a while. Around one, Cody and Joseph decided to go check on the horses and see whether they could pack out.

The door was just being shouldered shut when Kya turned to Latta beside her on the floor. "What the hell'd you do that for? The guy comes all the way out here in a goddamned blizzard to save your sorry ass and you break his nose? I don't know who's a bigger asshole, him or you. You two deserve each other."

Latta gripped the handle of the cup she was holding so hard, she thought it might snap off. "Just stay out of it, Kya. Take your bitchery someplace else. I've heard enough out of you to last a lifetime — twenty lifetimes — you and your brother. You Bennetts always have to get your fingers in everything. Well, this is one person who's telling you to butt out. So butt out." She unconsciously began to rub her belly again, as if the small swelling were the only comfort she had.

Kya's eyes followed the restless motion of Latta's hands. "He wants it, doesn't he? He'd have to —" Her voice softened, as if even she knew you had to speak in hushed tones around a baby. "You know he'd make a good father, Latta. He really would. You've seen him with the baby horses, calves. The guy doesn't have a mean bone in his body when it comes to something small and helpless."

"Like I said" — Latta hardened her eyes against the unexpected tone — "I don't want anything from any of you."

"What, you still pissed about your old man? He was scum, Latta."

Latta stood up abruptly. "He was *my* husband, Kya, not yours. No matter what he was. You don't know — you just don't know what you did." She folded her arms across her chest and began pacing, turning sharp corners at each wall. "Why couldn't you just have stuck to cowboys or boys your own age? What was the point, just tell me — if he was so horrible, why'd you do it?"

Kya raised her eyebrows, looked at the floor, and shrugged. "I honestly can't remember. He was probably just the first man I saw when I ran away from the ranch. He was Heywood's friend too, I don't know. I don't spend my time trying to figure this stuff out. Besides, I didn't want a bunch of romantic crap. I wanted sex. He knew a lot about that."

Stopping in front of Kya, Latta looked down at her, shaking her head. "Doesn't anything ever make you feel bad or sorry? Don't you feel anything?"

Stretching out her legs and pointing her toes so close to the fire that her damp socks started steaming, Kya thought for a moment. "If you think whining about how sorry you are every time shit happens makes a difference, then you have another thing coming, Latta. I always figured that guilt was about the most useless emotion a person could have. Don't do it if you can't handle it — I learned that. Anyone fucks with me, I get even or I forget it. You and Cody, though, you walk around feeling sorry for every little thing."

There was confusion on Latta's face. She didn't really have an answer for the girl's philosophy. It made a kind of sense, though she could feel there was something missing. "Okay, so don't apologize. The thing is, you're forgetting about consequences. That's not guilt. Me getting pregnant, for instance. Sleeping with Cody — my kid will be raised without a father, have a mother who's way too old, live this lonely life out in the sandhills or get sent away to boarding school and think I didn't like it. I see a lot of things happening to this person because of what I did. I don't have to bear the brunt of it — the child does." Latta stooped beside the fire, looking at Kya.

Kya shrugged. "You always take the most depressing view of things. Marry Cody. Give the kid a father. Cody didn't have the hottest start in life, so he probably has some pretty good ideas about what you don't want to do to a kid. You know, you got a pretty young guy hot for you, if you don't ruin his looks or kill each other first. You got money — what's the problem?"

Kya stood up and began touching the bits of rock, dried pods, and feathers on the mantel, holding some of them close as if she were nearsighted, then smelling them.

"I don't know how to make you see it, Kya, but I can't go through this thing with your brother. I'm just too —"

"Scared. But you know what? If it doesn't work out with Cody, kick his butt out and find someone it does work with. You won't die, he won't either. Plenty of women would love to take his sorry ass in and make everything better." She laughed in that brutal way that always made Latta want to slap her, but for the first time it seemed to be a joke that Latta understood too.

"You know," Kya went on, "men are always acting like

they're the brave, adventurous ones. It's really us women who're brave. We go out, no money or lives, and attach ourselves to these guys and have their babies and hold things together while they stumble around clueless, and we keep telling them everything'll be okay. Problem is, you spend enough time with men, you catch their fear after a while. Like you did with Jaboy."

"Jaboy's fear? What was he ever afraid of?" Latta turned and poked at the fire with a stick, sending out a shower of sparks that she had to brush away from herself. Kya stamped on the few that had landed on the wooden floor.

"Oh, Christ, Latta, the man was afraid of his own shadow. He was afraid he was just a short, fat greaseball. And you know what? He was. I told him so too. You should've seen how relieved he was to find out it didn't matter. I fucked him good anyway. I wasn't afraid of his looks, I told him."

"Or his wife, apparently." Latta shoved at the fire again, producing another shower of sparks.

Stepping on the few live coals that landed near Cody's bedroll, Kya said, "Will you stop, for chrissakes. You burn this down and we're in real trouble."

"Thought fear wasn't a problem." Latta grinned meanly.

Kya laughed. "Freezing to death isn't either, but I got a few things to do before that happens."

"You really told Jaboy that?"

Kya nodded. "I always tell the truth, especially to men. They ignore it or think they're tough 'cause they can take it. I figure hearing the truth about themselves will be such a novelty, they'll be thrilled."

"You include your brother?" Latta was studying the fire very hard now, letting the tip of the stick catch and glow red, trying to feel the heat that was beginning to pulse down the shaft into her hand.

"Oh yes. Only problem with him is he knows the bad things by heart. He has more trouble with the good stuff. He's not afraid he's homely — he knows he is. No offense, but that's why I think he's so awestruck by you."

"It's not about looks, Kya. Maybe it is for you, but —"

"Oh, don't start this B.S. Cody's one of the sexiest men alive and we both know it. If he looked like Jaboy, you wouldn't be pregnant, you wouldn't be breaking his nose, you'd be back on your ranch waiting out the snowstorm with your hand in your panties like the rest of us."

"Jesus, Kya, do you have to be crude about everything?"

"Yeah, I like it. I'll tell you something else. I just like sex, I like bodies, I like flesh, I like myself." She dusted her hands on her damp jeans like she'd just finished a big chore, folded her arms, crossed her legs, and leaned back against the mantel. "Just one more thing — don't hurt him again. I don't wanna see that. Twice now."

Latta stood up, not stepping back when it put her face to face with the other woman. "The first time was your doing, honey. Why the hell didn't you take care of your precious brother then? And why the hell'd you steal my horse? You took Stoney, didn't you?"

Kya tilted her head, looking down at Latta. "Stole him because I felt like it. You'd been bugging me since I was a kid, then you started messing around with my brother. I thought, You bitch, I'll show you. Besides, Burch Winants needed some money. We were going to bring him back, but things got all fucked up. Then he disappeared after Cody got shot. Anyway, what difference does it make? He's back now." She shrugged.

"Who, Cody? I know that."

"No, dummy, the stallion. I rode him up here. Joseph's cousin found him. But I don't know whether you're gonna want him back now." Kya picked up a crow's feather with separated and bent barbs, turning it in the light, trying to make the dull black shine.

"Is he hurt? Did they do something to him?" Latta took a half step closer to Kya. She could smell the mixture of sweat and animal on the girl, something like Cody's scent, only different, with a kind of wet sage odor too. It made Latta want to step away; it kept pulling at her, climbing up her nostrils and settling on her skin.

"He's fine. That's not what I meant. Jesus, calm down, will you. It's just that he's lost some weight. Tell you what — you take my brother, I take the horse — keep all the males happy, huh?" She laughed again, her sharp incisors two points of white against the dark of her throat.

Latta stared for a moment, wondering wildly if the girl ate raw meat with those teeth. "You're crazy. That stallion cost fifty thousand dollars. Just stay the hell away from me." She walked to her packs and began sorting things. "I'm getting out of here. I can't spend another minute with you crazy people. I'd rather die in a snowdrift than listen to any more of this crap."

There was the sound of the men stamping their feet, and the door yanked open. She kept pushing items into her packs, not looking up when the wave of cold came in with the men.

"Latta's leaving." Kya gestured toward the other woman and smiled at the look her words created on Cody's face. He and Joseph exchanged glances, then shrugged.

"Guess we'll all be going, then," Joseph said, and stooped to help Latta.

Latta went out the open door just as the stallion was trying to edge his way toward the mares on the other side of the geldings. Stretching his neck as long as he could, he sniffed the youngest mare's nose. She squealed and kicked out.

"That's him, that's Stoney. You —" Latta whirled on the three of them standing behind her, each wearing a different smile. She narrowed her eyes. "You knew all along — you had him all along. You're all shits and you can all go to hell."

She moved too quickly to the horse's side, and he shied, bumping the gelding next to him, who tried to get out of the way, and setting up a chain reaction. The stallion leaned back on the rope tying him to a pine tree, sending an ominous creak through the halter.

"Take it easy, big boy." Cody eased to the horse's rear end and tapped him lightly. The horse relaxed and stepped forward.

"Cody didn't know where he was, Latta," Joseph said as he began packing their equipment. "Horse has been at my cousin's. I was going to trade him to Cody as part of our rodeo bet."

Latta began packing her mare. "Cody knew Kya took him, and he lied for her. He even let Burch Winants get away with shooting him just so his sister wouldn't get in trouble. He's as guilty as she is." Latta brushed as much snow off the old mare's neck and face as she could.

"Generosity and bravery — good Lakota traits, Latta. He's right to take care of his sister. What kind of man would he be if he didn't? Nobody could trust him." Joseph spoke patiently, saddling the stallion.

"And while we're on the subject of trust, Joseph, how'd your cousin end up with my horse?" Latta asked.

Joseph smiled and slipped the bit between the horse's teeth. "Wisdom and fortitude — more virtues. I asked Ray to look around, and when Stoney came through the auction in Mitchell, he picked him up. You owe Ray, but you should be happy, Mrs. Jaboy. Your horse has come home. Your warrior brought him." He glanced at Cody's swollen face. "Well, almost, if this darn storm hadn't interfered."

Latta tied on the last of her equipment, and when Cody had saddled the other mare, she pulled the reins out of his hands. "Do me a favor, all of you, from now on? Stay the hell away from me. I'm not going to prosecute any of you because I couldn't stand to spend one minute more than this ride out of here will take, looking at you. Joseph, you ride my stallion — I don't want the Bennett brats near anything of mine ever again." Latta mounted, swinging her mare around so abruptly her haunch brushed Cody's chest. The stallion snorted and pawed, anxious to follow. "And I'm glad you're not pretty anymore, my friend," she whispered to Cody.

He shook his head and winced at the pain in his nose. Joseph and Kya had done a job on both of them. He knew Joseph had saved his life, but it looked like he'd just killed him again. "Thanks a lot, you two," he muttered as he mounted Marcus.

"To help out" in Lakota means *support* and includes both actively assisting and participating, as well as passively attending a ceremony or event. You measure the success of a communal event by the number of people there — whether they're watching or actually participating. "They depend on me" expresses the special kind of relationship Lakota feel with their families and community. "It's the Indian Way," to share and participate.

— from YUWIPI

O pal Treat didn't have time to write down the names of everyone there, describe the outfit Greta was dressed in, the flowers, and the service, so she took the mourners' registry from the little maple table in the vestibule, meaning to give it back when she was done with it. Years later, her nieces would discover it as they packed her house and wonder who Greta Vullet was, eventually agreeing that it must have been some close personal friend of their aunt's, and regretting that they hadn't spent more time with her in the difficult later years.

LaVeta Sheets sat beside Opal at the funeral, keeping an eye out for details that could be used in the newspaper article. They'd been doing it this way for several years, and both women found it suited them perfectly, though only Opal's name appeared on the byline. LaVeta was too shy. Radney, her husband, was back at Simon's Hardware, keeping the doors open for anyone who still preferred personal service to the Coast-to-Coast. He didn't much care for funerals anyway, La-Veta assured everyone, not since his mother passed on. The town merchants turned out because old Vullet had been in business there for so many years. A few ranch families came for the same reason, or because it was something to do on a wintry day, and they could go down the street to the Pizza Hut afterward.

Floral Haven had done a creditable job, everyone agreed. The girl was in a perfectly decent white lace and voile dress her father had picked out from the ones Dayle Gardner displayed on a rack in the casket room. She looked a little like a bride, but everyone assumed that was the German heritage or something. The casket was half closed, so they couldn't see the fancy cowboy boots the girl wore at Kya's insistence. They'd heard all about it, though, from Mildred Buck, who did the dressing, makeup, and hair, because the Gardner men didn't feel right taking care of female bodies, and the town ladies agreed that it wasn't proper to have a man dressing you at the end, for your last important appearance.

There wasn't much a person could do with the hair, Mildred Buck told anyone who commented on how nice she looked. Mildred knew they always said that to her face, then went home and talked about how the body looked wrong, so she'd learned to jump in and give the obvious mistakes an airing in public. Death had taken the shine from Greta's hair. Something about the carbon monoxide poisoning had made her skin difficult too, so Mildred had just coated the face with as much foundation as she could to hide the odd color. As a result, Greta looked like she'd been spending the past twenty winters sunning in Florida, her skin seemed so flaccid and wrinkled and brown. Mildred had made a slight miscalculation, she admitted to LaVeta while Opal was trying to keep an eye on the principal players.

Kya stood near the head of the casket, pulling at Greta's

dress, while Emil watched with his mouth gaping, one shaky hand extended helplessly. Kya Bennett had been making a fuss since she blew back in town. Opal and LaVeta thought she was going too far this time. She'd tried to take the body from Floral Haven the first night, had to be restrained by the sheriff, and her brothers had to be called. She was no doubt drunk or doped up — and dragging around that old Indian, Joseph Starr, too. She'd really scraped the bottom of the barrel. It was her fault Greta died anyway, they'd heard from the deputy in Chadron who had a cousin down in Babylon. Left the girl to freeze to death in the truck while she and the Indian rode off. Poor Greta — that was her epitaph around town. They'd all seen it coming when that psychic introduced the two girls. A worse thing couldn't have happened. Just lucky her mother had passed on, so she wouldn't have to see this. And Poor Emil, mixed up with the Bennetts. They'd probably kill him off too.

What worried the ladies most of all was the profusion of flowers that filled the Floral Haven chapel. Calla lilies, exotic purple irises, yellow and purple mums, and great herds of roses, red, yellow, and white, so many that it made a person wonder if there were any flowers left in the world at all. Opal said she hoped no one else planned on dying for the next month, unless they were willing to settle on plastic ones at their funeral.

"I will too."

The ladies swung their eyes back to the front of the chapel where Arthur was struggling with his sister over the coffin.

"Don't — they'll just steal it." He whispered so loudly everyone could hear.

"They better not — if I find out —" She gestured at the Floral Haven attendants standing to the side of the chapel, ready to give assistance.

Cody stood up from his seat in the front row and went to his brother and sister. "Let it go, Arthur." He put his hand on his brother's arm that was barring his sister's access to the body.

"It's my mother's ruby ring, dammit. They're just going to steal it when they close her up." Arthur's face was flushed red, his eyes bloodshot.

"Heywood gave it to her. It's hers. If she wants to throw it away, she can, Arthur. Just let it be." Cody had taken off his hat, and the rim had left a little indentation circling his head, flattening the hair on top. He was dressed in his newest jeans, boots, a grey western-cut suit jacket Heywood had given him, and a white shirt. It was the same outfit he'd buried his father in last April, and he was feeling so disarrayed, he couldn't understand how his brother and sister had the energy for this fight.

"Look, everyone's watching, Arthur," Cody said in a moment of inspiration.

His brother's head shot up, and his face flushed deeper. He quickly let his arm drop and stepped back from the eyes that faced him, unabashed in their curiosity. Only Emil was too dazed to realize what was going on. He'd been rigid with grief since seeing his daughter's body, simply staring into space, his hands clasped before him as if he were just about to pray but had forgotten the words.

Kya pushed Arthur back out of the way and picked up Greta's ring finger, sliding on the too big band with the big bloody stone, replacing the hand as if it were made out of marble, part of a sculpture she was arranging for exhibition.

When she leaned over the casket and planted a goodbye kiss directly on the lips Mildred Buck had so carefully painted the brightest red she carried in her makeup kit, a collective sigh went through the crowd. They had received what they had come for — paid the money for flowers and cards for — the one moment they would talk about for years to come. A piece of lore to add to the Bennett family myth. So Kya Bennett had after all ruined the girl, caused her death, even if it was a

suicide, as some would begin to suggest: Greta hadn't rolled
the window down because she was ashamed of what she'd
become and couldn't stand to hurt her father.

Opal and LaVeta watched Kya's every motion, certain now
that she'd gone Indian because she didn't dress properly for
the funeral; that she'd gone crazy because she was louder and
more obnoxious than usual; and that she should be run out of
town because she'd finally done what they'd predicted for
years — managed to kill someone with her wild ways.

The minister took the pulpit and did his short service without causing much of a distraction from the real business of the
funeral. People noticed that all the Bennetts except Cody cried,
though he kept an arm around his sister's shoulders the whole
time. He had a broken nose too — another barroom brawl,
people whispered. Arthur was the real hero, because he gave
Emil his handkerchief and helped the old man stand up and
follow the coffin out. When Cody and Arthur and Kya took
their places with the Floral Haven men to carry it, another hiss
of collectively drawn breath passed through the onlookers. The
steps were still a little slippery, and when Arthur and Cody
both slid on the ice, threatening to let the coffin fall, it was Kya
who jerked it up at her end, cursing quietly. Another piece of
Bennett pride, that girl hauling around a casket, Opal Treat
would later comment.

The sun shone aggressively against the acres of undisturbed
snow at the cemetery, making people squint and shield their
eyes while they tried to watch. The wind was blowing strong
enough to slide right up Opal's and LaVeta's stockinged legs,
turning their nylon slips into icy sheaths on their thighs and
hips, making them hunch their shoulders as the cold breathed
down the back of their coats, freezing dress zippers against
their spines. LaVeta held her Bible firmly, and Opal gripped the
handle of her purse in front of her with the same determina-
tion, staring straight ahead at the box, poised in its white case
over the indoor-outdoor–carpeted hole. The casket shone as

pure as a block of salt in the light. They had been to this moment many times, and they meant to see it through again.

It was death's elegant reminder to them, and they didn't want to whisper to each other now. This was the part that turned them silent, that defeated them as they felt the defeat of the dead. They watched, setting aside personality, as anonymity settled over the small crowd, making them faceless, without gesture or distinction.

Even Kya was still, held in the palm of that one moment. She joined with them as they let the final words be said, against their will, struggling against the last amen that would slip Greta away into the ground. This was really the end. And they turned reluctantly from it, as if each time they went this far, they had to leave a piece of themselves for the dead to take on ahead with them.

As they walked toward their cars, there were approving murmurs for the fake marble case, the minister's final words, the decorum that had been observed. They thought the ragtag group of Indians coming toward them were there for another funeral, and they didn't pay them special attention at first, but when Joseph with long grey braids cut in front of the departing mourners, leading the others to the Vullet site, they turned and stopped and stared.

A man placed a white wooden cross, obviously homemade, in the mound of dirt he exposed beneath the plastic grass. Another began to beat softly on the drum he carried, while another played a sad melody on a homemade wooden flute. The other men and women took up the voice of the song and began chanting slowly in soft Lakota syllables. One by one, the four men and three women walked to the white case and placed a token on top of it: tobacco, feather, beaded bag, turkey claw, piece of fur, stone, seedpod. The music continued as Joseph and an old woman laid garlands of tobacco ties on the cross. The entire ceremony appeared smooth and dignified, like the performance of an ancient play, so familiar that it was the inexorable unwinding that mattered, carried by its own weight. All other interests were subsumed, diminished, swallowed into something larger, and finally annihilating.

Joseph, who was leading the ceremony, stopped in front of Kya, taking her by the hand, placing something in it, and leading her to the cross and back again to the box. As the others watched, she sang "Goodbye Greta, go home now," lifting her head to the sky and spreading her arms. Then she drew a figure within a circle on the case with a stick of charcoal he had given her, and dusted it with yellow and red powders. The coffin was so white, and the desecration so large, but no one stopped her. Not even Emil, who was waiting, it seemed, simply waiting for it to be over — whatever *it* was that had to happen.

After a few minutes, everything did stop, and the figures around the grave stood silently, as if they were considering becoming permanent gestures there. The uprightness of their bodies and of the cross was emphasized because there were no vertical gravestones, only flat bronze plaques and foot-high vases for flowers, which were now drifted over with snow, leaving only colorful peaks of weathered plastic. It occurred to the onlookers that maybe the native people *did* know something they didn't, and even if the native people didn't know *what* it was they themselves knew, it was still there.

Turning away, the onlookers shrugged and stepped into their cars, glancing over at the gravesite one last time as they sped off.

Driving back through the acres of cemetery, laid out in subdivisions called Apostles, New Jerusalem, Prophets, Married Love, Suffer the Children, and Eternal Friendship, where Greta was, LaVeta Sheets wondered at the size of it all, doubting that there would ever be enough dead in Babylon or the surrounding hills to fill Dayle Gardner's ambitious dream.

LaVeta decided not to tell Opal that she'd seen Arthur Bennett handing a ten-dollar bill to Tom Lacy, who'd closed the coffin lid, in exchange for the ring that flashed like a blood-filled eye in the sun before it disappeared into Arthur's pocket. She didn't know why she felt like hanging on to what she'd seen, but she was determined. It made her uncomfortable, as if she'd witnessed someone robbing the dead, and gave her a little shiver of satisfying sympathy for the dead girl and even for Kya Bennett, who was willing to give her friend what was probably the only thing of value she owned. She snugged the thought into her chest, squeezing her arms tighter against herself.

Opal glanced at her and stepped on the gas to get them back to town faster, where they would sit in the back booth at the Buckboard, in the warm restaurant part, and discuss the whole thing over tea and some of their frozen specialty cheesecake, amaretto raspberry, she'd have them microwave to the point of melting because it was cold today. The reception was at the Bennett house on Main, but they'd have time to talk about things and get over there before anything really happened.

When Cody, Arthur, and Emil got back from the funeral, Latta was already at the house for the reception. As people filtered in, taking paper plates of the food Wanita Cone had set up with several of the other ladies, few people spoke to Latta. When they did, it was with such courtesy, Cody felt embarrassed. He wanted to stand behind her chair, force people to acknowledge her. He'd put the fierceness back in her face and eyes that was missing now, as if she were agreeing with their assessment of her.

She was wearing a suede buckskin split skirt and a dark green silk blouse. The way the green sat at her throat reminded him of the soapweed against the sandhills in a certain light. Her jaw line was tight. He filled a plate with food, got a cup of punch, and brought it over to where she sat. Kneeling, he put the plate in her hands, letting his fingers brush hers. She looked away and said "Thank you," so low he had to lean forward to catch it.

That was when Kya flung the front door open with a rattling bang, followed by Joseph Starr and the group that had been at the cemetery. Cody wanted to duck, but his sister's eyes found him immediately.

"What's she doing here?" Kya stopped in front of him.

"She wanted to give her condolences to Emil," Cody said in a clear, sharp voice that sent a look of surprise to Latta's face.

"No, she came to take you." Kya was reaching for Latta when Cody caught her arm.

"Come on, Kya. Don't make a fuss, you'll upset Emil. It's his daughter's funeral, for God's sake," Cody said quietly, trying to pull her away. "Come on, we'll discuss this in the kitchen."

In the dining room, Emil was surrounded by people and seemed to be more his old self, smiling and telling a story in a voice just a little too loud, with his German accent rising and falling oddly in English inflections. John Long was in the kitchen arranging carrot sticks and radishes, but when he saw the family gathering there, he quickly took his platter and left. Kya was crying and talking in a furious low voice to her brothers, who were standing in front of her, as if to cage her, when Latta came through the door.

"If she hadn't gone off — if she'd just stayed home — if she hadn't made you love her — if —" Kya sobbed like a child, and both brothers tried awkwardly to comfort her. For the moment, the competition between them had evaporated. "It's my fault, I took the horse. She'd be alive if — I should be the one — it's my fault. I didn't take care of her." She struggled, but her brothers held on. "She was my friend," she wailed.

Arthur caught Cody's eye, and a grim expression passed between them. They'd never seen her so inconsolable, so without power, and it scared them. She started to go limp, letting herself slide out of their arms, and because she was almost as tall as they were, they had trouble keeping her on her feet. Finally they eased her to the floor, where she sat collapsed, one leg bent up, the other sprawled like a doll dropped by a heed-less child. She wasn't trying to hide her face or her grief. Her hands lay useless in her lap, palms up, her shoulders slumped. Kya was looking in Latta's direction, obviously not seeing any-thing but what was playing in her head. The two men stood helpless on either side of her like superannuated soldiers who had failed at the one job they'd been given.

"Get her some whiskey," Latta ordered.

Arthur stared blankly at her, but Cody turned to the cabi-nets behind him and reached down a bottle of Jack Daniel's.

"Now get her to take a drink," she directed. Cody and Arthur knelt by Kya, one with his hand behind her head to hold it in place, the other putting the glass to her lips and urging her to take a sip. At first she tried to shake her head and pull away, but then she drank. The first gulp sent a shudder of recognition through her, and she tried to push the glass away, slopping some over on her jeans and shirt, but Cody held on to it and put it back to her lips.

"This'll help," he said in a low voice.

"Don't wanna — don't wanna drink," she whimpered.

"Just another sip, it'll help," Cody urged.

She gazed at Arthur's face and he nodded, then she looked at Cody, who said, "It will," and she drank, closing her eyes and letting it settle inside her, smoothing out the hiccups and making the sobs trail off. When she took the glass herself and drank again, Arthur stood up, looking around the kitchen as if there had to be something he could do to make himself busy. The worn grey paint on the cabinets and walls stared back emptily. His eyes were red-rimmed.

They were all quiet, waiting, as if this were the intermission or commercial break and they were too tired to leave their seats. From the other rooms, they could hear the murmuring of Babylon's people, who were trying to keep the boisterous-ness out of their voices, trying to keep themselves from sound-ing too alive in the house where death was being paid attention to. But they couldn't help it. More bursts of laughter were heard, and every once in a while they could hear even Emil Vullet's voice rise above the others, as if his living were a defiance to his child, as if only in some riotous exhibition could he show her that what she had done was wrong, that always, living was better than dying.

"Must be hitting the booze out there," Arthur said, which sounded like the best idea he'd heard all day. He got himself a clean glass. "Want some?" he asked Latta as he picked up the bottle.

"No." She didn't want to make a mess of her insides, with the baby.

He held the bottle up and raised his eyebrows at Cody, who shook his head, glancing quickly at Latta, then away, sucking in his lips.

"Doing it for you, Latta," Kya said. "Tell him cut off his hand, he'd do that too." She was slurring her words. Her face was settling back to its normal configuration, though, and her eyes had a glint of dull amusement.

Latta shrugged.

"I just gotta clear a little of the mess," Wanita apologized, bustling in with a small stack of plates smeared with melted puddles of purple and cherry Jell-O and greasy yellow islands of potato salad. Actually, Opal had sent her in to see what was going on, so she tried to get a mental picture of them — Kya practically passed out on the floor, Arthur and Cody getting drunk, and Latta telling them all what to do.

Kya put an arm around Cody's leg, pulling him off balance so he had to grab the counter. "Can't have 'im, mine." The grief in her eyes kept trading places with rage and craziness, and a childish humor.

Cody was blushing, looking down at his sister, anything to keep his eyes away from Latta.

"Tell her 'bout swimming, Cody. Tell her 'bout summers you and me —"

"That's enough, Kya." Arthur's knees cracked as he squatted beside his sister and poured more whiskey in her glass.

"Just jealous." Kya smirked and drank. Arthur paused and then shook his head, turned and leaned back against the counter, easing his bulk down on the floor beside his sister. Kya leaned her head on his shoulder, and Arthur put his arm around her. She closed her eyes and tears made their way slowly down her face again.

"Love both you, don't fight anymore, please?" Her voice was plaintive, and both men tried to concentrate on a detail of their clothing. "Please? Can't we just stop — she died 'cause of us." Kya choked, took a deep drink of whiskey, and went on. "My fault, I know — but now, isn't this 'nough — got to carry this, Greta, till I die." She buried her head in Arthur's chest, letting the sobs ripple out gently across her shoulders and down her back. Cody knelt down again, put his face in her hair, whispering, rubbing her shoulders, trying to soothe the crying down and away. Arthur hugged her more tightly. Her fingers around the glass started to loosen, and Cody took it before it fell and set it aside.

Latta realized that it wasn't only Kya's affection for the other girl, but also the fact that she had been so directly involved in bringing Greta to her death that was afflicting Kya. Kya, who never regretted anything, who never looked back, had come to find grief in her path. It was the kind of grief that stayed, that she would carry with her. And she was mourning for herself too, Latta saw, for the life that she would never be free enough again to have. Without grief, Kya would never have been complete, but something in Latta hated to see the girl taken down this way. She'd hated her for fourteen years, held her responsible for the worst turns in her life. Kya had been the symbol of everything that was wrong about people, about sex, about her husband, and now that she was broken, Latta regretted it. She had made a mistake, as Kya had. She had wanted this wild thing bitted and saddled, harnessed and forced to the hand. Now all she saw was some extinct animal dying.

"Time to go." Joseph came in and knelt in front of Kya, his hands shoved in the side pockets of his jacket.

The girl looked at him and squinted as if she could barely recognize him.

"Get your coat," he said. "Ray wants to get back now. Has to feed the animals." He looked at Cody. "She better come with me for a while." Cody searched the older man's face, then nodded.

Arthur opened his mouth to say something, but Cody said, "It's okay, Arthur," and they both relaxed away from their sister. "Get up, Kya. I'll get your coat." Cody stood, touching the bridge of his nose as blood rushed painfully, and walked quickly out of the room. When he came back, Arthur and Kya were standing, and Arthur was sliding the sterling silver dollar-sign money clip off a wad of bills and stuffing them in her jeans pocket. Then he hugged her awkwardly.

Cody helped her put the coat on, his old blue down parka with a wolf fur–trimmed hood he'd always hated. He handed her his new gloves and wrapped his new scarf around her neck, kissing her cheek and hugging her until she hugged him back. "Take care."

Joseph put his arm around Kya's waist and half led, half carried her down the hall toward the front door. "Thanks, Joseph," Cody called. Opal Treat and Wanita Cone had to flatten themselves against the wall right in the middle of their conference to let the group of Indians go by. Wanita didn't want them in her store, and she held her breath until the whoosh of fresh air from the open door chased whatever smell she imagined they carried. Opal, who never got enough opportunity to express herself on the subject of Indians because LaVeta didn't mind them, felt a kindred spark growing in her breast when Wanita pinched her nose between her two fingers and laughed.

"Back where she belongs," Opal remarked, and Wanita nodded as the door closed softly against the cold outside. "Heywood Bennett always did just what he wanted, and look at things now. I hope he's happy." Wanita nodded again.

The phone rang at midnight and Cody picked it up. They had all stayed in town for the night. Colin couldn't get back for Latta, and Cody didn't want to leave her alone with Arthur. He was going to drive her back in the morning, whether she wanted him to or not. He'd been awake trying to read a book, but he was having a hard time making the sentences enter all the information they were trying to give him. He wanted a drink — that was how he usually got to sleep on nights like this — but he didn't want to get up with Latta down the hall. He needed to go back to work, to make himself blind tired.

Arthur had been in bed for an hour, and an hour before that, Latta had gone to the room Kya usually used. Cody had gone to check on her, but she was sleeping soundly, snoring lightly. When the phone rang, it startled him. He hated calls in the middle of the night.

"Cody?" His sister's breathless whisper scared him.

"What's wrong?"

"Nothing. I don't know. I just —"

There was such a long pause, it worried him. "Kya? You okay?" He tried to keep his voice soft, encouraging.

"Yeah, no. I had a bad dream. Joseph's sleeping. I just wanted to talk to you."

"What was it? Tell me."

"Are you awake?"

"Yes."

"I dreamed I was lost. I was in a strange town and I was supposed to be living there. Nothing seemed familiar, but at the same time it was, a little bit. I didn't even know my name. I thought if I found someone they'd tell me, so I followed this girl home. She was nice to me, see, and spoke to me, and once we were in her apartment, I told her I didn't even know who I was. I didn't recognize myself. I couldn't find my house. I was so sad, and then I told her I had no one in the whole world who knew how I felt. No one I could tell it to. I was alone, completely alone. But she couldn't help me, and I woke up."

"That's a bad dream, all right. But I'm here, Kya. You can tell me, like you're doing." Cody was whispering now because she was.

"It's not the same, Cody," she sighed.

"What?"

"I need a person I can be really close to, the other way too. You're my brother. You're always going to be close to Latta or somebody else."

He couldn't think of anything to say. She was right. It did make you closer to sleep with another person. But even more than that, Kya wanted a person she could possess; she wanted sole ownership.

"Will I be alone now?" she asked hesitantly, afraid it might be the truth.

"No. You'll never be alone unless you want to be. Who could resist you, Kya? You know that."

She laughed softly. The sound made him glad.

"Go wake Joseph up." He laughed.

"Think so?"

He laughed again. "Know so. He'll be pleased as punch."

"Okay. Cody?"

"Yeah?"

"Thanks."

"You bet. Anytime." He held on to the receiver after she was gone, listening to the blank space that hummed between Babylon and Mission. His sister was out there, coasting like a big star burning too close. He just hoped she could stay there, hanging in some infinite brightness, not crash to earth with the rest of them.

The four directions, four seasons, and four quarters mark the circle of earth, sky and all related life attached to sacred colors and animals that represent the Sacred Hoop ⊕. In the center is Mother Earth (Turtle). The north (white) is watched over by Snowy Owl, Polar Bear and Bald Eagle. The northwest quarter is Winter Dragonfly, Nymph beneath the ice. The west (black) is Thunderbird and Black Horse. The southwest quarter is Blue, Autumn Dragonfly. Buffalo and Bear sit at the south pole (yellow). The southeast quarter is yellow, Summer Dragonfly. The east (red) is Red Hawk and Wolf, and the northeast quarter is Red, Spring Dragonfly.

— *from MOTHER EARTH SPIRITUALITY*

Cody and Arthur had just finished their accounting on the fall calf sales. Arthur tore the check out and handed it to his brother, who folded it neatly and slipped it into the front pocket of his jeans.

"You're going to freeze to death in that outfit." Arthur shook his head at the holey jeans and denim jacket. "Where are you going tonight?"

Cody stared at him a moment, then shifted his gaze to the dining room windows, sheeted black from the dark outside. They both knew that Clark's was his usual destination with fall calf money in his jeans. "Supper at the Buckboard, then back to the ranch, I guess."

Arthur looked at him with surprise. Maybe what he'd been hearing was true — his brother was on the wagon. Ever since that girl's funeral, it had been very quiet at the ranch. Nothing from Kya either, though he'd left word at the Sioux Trading Post in Mission that he wanted Kya to call him. Thanksgiving was coming up in two days, and he wanted her home for the first holiday without Heywood.

"Wanna see something?" Arthur asked, pointing toward the coffin elevator.

"Long as it doesn't take much time. I gotta get back."

"Won't take long, come on." Arthur picked up a small note-book and led the way to the narrow elevator they had to stand single file in, and pushed the button for the basement. "Ever been down here?"

Cody shook his head.

"You never cared much about this house, did you? There's two interesting places here — the attic with Heywood's files and boxes, and the basement."

Arthur led the way down a dark hallway, wide enough for coffins and equipment to pass through, and stopped before the last door, which was wider than the rest and made of heavy grey steel, like a fire door. The little black and gold sign said EMBALMING ROOM.

"Forget it." Cody turned to go, but Arthur caught his arm.

"Come on, Cody. You can't be afraid. Don't you want to see this?" Arthur turned the knob slowly and pressed the light button beside the door.

They entered in a flood of fluorescent glare from the heavy metal fixtures hanging by chains that marched across the ceiling, casting a silvery glitter on the walls clad in light grey ceramic tile. The floor was unpainted concrete, as smooth as a newly poured driveway. Along the wall facing them were a series of stainless steel sinks as deep as potato bins, each presided over by the arched neck of a chrome faucet, as curved as a crane's. Steel counters lined the wall on either side of the deep sinks. The other walls held a series of cabinets and closets, and in the middle of the room were three elevated tables bolted to the floor, also stainless steel. Upon closer inspection, it was possible to see little dents, specks of rust, and stains in the surface from the years of harsh chemicals and clanging tools. Despite the obvious care taken to keep the room clean, there lingered the disturbing medicinal smell of a high school biology lab, dentist's office, or hospital that any animal knew to run from, by the way it threatened to insinuate itself into the thin layers of the skin, seeping and staining the blood itself with its implications. There were some things you were better off not knowing, that smell suggested.

Cody went to one sink and turned a knob. The pipe rumbled, resisted, then spat orange water. Turning it off, he tried another knob, but nothing happened.

"That was for formaldehyde, or one of the other chemicals they used, I think." Arthur hoisted himself onto one of the waist-high tables, letting his feet dangle and bang against the legs, like a kid visiting a doctor's office, and he placed the little notebook next to him.

"No windows," Cody remarked, and slid onto the table opposite Arthur's. The room was chilly despite the heat blowing in the little vents along the inside wall, as if the tile-clad surfaces refused the solace of warmth, and sent it back through the outtake air vents along the baseboards. Both men shivered, then laughed.

"This is kind of weird down here," Cody said.

"They must of needed all the stainless steel so they could keep things hosed down. Like a rendering plant. Ever see the slaughter and gut rooms? They're always hosing those fuckers down, some poor bastard in hip boots coated with shit and blood, trying to get it to go down some little drain. Heywood took me to one in Sioux Falls. One of his big education deals — give Arthur a glimpse of the real-world thing. You remember."

"So this is where it all ends up, huh? Kinda sickening. Bodies laying on these tables like this —" Cody lay down, crossing his feet at the ankles. "This it?"

Arthur shrugged. "Guess so."

"Well, this is your little horror show, Arthur. What're we doing down here?" Cody watched a centipede stick its pale furry head out of a vent on the wall in front of him, then enter the room with a rush, legs as fine as baby hair, moving so quickly he couldn't make them out individually as it hurried down the wall. When it entered the shadow his boots cast on the wall, he crossed his feet the other way and it stopped, as if it could become invisible by the mere lack of motion.

"This deal I was doing . . ." Arthur began, and Cody phased out. What did centipedes eat? The idea that it might have eaten human flesh in this room was disturbing. Silverfish did. They nibbled the dried skin that flaked off you at night. Sometimes they didn't wait for it to flake off. Spiders bit you, mosquitoes got your blood. Humans were just a feedlot.

". . . So it looks like it's not happening. Sid couldn't come up with the extra cash. We owed Latta, but —"

"What?" Cody was suddenly paying attention and swung his legs over the side to sit facing his brother. "What the hell are you doing, Arthur? I mean, why can't we just do what we do? Why can't we just be regular? I mean, Kya be a regular person who doesn't go out stealing and fucking things up. And you just be a guy who runs a business and whatever it is you do that makes you happy. And I can just — I don't know — this whole thing with Latta is making me crazy." He hugged himself and paced back to the end of the room.

Arthur watched him carefully. "We aren't regular, whatever that means — nobody is. Who's regular? average? Lift the roof off any house in Babylon, any ranch in the sandhills, the whole fricking state of Nebraska, Iowa and the Dakotas even, the whole country, everybody's sitting around doing the same thing we are."

Cody raised his eyebrows and laughed. "Yeah, sure. Sitting in the embalming rooms in their basements, coupla bastards — excuse me, one bastard son, one regular son, and a bastard daughter, trying to sort out who stole what for which and —"

"You're missing the point." Arthur waved at him impatiently. "Every family's trying to figure things out. Maybe not the exact things we are, but everybody's got the same things going on: parents mixed up about their own lives, kids not trusting each other, trying to figure out how to live. Nobody gets a map anymore. And despite Heywood's grand plans, he left out all the important things."

Cody squatted down and looked under the sinks, then straightened and came back to the tables, sweeping the metal surface with his palm. "So?"

"So, he wanted the least common denominator in each of us to be the biggest. He undersold all of us, Cody. You too. You think he would let you marry Latta Jaboy if he was alive? You think he'd say fine, have that kid and call it yours? No, he made each of us live a secret life, hide everything about ourselves. You crawled into a bottle and waited. Kya crawled into another hole, and me another. Now we all want out. That's the problem. We don't know how to do it."

Cody was pacing, measuring his brother's words with his steps, using the rhythm to send himself around the room. He didn't know how long he could stand listening to this stuff. "So? So now what?"

Arthur watched his brother, seeing the tension, fascinated by the way energy built up in him, then erupted. They were close to that point now, he could tell, and he wasn't ready yet. Cody pulled open the doors of the cabinets, lifting and dropping objects, until he found a cigar box of wedding rings. He stirred them with his finger, then brought the box over and set it down beside Arthur.

"You know, when the deal for the resort condos started to

go sour this summer, I was really going crazy. I thought I had blown it. I thought we'd lose everything. It took me eight, ten hours to realize nothing was at stake. We have plenty. What the hell was I doing it for? For Heywood. I was taking orders from a dead man. He was still running my life. It was weird." Arthur stretched and rubbed the back of his neck with both hands, flexing his jaw from side to side to relieve the pressure. "When I stopped including Heywood's voice in everything, I figured out how to make some real money from the deal. And it worked. It really worked." Arthur smiled as he remembered Sid Greenway's plaintive voice that afternoon. His success made him feel generous.

"That's what this is all about? That's why we're down here? So you can tell me you decided not to take orders from the dead anymore?" Cody leaned back against the opposite table, cocked one leg and tilted his head.

Arthur rolled his shoulders and scooted his butt around to adjust the soreness that was developing. "Cody, sit down. You're driving me nuts with that pacing. I'm getting to it now, okay?"

Cody started walking again, then turned back and lifted a long leg and hiked himself up on the table opposite Arthur again.

"I think it's time we let each other in on our lives. All of us. Don't worry — I'm willing to start. It's just that I have to know, I have to feel like you're not going to do anything when I tell you this stuff. You have to promise not to throw it up to me, overreact or anything, okay?"

Arthur pulled a piece of paper from the notebook and unfolded it. "It seems that Heywood had a little secret of his own, Cody. One that affects you and me most of all. Here." He held the paper out. Cody hesitated, then took it and read it twice.

"Heywood and Caroline were married?" he asked, looking at Arthur.

"They were married and never divorced. Which makes me,

well, the bastard I always claimed you were, I guess." Arthur was surprised at how hard it was to say those words. "Pretty funny, huh?"

Cody waved the paper as if he were trying to extinguish a fire, then laid it on the table. "How long have you known?"

"Found it last month when I was looking for the other will giving me everything, like Heywood used to promise. Just another lie, it turns out."

"You weren't going to tell me. What changed your mind?" Cody eyed him wearily.

Arthur shrugged. "Kya, I guess. That bit of time thinking she was dead and all. I've had a lot of time to think lately. Things have gotten clearer, you might say."

Noticing the centipede's progress toward the darkness under the sink, Cody slipped off the table and squatted on his heels with his back against the wall by the door. "It doesn't matter. What difference does it make? You'll always be Arthur Bennett, Heywood's *real* son, and I'll always be Cody Kidwell, the bastard son. He claimed you. Kya and me — we were just some messes he had to clean up." Cody pushed up and paced the room again. "You don't know how much I wish you hadn't found that or told me. You don't see what it really means, do you? You're such a fat, self-satisfied fuck, you don't begin to get it, Arthur. We lived on nothing — everything hand-me-down and second rate. My mother in your mother's old coat, for chrissakes. It doesn't make me feel better to trade places with you, Arthur. We'll never trade places — for all your whining, you *had* a father."

Arthur slammed his fist onto the stainless counter. "He was always at *your* place. He was never around when I was growing up. The affair with your mother made my mother kill herself. Then you show up here and become king of the cowboys, out there riding the range with him. You were even with him when he died."

Cody stopped pacing. "You went to sleep. You left me with the dirty work, like always. Don't bullshit me. He was calling your name right along with everyone else's that night." He stood with his fist half cocked, ready for the fight.

Arthur put his hands on the table behind him so Cody would see he wasn't going to brawl with him.

Cody finally exploded. "Say something, goddamn it!"

Arthur could feel his old antagonism for his brother rising up. He didn't know why it came now, after he'd opened himself up, but there it was. "Listen, you son of a bitch, I'm trying to do something here. I didn't have to tell you anything. But it's always Arthur this, Arthur that, isn't it? You're always blaming me for everything that goes wrong in your life — and your mother's life. Let me tell you something, buddy boy, it ain't so. I am *not* the source of your problems. Let's look at it another way. You move in and Kya stops talking to me. My father spends even *less* time with me than he did before. The help takes up your cause, except for the few you nearly beat to death, who leave. And then you end up owning a third of something I was led to believe was all mine."

Cody knew that tone in his brother's voice. He was about to pay for what Arthur had told him now. He put his hand on the doorknob. "I'm outta here."

Arthur jumped off the table, knocking over the box of wedding bands, which went rolling across the floor with a tinny ringing sound. In two big steps he was at the door, facing Cody. "No, you have to wait and hear the rest of this, really." He grinned and the familiar malicious look glinted in his eyes despite his intention of simply sharing a piece of information that might free his brother from the past.

Cody stepped back, folding his arms. "What." He tried to empty his face and look bored.

"You know that man you shot? The one stealing the pig?"

"Turkey. Carl the turkey."

Arthur nodded. "Carl the turkey, then." He opened the battered spiral notebook in his hand and thumbed the pages. "Here it is, written by Caroline Kidwell, your mother, the day after you shot John Axel."

"Don't, Arthur."

"No, really, listen to this: 'Cody was supposed to be gone all day with the gun Heywood gave him, but then we heard him ride up, calling my name. John barely had time to get out of my bed and to pull his pants on. Oh God, I sent him out that window.

" 'The shots rang so, it felt like I was underwater, trying to make out what people were saying. The window smashed into the room. John was lying in the powdery dust outside, an arc of red shooting up from his leg. The third shot caught him in the stomach. He was bleeding to death so fast he never opened his eyes again. I stood there, sheet dragging in dust and blood, staring at Cody on the other side of the body. He finally shut me up, I kept thinking.

" 'Cody's pet turkey, Carl, started pecking the body on the ground, leaving angry red triangles on his arm. I grabbed it by the neck and dragged it to the pile of broken blocks by the new cistern. Picked up a chunk of cement and hammered its head flat.

" 'That's when Cody threw up, not before, and I saw then he wasn't anyone I knew. He could kill a man in the blink of an eye. It was the stupid bird he cared about. I wish there'd been twenty turkeys, I would have killed every single one of them. I'd been fooling myself into thinking I could raise him alone. Make him better, different, but he's turned out just like the rest of them, only worse. I can't live under the same roof anymore. John Axel's dead. Cody killed him because he's sick with jealousy, wants me all to himself. I can see it in his eyes, he doesn't even feel ashamed. Maybe it'll be Heywood next time. I can't risk it. I just don't see how he went so wrong.

" 'The sheriff wanted to charge him with murder, send him

away, but we've taken care of it. Said it was a thief stealing a turkey.' "

Arthur eyed Cody as he shut the notebook and laid it on the table. "I guess it was a mistake —"

"That's wrong." Cody closed his eyes, feeling the redness rush over his head. The whole scene, his years of rage and hurt, came pouring up as if a vacuum lid had been released.

"Now don't go off half cocked."

"It didn't happen that way. It didn't. I *didn't* know him." Cody yelled and pounded the door frame with his fist, ignoring the shooting pain.

"Cody —" Arthur started to touch his arm, but stopped.

"All that time she thought I was a murderer. *That's* why it never made sense. She made me lie because she believed a lie. 'Protect your mother,' Heywood said. Then he handed me the rifle." He pounded the door frame again, but not as hard as before. If he broke his hand, he couldn't get to Clark's. If he couldn't get to Clark's, he'd stay sober and kill somebody. "Christ, I feel like I'm going crazy. Just like Caroline." He looked wildly around the room, but there was nothing to stop him.

"Blood, there's too much blood." He pushed Arthur out of the way as he crashed out into the hall, running by the time he hit the stairs.

29 ✧ BLAME THE DEAD

POLICE REPORTS

10:45 A.M. A woman was worried about fire possibility in a lot full of weeds.

12:43 P.M. More weed complaints.

3:30 P.M. A cow and calf were at large.

7:25 P.M. A man wanted assistance in opening a trap door in the floor. He said he heard voices under the floor and thought someone had dug tunnels under the house. The owner of the property said the trap door was under the carpet and had not been opened in years.

— *BABYLON CALLER*

Cody woke with a start. It was another dream of his mother. Since the scene with Arthur, he found he could sleep for only an hour or two at a time without the dreams coming again. Their pain and insistence made him leave the house and ranch to drive the hills. He got up and went out to his truck; he figured he'd go to the Niobrara valley and doze there while he fought off the cold and time. In the morning he'd wake up and there'd be one of those bald or golden eagles that wintered around Babylon, hunting the river valley where game was still plentiful despite the cold and snow. He often saw the eagles hanging in the drafts overhead, like kites or scraps of paper caught by some invisible wire, holding them aloft. Then suddenly they'd come plunging down to a place their incredible eyes had found: the small body of a vole, whose tan ears, pulsing with pink blood so thin you could see light through it, had given it away.

He'd wanted to wake up to something beautiful. Something alone. He had to get rid of those old voices and dreams, he decided, combing his fingers through his hair until they got caught in the knots and tangles, and he'd start over.

The truck found the way to the Niobrara valley sooner than he did because he was so tired. The road humped and dropped with the regularity of a chest breathing in and out, threatening to lull him to sleep. He pressed the gas harder; he'd have to get there before the exhaustion dropped him.

He didn't know which happened first — the truck sliding or the several deer that appeared in front of it, solid and alive one moment, then smashed and flung up and up into the air the next. He managed to stop at the edge of a ditch after spinning around twice, hitting another deer that was following the first group. The engine ground to a burning halt as the parts seized up from both the radiator and the oil pan being ripped open. Cody turned the key off. He'd bumped his forehead at some point, but otherwise he was fine. Probably so tired he'd simply flowed with the bashing and jerking of the truck.

He sat for a few minutes trying to steady his body, which had started shaking, then he gave up and pushed open the door. He didn't want to see the deer, but he knew he had to check. He leaned across the seat and dug around in the glove compartment, which had popped open. The cold of the pistol came to his fingers. He leaned a little farther and the truck groaned, but he got the gun in his hand and pulled his weight back. He really didn't want to be in a rollover.

There was so much blood, he wondered if he'd hit all of them. His shaking got worse and he gripped the handle of the gun harder, putting his finger on the trigger as if to steady himself. Blood all over the highway, he slipped and went to one knee, and had to put his hands in it, and wipe it on his jacket. Jesus Christ, maybe he'd killed them all. He started to feel like throwing up, but nothing would come. He wanted to run, but there was blood and body parts everywhere, and a mewling sound, a groan.

He staggered toward the noise. On the other side of the road, lying on the bank of the ditch, was a doe, her hind end smashed, stomach ripped open, but somehow still alive, bloody foam on her lips, eyes full of fear as he knelt beside her head, laying the gun down. "Don't die," he begged. It was as if he held in his arms all the things he'd ever touched and loved and lost. The deer thrashed with her front legs, and a tiny sharp hoof struck him on his bare knee sticking through the holes in his jeans, scraping the skin and flesh to the bone in one white slash that waited, turned light blue, before blood came seeping up and began to flow down into the already bloody snow. He didn't feel anything except the huge boom of her heart in the rasping breath she moaned out.

"You know what to do," he said in a voice that was not his but more his father's — Heywood, who had taught him the gun, the mercy of the gun. "No," his mother had whispered that day he shot the thief. He had a name, but Cody had lost it the minute the gun resounded around the house and barn, like it was barbed wire circling them, tying them in its cruel rupture forever.

"Pick up the gun," he ordered. "Put it under her eye. Squeeze." There was the sound that closed his eyes, then his ears and heart, then nothing. The wind sent the soft snow onto the scene, turning the spilled blood milky pink after a while. Cody sat beside the doe, feeling the grid of memories tracing back and forth over him, leaving every cut open, every scar unscarred and new. He couldn't move. What could he do? At last it came to him. Bury the dead. Bury all the dead. That was the demand. The reparation.

He got up slowly and walked through the bloody ice on the

road. There was a small shovel in the back of the truck, in case he got stuck. He began to dig in the deep drift of the ditch, below where the doe lay. The surface of the ground was crusty hard when he hit it, but he finally broke through to the sand that gave easily, though with each shovelful, more rushed in to fill the hole again, collapsing it from the sides, so all he was producing was an indentation.

He had to bury every one of them. It was their due respect. He dragged the stiffening doe down the hill and laid her carefully in the shallow trench he'd made. She stuck up too far; her legs wouldn't fold into the trench. He couldn't force them to bend far enough, and stopped himself just as he was about to use the sharp edge of the shovel to cut the joints loose. Respect. He shoveled the sand and dirt, then the snow, as best he could on top of the corpse. Then he began on another.

Each shovelful took him a little further away, a little further back to his past. It was the only way he could keep at it. Thinking, remembering, letting the pictures twist and turn him with their pins of accurate failure and love. At times, single words caught and spun, Caroline's and Heywood's words, coming around and around, then down, like a drain whose face became Latta's, and he wept. Digging and digging, his shoulders and arms ached, his head throbbed, almost blinding him with stabbing pain.

Kya, Joseph, and Arthur were coming back from the Thanksgiving program at the Babylon Consolidated High School. The senior class had invited their counterparts from the high school in Mission, to include Native American views in their pageant for a change, and the uneasy marriage of interests had produced some moments of drama and humor. Whites in the audience shifted uncomfortably at the surprisingly long list of native contributions to the world they shared. A few got up and left during the more vitriolic reference to Wounded Knee and Leonard Peltier. But in the end, there had been a genuine attempt at making peace when the two groups on stage exchanged handmade gifts and burned sage and sweet grass. And when the smoke set off the fire alarms, the fire chief just laughed and sent someone to shut off the noise. The audience applauded, and there weren't any fights in the parking lot afterward.

"Pretty nice deal tonight," Joseph said as they got into his truck.

"I thought it was great." Kya unwound the long turquoise scarf from around her neck and head. She was wearing gloves with the fingers cut out, and Cody's old parka. Her face was flushed with the cold. She lifted her long black hair and shook it out, then let it flop back on her shoulders. "Opal Treat looked happy, 'bout like she had a mouthful of toad." Kya laughed.

Arthur rubbed at the frost on the side window. "It was okay. Too cluttered maybe, too many people on stage. And I'm sorry, but this Wounded Knee thing . . ."

Joseph glanced at Arthur's pensive face. He was a person not unlike most, whose salvation would always remain only half realized. The important moments of revelation and sorrow would provide Arthur momentary relief. Later he would discover how difficult it was to put his new understanding into practice, or he would just forget about it, feeling vaguely uneasy when those insights resurfaced for a moment or two, as they always did. Arthur wasn't a bad man. He had good in him, but he was, in the end, only an ordinary man.

"Long as everyone's included, there's enough for everyone, Arthur. U.S. government may not like it —"

"What's that?" Kya said, pointing ahead of them.

"What the hell?" Arthur muttered, and Joseph slowed to a stop a few yards away from the mess in the road.

"Oh God, that's Cody's truck." Kya jumped out and ran in the path of the headlights to the vehicle leaning precariously on the edge of the ditch. Joseph and Arthur got out and walked toward the dark clumps in the snow-slick road.

Cody didn't hear the truck brake or see the lights, but when Kya said, "Cody, what're you doing," he ignored her. She was just a ghost taking over the voice in his head. "Stop." She pulled his arm and he shoved at her.

"Got to bury them. Too many dead. Got to be right again. Clean up the blood. Got to start over. Put 'em back to places. Pieces."

"Arthur, Joseph, help me — he's covered with blood — I can't tell —" Kya called, grabbing the shovel and pulling so hard that when he pulled back, she lost her balance and fell on top of him. She lay there, pressing down with all her weight. He could feel the hoof of the dead animal beneath him and wanted to twist away when it began to wiggle and dig into him.

"It's alive," he gasped, and tried to push her off, but she held him down.

"Stop it. Just stop. There's nothing you can do. It's over — they're dead. We have to go home now, hear? We're going home. You need to sleep. I'm going to hurt you if you don't stop." Her voice was rough, and he knew she'd use the shovel if she had to. But he didn't care. "You can come back tomorrow. We'll all come back."

"I have to bury 'em, Kya. I can't leave," but he could feel his strength draining, flattening into the ground, flowing away with the dead. "I didn't know she loved him, didn't know they — he was — I thought he was going to hurt her, that's why I shot him. All those years, she thought I killed him on purpose. She made a lie out of it, Kya. Now she'll never know the truth. Everything I love turns. I have to stop it. I have to change. I'm so sorry, so so sorry." He closed his eyes against the images.

Kya sat up and rolled off him.

"Come on, buddy, let me help you here," Arthur said, and half carried, half pulled his brother up the hill to the waiting truck. It was so warm in the cab, he couldn't keep his eyes from closing and found himself floating in the smooth heat while his brother's and sister's bodies supported his shoulders, keeping his head just above the dark dreamless waters as the windshield wipers clicked the snow away.

"Aren't you celebrating Thanksgiving?" Latta asked when she saw Joseph in the doorway.

"Not my holiday." He smiled and stepped into the sunroom. "How's the baby?" He took her hand before she could stop him. Then she remembered she wasn't so mad at him anymore.

"Fine. I'm just supposed to stay off my feet twenty-four hours a day or risk losing it. No problem. I'm only going a little crazy."

She was settled on a white wicker couch with big floral pillows. "I hope this isn't a bunch of B.S. you think you're going to snow me with, Joseph. I'm not forgetting you had my horse all along."

"My cousin Ray found him, remember?" He looked around and cleared his throat. "I think you should talk to Cody, Mrs. Jaboy."

With the use of her married name, he had told her to behave, and she sighed. Looking out the wall of glass behind Joseph, she noticed that the squirrels had made a pattern between the walk and the huge old elm where they lived, going back and forth, never using the same path, until the blue steps in the snow stitched a shawl around the tree.

"You should marry Cody."

She looked at him sharply. He stared back.

"I shouldn't marry anyone." She said it flatly, so he'd hear her and know she wasn't being taken in.

"He's a good man. He doesn't lie, and he doesn't want a lot. He'd work himself to death for you and the baby."

Latta laughed. "You make him sound like a loyal dog or something. Besides, it looks like he's more interested in drinking himself to death. I don't need that. I told him I can't have that going on in the house with a child. And I don't want to put up with it."

Joseph rubbed his hands on his thighs. "He hasn't had a drink since the cabin."

Latta closed her eyes for a few minutes before she spoke again. "Okay, you're right. I do love him. I just need some time to think — okay?"

"He can come and work here while you're laid up."

They were quiet, listening to the crows arguing over the suet Inez had thrown outside the back door. Finally Latta nodded. "Okay. All right."

"I also came to ask for my ghost shirt back." Joseph stood quietly in front of her, holding the brim of his worn hat. It was as stained and wrecked as any old cowboy's had a right to be. The beaded band looked new, though, with an intricate pattern of blue, red, white, and yellow beads on deerskin that ended in two thin trailers tied with feathers off the back.

"I told you before — it's yours. Anytime you want it." She relaxed and put her hands around the baby again. Lately she'd felt it shifting and kicking, and she was in the habit now of waiting for it to happen again, as if the child were starting to respond to her taps.

"It has to be a trade. So I'm painting the inside of the church in exchange."

She stared at him. "You are?"

He nodded, with a tiny smile curving his lips. "It's very beautiful. I've been using some of the old Lakota designs."

The church was her responsibility because it was on her land, but she had always understood it belonged to everyone in the hills around her. "I hope you aren't making it too —"

"Too Indian? You'll see, Latta, I'm following my vision. Kya's helping. I'm teaching her. You're coming to the services Christmas Eve, aren't you?"

She looked away, trying not to react to the idea of Kya on her land. "I hadn't thought about it. I suppose I could get Curt or Colin to drive me up in the truck if it isn't snowing too hard."

"I'll come and bring you. You should come. It's important for you to be there, to be in the church with the rest of the people."

She shrugged. "All right. An hour of sitting up shouldn't hurt. You pick me up."

He smiled more broadly and took her hand. "You're a good woman, Latta Jaboy. You shouldn't be so hard on yourself. Not good for the baby to have a mother so worried all the time. Old Indian saying."

She laughed and pushed his hand back. "Go get the shirt and tell Inez I'm all right. I just want to be left alone for a while, okay?"

They were careful to avoid staring at each other rudely, and the respect that had always been there between them returned, leaving a small circle of peace in the room after he had gone.

She didn't want to think about this Cody business. She couldn't deny that she loved him. She dreamed about him every night. He came to her in sleep like a dark mysterious lover, the faceless one she'd seen for years, knowing every move that could touch her and bring her to her private sensuality, to the place of love no one had ever found before. In a way, having him gone felt like a relief — a responsibility she wasn't sure she'd wanted finally. It had been a dream, but maybe not the right one. Maybe not one she had the time for anymore. Not with the baby, not with the rest of her life, which had grown so terribly complicated over the past year. Yes, it was true, she told herself, she loved Cody Kidwell, but she wasn't sure she could ever trust him in person. Whether she could ever trust anyone but herself. She just didn't know, and it irritated her that everyone else could see her feelings so clearly. A part of her was resisting on those grounds alone. And she'd be damned if she'd give Opal Treat one more piece of gossip.

LETTERS TO THE EDITOR

To the editor:

It all started with a flat tire on December 18.

I came out of the Oasis Motel and the manager told me my tire was flat. I was going to change it and discovered I had no jack. He got his jack out of his pickup and we changed the tire. I didn't expect that.

Then I took my tire to B&E Tire where I was greeted by Chris Jones. He said he could probably fix the tire. When we went out to the car to look at the tire, he noticed a gasoline leak but said they were too busy to fix it and suggested I try Fred's Auto Repair. Fred treated me more than fair and I was out of his place in less than 15 minutes.

When I went back to pick up my tire at B&E, Chris Jones said the tire was unfixable and had a new tire on the wheel. I expected to be charged a high price because I was from out of town but I was treated like a local repeat customer.

I have traveled this area for 38 years and without exception the ranchers and townspeople have always treated me good. You have a very great community with a lot of very good people. That's why for years it has been one of my favorite towns. I hope you keep it that way.

Paul Joseph
Nevis, MN

— *BABYLON CALLER*

*I*t was snowing again. In the white outlines of solid objects the world doubled, dark and light, as if the snow were a mirror that told the future. The hills smoothed in the snow, rounded and curved around the houses and valleys, as if their sole purpose were protection and the wisest of people and animals understood that and had sought the shelter, found it, and settled there. There was a kind of utter silence in the sandhills winter, unimaginable in the rest of the world, a silence that was achieved elsewhere only after a blasting away of anything living. But this was a natural absence, a form of comfort.

The snow was a light exhalation of white, not gathering or irritating. It was as if the air itself had become visible to the living eye and it was possible to make out the elaborate curls of currents, the paisley design that would appear if each flake were colored.

Cody had been tracking Latta's mares all morning after they'd broken through one fence after another the night before, as if chased by something. The hot wires in the corrals hadn't been a problem. The boards on the fences were old and had simply pushed away from the posts they were nailed to, or splintered in two. It hadn't looked like there was much hair and blood on those, so he wasn't worried. By the time the horses got to the barbed wire, he did start to worry. From the tangle he found, it was clear he was going to find some damage when he rounded them up.

He'd been coming to Latta's every morning since the day after Thanksgiving. Latta had been so used to directing and doing the work herself, the place was short a hand without her. Besides, Chris had taken up permanent residence at Bennett's. Cody had been too busy over the past weeks to think much about it, but he could tell Arthur was once again in the middle of something. He always got edgy and spent a lot of time on the phone, then haggled about the price of groceries or any little thing, a pair of pliers, when he was doing a financial deal. It reminded Cody of Heywood's economies: never throw away a piece of wire, no matter how rusty; always straighten bent nails.

He'd never known how to please that man, and he hated it that he'd had to try and fail so often. In the end it hadn't mattered; Cody was sure he hadn't pleased his father and mother, and now they were dead, so it was too late to try. But he had kept trying, that was the bitch of it, he thought, you kept trying even after they were gone. They never let go of you. They were like the little scabby plants that came up when the soil started to blow from overgrazing or erosion. Everything wanted life, anything fought for it, even the dead.

It was the reason for families that should've scattered in pieces, the reason for runts that clung to the edges of the herd and made it, the reason for these hills and the people in these hills like Latta and him. Despite drought and wind and cold, they all stayed, and gradually lived their lives, dying satisfied that when all was said and done, they'd managed to survive, to perpetuate something for a little longer. He was going to make Latta understand that.

This side of the hill was unprotected to the southwest, and erosion had stripped much of its thin soil crust, so the prickly pear cactus were starting to invade. A while back he'd seen evidence of jimson and spurge, noxious weeds that needed killing too. He reached the top of the hill, and below him stretched a wide valley where he could see in the distance the five mares nosing for marshgrass at the shoreline of a small lake. As he watched, letting the horse blow, one of the mares seemed to be dragging her hind leg. He'd been seeing splatters of blood in the snow for quite a while now, and he worried that she might have hit a vein or an artery. She'd bleed to death if that was the case. He had a portable two-way radio with him, but he doubted he could get through to anyone this far out.

When he got close enough to the mares, he dismounted and untied a sack of corn he'd brought to lure them with. Dumping the ears in a pile on the ground, he called softly to them and held out a single yellow ear so they could see. All five eyed him curiously until the leader of the little group, a big brown mare with a finely modeled head and ears that were small and delicately curved toward each other, stepped forward cautiously, blowing along the ground for the smell of the corn. With each step she grew bolder, licking her big lips with her tongue as she neared the corn. When she was safely planted with a cob in her teeth, crunching away, the other mares followed, jostling each other for a position around the pile that wouldn't make them turn their backs to him.

The last was the injured horse, who was definitely dragging her leg. She stopped outside the circle around the corn and gazed at him. He held out the ear of corn and crooned, walking around the mares pawing and turning the cobs with their noses. The mare, a black with a thin white strip on her face, waited patiently, her injured leg cocked. When he presented the corn, she lipped it politely, but didn't bite at it. He shoved it in his coat pocket and pulled out a soft rope he'd tied around his waist for catching them. He hobbled the mare, slid his hand along her side, talking softly to let her know where he was, and worked his way to her haunches. Kneeling, he saw that the leg had gotten tangled in wire and that her struggle had cut the flesh in strips that hung away from the bone, which was poking out yellow-white from the bloody pink flesh around it. He had no idea how she'd made it this far. The snow and ice had helped control the bleeding, and he knew if he started doctoring it now, he'd get it going. Somehow she'd missed the big blood vessel. Examining the other legs, he found several other deep cuts and scratches, as well as long stripes across her chest where she'd hit the wire and kept going. She was a pretty, small mare, but she wouldn't be anymore, he thought grimly. He wondered if she was in shock, she was standing so still. Pulling her upper lip out, he pressed his forefinger against her pale gum. Then he pinched the skin on her neck and held it for a moment. It stood up too long: needed liquids too. He was a couple of hours away from the ranch.

Leaving the mare where she was, he walked back to his horse, unlashing the two ropes he'd brought and his saddle-bags, which contained some of the vet supplies he thought he might need. Cattle hide was tough enough to take a lot of barbed-wire cuts, but horsehide was different. That was the problem with keeping horses in wire fencing. The other horses were still busy with the corn, and the injured mare stood now with her head hanging. Another bad sign. He didn't want her to go down; he'd probably never be able to get her up on that leg again without help.

Horses were funny, he thought as he doctored her. A horse could go miles, injured the way she was, and then sudden-ly drop, as she was now. They were much more emotionally charged than cattle, and that emotion carried them past reason and pain, the way it did humans sometimes. He'd seen a horse with a smashed shoulder run a hundred yards before it stopped, and there were all those stories of horses with broken legs finishing races. They were so damn brave, it made you mad.

You could break a horse's spirit too, ruin it. They wanted a relationship. "Like women," Cody muttered as he sorted out the catgut and big curved needle for sewing the wounds. He wasn't going to put in the neat stitches a vet would, but he'd do the best he could and hope they held long enough to get her back.

The painkiller was helping the mare relax, her eyelids droop-ing as she found a place that didn't hurt anymore. He wanted to give her a tranquilizer too, but didn't dare since he couldn't risk her stumbling around and falling if she got too dopey.

He hoped she was in enough shock to ignore the needle piercing her skin and pulling. She twitched and shook her head when she felt the sting, but quickly settled down again. The hind leg was trickier and he decided to use the gauze and cotton he'd brought, to dress it instead of trying to sew anything. He wrapped the bandage as tight as he dared, to keep it from sliding off in the snow as she moved.

Disturbing the surface made it bleed more, and his hands and the bandage itself were splotched red by the time he was through. He stood up, tried brushing the bloody snow from his knees and hands, and went to her head. "Now listen, we're going back, you're gonna be okay. You just gotta try this one last time, okay?" He slipped the hobbles off, unwound the lead, and put it in his pocket. He picked up one of the lariats and fashioned a halter around her head and neck. He'd do the same with the lead mare, and the others would follow.

He tried the radio, but there was nothing but static. He knew it wouldn't work, but Inez had insisted. As he rode off that morning, he'd tipped his hat at Inez and Latta, whose faces he could see watching him out the kitchen windows where they were having the breakfast he'd missed. Inez had waved, but Latta had turned away. She'd been like that since the cabin. Not talking to him, accepting what she had to stoically.

The lead mare wasn't too happy about the rope, and swung her big flank at him after it settled around her neck. He dodged the kick and jerked the rope tight to remind her that breathing was more important than getting even. She kept her ears flat against her head the whole time he made her halter out of a series of loops and knots, trying to bite him as he turned to collect the other rope. Her teeth clacked in the air next to his ear and he spun, catching the side of her nose with the flat of his hand. She jerked her head up from the slap and rolled her eyes. "Now behave," he ordered, and the mare snorted and looked away. "That's better." He reached his hand out slowly and rubbed her shoulder to show there were no hard feelings. The other horses watched him warily.

Starting off, he had to tug at the injured horse to get her moving. The three that were loose waited a few minutes, grab-

bing anxious mouthfuls of corn and whinnying at the horses
that were being led away, until finally they came trotting, then
loping to catch up. They were all pregnant, he noticed, their
big bellies swinging heavily as they moved.

Cody had to stop frequently to let the wounded animal rest,
and he worried that the free ones would mill up and hurt her
or get tangled in the ropes. He had only one bad moment, and
that was when they got to the barbed-wire fence the mares had
torn down. Cody had to get off and keep them from trying to
crowd through while he used his nippers to cut the wire and
pull it out of the way. The horses could smell the ranch again,
and were ready to get back to their safe corral and hay after
their excursion.

"Tired of eating snow, huh?" He remounted and started
through the gap with the loose horses bodying up on the
others, forcing the lead mare to surge ahead, almost pulling
him off his horse as she spun to face him at the end of the rope.
The injured mare lagged behind.

"Jesus Christ." He stopped his horse, not daring to get off
again, while the three loose mares trotted off toward the ranch,
a half mile away at the end of the valley. "Come here, then."
Pulling the lead mare toward him, he snubbed her head on his
leg and unlooped the halter gradually so she wouldn't lunge
away too quickly. He patted the wide space between her eyes
when the rope was off, and it seemed to take her a moment to
realize she was free.

"Go on." He waved, and she spun and kicked her hind legs
at him, narrowly missing his leg and his horse's shoulder, then
galloped after the others in a whirl of snow. The mare reminded him of his sister, and he laughed. She'd been going
off for several days with Joseph, coming back late, dirty and
speckled with paint. He wondered what they were doing, but
didn't ask. She seemed happy for a change, not bored and
energized to cause trouble. If anything, she was working to
keep peace between all of them. Whatever else he was doing,

Joseph was a good influence on Kya, Cody decided. Maybe on Arthur too, who had eased up on stuff lately.

The wind was coming up the valley, lightly twisting the snow, gusting it into finely sifted clouds and dropping it in crosshatches as if there were several different storms at work here, each with its own purpose and meaning. The injured mare was moving slower and slower, and Cody wondered if she was going to make it. He reached back and pulled the radio out. This time he was able to make contact and alert the house to call the vet immediately.

He sighed and hunched his shoulders. He'd have to check the rest of the corrals; make sure the other mares weren't carrying wounds he hadn't spotted; get on Colin's boys to clean the stalls better, because that was one thing he knew Latta was particular about; move some more hay closer, because they'd already gone through a lot from the last storm; make sure the oats got delivered; check to see that the water tank heaters were working; and see what lists Inez had. Colin had been too busy for trips to town, so Cody had been shopping too, bringing the groceries and things for Christmas baking with him every day or so. How women could be such poor planners, he couldn't figure out. They always needed something, especially now that they had him to run it out to them. He'd finally gotten his wish, he was mostly too tired to think, between the Bennetts and the Jaboys.

He blanketed the injured mare and offered her fresh water. She nosed it, wetting her lips, then let them hang in the bucket for a moment, her eyelids half closed.

"Come on, have a drink," he urged, stroking her ears and rubbing her neck. She sipped a little, sucking water in and swallowing in slow, long gulps. When she finished, she'd hardly lowered the level in the bucket. He set it down and continued rubbing her head, talking to her. The mare tucked her nose in between his arm and body, shoving against him as if she needed his warmth. He held her that way, humming and talking to her, letting his face sink into the furry heat of her neck, smelling the spicy must he loved with each breath.

"You're gonna be all right," he kept saying, "all right," trying to will her to believe it. Inside her big body, a foal was nestled, sleeping in its dark well, waiting, like its mother, depending on another world for safety and comfort. Above them in the rafters, the sparrows and barn swallows were drowsing away the afternoon, as they did every day. Toward dark, they flitted about the barn, gathering dropped grain, searching manure and collecting straw to fortify their nests, chattering, arguing, bullying, and singing until they were exhausted back into silence again.

He was holding her when her knees buckled and she started to go down. He did the irrational thing — tried to hold her up, tried to keep her head so she wouldn't give in, but she did. Her legs folded and he went down on his knees with her. Even as she heaved a huge sigh ending in a long groan, he tried to pull her head up, lifting it and stretching her neck as the last rattling breath collapsed from her huge lungs and her sphincter opened and the stall filled with the scent of liquefied manure.

"No, come on, don't," he kept saying, until he rocked back on his heels, hands dangling uselessly between his legs. The mare's shredded leg had soaked the bandage red and stained the straw around it. He didn't know what had stopped her — blood loss, shock, stress. It didn't matter. He hadn't been able to save her. Everything seemed just beyond his control, and the more he tried to affect it, the more screwed up it got.

He was still sitting there when Judy, the vet, found him. "Dead," he said, standing up and shoving his hands in his pockets. "Got into wire. Died anyway. I'd better tell Latta." He pushed past her, stumbling on the step down from the stall to the aisle, half running out of the barn to the old jeep he was using now that his truck was wrecked.

He sat there in the failing light, not bothering to turn the jeep's heater on. It barely worked anyway. This was when he needed a drink, needed a place to hide. Here he was again, his hands shaking, blood on his clothes — a state he hadn't been able to escape for fifteen years. Even drunk. The only time it let go a little was with Latta last summer and fall. The good days he'd spent with her.

Half an hour later, he made himself climb out of the jeep and walk to the back door of the house and knock. He nodded to Inez when she opened the door and pointed the way into the sunroom where Latta had spent the afternoon reading.

Her eyes were closed, her lips curved in a smile, a healthy flush on her skin as he watched her sleep. He hadn't been this close to her in weeks. She was growing so beautiful it almost hurt him. He was surprised by the size of her belly now too.

When she opened her eyes, they were soft and glad, and the smile stayed for a moment before he looked away.

"We lost one of the mares that broke out this morning. Tangled up in wire. I tried to — save her, but she didn't make it. I'm sorry." He concentrated on the top of her head. It was his fault, he knew, it always was. Someone had to be responsible.

"Which one was it?" Latta asked quietly.

"Neat little five-year-old black mare."

"A good one," Latta sighed.

Cody nodded and glanced quickly at her face. She didn't look mad at all. "I am sorry."

"It's not your fault. If I had the money, I'd replace every inch of that barbed wire. I know you tried — you never let up with the animals."

The way she said it almost made him flinch, though her face remained open. She picked up the book she was reading, folded the corner of a page, and closed it. She was letting her hair grow, and he liked it, but didn't dare say anything too personal.

"I appreciate your help, Cody. I really do. I guess it makes me feel a little hopeless, not being out there with you when something like this happens." She glanced at the dark smears of blood on his jacket. "I know how hard it is alone." She blushed and looked out the dark windows.

For the first time since the cabin, he sensed a slight give in her feelings toward him. He bit his lower lip and sucked in his breath, lest he scare her away again.

"Well, that's that," she sighed, and shook her shoulders loose of the shawl around them. "If I don't see you again, have a Merry Christmas. Inez has something for you — from all of us, a thank you." She smiled and held out her hand as if she wanted it kissed.

Confused, Cody took it and held it lightly, as if it could shatter like a porcelain teacup. "Merry Christmas," he mumbled as she gently pulled it away.

When he was out of sight of the house, he stopped the jeep and opened the package Inez had given him as he'd left. Inside was a pair of golden tan elkhide chaps with silver conches at the hips. CODY, in fancy letters, was cut out in dark brown along the back. "Special order," he said to himself. She must have decided on the gift weeks ago.

31 ✧ ABOVE THE DISMAL RIVER

*We spin the globe, drawn through the hair of time, the single strand,
aligned perfectly and casually, rooted to the head of something we
won't know, but always recognize, the light that smothers us, the
light that smooths us waiting in line for the traffic to move on, for
the ancient creak of springs, of thumping car doors, of arrival to and
from, the well of work, that waters the day, the pantry with blue
light, the steam of morning air, the kettle's heating polishes the metal
to untouchable bright, I go to take my bath each day in the enameled
tub of light.*

— Caroline
December 25, 1962

*L*atta was waiting for the ride Joseph had promised, having
sent Inez on ahead with Curt Sykes. It had been snowing
on and off, and Curt had spent the evening keeping the road
to the church scraped clear for people coming to the Christmas
Eve service.

She'd called her parents earlier and had the same conversation she'd had for the past twenty-some-odd years. She
couldn't bring herself to tell them of her pregnancy. They'd be
shocked, especially because she wasn't married, wasn't even
living with a man, and she had planned on telling them she
didn't know who the father was. Some Christmas present, so
she hadn't mentioned it. She had plenty of time. Five months.

When she saw the new Chevy truck drive up, its big headlights searching the house, she stood and struggled into her coat, calling for Joseph to come in the door.

Cody's pale face bobbed behind and above the older man's like a yard light in snow. He looked everywhere but at her, but she could tell he was seeing her too. He looked so pale — she hadn't noticed it that afternoon. Different. He held his hat in his hand, that was it. His face was exposed, naked, and he seemed ashamed of it almost, the way he kept his head turned away.

She hadn't realized she was staring quite so intently until Joseph shuffled his feet and said, "Ready to go, Latta?" She nodded, and began to work her way slowly across the front sitting room.

"I thought Cody here could carry you to the truck. You won't make it. Too slippery." Cody stepped around him and bent to lift her.

"No — I —" she protested as his arms fit neatly around her back and under her knees, lifting her easily so she had to put an arm around his neck to balance them both. His cheeks burned pink, and she felt the glow of hers as well. She could smell the scent she always associated with him, the one that drove an arrow into her, something spicy lemon and nutmeg and earthy that made her want to bury her face in his neck. As they cleared the door frame, with Joseph behind them carrying Cody's hat, she felt the imprint of each of his fingers — the ones on the side of her breast, the ones on the side of her knee. She hoped she wasn't heavy, hoped the baby didn't make her seem too clunky. "Damn you, Cody Kidwell," she whispered so he'd hear her but Joseph wouldn't.

He tried not to smile and hugged her body tighter against his. She called on all the anger and resistance she'd felt in recent months, but they wouldn't listen. "This isn't fair." He raised his eyebrows and kissed her head softly, banging her feet into the gatepost in the process.

"Watch out," Joseph called after them. "You two are about

the clumsiest people I've ever seen." Then he muttered, "Must be made for each other."

Cody was breathing a little hard, his hands shaking, when he shut the door on Latta. He caught her looking at him and turned away. "Little out of shape, I guess." He put his hands on his legs and pressed the knuckles white trying to stop the tremor. In fact he felt sick, but didn't dare show it. Joseph had given him this chance; he wasn't going to mess it up. When he'd gotten home earlier, Joseph had taken one look at him and made him sit down for a talk. He reminded Cody that he'd been walking a line of fear, wondering if it was worth it to come back into the world. Then Joseph told him to come bring Latta to church, and not ask a lot of questions. Just do what he was told. He'd figure it out in due time.

"Nice truck," Latta commented when they were settled in its vinyl-scented warmth.

Joseph shifted and smiled. "Cody's — he's letting me try it out, see if I should get me one too. Maybe I'll trade him something."

They laughed and Cody said, "Kya and Arthur's surprise, I guess. Her color, red. It's loaded with all the options. Guess he got a deal, some demo thing." His face wore the fresh happiness of a child who has received exactly what he would've asked for if he'd been able to imagine it.

The new truck shivered and bellied through the snow, lurching with the ruts and spinning its tires on the clear icy flat parts up and down the several hills that took them through the pastures to the church. The night was lovely, with a waxing moon crowding out of the clouds every few minutes, catching the big soft flakes and turning them over and over so they glittered and shook. The snow was iridescent purple and blue. In some places it shone like the wet summer hide of a horse, in other places it grew furry and thick like the winter coats of animals living under it.

Halfway up the last hill before the church, Joseph paused

ABOVE THE DISMAL RIVER 399

so they could look at the Dismal River, capped with ice except where the rush and gurgle of water burst through in dark silver swirls. While they watched, several deer came up so silently they might have been a mirage, and drank out of an open place, then pawed at the grass beneath the snow with their sharp hooves.

Cody's hand went instinctively to his knee. He remembered only partially how that accident had happened, but he knew he was glad for the deer by the river. As glad as he'd ever been. He wished them well, in his heart, and hoped they could find their way to the stack yard when the snow got too deep. Maybe they would be there tonight even, lying down in the shelter of the towering mounds, resting their heads in the warm hay, dreaming of the open hills next summer as the ripe green smell inside the stack worked its way up their nostrils.

He lifted his arm and set it along the back of the seat behind Latta, and when Joseph put the truck in gear again, the thrust pushed her head back against his arm, and she left it there. As the truck ground its way up the rest of the hill, he felt her leg outlining the heat of his, her arm tucked between their bodies. This is worth everything, he wanted to tell her. This is worth the rest of what has happened to both of us.

Opal Treat would have given her right arm to be inside that little church. A hundred people crowded the benches, lining the walls in their folding chairs, when Cody Kidwell carried Latta Jaboy inside, walking her down the aisle every bit like a groom bringing his bride home. He placed her in the front pew, usually reserved for the Jaboys, this year filled with Bennetts too. Latta sat right next to Kya, whom she wouldn't look at, while Cody helped her off with her coat and fussed over her. That was the way it was described later, and Opal was real sorry that LaVeta Sheets hadn't asked her to go along with her, like she had last year. But over the past few weeks, Opal had spent more time with Wanita Cone than with LaVeta, and it hurt her old friend enough that she'd gone with Radney instead. They always got an invitation from one of the old ranchers in town who returned yearly to the Christmas Eve service they'd loved so well all of their lives. John Long and Emil Vullet slipped in beside Arthur at the other end of the bench.

No one thought about Joseph's being there once they lifted their eyes to the walls, newly decorated with Lakota designs in brilliant primary colors on the white wood. The painted hide shields that decorated the walls under the lit kerosene lamps in antique glass shades depicted a series of animals and symbols and actions that were mysterious and disturbing to the ranching families, who were making their first pilgrimage of the year to the church. For the past forty minutes, they had been whispering about whether Latta had any right to let this happen, and whether it was unchristian. Her appearance brought its customary silence, and for once she knew she should be grateful.

"It's kinda pretty, isn't it?" Cody whispered in her ear. His hot breath made her wiggle in her seat, which he took to mean it was okay for him to put his arm around her again, and he did. She wasn't sure if that was what she wanted exactly, but since it felt okay, she didn't resist. She wasn't going to give in so easily this time, though. He was going to have to work for it.

Kya glanced at them and smiled. She was satisfied with her work. The church she'd helped paint had taken on new meaning for her. She'd already found out what some of the symbols meant — the red bear walking west, with the yellow lightning rod overhead, the white pony with the black handprint. She ran her thumb over the medicine-wheel bracelet on her wrist, the same symbol she'd painted above the hand-hewn pine cross behind the altar. They'd hung the ghost shirt opposite the altar, over the door. Only a few people had noticed it, and they immediately dropped their eyes away from its white glare.

Kya was going back to Rosebud with Joseph. She had so

much to learn; so much had been coming clear. She hadn't had a drink since the night of Greta's funeral, couldn't afford to cloud her mind now. They had traveling to do, she and Joseph.

This year it was Arthur Bennett's turn to conduct the service, and when he rose with the first chords of "O Come, All Ye Faithful" from the wheezing pump organ, Joseph Starr appeared in the front of the church also, to take his place beside him. They had talked earlier, and Joseph had explained what he had done, and what he was about to do. Arthur had tried to put it off, but finally agreed. When all was said and done, Arthur didn't have much religion, and this was a social, community event mostly. Maybe it was time for things to be a little different, like Joseph and Kya said.

Arthur gave a prayer in English, and Joseph offered one in Lakota, sharing equally the attention of the congregation. Then Arthur said his words of greeting, thanking the families for coming and for bringing the poinsettias and flowers that now banked the altar. He turned to Joseph and thanked him for coming and bringing the Lakota decorations to their church, and asked him to explain their significance. Joseph gave a brief introduction without revealing any of the deep meanings that the uninitiated should not hear.

Cody felt himself lulled by the quiet assurance of Joseph's voice, almost chanting the syllables that seemed to rise and fall with a special rhythm taken from Lakota itself. He remembered being in the sweat lodge with Joseph that summer, the frustration of the older man about the church on the hill and what it was taking from his people. Now he saw what Joseph had discovered: a momentary blending of the two worlds without their doing battle, without their trying to take away from each other as if there were only one economy possible, one that must take and swallow all others. He felt the walls of the church growing stronger by the minute under the flickering dance of the kerosene light, the way the paint seemed to murmur the figures alive again, so that the bear was marching, the lightning on his trail, protecting him; the horses, eager to be galloping, were trotting high-kneed in place. The birds began to swoop and hover over the people listening intently, their heads bent or cocked. The light came down and caught their hair and wove it in a fantastic display, lifting the collecting light of their hair, their bodies in a wild kinetic aura, until they all seemed to wear halos, neon and wonderful, like the marks left on the heads of the cowboys after they removed their hats.

Joseph's words caught at him and pulled his eyes forward, where the cross seemed straighter. Even the mouse-chewed bark seemed gnawed to the exact measure of natural beauty it needed. The cross had hung there for a hundred years, from when the church was first built, and never had it seemed more alive since the day it was cut and roped together from two trees whose sacrifice was blessed and then forgotten.

A few hours earlier, Arthur and he had discussed Heywood's two marriages. At first, Cody had been hurt that his father had never acknowledged Caroline as his true wife. Then he'd realized that in the way of things in Caroline's world, it had been her desire to keep the marriage secret too. Making Heywood a bigamist and Arthur illegitimate would have an odd appeal to her. When his brother offered the boxes of his mother's possessions, so he could read what she'd left, Cody had immediately refused. He'd spent a lifetime listening to his mother's voice. It had distracted, shamed, confused, and almost ruined him. He was happy to know that the writings were intact for some future generation, but for now he just wanted to keep the silence he'd found on the night he'd tried to bury the deer.

He remembered that Caroline was the one who always wanted to stop the truck and pick up roadkills and take them home for a proper, respectful ending. When he was tall enough to drive, he simply stepped on the gas and flew past the mashed forms. He'd had enough of struggling to scoop up the remains on the shovel she kept in the back, lifting them carefully into the truck bed so the gases wouldn't burst the bloated bellies, or the crust of skin and bones fall away into maggoty puddles.

She'd tried to smack his face as he drove past the dead, but he'd raised his arm and laughed to show it didn't hurt as she flailed away, leaving red blotches from his shoulder to his wrist. It wouldn't have cost so much to stop, to let her have her way, he realized now, but he was a kid then, and it was important to show her how brave he was becoming. Now it seemed silly. His parents had never been as strong and powerful as he'd imagined. They'd never acted out of true courage — declaring their love openly enough to save their son.

It was that recognition that led him to his decision about Latta. He simply would not leave her, ever. They needed to love each other. And more important, he wasn't going to let another child grow up without enough love. Maybe Caroline had been right, maybe there were angels here on earth, lost and strange: Heywood and Caroline, and Arthur's and Kya's mothers, Joseph, Greta and Emil, John Long, even Opal Treat. And maybe it was desire that made them angels, he suddenly realized. Desire, not need, that made them strange angels. A desire you were born with that made you strange to yourself until love made you visible, known. It wasn't like looking in a mirror. It was better. It made you capable of extraordinary things.

"The man buried beneath this church was a great spirit," Joseph was saying, "a great leader in old times, and his spirit has been calling out to me. It took me a long time to find him, and I spent a long time praying for a way to satisfy his need. The decoration you see is homage, my people's homage. The ghost shirt is his. He wanted it hung here, to take its rightful place, so his spirit on occasion might come to meet the one you worship. There is enough space in this church for all of them, for all of us, as you can see. Years ago, the people of the hills here, your people, made a grave for a small child, a baby, because it was right, and built a church and a place for the dead. No one even knew the name of that child, but it was a spirit that needed shelter, needed a home, and they opened their hearts and gave it one. Let us open our hearts again tonight, and welcome all the spirits, all the souls, living and dead, home again, that they might make us strong, and we might live on earth, with peace toward her."

A hush filled the church when his words ended, and he lit the tobacco and sent it in the four directions. Everyone felt their bodies give a little, as if some weight, some burden they hadn't even known, was there, was lifted from them, if only momentarily, and they were lighter, and they could straighten their backs and chests, taking deep breaths for the first time since they were small children, in the grips of wonder again.

Outside the snowflakes fattened, and hidden in the dark space beneath the church floor, the skunks wheezed and shuffled their feet, waking sleepily, then closed their eyes again. Somewhere within the walls, between the wood lathing and the outside planks, the mice were chewing a new tunnel to the back of the organ. They would work on it all winter long, and in the summer someone would open the organ and discover that the stop with the brass plate that read *Flute* was now ringed with the perfectly symmetrical indentations of yellow teeth.

Arthur took his place beside Joseph, and instead of giving his little prepared sermon, motioned to the organist to begin the series of carols they always closed the evening with. Some people stood, some sat, but they all sang the familiar words of "O Little Town of Bethlehem" and "It Came upon a Midnight Clear."

Cody, on the bench beside Latta, holding the hymnal for them with his arm around her shoulders, let his free hand rest lightly on the swollen belly where their baby was growing. Latta closed her eyes against the tears and let herself rest against the comfort of his body, strong and battered as it was.

She had to believe in it — there wasn't anything else but herself that had ever been so good to her. And maybe that was all that love ever could teach a person.

She'd try again, maybe just until the baby was born. Or a little longer, until it grew up. You can always kick him out, she assured herself. Heywood had left her the choice of anything she wanted in his will, and she'd finally decided: she would take Cody, his son.

Kya caught her brother's eye and winked. Grinning and looking at Latta's belly, then pointing to herself, she mouthed, "Name it after me."

He smiled. There'd be a good fight over that one.

Up front, Arthur and Joseph stood side by side, momentary allies as oddly matched as any of the couples sitting in front of them, but perfectly suited for the job they had done that night.

On their way outside, singing the last verse of "Joy to the World," only a couple of people stepped into the snowy dark of the graveyard and noticed the white crosses, two of them, draped with tobacco on colored strips of cloth. One cross said *Chief John Starr*, the other said *Greta Vullet*, to honor their spirits. The crows, filling the trees like black leaves, lifted together into the suddenly clear sky, paused like black stars, then dropped back like tatters of ash onto the trees again. And on the very edge of the graveyard the small pink marble headstone, elaborately engraved *Our Baby*, stood guard over the Dismal River, winding its way through the deep heart of the sandhills.

ACKNOWLEDGMENTS

Dwight Yoakam for the magic of hillbillies and honky-tonks I rediscovered through his music; Chris Mosner for taking time to show me so much of Rosebud and for sharing his imagination; the Tucker family, Mike Young, and David Beman for sharing their sandhills lives.

Paul McDonough for his support, understanding, and wonderful intelligence; Lon Otto, again, for friendship and tough criticism; Cindy Boettcher, Jackie Agee, Alvin Greenberg, Marilyn Hart, Susan Welch, JoJo Kramer, Cecil Drummond, Tom Redshaw, George Rabasa, Juanita Garciagodoy, Chris Jones, Jane Barnes, Lisa Rogers, Angela Kramer, Greg Hewett, and Tony Hanault.

The Loft and the College of St. Catherine for giving me support and time to write; Laurie Gray for her patient production of the manuscript.

Ned Leavitt, my agent, for his friendship, support, and belief over the years and for pushing me when I need it.

Jane von Mehren for being my teacher, friend, and mentor, for having faith in my work even when I don't, and for being a wonderful editor who helps midwife the voices.